POKÉMON ADVENTURES:
DIAMOND AND PEARL/
PLATINUM
Volume 3
Perfect Square Edition

Story by **HIDENORI KUSAKA**
Art by **SATOSHI YAMAMOTO**

© 2011 The Pokémon Company International.
© 1995–2009 Nintendo / Creatures Inc. / GAME FREAK inc.
TM, ®, and character names are trademarks of Nintendo.
POCKET MONSTERS SPECIAL Vol. 3 (32)
by Hidenori KUSAKA, Satoshi YAMAMOTO
© 1997 Hidenori KUSAKA, Satoshi YAMAMOTO
All rights reserved.
Original Japanese edition published by SHOGAKUKAN.
English translation rights in the United States of America, Canada, the United Kingdom,
Ireland, Australia, New Zealand and India arranged with SHOGAKUKAN.

Translation/Katherine Schilling
Touch-up & Lettering/Annaliese Christman
Design/Yukiko Whitley
Editor/Annette Roman

The stories, characters and incidents mentioned
in this publication are entirely fictional.

Printed in the U.S.A.

Published by VIZ Media, LLC
P.O. Box 77010
San Francisco, CA 94107

10 9 8 7 6 5
First printing, October 2011
Fifth printing, January 2018

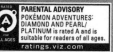

www.viz.com

Art

Satoshi Yamamoto

Pokémon Adventures™
Diamond and Pearl
Platinum

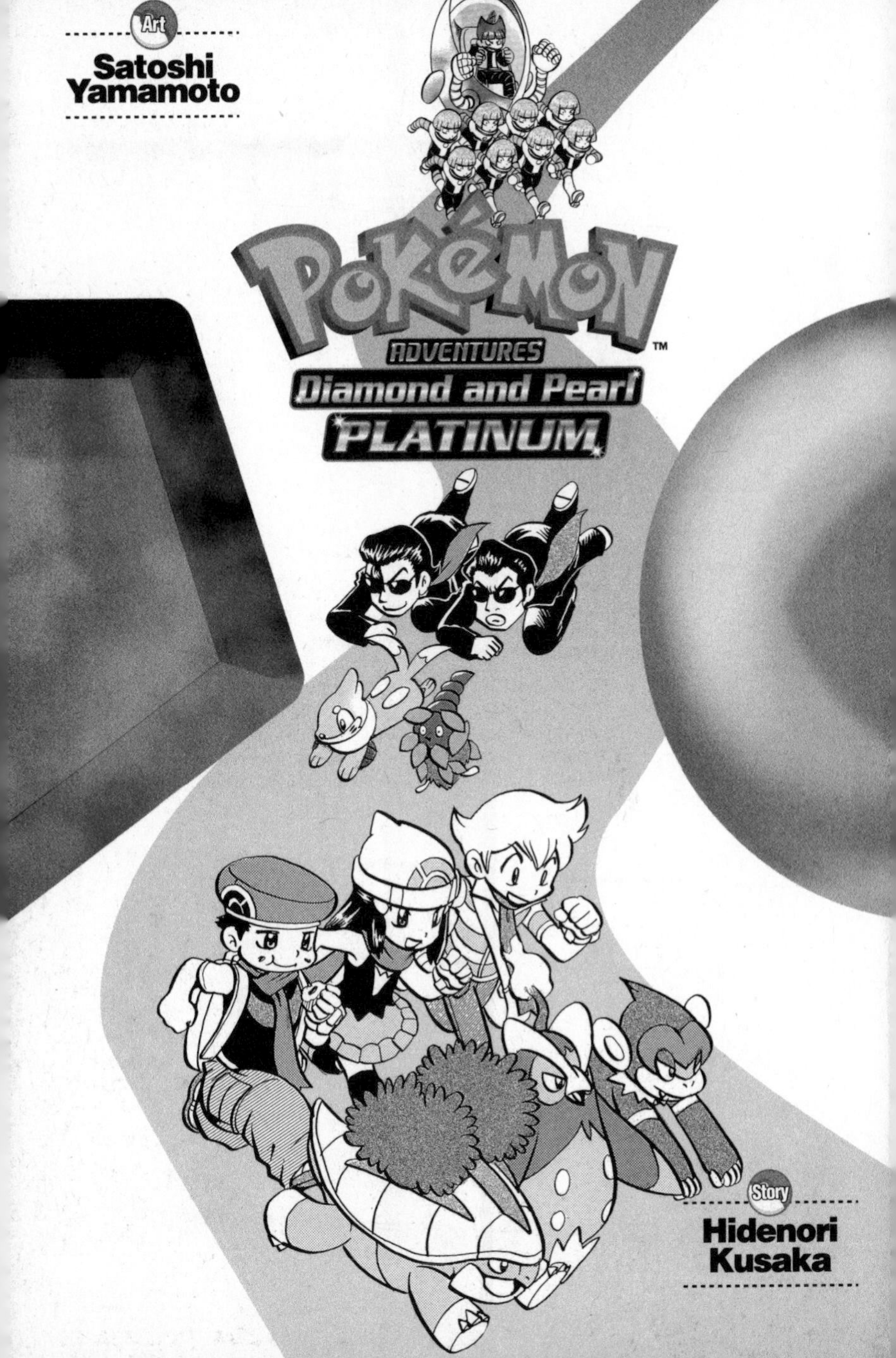

Story

Hidenori Kusaka

Lady
Diamond
Pearl

A STORY ABOUT YOUNG PEOPLE ENTRUSTED WITH POKÉDEXES BY THE WORLD'S LEADING POKÉMON RESEARCHERS. TOGETHER WITH THEIR POKÉMON, THEY TRAVEL, DO BATTLE, AND EVOLVE!

SOME PLACE IN SOME TIME... THE DAY HAS COME FOR A YOUNG LADY, THE ONLY DAUGHTER OF THE BERLITZ FAMILY, THE WEALTHIEST IN THE SINNOH REGION, TO EMBARK ON A JOURNEY. IN ORDER TO MAKE A SPECIAL EMBLEM BEARING HER FAMILY CREST, SHE MUST PERSONALLY FIND AND GATHER THE MATERIALS AT THE PEAK OF MT. CORONET. SHE SETS OUT ON HER JOURNEY WITH THE INTENTION OF MEETING UP WITH TWO BODYGUARDS ASSIGNED TO ESCORT HER.

MEANWHILE, POKÉMON TRAINERS PEARL AND DIAMOND, WHO DREAM OF BECOMING STAND-UP COMEDIANS, ENTER A COMEDY CONTEST IN JUBILIFE AND WIN THE SPECIAL MERIT AWARD. BUT THEIR PRIZE OF AN ALL-EXPENSES PAID TRIP GETS SWITCHED WITH THE CONTRACT FOR LADY'S BODYGUARDS!

THUS PEARL AND DIAMOND THINK LADY IS THEIR TOUR GUIDE, AND LADY THINKS THEY ARE HER BODYGUARDS! DESPITE THE CASES OF MISTAKEN IDENTITY, THE TRIO TRAVEL TOGETHER QUITE HAPPILY THROUGH THE VAST COUNTRYSIDE.

Paka & Uji
THE REAL BODYGUARDS HIRED TO ESCORT LADY.

Sebastian
THE BERLITZ FAMILY BUTLER, WHO IS ALWAYS WORRYING ABOUT LADY.

Mr. Berlitz
LADY'S FATHER, WHO ASSISTS PROFESSOR ROWAN.

Professor Rowan
A LEADING RESEARCHER OF POKÉMON EVOLUTION. HE CAN BE QUITE INTIMIDATING!

Cynthia

THE MYSTERIOUS WOMAN WHO SOLVED THE CASE OF THE KIDNAPPED BIKE SHOP OWNER.

Fantina

THE ALLURING SOULFUL DANCER OF HEARTHOME.

Gardenia

THE CHEERFUL GYM LEADER OF ETERNA GYM.

Roark

THE FOSSIL HUNTING GYM LEADER OF OREBURGH GYM.

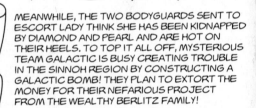

MEANWHILE, THE TWO BODYGUARDS SENT TO ESCORT LADY THINK SHE HAS BEEN KIDNAPPED BY DIAMOND AND PEARL AND ARE HOT ON THEIR HEELS. TO TOP IT ALL OFF, MYSTERIOUS TEAM GALACTIC IS BUSY CREATING TROUBLE IN THE SINNOH REGION BY CONSTRUCTING A GALACTIC BOMB! THEY PLAN TO EXTORT THE MONEY FOR THEIR NEFARIOUS PROJECT FROM THE WEALTHY BERLITZ FAMILY!

THE CURTAIN RISES ON AN INCREASINGLY CONVOLUTED CHAIN OF HOT PURSUITS: OUR CLUELESS TRIO OF HEROES ARE BEING TAILED BY CONFUSED BODYGUARDS PAKA AND UJI WHO IN TURN ARE BEING TAILED BY TEAM GALACTIC!

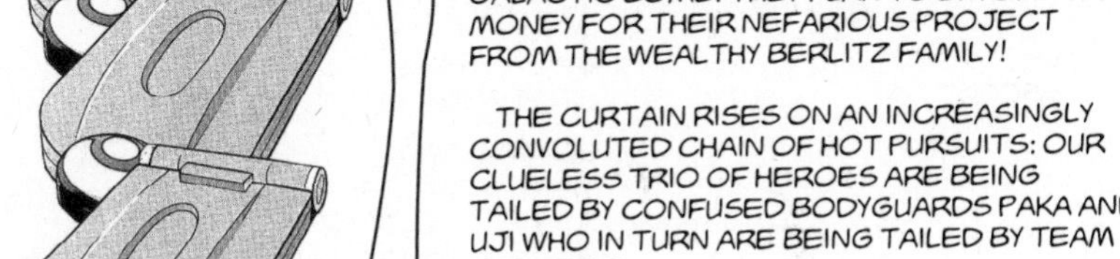

Cyrus

TEAM GALACTIC'S BOSS. AN OVERBEARING, INTENSE MAN.

Galactic Grunts

THE TEAM GALACTIC TROOPS, WHO CARRY OUT THEIR LEADER'S BIDDING WITHOUT QUESTION. CREEPY!

Saturn

HE IS IN CHARGE OF THE BOMB AND RARELY STEPS ONTO THE BATTLEFIELD HIMSELF.

Mars

A TEAM GALACTIC LEADER. HER PERSONALITY IS HARD TO PIN DOWN.

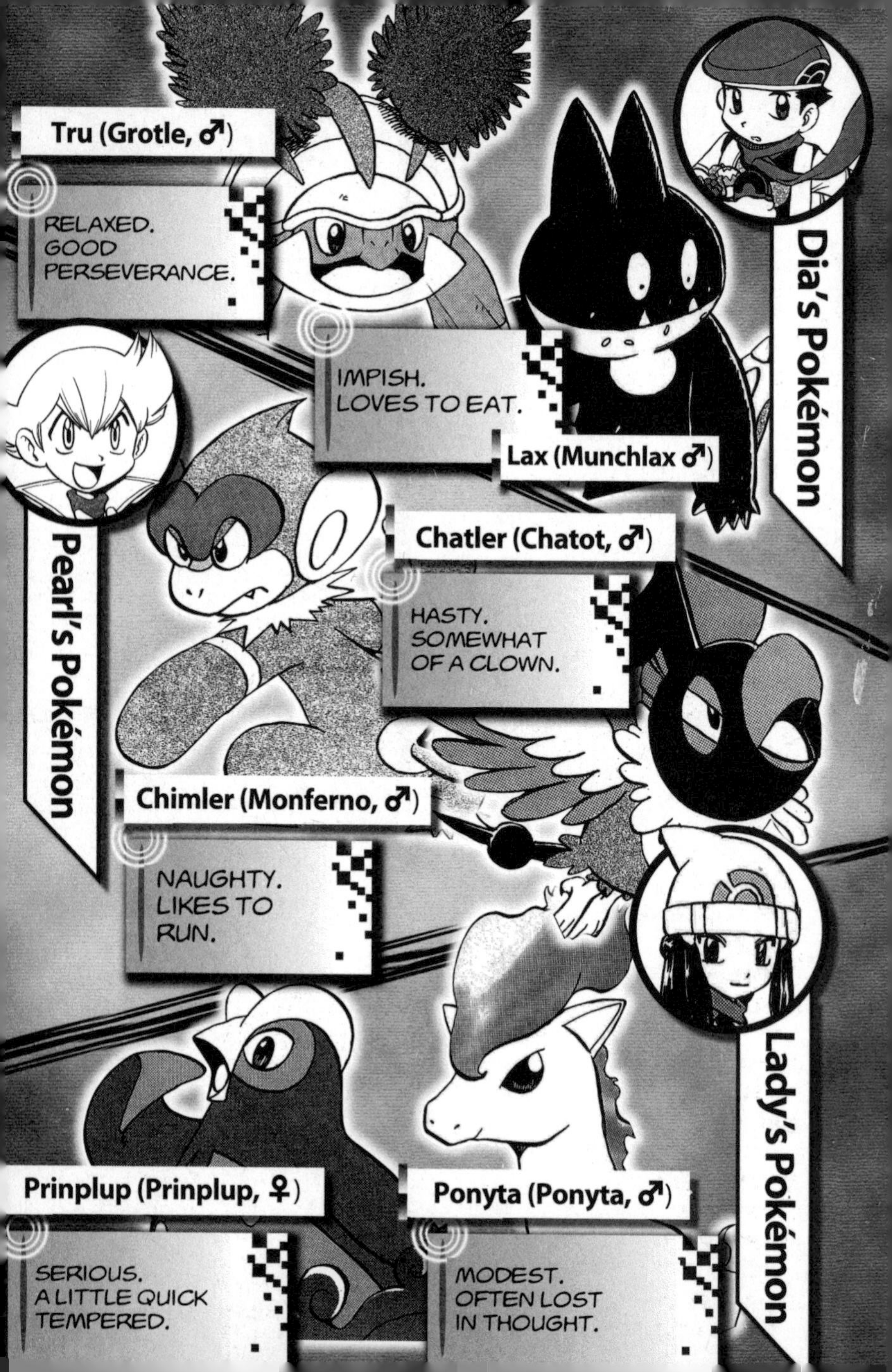
Dia's Pokémon
Tru (Grotle, ♂)
RELAXED. GOOD PERSEVERANCE.
Lax (Munchlax ♂)
IMPISH. LOVES TO EAT.
Pearl's Pokémon
Chatler (Chatot, ♂)
HASTY. SOMEWHAT OF A CLOWN.
Chimler (Monferno, ♂)
NAUGHTY. LIKES TO RUN.
Lady's Pokémon
Ponyta (Ponyta, ♂)
MODEST. OFTEN LOST IN THOUGHT.
Prinplup (Prinplup, ♀)
SERIOUS. A LITTLE QUICK TEMPERED.

POKÉMON
ADVENTURES
Diamond and Pearl
PLATINUM

CONTENTS

19

Magnificent
Meditite
& Really
Riolu I

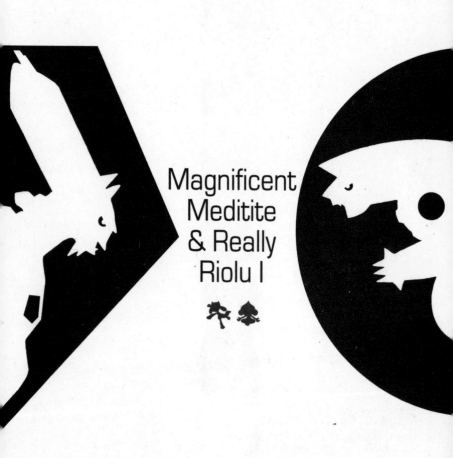

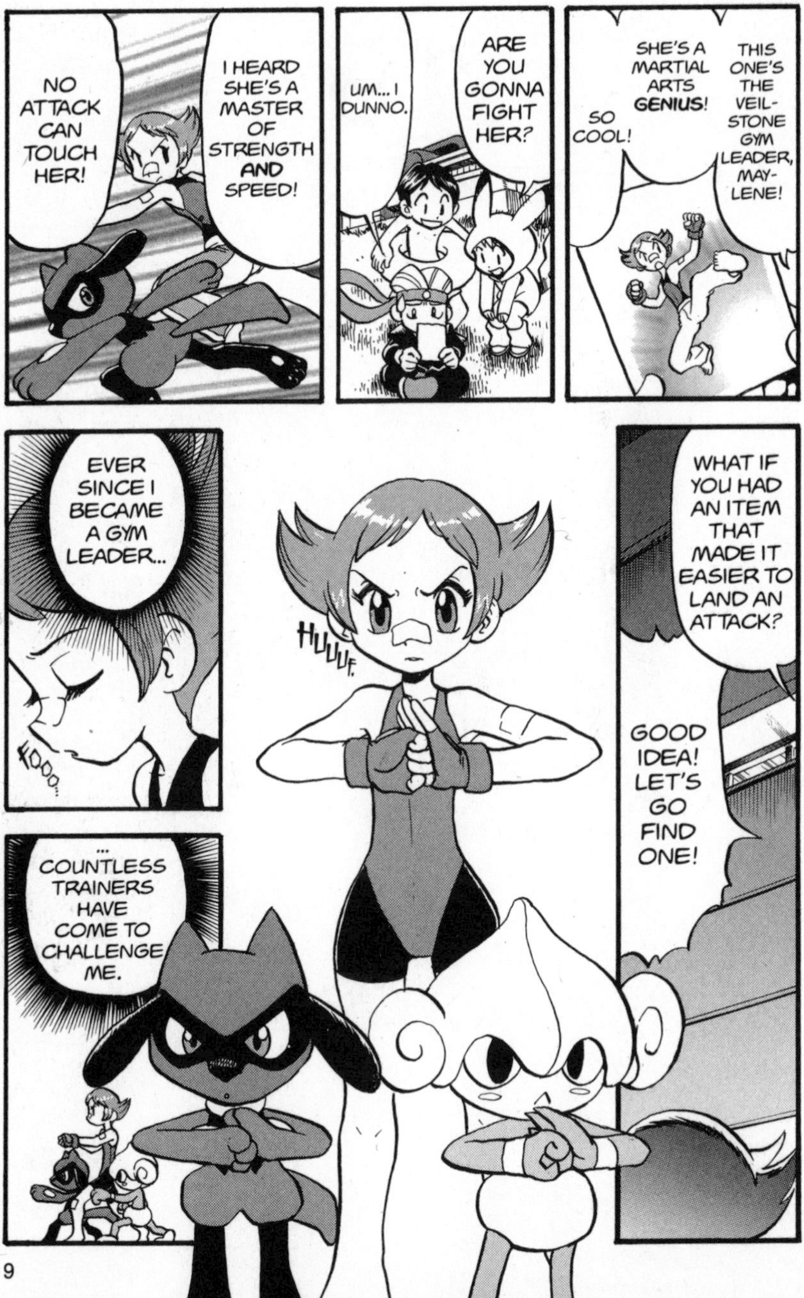
THIS ONE'S THE VEIL-STONE GYM LEADER, MAY-LENE!
SHE'S A MARTIAL ARTS **GENIUS**!
SO COOL!
ARE YOU GONNA FIGHT HER?
UM... I DUNNO.
I HEARD SHE'S A MASTER OF STRENGTH **AND** SPEED!
NO ATTACK CAN TOUCH HER!
WHAT IF YOU HAD AN ITEM THAT MADE IT EASIER TO LAND AN ATTACK?
GOOD IDEA! LET'S GO FIND ONE!
HUUUF.
EVER SINCE I BECAME A GYM LEADER...
FOOO...
...COUNTLESS TRAINERS HAVE COME TO CHALLENGE ME.

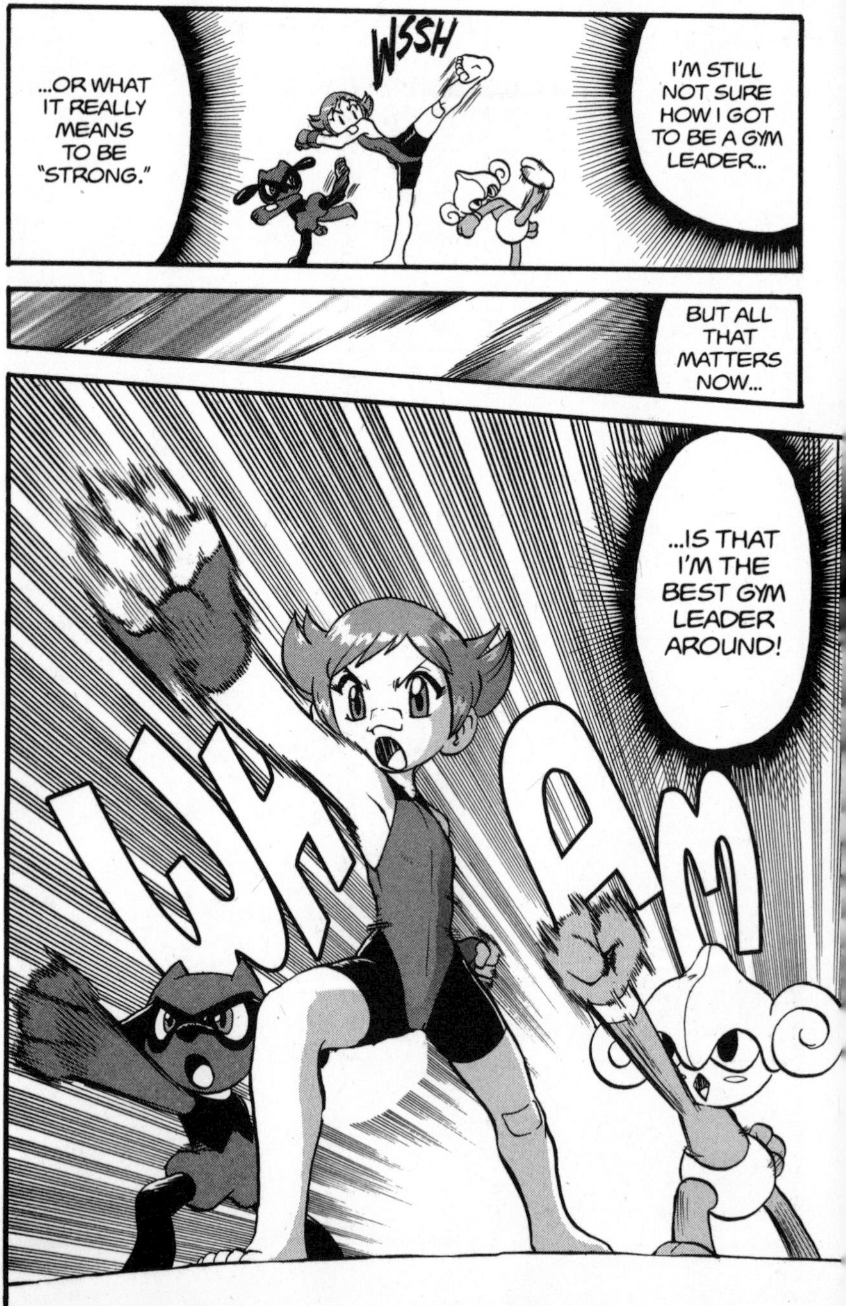
I'M STILL NOT SURE HOW I GOT TO BE A GYM LEADER...
WSSH
...OR WHAT IT REALLY MEANS TO BE "STRONG."
BUT ALL THAT MATTERS NOW...
...IS THAT I'M THE BEST GYM LEADER AROUND!
WHAM

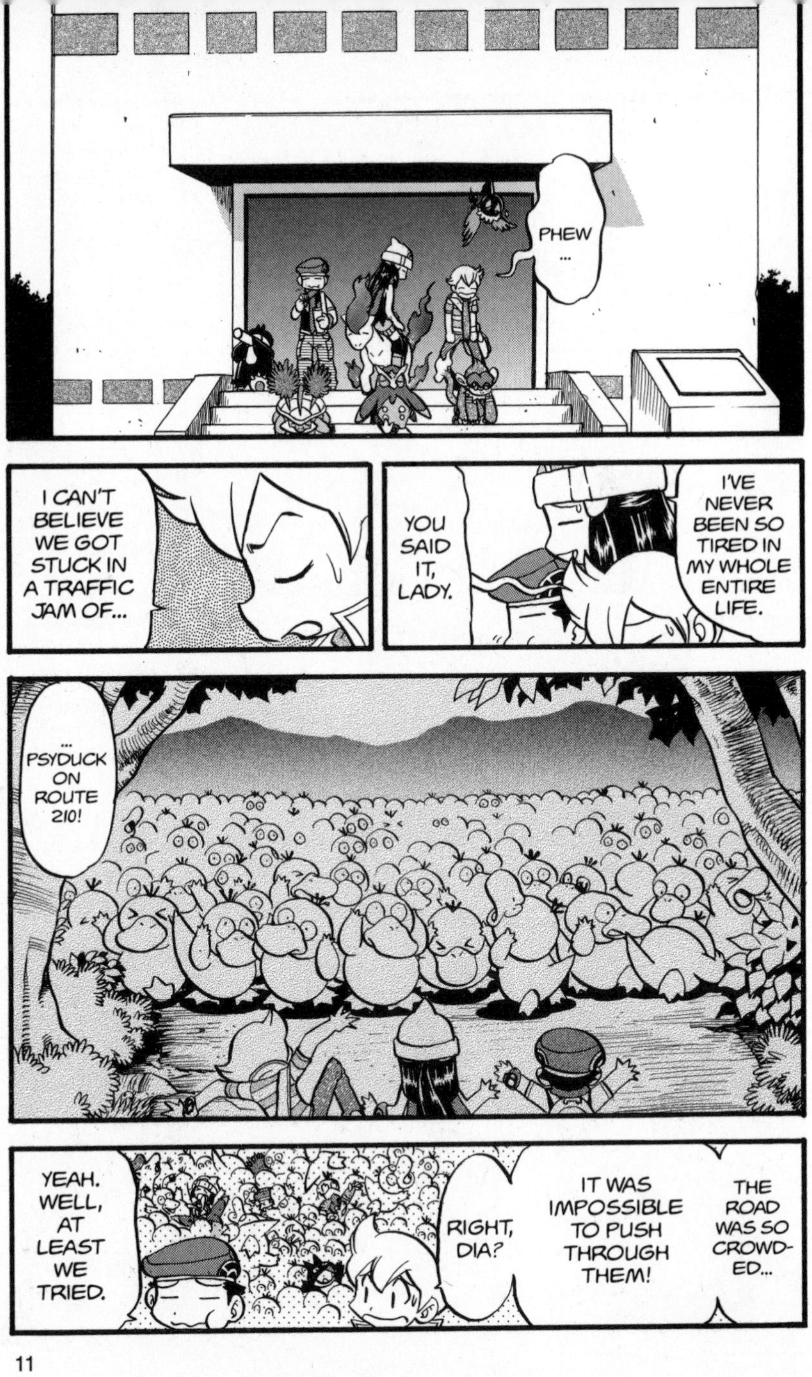
PHEW...
I'VE NEVER BEEN SO TIRED IN MY WHOLE ENTIRE LIFE.
YOU SAID IT, LADY.
I CAN'T BELIEVE WE GOT STUCK IN A TRAFFIC JAM OF...
...PSYDUCK ON ROUTE 210!
THE ROAD WAS SO CROWD-ED...
IT WAS IMPOSSIBLE TO PUSH THROUGH THEM!
RIGHT, DIA?
YEAH. WELL, AT LEAST WE TRIED.

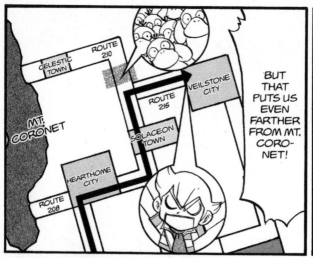

WE DIDN'T HAVE A CHOICE IN THE END. WE HAD TO TAKE THIS DETOUR ONTO ROUTE 215 TO VEILSTONE CITY.
BUT THAT PUTS US EVEN FARTHER FROM MT. CORO-NET!
ROUTE 210
CELESTIC TOWN
VEILSTONE CITY
ROUTE 215
MT. CORONET
SOLACEON TOWN
HEARTHOME CITY
ROUTE 208
THERE'S NO POINT WHINING ABOUT IT NOW.
LET'S REST WHILE WE RETHINK OUR ROUTE.
THE SUN'S ALREADY SETTING.
LOOK!
I SEE LOTS OF GLITTER-ING NEON LIGHTS THAT WAY!
THE CITY ISN'T THAT BIG, BUT THEY MUST HAVE AT LEAST ONE DECENT HOTEL.
IT'S A PLAN, LADY. WE'LL REHEARSE OUR NEXT SKIT TO CHEER OURSELVES UP...
...WHILE YOU CHECK US IN TO A HOTEL.
Later!
ALL RIGHT.

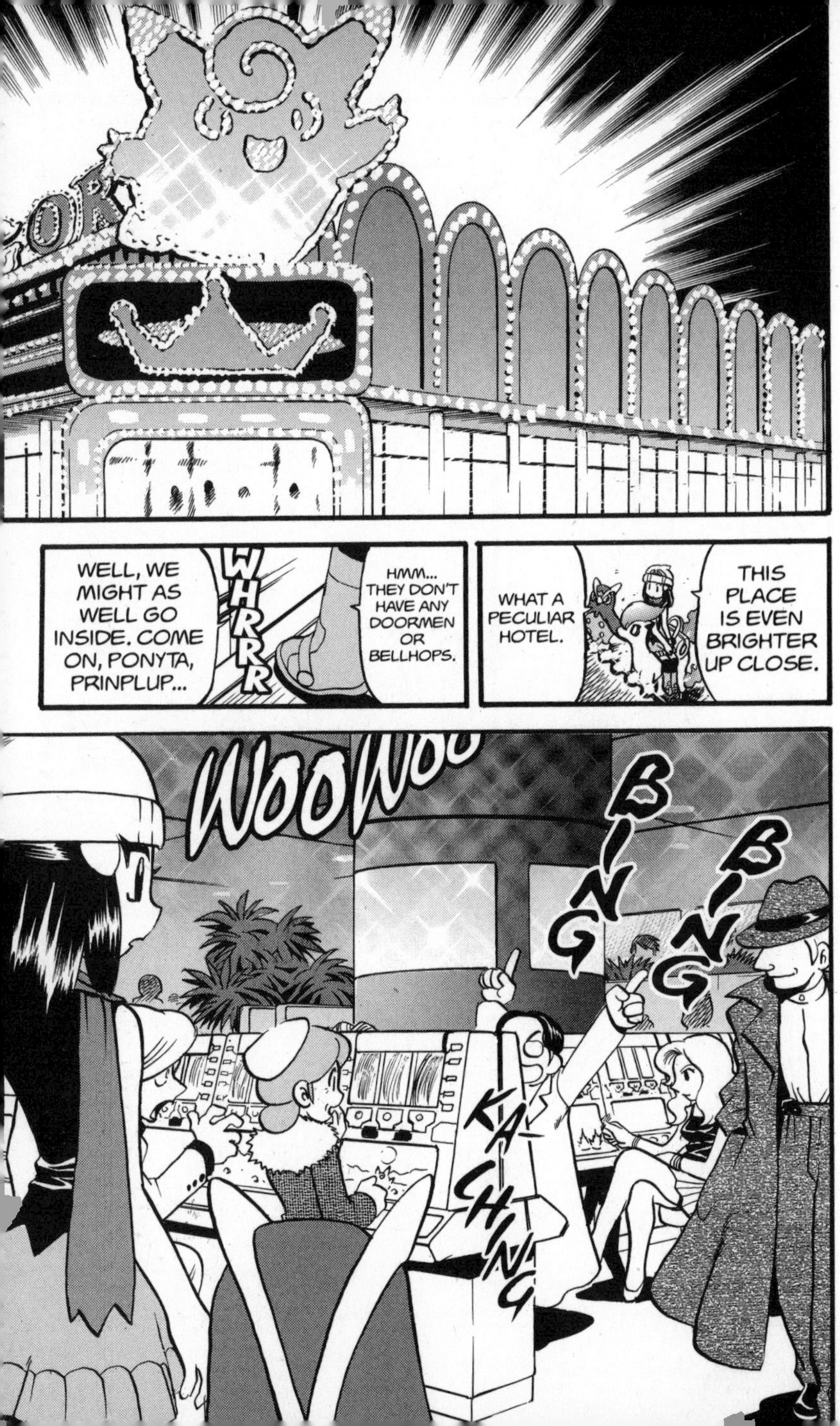

THIS PLACE IS EVEN BRIGHTER UP CLOSE.
WHAT A PECULIAR HOTEL.
HMM... THEY DON'T HAVE ANY DOORMEN OR BELLHOPS.
WHRRRR
WELL, WE MIGHT AS WELL GO INSIDE. COME ON, PONYTA, PRINPLUP...
BING
BING
WOOWOO
KA-CHING

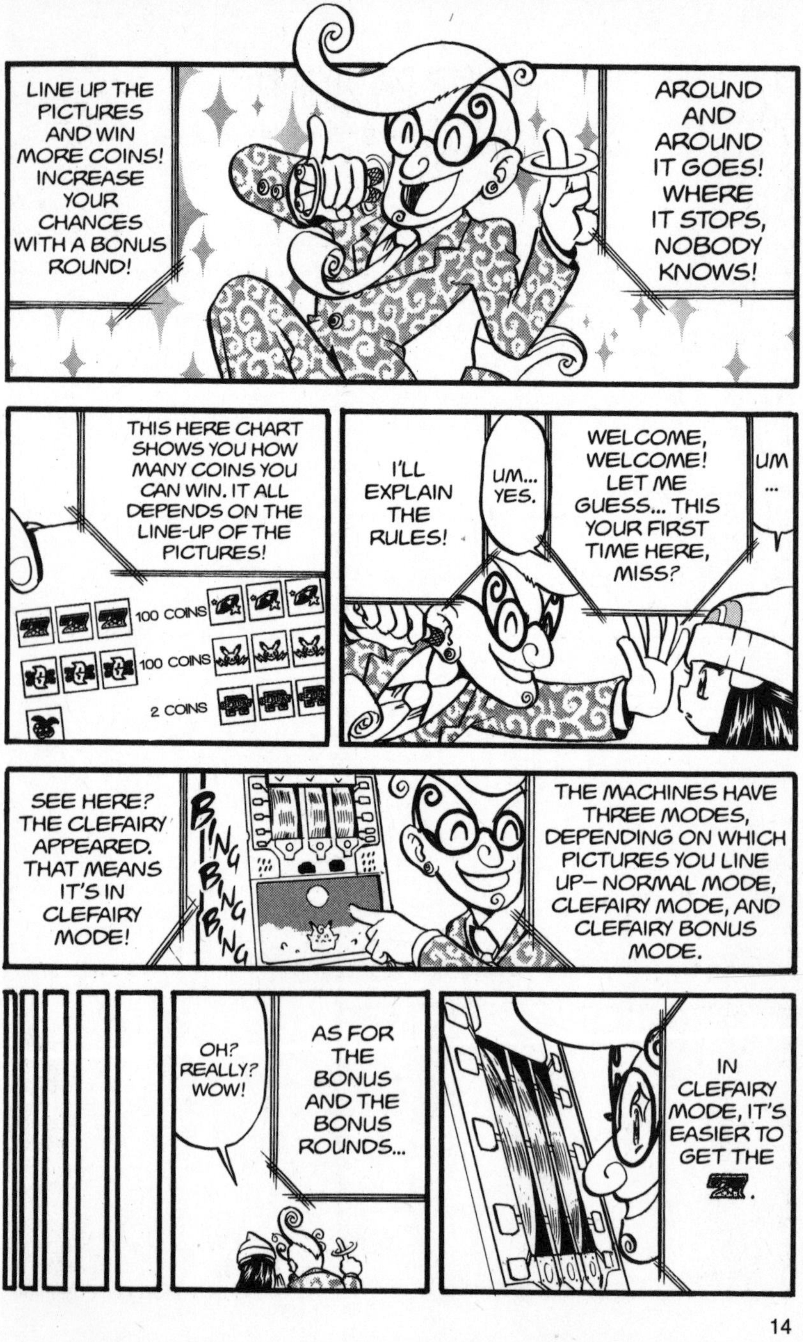
AROUND AND AROUND IT GOES! WHERE IT STOPS, NOBODY KNOWS!
LINE UP THE PICTURES AND WIN MORE COINS! INCREASE YOUR CHANCES WITH A BONUS ROUND!
UM ...
WELCOME, WELCOME! LET ME GUESS... THIS YOUR FIRST TIME HERE, MISS?
UM... YES.
I'LL EXPLAIN THE RULES!
THIS HERE CHART SHOWS YOU HOW MANY COINS YOU CAN WIN. IT ALL DEPENDS ON THE LINE-UP OF THE PICTURES!
100 COINS
100 COINS
2 COINS
THE MACHINES HAVE THREE MODES, DEPENDING ON WHICH PICTURES YOU LINE UP– NORMAL MODE, CLEFAIRY MODE, AND CLEFAIRY BONUS MODE.
BING BING BING
SEE HERE? THE CLEFAIRY APPEARED. THAT MEANS IT'S IN CLEFAIRY MODE!
IN CLEFAIRY MODE, IT'S EASIER TO GET THE .
AS FOR THE BONUS AND THE BONUS ROUNDS...
OH? REALLY? WOW!

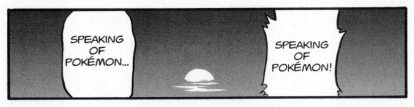

SPEAKING OF POKÉMON!
SPEAKING OF POKÉMON...
EVERY JOURNEY COMES WITH ITS SHARE OF ROADBLOCKS. AND THAT FLOCK OF PSYDUCK WAS NO EXCEPTION!
YOU CAN SAY THAT AGAIN! DID YOU NOTICE THEY ALL SEEMED TO HAVE HEADACHES ...?
HUH? REALLY?
SURE. POKÉMON CAN GET ALL KINDS OF ACHES.
LET'S SEE...
THEY CAN GET A HEADACHE, TUMMY ACHE, BACKACHE, RATICATE...
IDIOT! THAT LAST ONE IS A POKÉMON!
WHEN THEIR HEADS HURT TOO MUCH, PSYDUCK UNLEASH THEIR PSYCHIC POWERS.
REALLY? PSYCHIC POWERS?
OOH, LET ME TRY! NNNGH! COME ON, POKÉ BALL—FLOAT!
DIA! WHAT THE HECK ARE YOU DOING?
YOU WHACK ME IN THE HEAD SO MUCH, I THOUGHT I MIGHT HAVE DEVELOPED PSYCHIC POWERS TOO!
THAT'S JUST PART OF THE ACT!
DON'T MAKE ME LOOK BAD!
WELL, I THINK WE'VE GOT SOME GOOD NEW MATERIAL!
LET'S GO MEET LADY.
OKAY!
HUH?
IS THIS THE "HOTEL" LADY WENT INTO...?
LOOKS MORE LIKE A **CASINO** TO ME!

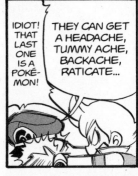

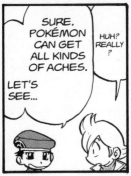

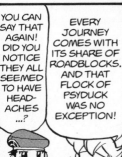

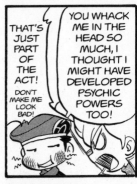

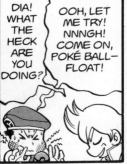

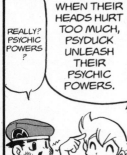

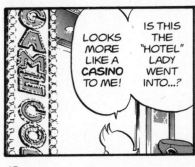

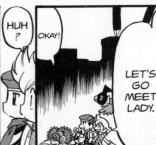

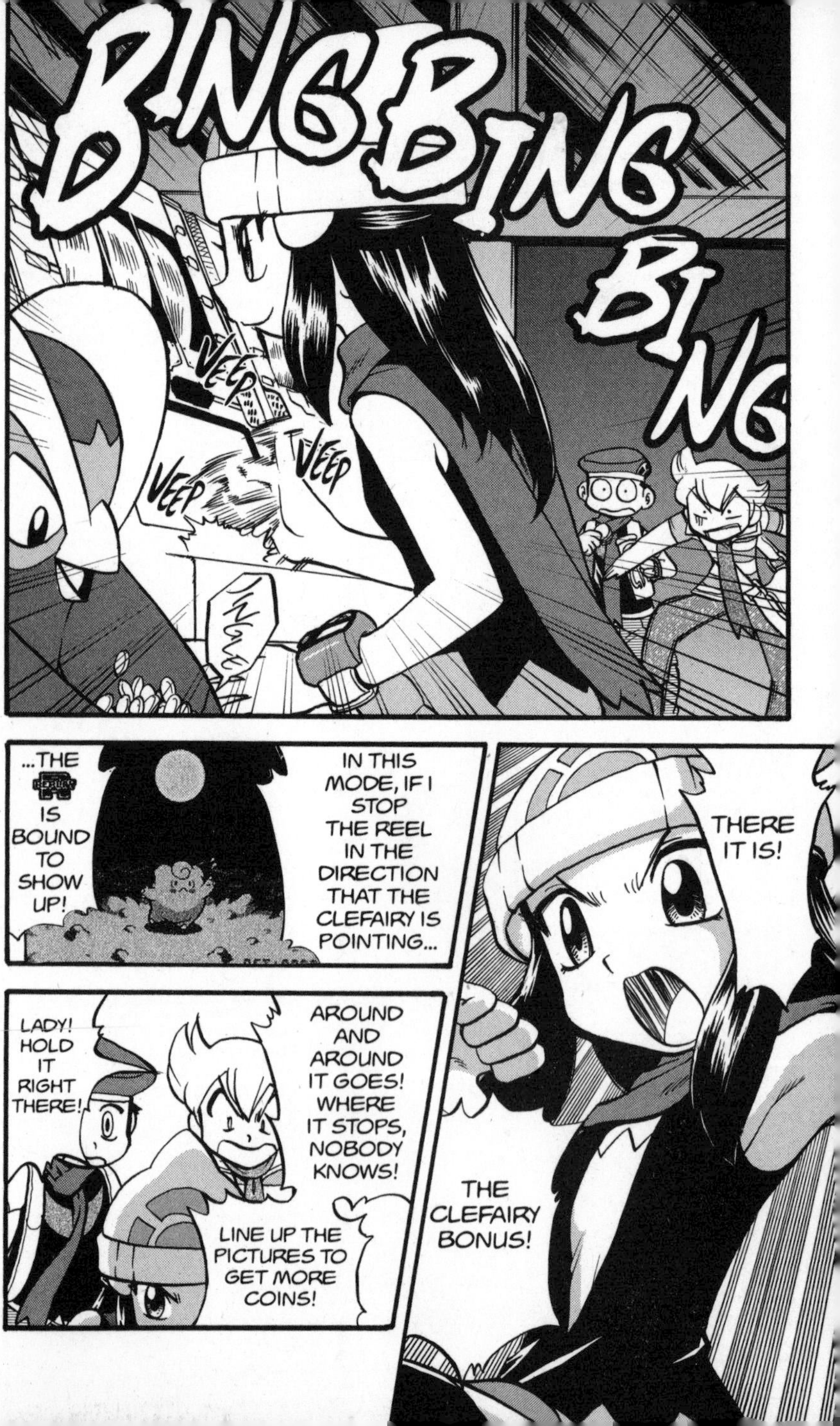
BING BING BING
VEEP
VEEP
VEEP
JINGLE
THERE IT IS!
THE CLEFAIRY BONUS!
IN THIS MODE, IF I STOP THE REEL IN THE DIRECTION THAT THE CLEFAIRY IS POINTING...
...THE
IS BOUND TO SHOW UP!
AROUND AND AROUND IT GOES! WHERE IT STOPS, NOBODY KNOWS!
LADY! HOLD IT RIGHT THERE!
LINE UP THE PICTURES TO GET MORE COINS!

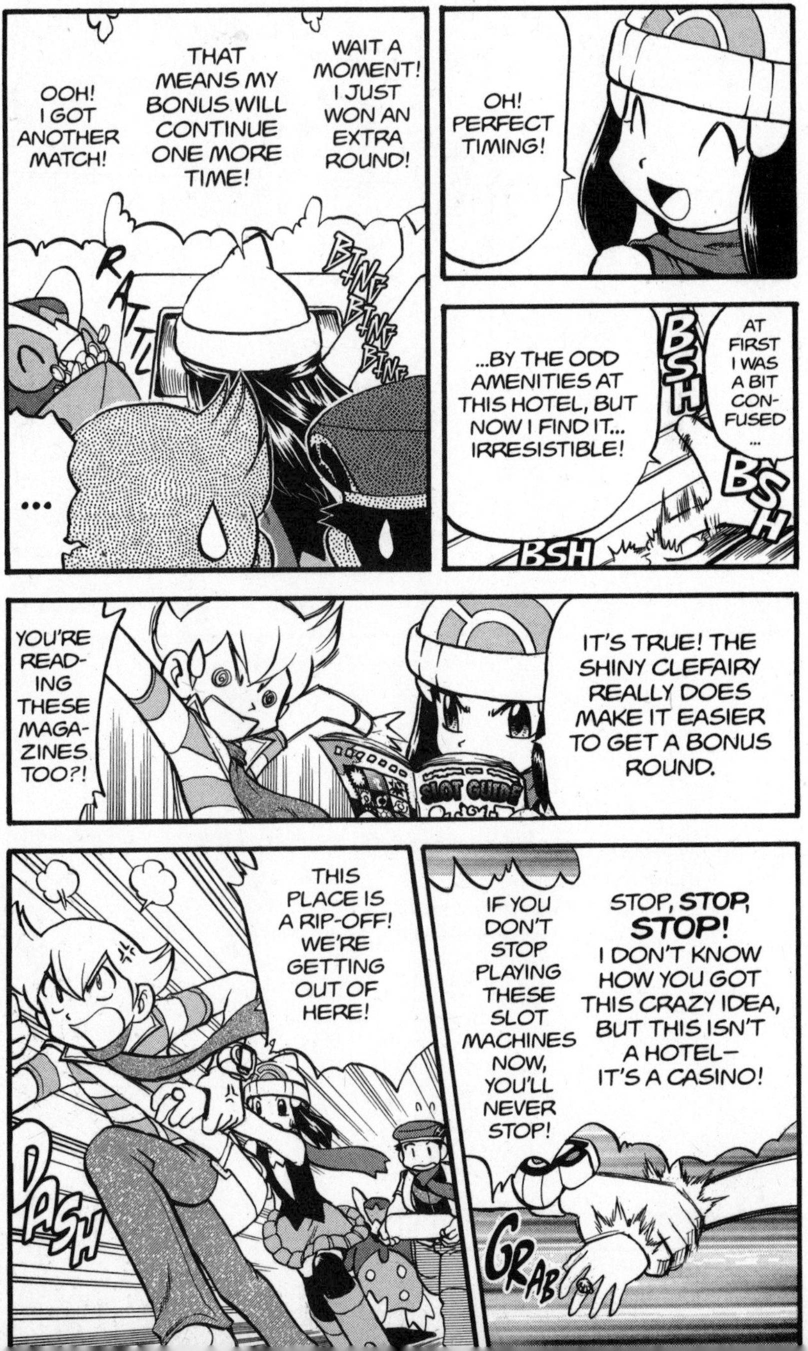
OH! PERFECT TIMING!
AT FIRST I WAS A BIT CON-FUSED...
BSH
...BY THE ODD AMENITIES AT THIS HOTEL, BUT NOW I FIND IT... IRRESISTIBLE!
BSH
BSH
WAIT A MOMENT! I JUST WON AN EXTRA ROUND!
THAT MEANS MY BONUS WILL CONTINUE ONE MORE TIME!
OOH! I GOT ANOTHER MATCH!
BING BING BING
RATTL
...
IT'S TRUE! THE SHINY CLEFAIRY REALLY DOES MAKE IT EASIER TO GET A BONUS ROUND.
YOU'RE READ-ING THESE MAGA-ZINES TOO?!
SLOT GUIDE
STOP, **STOP**, **STOP!** I DON'T KNOW HOW YOU GOT THIS CRAZY IDEA, BUT THIS ISN'T A HOTEL— IT'S A CASINO!
IF YOU DON'T STOP PLAYING THESE SLOT MACHINES NOW, YOU'LL NEVER STOP!
GRAB
THIS PLACE IS A RIP-OFF! WE'RE GETTING OUT OF HERE!
DASH

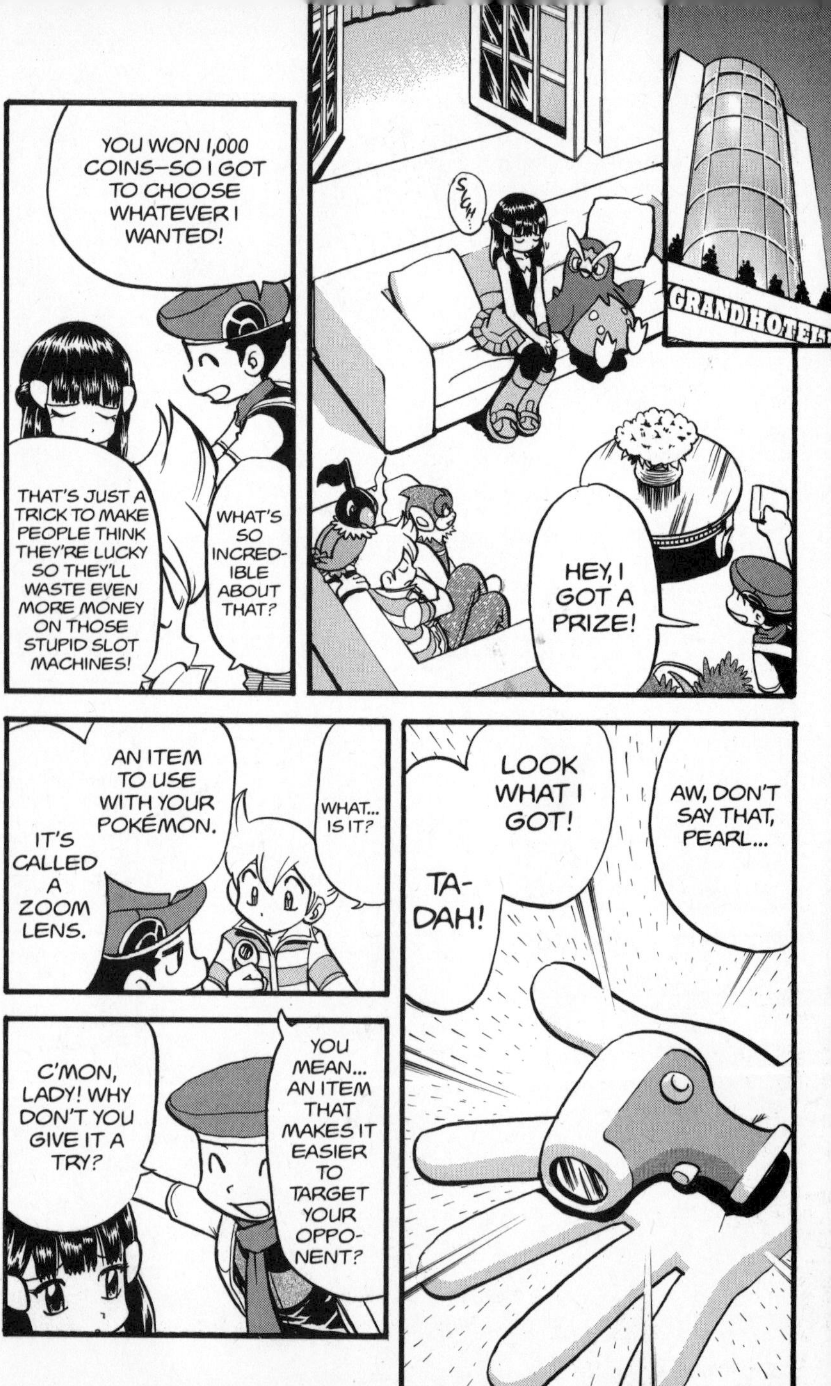
GRAND HOTEL
SIGH...
HEY, I GOT A PRIZE!
YOU WON 1,000 COINS—SO I GOT TO CHOOSE WHATEVER I WANTED!
WHAT'S SO INCRED-IBLE ABOUT THAT?
THAT'S JUST A TRICK TO MAKE PEOPLE THINK THEY'RE LUCKY SO THEY'LL WASTE EVEN MORE MONEY ON THOSE STUPID SLOT MACHINES!
AW, DON'T SAY THAT, PEARL...
LOOK WHAT I GOT!
TA-DAH!
WHAT... IS IT?
AN ITEM TO USE WITH YOUR POKÉMON.
IT'S CALLED A ZOOM LENS.
YOU MEAN... AN ITEM THAT MAKES IT EASIER TO TARGET YOUR OPPO-NENT?
C'MON, LADY! WHY DON'T YOU GIVE IT A TRY?

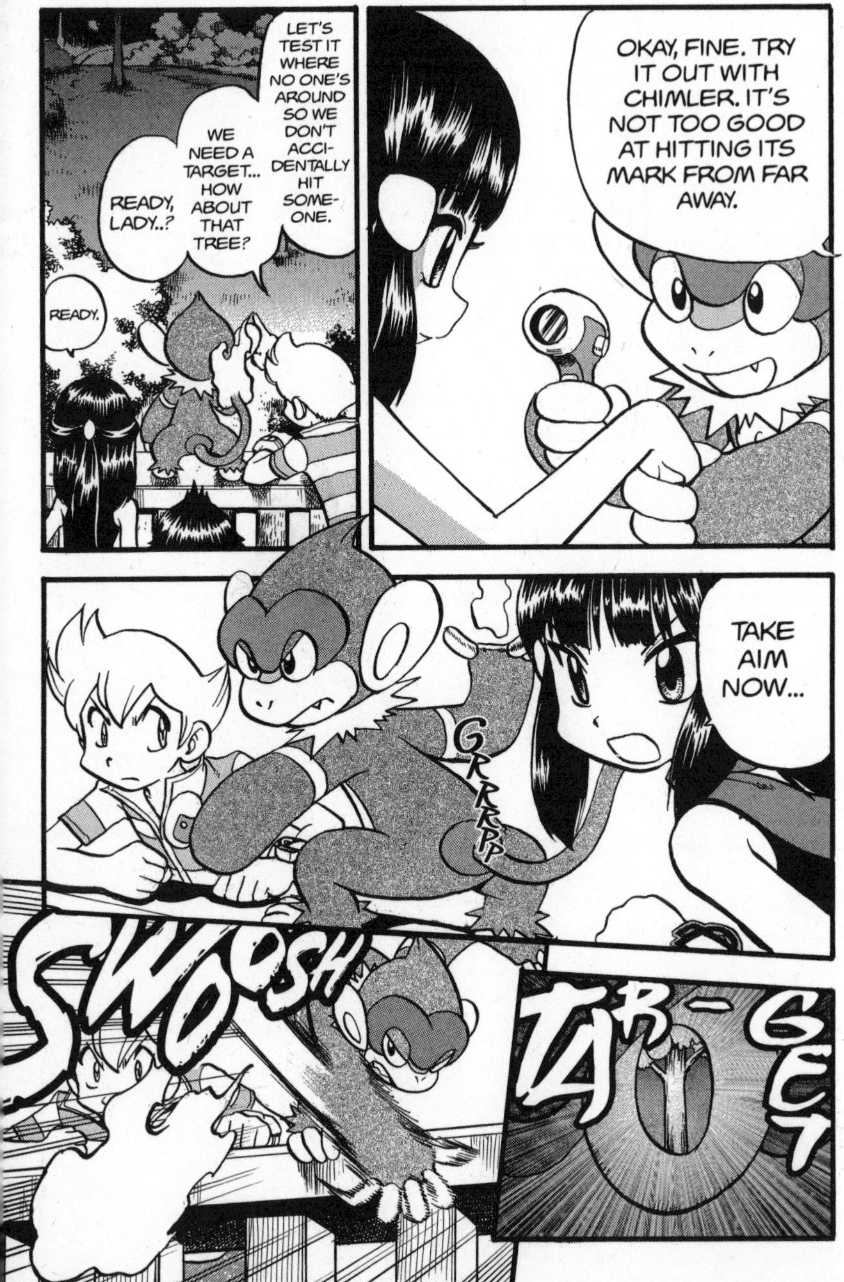
OKAY, FINE. TRY IT OUT WITH CHIMLER. IT'S NOT TOO GOOD AT HITTING ITS MARK FROM FAR AWAY.
LET'S TEST IT WHERE NO ONE'S AROUND SO WE DON'T ACCI-DENTALLY HIT SOME-ONE.
WE NEED A TARGET... HOW ABOUT THAT TREE?
READY, LADY..?
READY.
TAKE AIM NOW...
GRRRPP
TAR-GET
SWOOSH

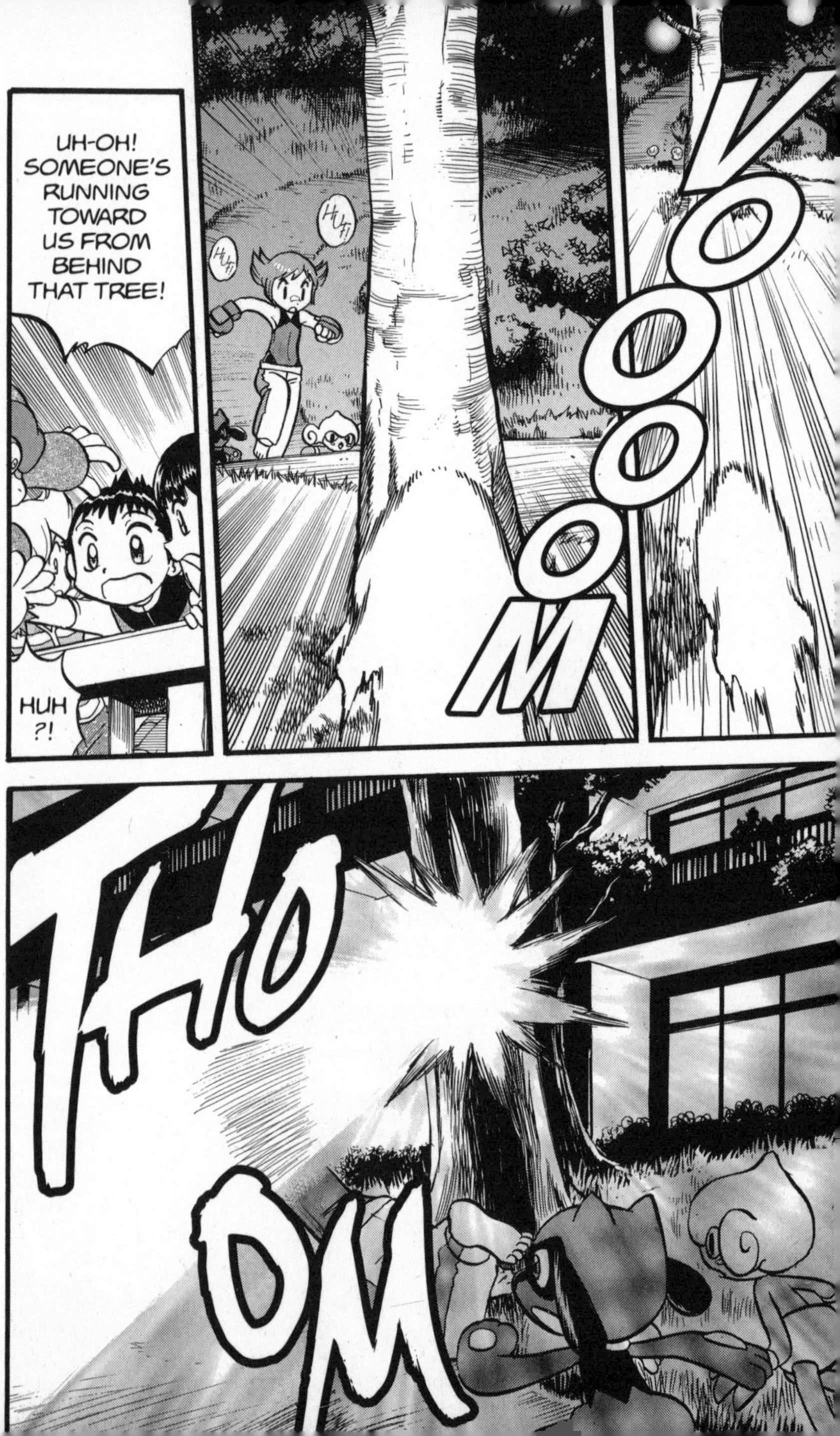
VOOOOOM
HUF!!
HUF!!
UH-OH! SOMEONE'S RUNNING TOWARD US FROM BEHIND THAT TREE!
HUH ?!
THOOM

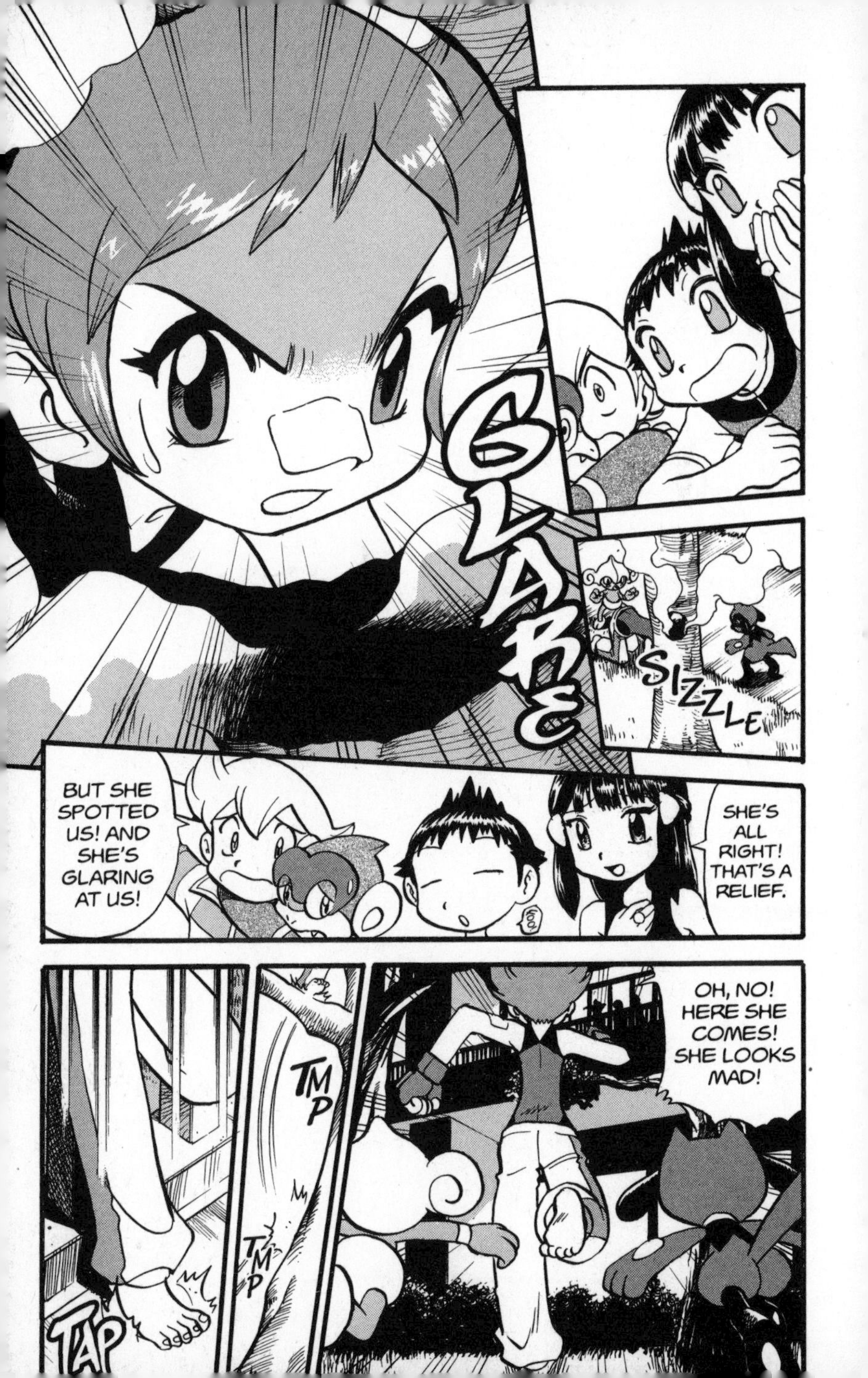
SIZZLE
GLARE
SHE'S ALL RIGHT! THAT'S A RELIEF.
BUT SHE SPOTTED US! AND SHE'S GLARING AT US!
OH, NO! HERE SHE COMES! SHE LOOKS MAD!
TMP
TMP
TAP

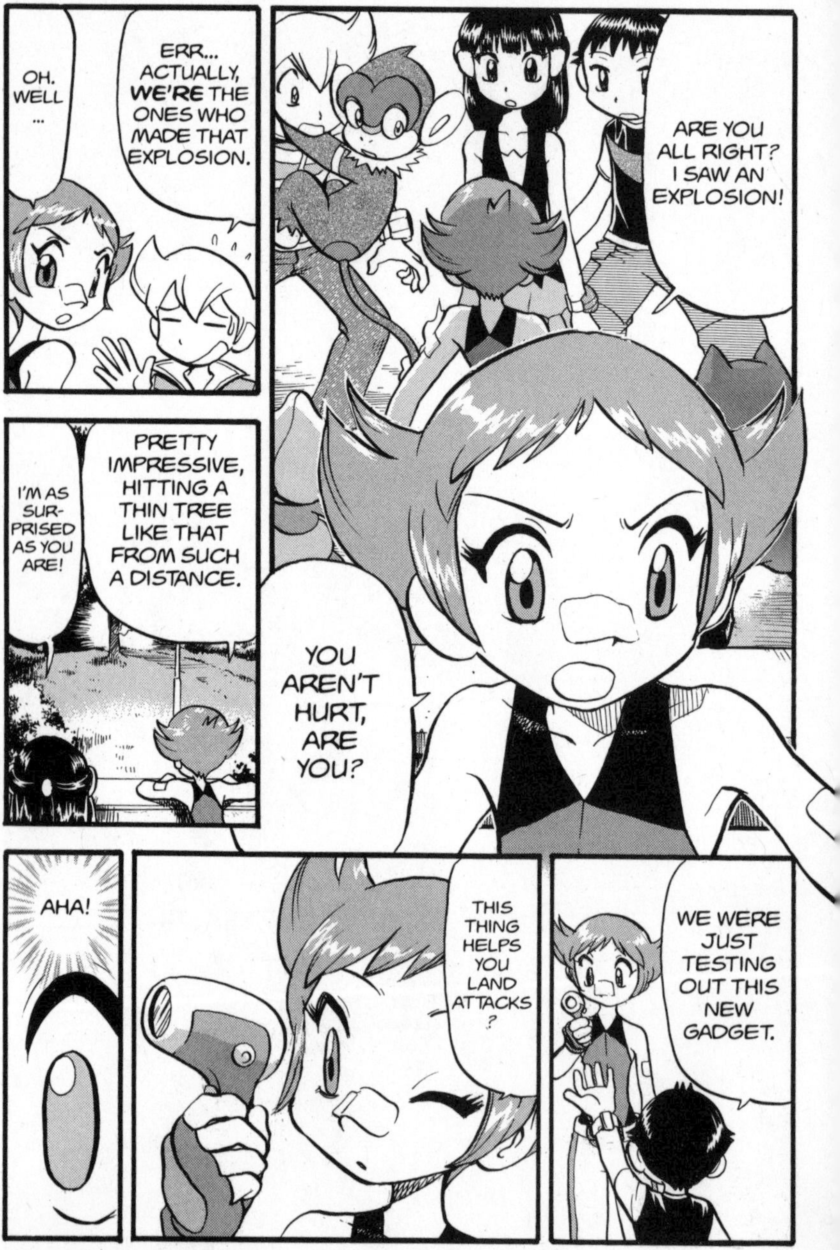
ARE YOU ALL RIGHT? I SAW AN EXPLOSION!
YOU AREN'T HURT, ARE YOU?
ERR... ACTUALLY, WE'RE THE ONES WHO MADE THAT EXPLOSION.
OH. WELL ...
PRETTY IMPRESSIVE, HITTING A THIN TREE LIKE THAT FROM SUCH A DISTANCE.
I'M AS SUR-PRISED AS YOU ARE!
WE WERE JUST TESTING OUT THIS NEW GADGET.
THIS THING HELPS YOU LAND ATTACKS?
AHA!

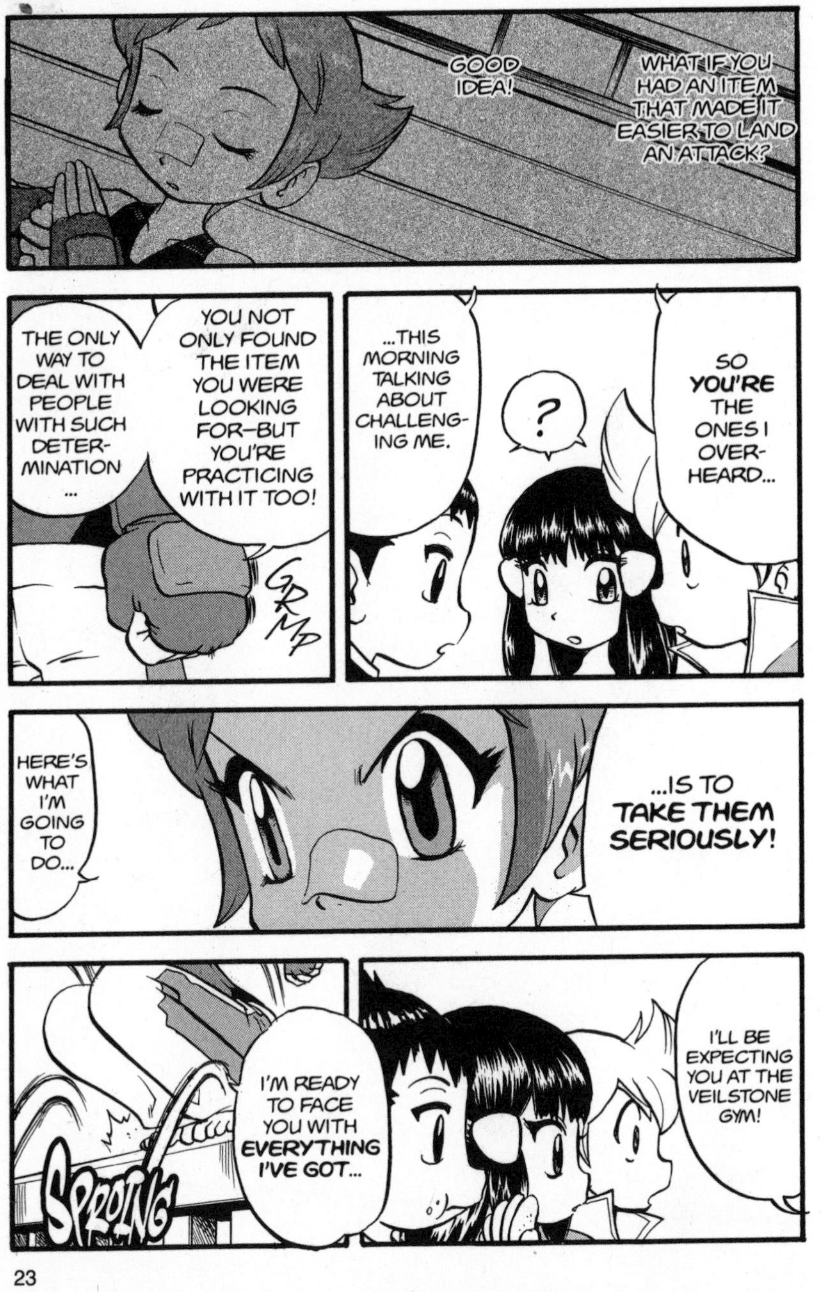
WHAT IF YOU HAD AN ITEM THAT MADE IT EASIER TO LAND AN ATTACK?
GOOD IDEA!
SO **YOU'RE** THE ONES I OVERHEARD...
?
...THIS MORNING TALKING ABOUT CHALLENGING ME.
YOU NOT ONLY FOUND THE ITEM YOU WERE LOOKING FOR—BUT YOU'RE PRACTICING WITH IT TOO!
THE ONLY WAY TO DEAL WITH PEOPLE WITH SUCH DETERMINATION...
GRMP
...IS TO **TAKE THEM SERIOUSLY!**
HERE'S WHAT I'M GOING TO DO...
I'LL BE EXPECTING YOU AT THE VEILSTONE GYM!
I'M READY TO FACE YOU WITH **EVERYTHING** I'VE GOT...
SPROING

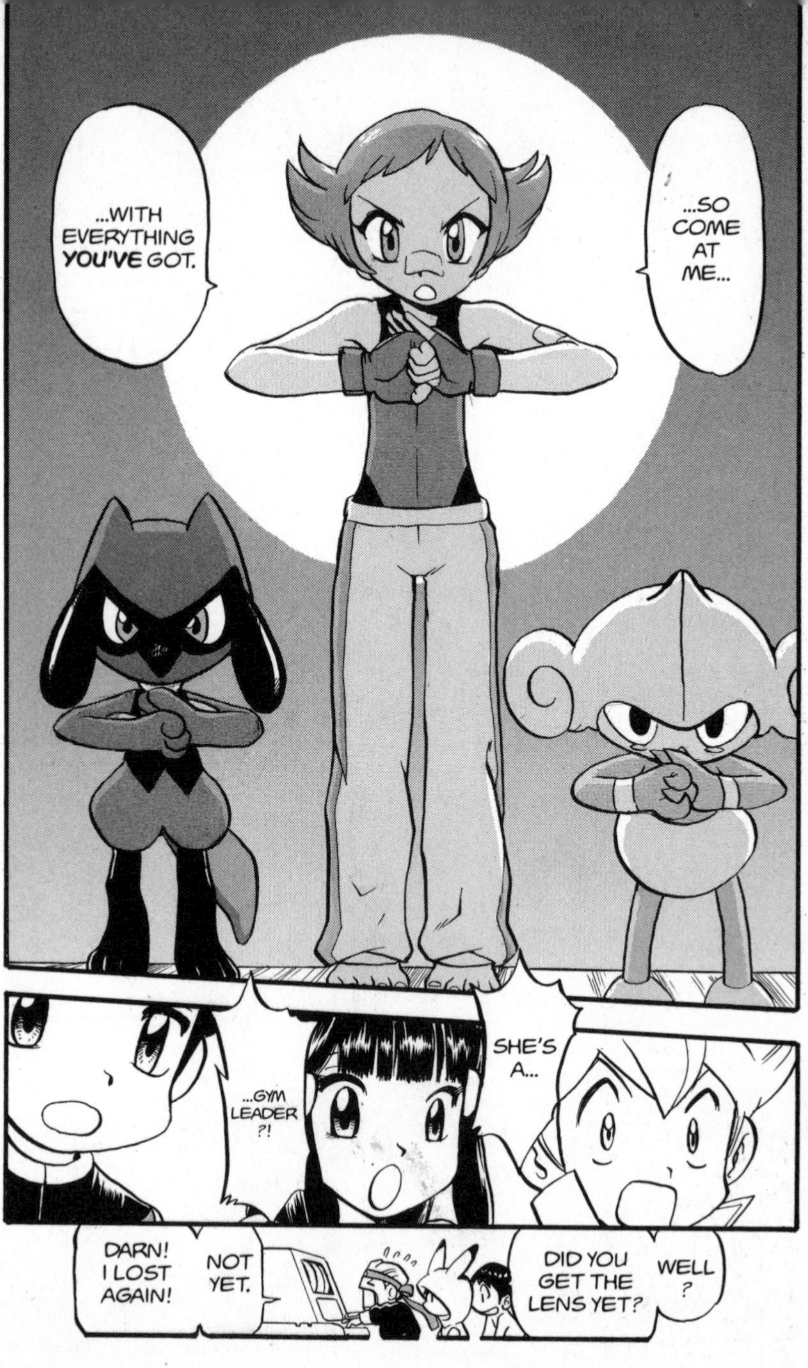
...SO COME AT ME...
...WITH EVERYTHING YOU'VE GOT.
SHE'S A...
...GYM LEADER ?!
WELL ?
DID YOU GET THE LENS YET?
NOT YET.
DARN! I LOST AGAIN!

ADVENTURE MAP

Veilstone City ◄

Oreburgh VS Roark Coal Badge	Eterna VS Gardenia Forest Badge						

DIAMOND

PEARL

LADY

► TRU
Grotle ♂

LAX
Munchlax ♂

► CHIMLER
Monferno ♂

► CHATLER
Chatot ♂

► PRINPLUP
Prinplup ♀

► PONYTA
Ponyta ♂

20

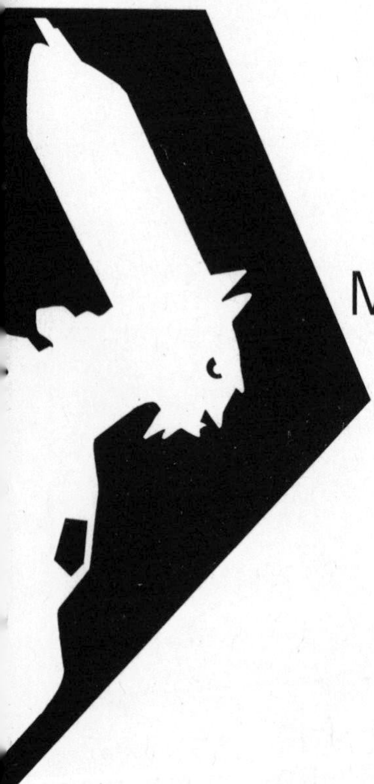

Magnificent Meditite & Really Riolu II

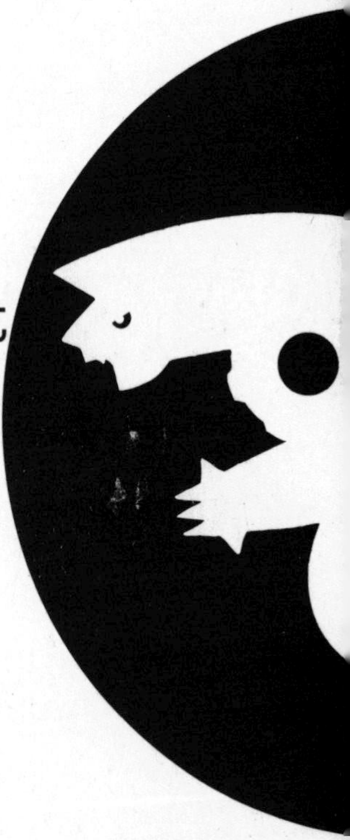

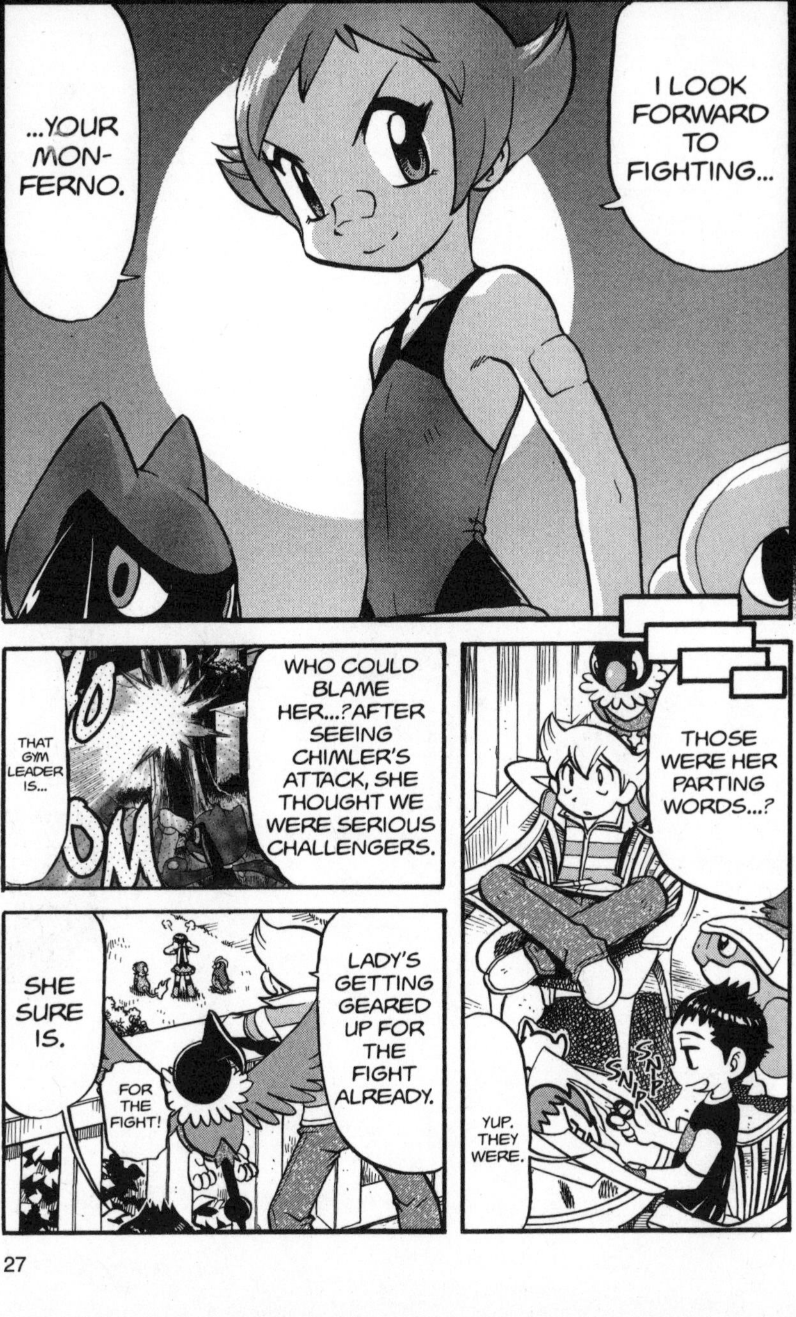
I LOOK FORWARD TO FIGHTING...
...YOUR MON-FERNO.
THOSE WERE HER PARTING WORDS...?
SNIP SNIP
YUP. THEY WERE.
WHO COULD BLAME HER...?AFTER SEEING CHIMLER'S ATTACK, SHE THOUGHT WE WERE SERIOUS CHALLENGERS.
THAT GYM LEADER IS...
LADY'S GETTING GEARED UP FOR THE FIGHT ALREADY.
SHE SURE IS.
FOR THE FIGHT!

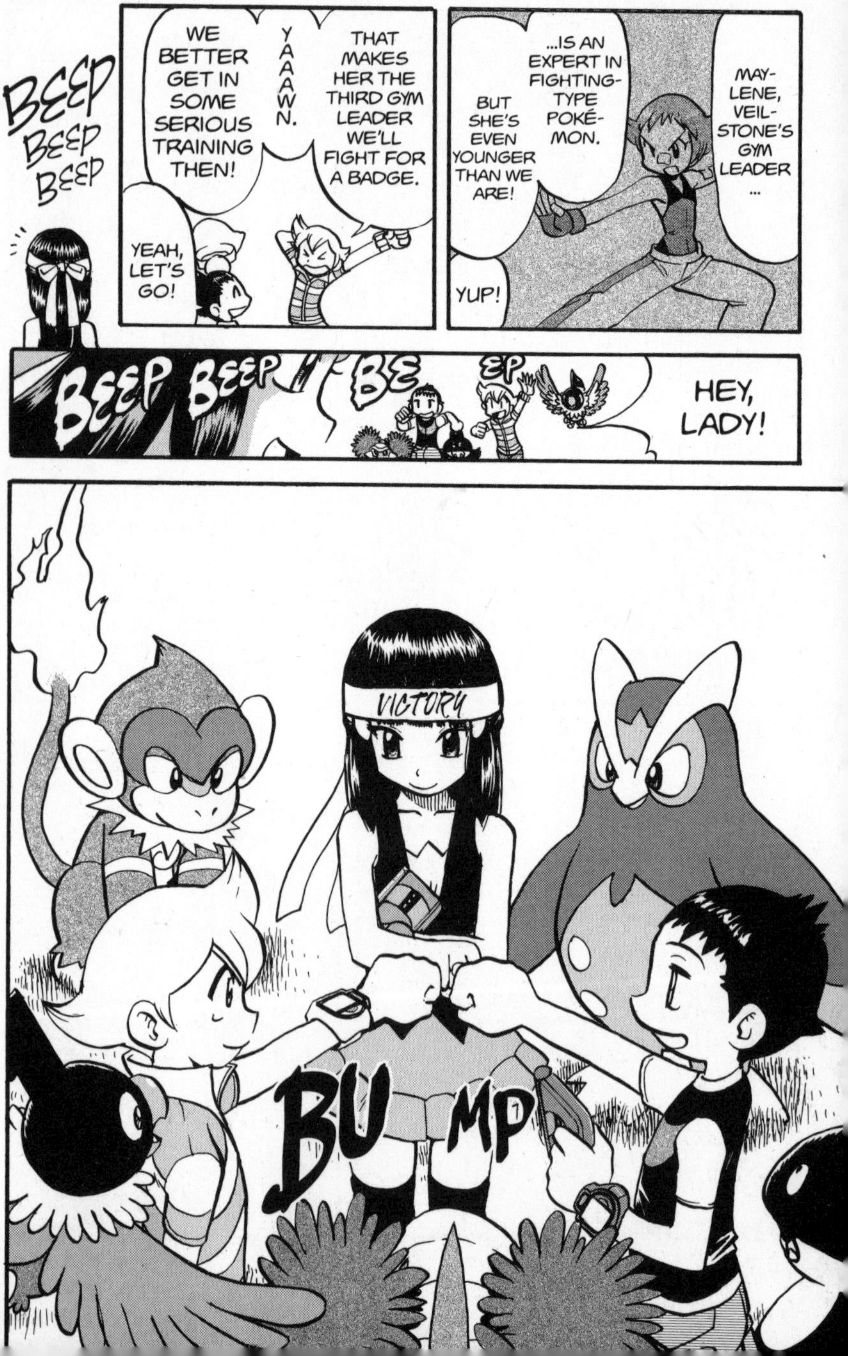
MAY-LENE, VEIL-STONE'S GYM LEADER ...
...IS AN EXPERT IN FIGHTING-TYPE POKÉ-MON.
BUT SHE'S EVEN YOUNGER THAN WE ARE!
YUP!
THAT MAKES HER THE THIRD GYM LEADER WE'LL FIGHT FOR A BADGE.
YAAAAWN.
WE BETTER GET IN SOME SERIOUS TRAINING THEN!
YEAH, LET'S GO!
BEEP BEEP BEEP
HEY, LADY!
BEEP BEEP BE EP
VICTORY
BU MP

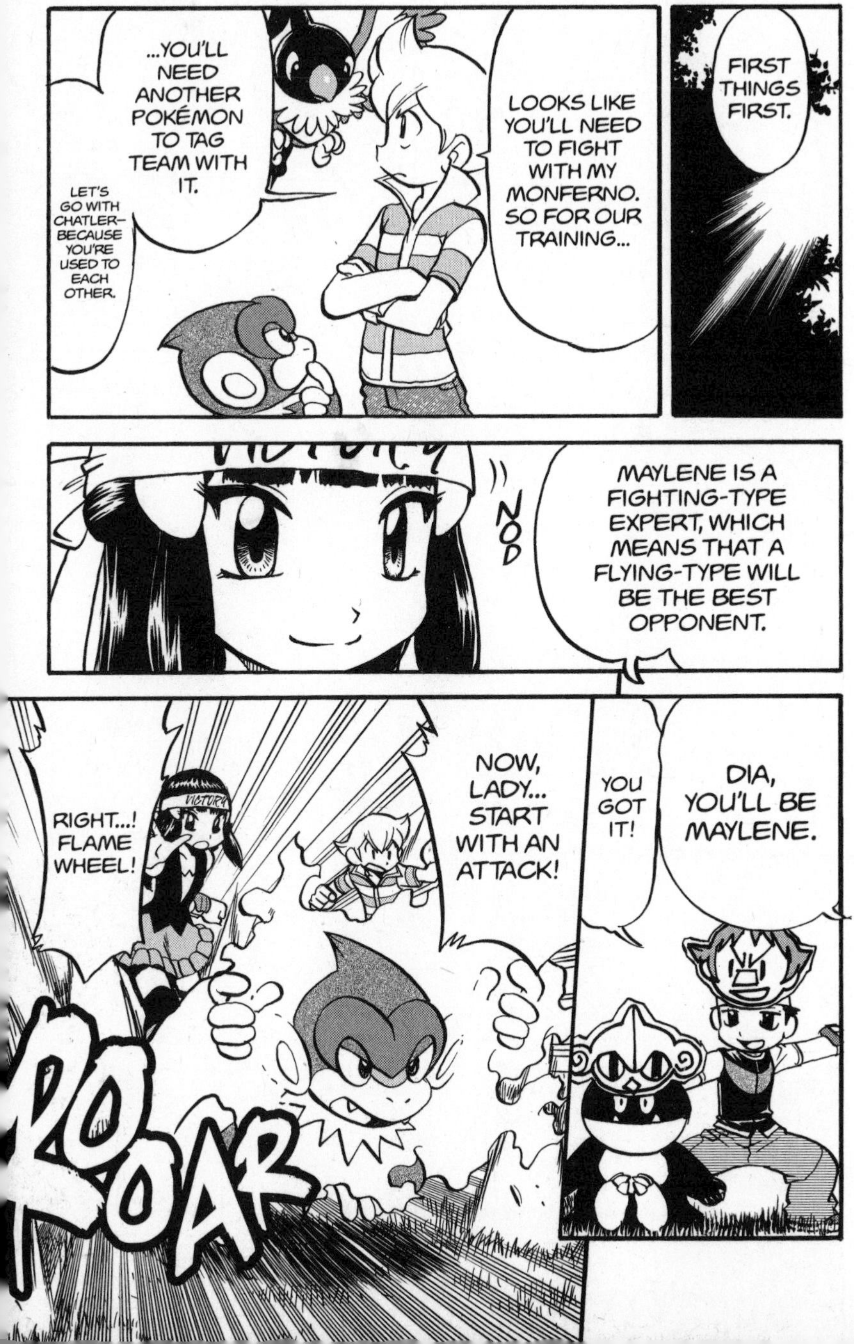
FIRST THINGS FIRST.
LOOKS LIKE YOU'LL NEED TO FIGHT WITH MY MONFERNO. SO FOR OUR TRAINING...
...YOU'LL NEED ANOTHER POKéMON TO TAG TEAM WITH IT.
LET'S GO WITH CHATLER—BECAUSE YOU'RE USED TO EACH OTHER.
MAYLENE IS A FIGHTING-TYPE EXPERT, WHICH MEANS THAT A FLYING-TYPE WILL BE THE BEST OPPONENT.
NOD
DIA, YOU'LL BE MAYLENE.
YOU GOT IT!
NOW, LADY... START WITH AN ATTACK!
RIGHT...! FLAME WHEEL!
ROOAR

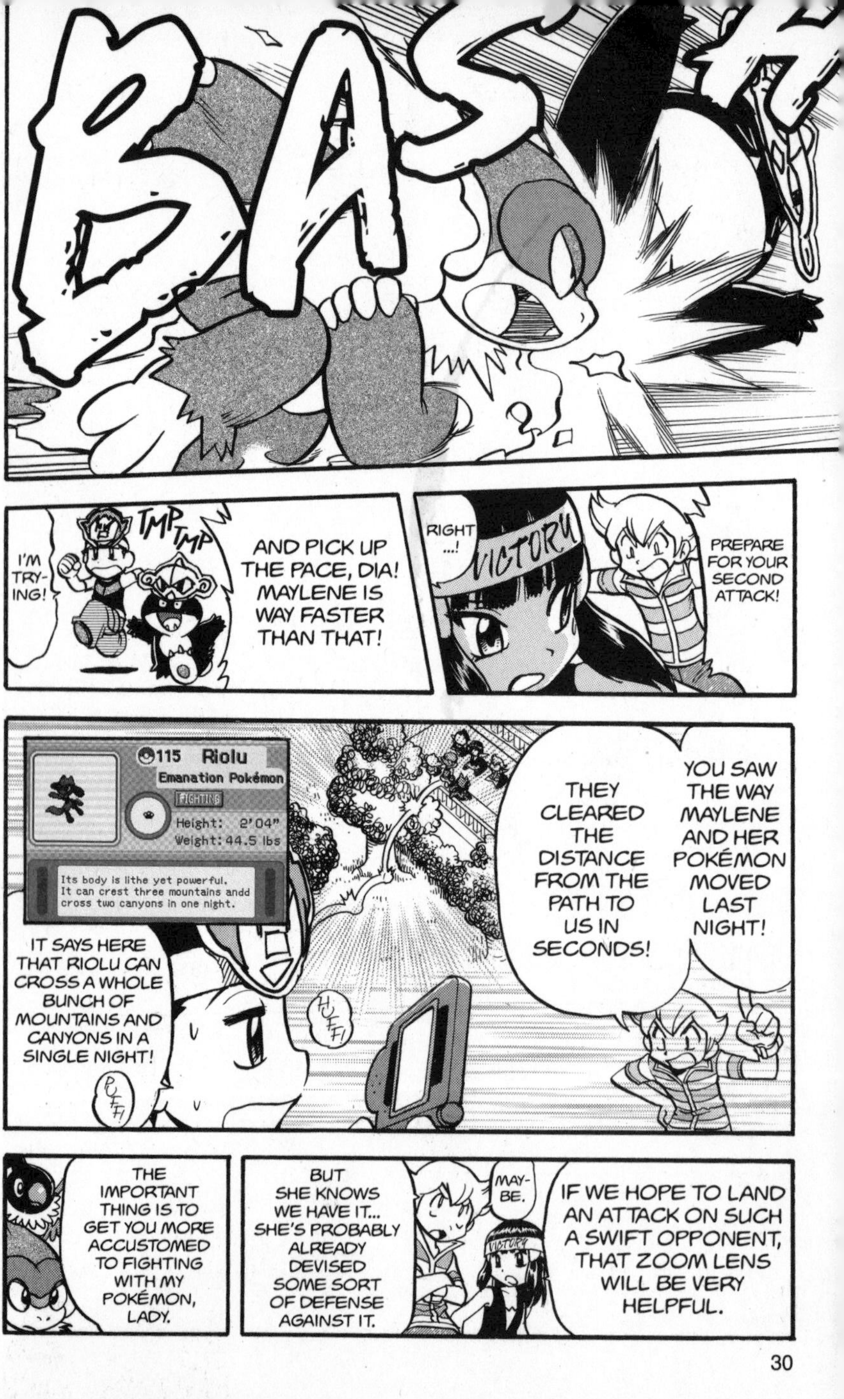
BASH
PREPARE FOR YOUR SECOND ATTACK!
RIGHT ...!
VICTORY
AND PICK UP THE PACE, DIA! MAYLENE IS WAY FASTER THAN THAT!
TMP TMP
I'M TRY-ING!
YOU SAW THE WAY MAYLENE AND HER POKÉMON MOVED LAST NIGHT!
THEY CLEARED THE DISTANCE FROM THE PATH TO US IN SECONDS!
115 Riolu
Emanation Pokémon
FIGHTING
Height: 2'04"
Weight: 44.5 lbs
Its body is lithe yet powerful. It can crest three mountains andd cross two canyons in one night.
IT SAYS HERE THAT RIOLU CAN CROSS A WHOLE BUNCH OF MOUNTAINS AND CANYONS IN A SINGLE NIGHT!
HUFF!
PUFF!
IF WE HOPE TO LAND AN ATTACK ON SUCH A SWIFT OPPONENT, THAT ZOOM LENS WILL BE VERY HELPFUL.
MAY-BE.
BUT SHE KNOWS WE HAVE IT... SHE'S PROBABLY ALREADY DEVISED SOME SORT OF DEFENSE AGAINST IT.
VICTORY
THE IMPORTANT THING IS TO GET YOU MORE ACCUSTOMED TO FIGHTING WITH MY POKÉMON, LADY.

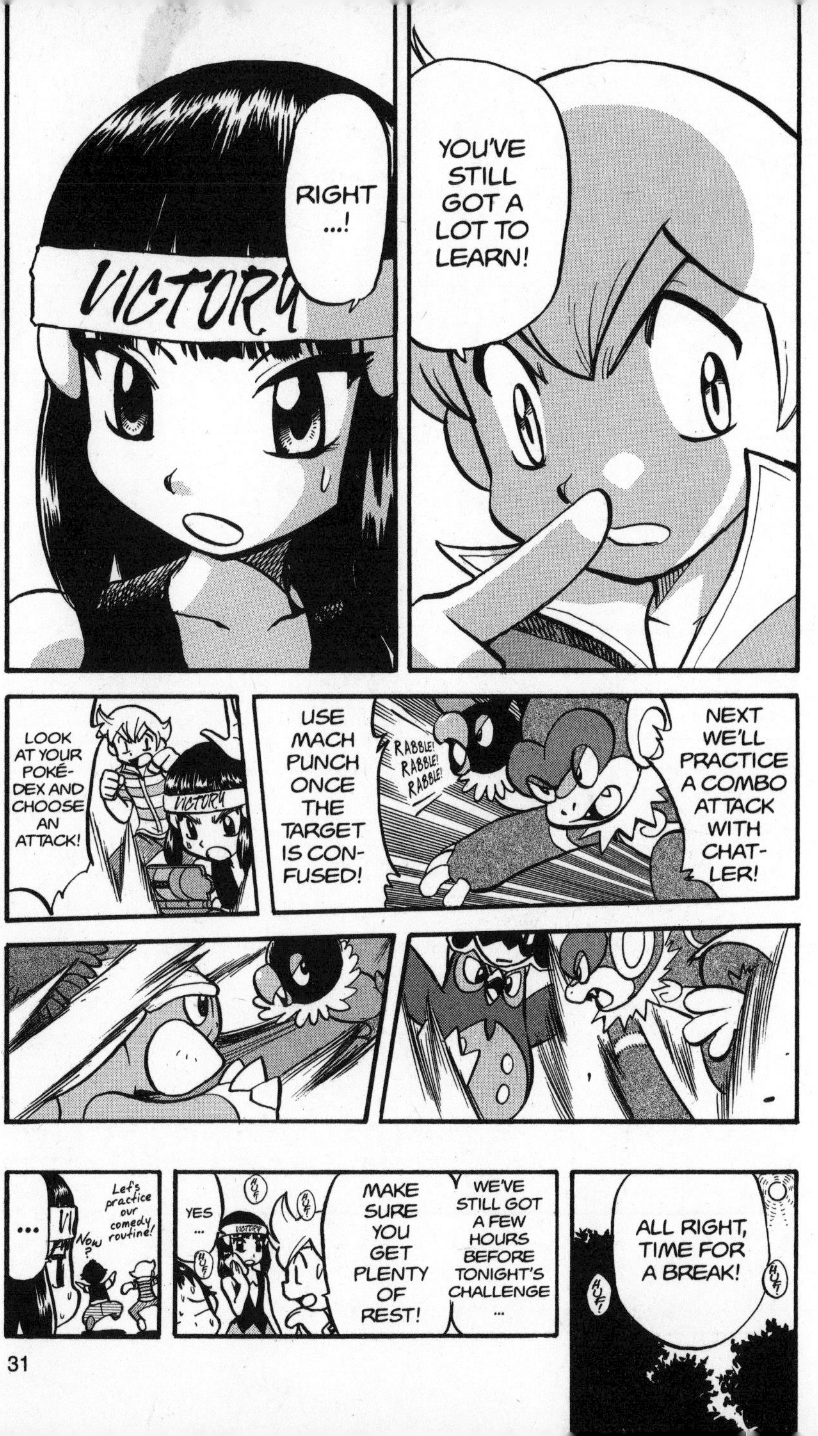
YOU'VE STILL GOT A LOT TO LEARN!
RIGHT ...!
NEXT WE'LL PRACTICE A COMBO ATTACK WITH CHATLER!
RABBLE! RABBLE! RABBLE!
USE MACH PUNCH ONCE THE TARGET IS CONFUSED!
LOOK AT YOUR POKÉDEX AND CHOOSE AN ATTACK!
ALL RIGHT, TIME FOR A BREAK!
HUF HUF
WE'VE STILL GOT A FEW HOURS BEFORE TONIGHT'S CHALLENGE ...
MAKE SURE YOU GET PLENTY OF REST!
HUF HUF
YES ...
HUF
VICTORY
Let's practice our comedy routine!
Now ?
...

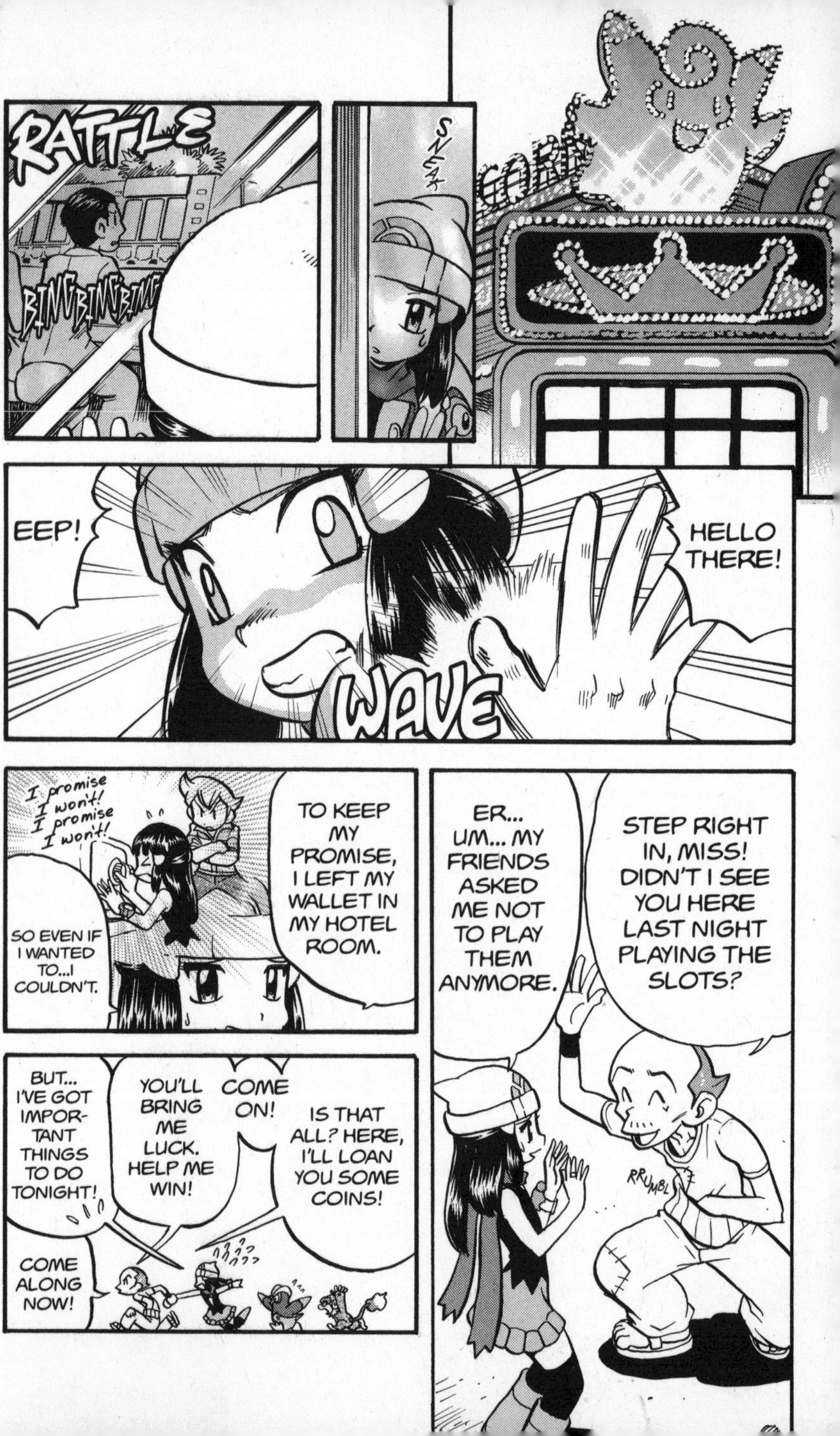
SNEAK
RATTLE
BINGBINGBING
HELLO THERE!
EEP!
WAVE
STEP RIGHT IN, MISS! DIDN'T I SEE YOU HERE LAST NIGHT PLAYING THE SLOTS?
ER... UM... MY FRIENDS ASKED ME NOT TO PLAY THEM ANYMORE.
RRUMBL
TO KEEP MY PROMISE, I LEFT MY WALLET IN MY HOTEL ROOM.
I promise I won't! I promise I won't!
SO EVEN IF I WANTED TO...I COULDN'T.
IS THAT ALL? HERE, I'LL LOAN YOU SOME COINS!
COME ON!
YOU'LL BRING ME LUCK. HELP ME WIN!
BUT... I'VE GOT IMPORTANT THINGS TO DO TONIGHT!
COME ALONG NOW!

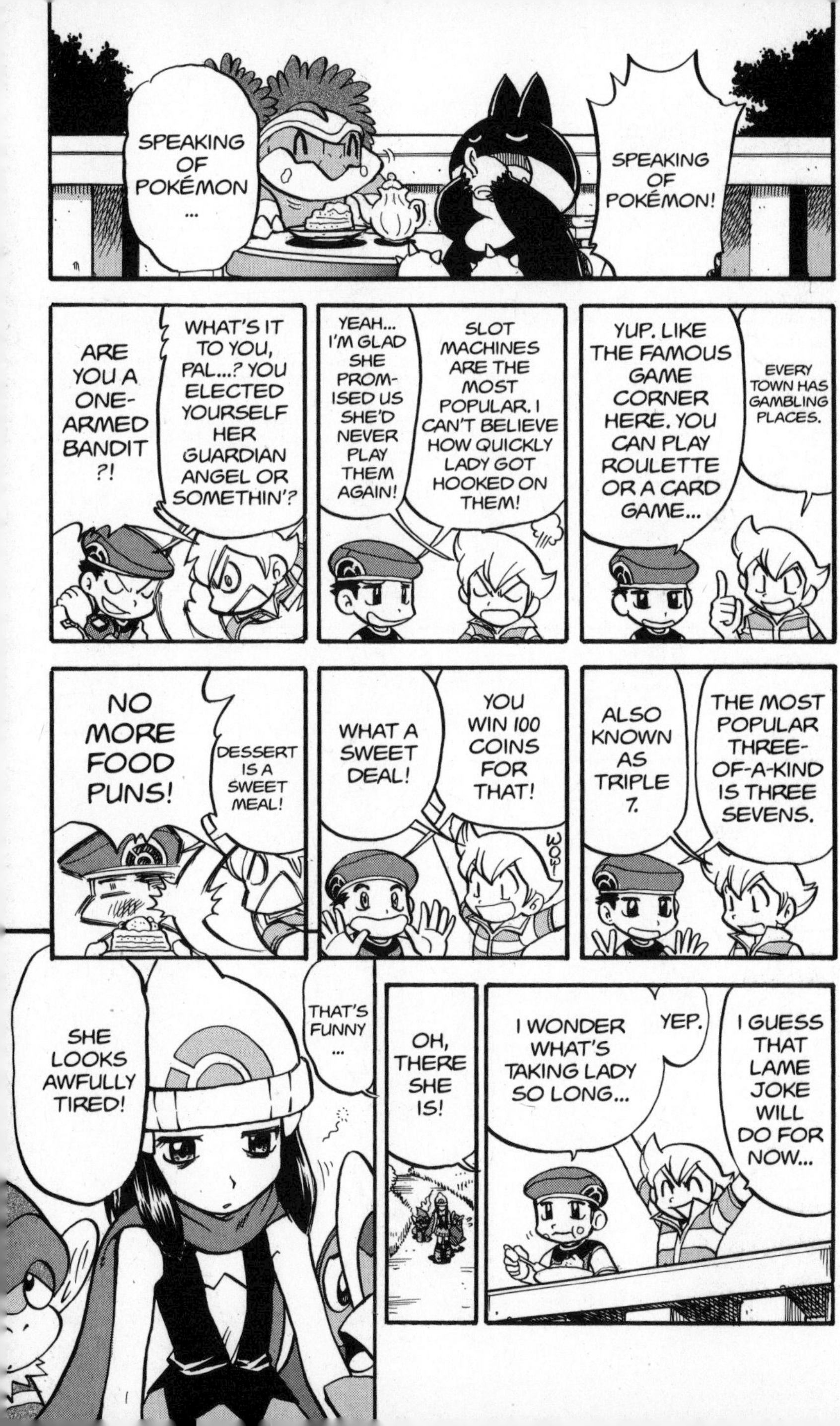
SPEAKING OF POKÉMON!
SPEAKING OF POKÉMON ...
EVERY TOWN HAS GAMBLING PLACES.
YUP. LIKE THE FAMOUS GAME CORNER HERE. YOU CAN PLAY ROULETTE OR A CARD GAME...
SLOT MACHINES ARE THE MOST POPULAR. I CAN'T BELIEVE HOW QUICKLY LADY GOT HOOKED ON THEM!
YEAH... I'M GLAD SHE PROMISED US SHE'D NEVER PLAY THEM AGAIN!
WHAT'S IT TO YOU, PAL...? YOU ELECTED YOURSELF HER GUARDIAN ANGEL OR SOMETHIN'?
ARE YOU A ONE-ARMED BANDIT?!
THE MOST POPULAR THREE-OF-A-KIND IS THREE SEVENS.
ALSO KNOWN AS TRIPLE 7.
YOU WIN 100 COINS FOR THAT!
WHAT A SWEET DEAL!
WOW!
DESSERT IS A SWEET MEAL!
NO MORE FOOD PUNS!
I GUESS THAT LAME JOKE WILL DO FOR NOW...
YEP.
I WONDER WHAT'S TAKING LADY SO LONG...
OH, THERE SHE IS!
THAT'S FUNNY ...
SHE LOOKS AWFULLY TIRED!

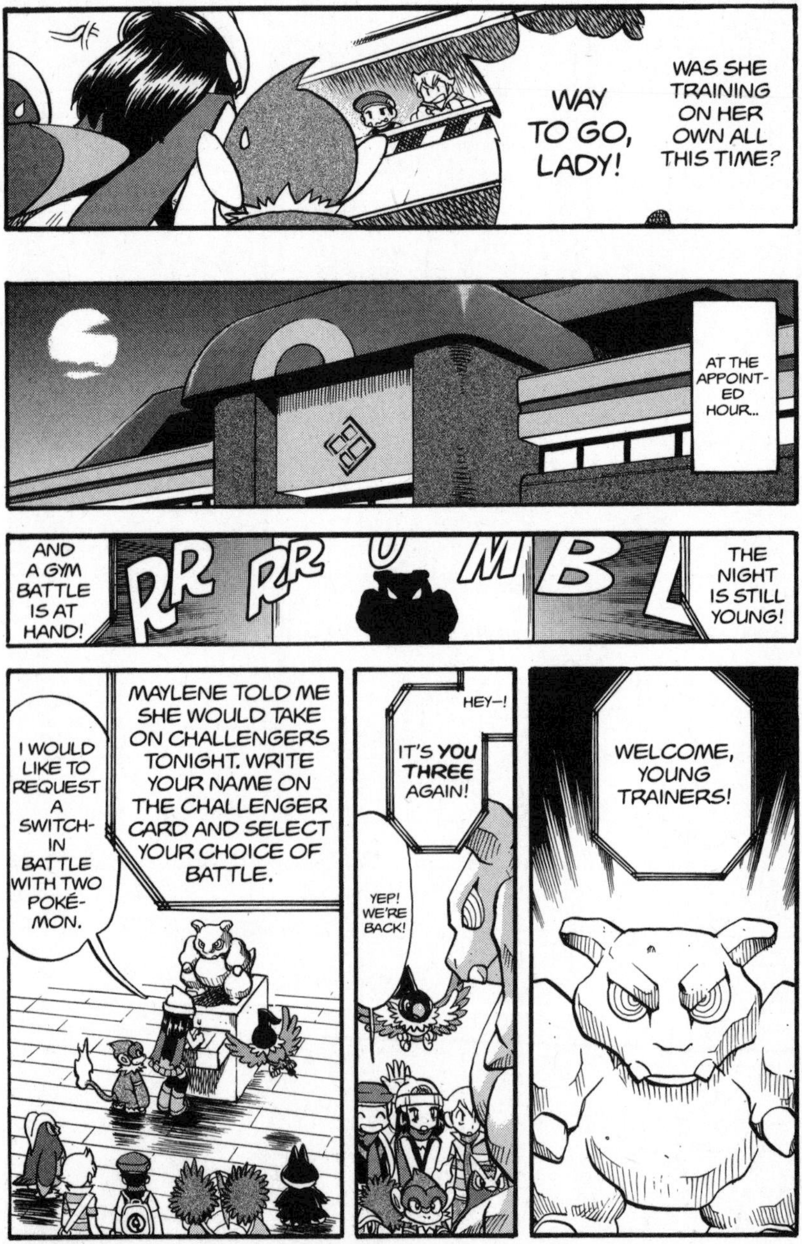
WAS SHE TRAINING ON HER OWN ALL THIS TIME?
WAY TO GO, LADY!
AT THE APPOINTED HOUR...
THE NIGHT IS STILL YOUNG!
RRRRUMBL
AND A GYM BATTLE IS AT HAND!
WELCOME, YOUNG TRAINERS!
HEY—!
IT'S **YOU THREE** AGAIN!
YEP! WE'RE BACK!
MAYLENE TOLD ME SHE WOULD TAKE ON CHALLENGERS TONIGHT. WRITE YOUR NAME ON THE CHALLENGER CARD AND SELECT YOUR CHOICE OF BATTLE.
I WOULD LIKE TO REQUEST A SWITCH-IN BATTLE WITH TWO POKÉMON.

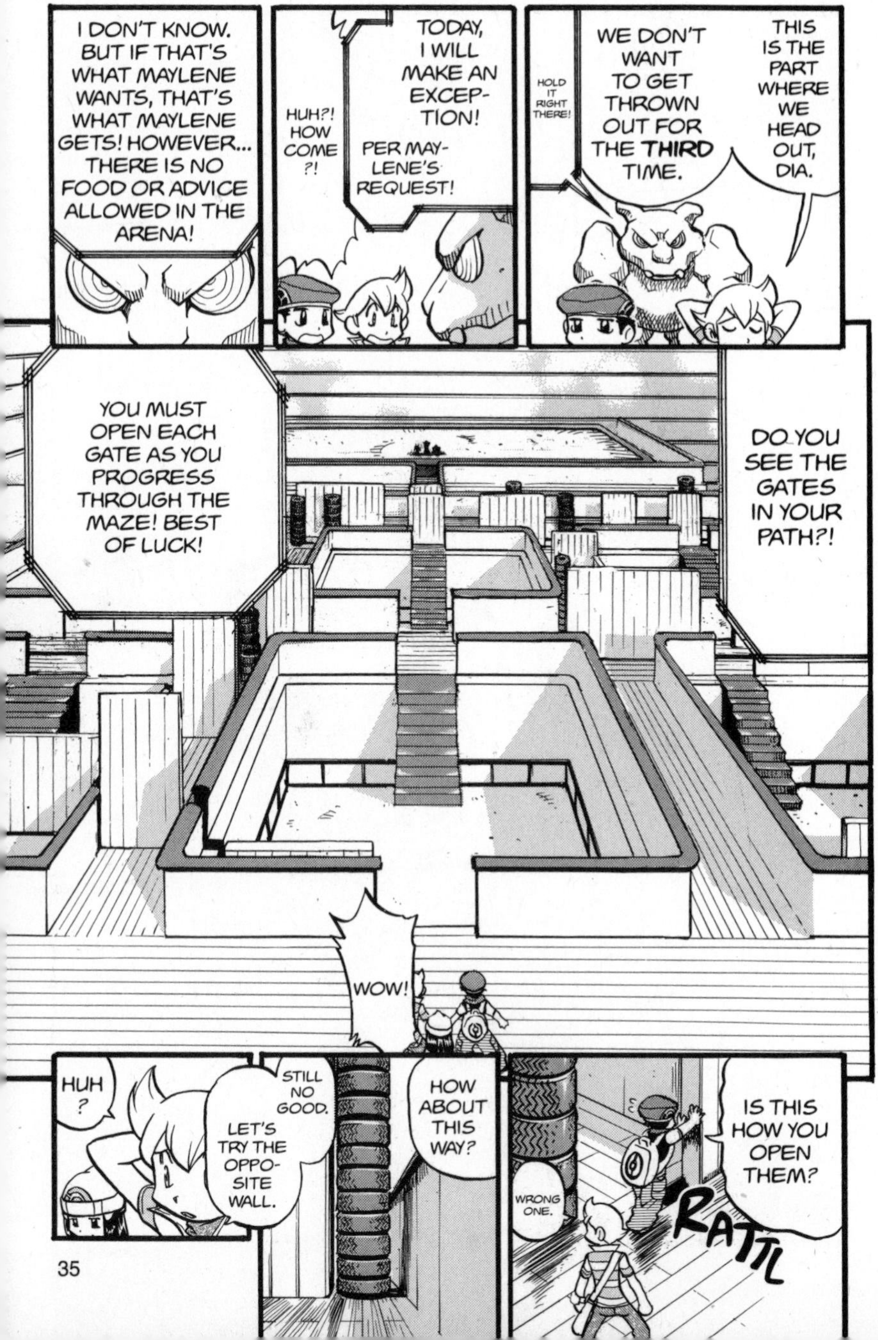
THIS IS THE PART WHERE WE HEAD OUT, DIA.
WE DON'T WANT TO GET THROWN OUT FOR THE **THIRD** TIME.
HOLD IT RIGHT THERE!
TODAY, I WILL MAKE AN EXCEP-TION!
PER MAY-LENE'S REQUEST!
HUH?! HOW COME?!
I DON'T KNOW. BUT IF THAT'S WHAT MAYLENE WANTS, THAT'S WHAT MAYLENE GETS! HOWEVER... THERE IS NO FOOD OR ADVICE ALLOWED IN THE ARENA!
DO YOU SEE THE GATES IN YOUR PATH?!
YOU MUST OPEN EACH GATE AS YOU PROGRESS THROUGH THE MAZE! BEST OF LUCK!
WOW!
IS THIS HOW YOU OPEN THEM?
RATTL
WRONG ONE.
HOW ABOUT THIS WAY?
STILL NO GOOD.
LET'S TRY THE OPPO-SITE WALL.
HUH?

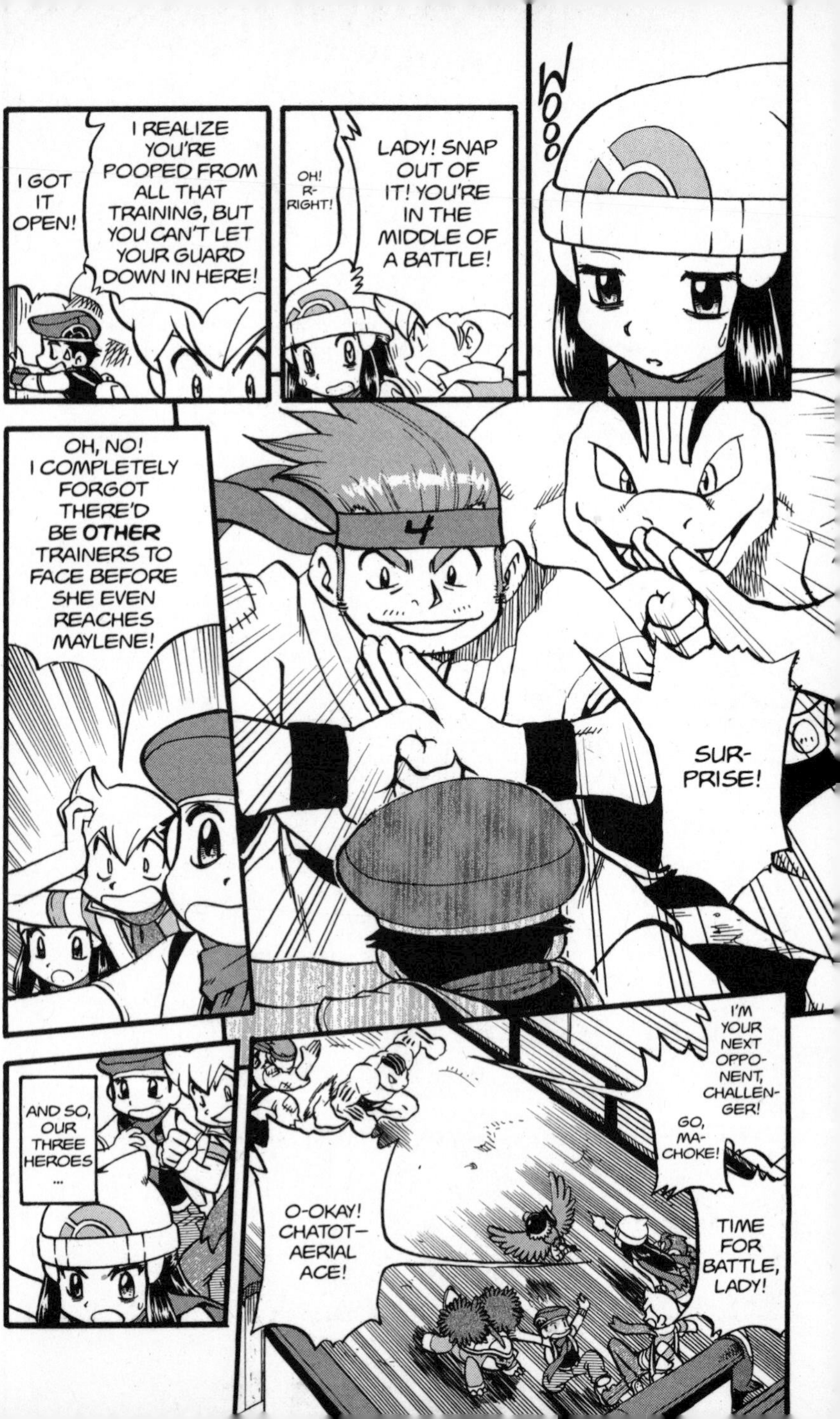
WOOO
LADY! SNAP OUT OF IT! YOU'RE IN THE MIDDLE OF A BATTLE!
OH! R-RIGHT!
I REALIZE YOU'RE POOPED FROM ALL THAT TRAINING, BUT YOU CAN'T LET YOUR GUARD DOWN IN HERE!
I GOT IT OPEN!
SUR-PRISE!
OH, NO! I COMPLETELY FORGOT THERE'D BE **OTHER** TRAINERS TO FACE BEFORE SHE EVEN REACHES MAYLENE!
I'M YOUR NEXT OPPO-NENT, CHALLEN-GER!
GO, MA-CHOKE!
TIME FOR BATTLE, LADY!
O-OKAY! CHATOT—AERIAL ACE!
AND SO, OUR THREE HEROES...

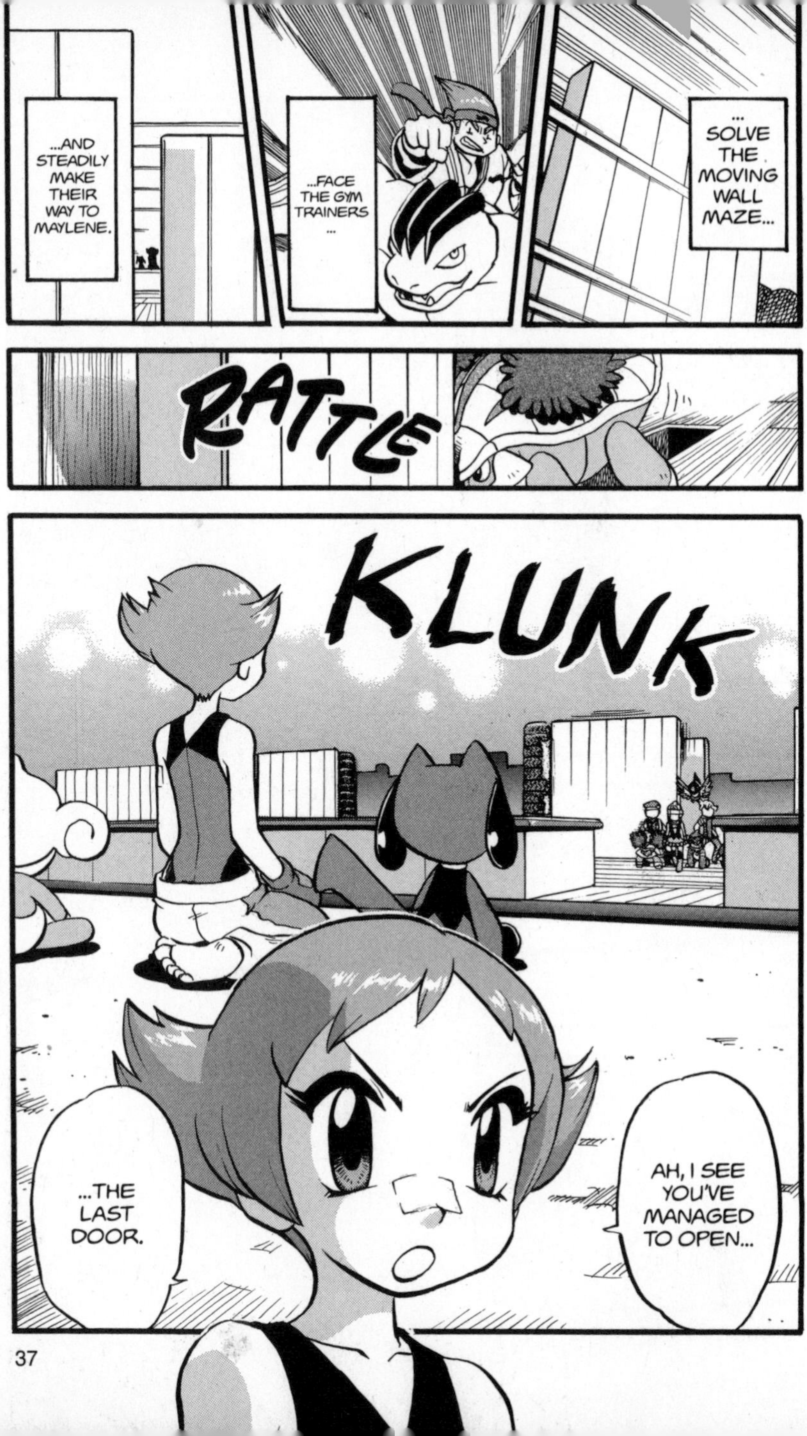

... SOLVE THE MOVING WALL MAZE...
...FACE THE GYM TRAINERS ...
...AND STEADILY MAKE THEIR WAY TO MAYLENE.
RATTLE
KLUNK
AH, I SEE YOU'VE MANAGED TO OPEN...
...THE LAST DOOR.

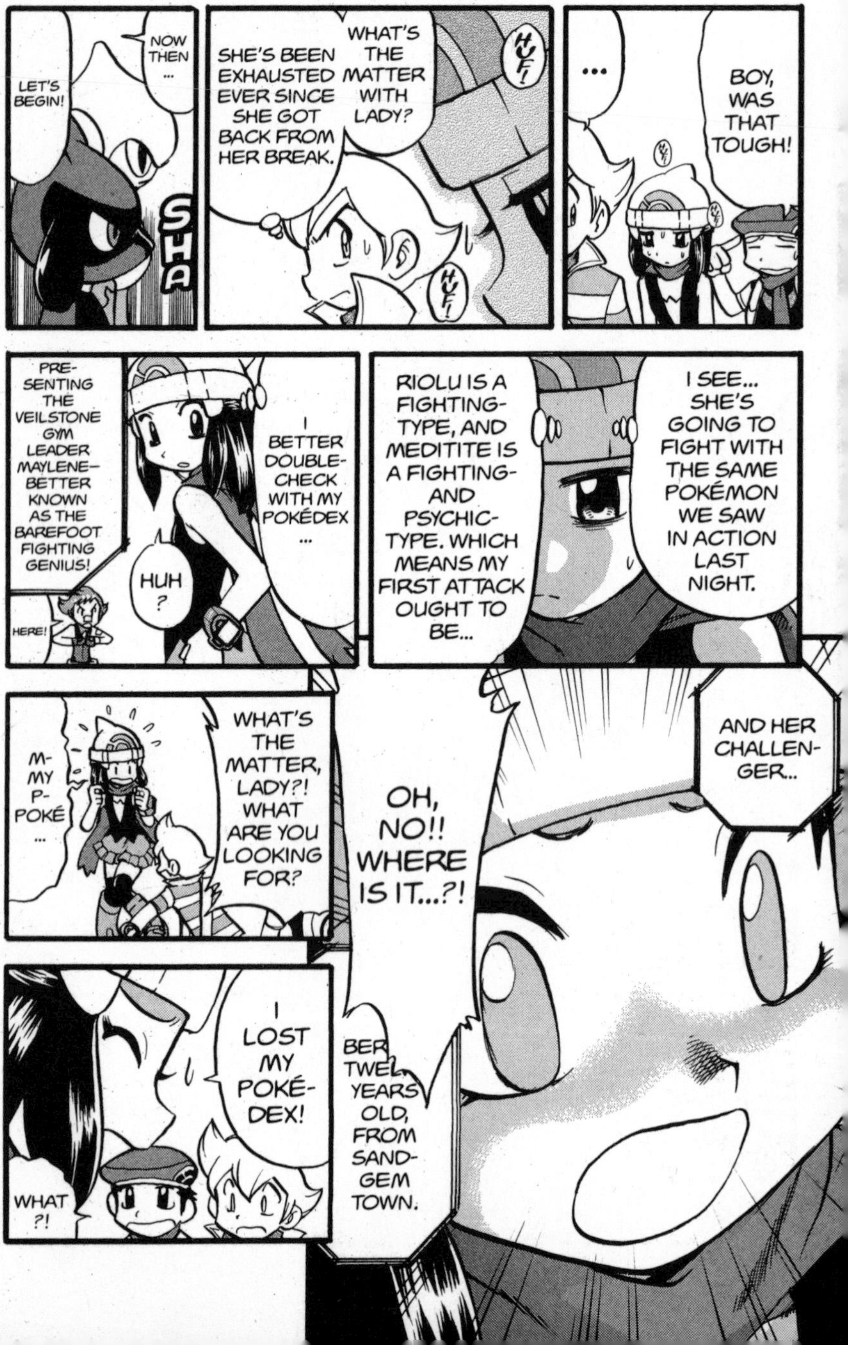
BOY, WAS THAT TOUGH!
...
WHAT'S THE MATTER WITH LADY?
HUF!
SHE'S BEEN EXHAUSTED EVER SINCE SHE GOT BACK FROM HER BREAK.
HUF!
NOW THEN ...
LET'S BEGIN!
SHA
I SEE... SHE'S GOING TO FIGHT WITH THE SAME POKÉMON WE SAW IN ACTION LAST NIGHT.
RIOLU IS A FIGHTING-TYPE, AND MEDITITE IS A FIGHTING- AND PSYCHIC-TYPE. WHICH MEANS MY FIRST ATTACK OUGHT TO BE...
I BETTER DOUBLE-CHECK WITH MY POKÉDEX ...
PRESENTING THE VEILSTONE GYM LEADER MAYLENE—BETTER KNOWN AS THE BAREFOOT FIGHTING GENIUS!
HUH?
HERE!
AND HER CHALLENGER...
BER TWEL YEARS OLD, FROM SANDGEM TOWN.
OH, NO!! WHERE IS IT...?!
WHAT'S THE MATTER, LADY?! WHAT ARE YOU LOOKING FOR?
M-MY P-POKÉ ...
I LOST MY POKÉDEX!
WHAT ?!

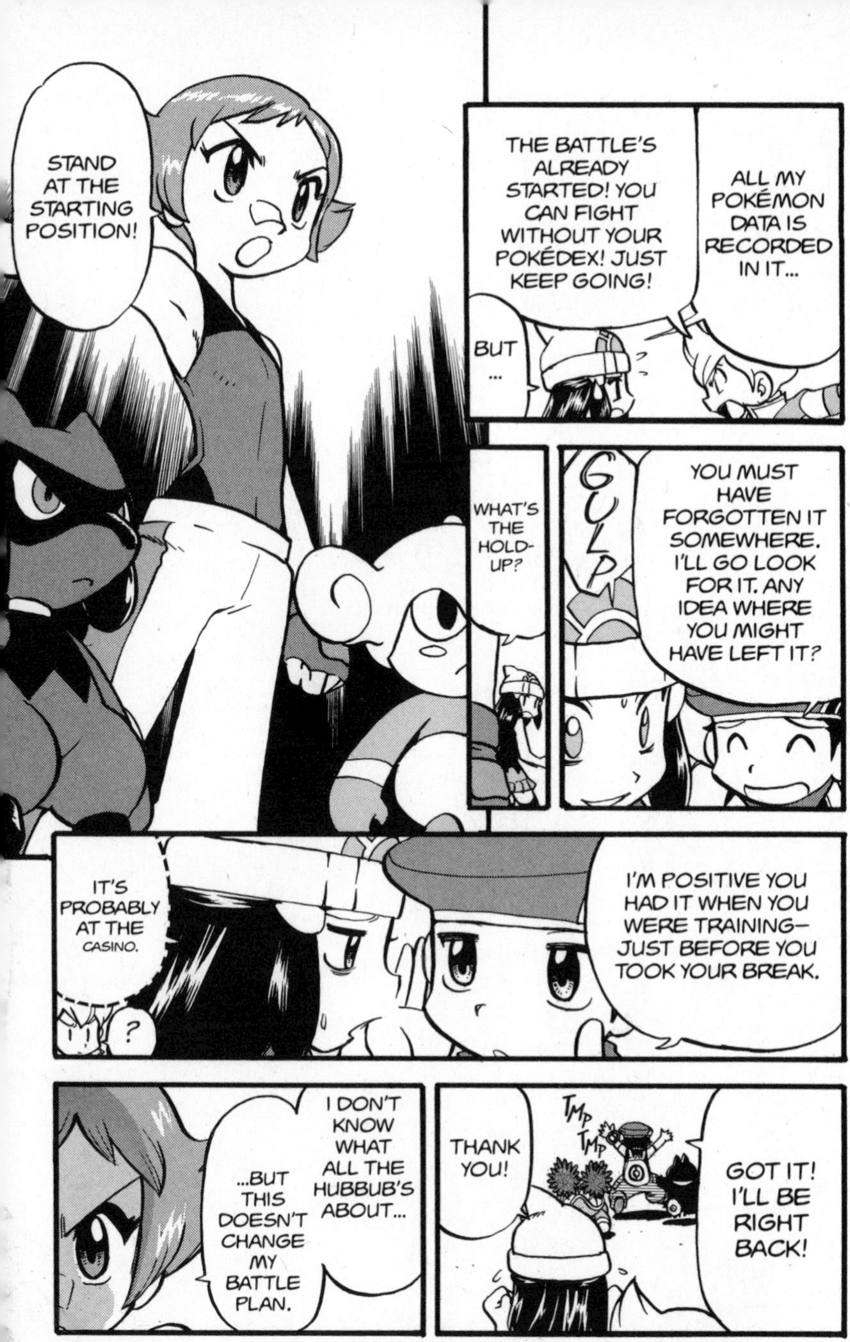
ALL MY POKÉMON DATA IS RECORDED IN IT...
THE BATTLE'S ALREADY STARTED! YOU CAN FIGHT WITHOUT YOUR POKÉDEX! JUST KEEP GOING!
BUT ...
GULP
YOU MUST HAVE FORGOTTEN IT SOMEWHERE. I'LL GO LOOK FOR IT. ANY IDEA WHERE YOU MIGHT HAVE LEFT IT?
WHAT'S THE HOLD-UP?
STAND AT THE STARTING POSITION!
I'M POSITIVE YOU HAD IT WHEN YOU WERE TRAINING—JUST BEFORE YOU TOOK YOUR BREAK.
IT'S PROBABLY AT THE CASINO.
?
GOT IT! I'LL BE RIGHT BACK!
TMP TMP
THANK YOU!
I DON'T KNOW WHAT ALL THE HUBBUB'S ABOUT...
...BUT THIS DOESN'T CHANGE MY BATTLE PLAN.

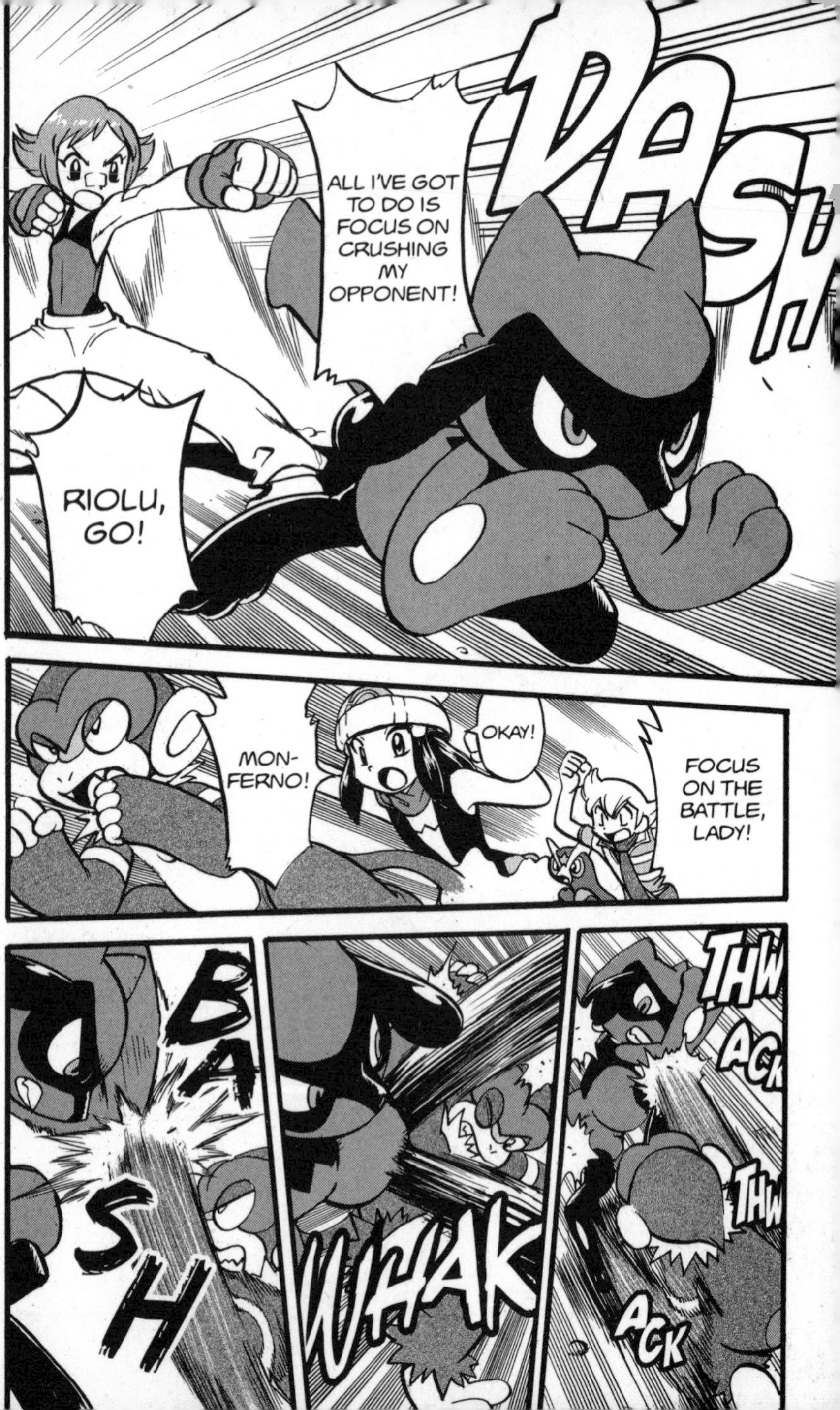
DASH
ALL I'VE GOT TO DO IS FOCUS ON CRUSHING MY OPPONENT!
RIOLU, GO!
FOCUS ON THE BATTLE, LADY!
OKAY!
MON-FERNO!
THWACK
THWACK
WHAK
BASH

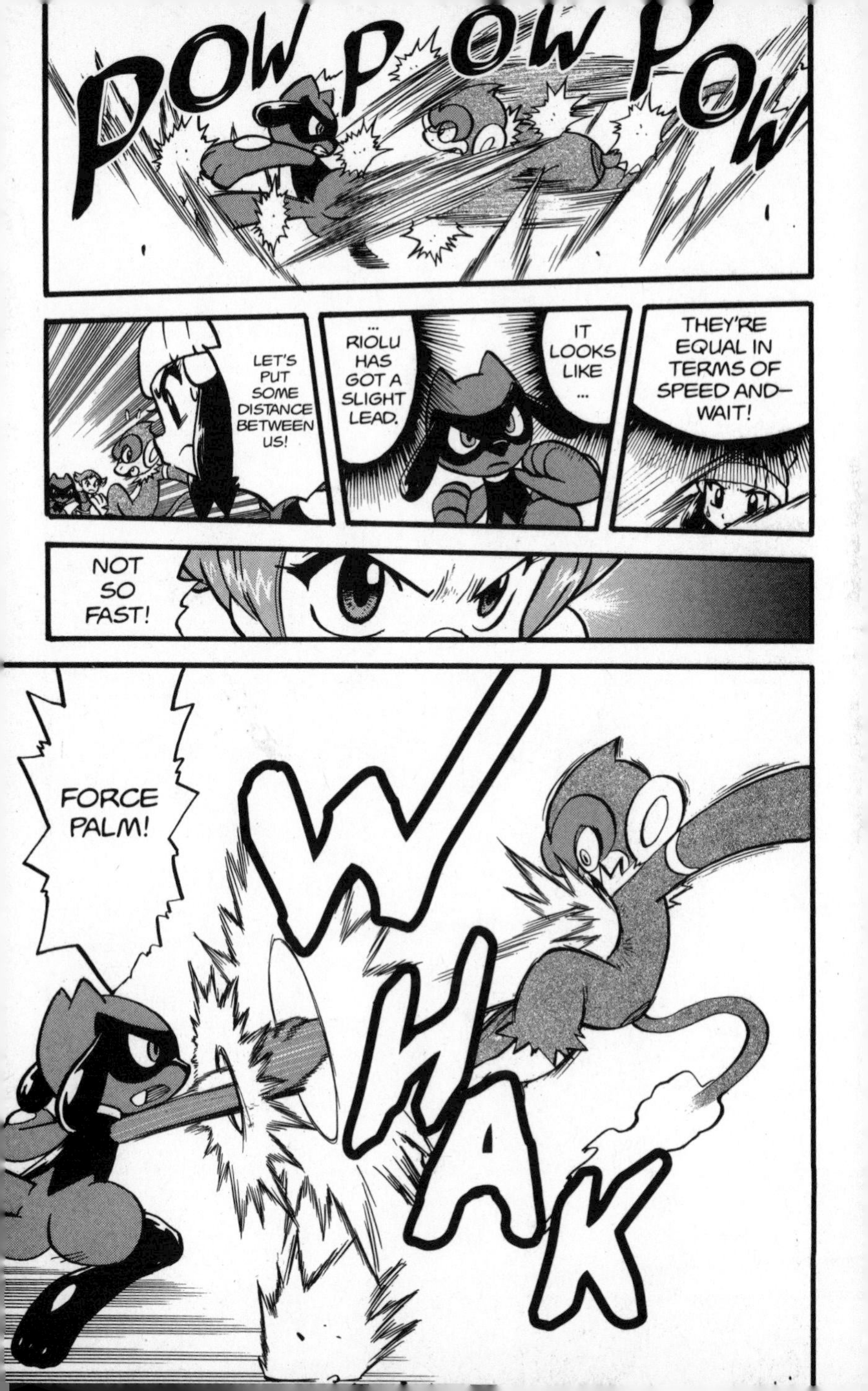
POW POW POW POW
THEY'RE EQUAL IN TERMS OF SPEED AND— WAIT!
IT LOOKS LIKE ...
... RIOLU HAS GOT A SLIGHT LEAD.
LET'S PUT SOME DISTANCE BETWEEN US!
NOT SO FAST!
FORCE PALM!
WHAK

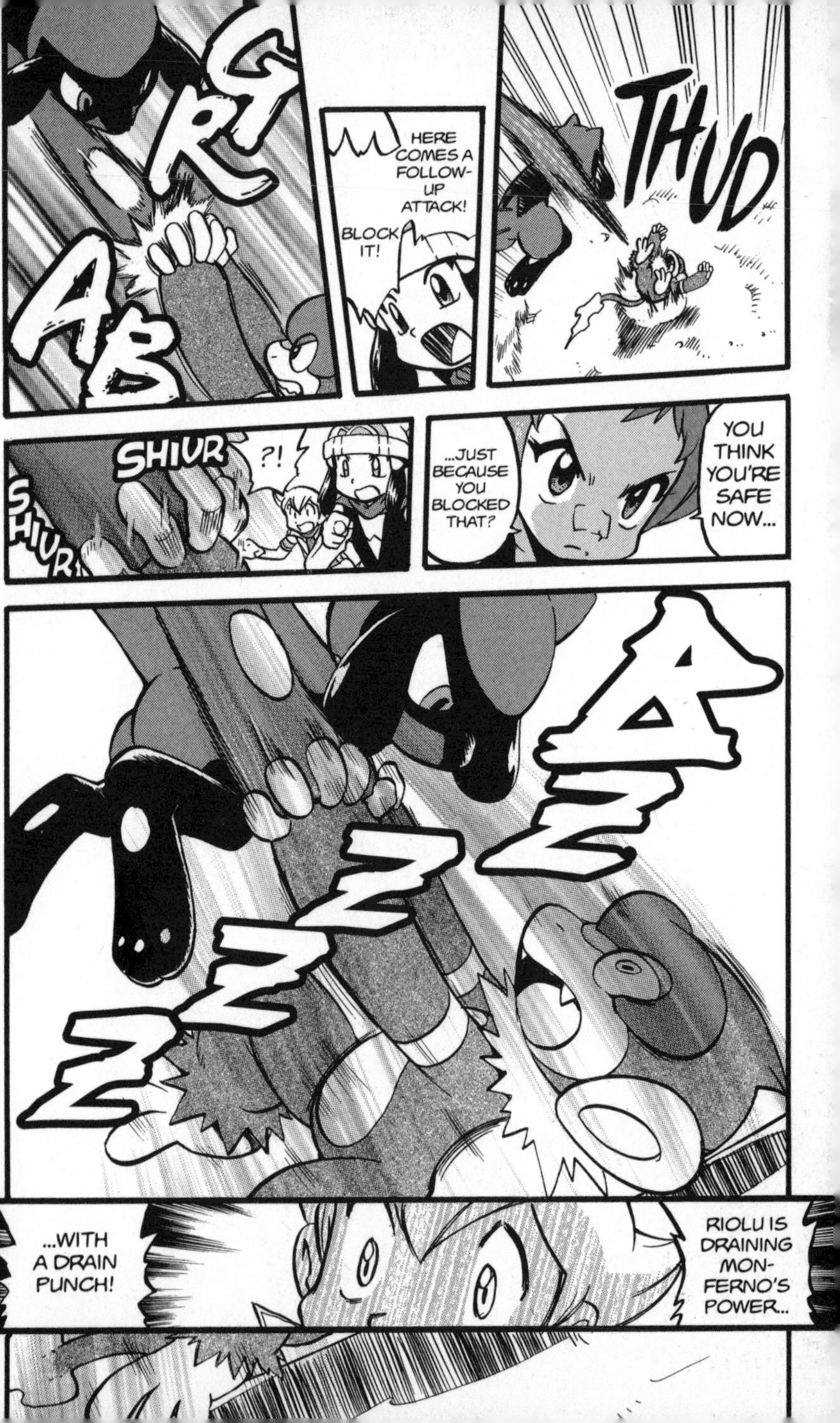
THUD
HERE COMES A FOLLOW-UP ATTACK!
BLOCK IT!
YOU THINK YOU'RE SAFE NOW...
...JUST BECAUSE YOU BLOCKED THAT?
?!
SHIVR
SHIVR
RIOLU IS DRAINING MON-FERNO'S POWER...
...WITH A DRAIN PUNCH!

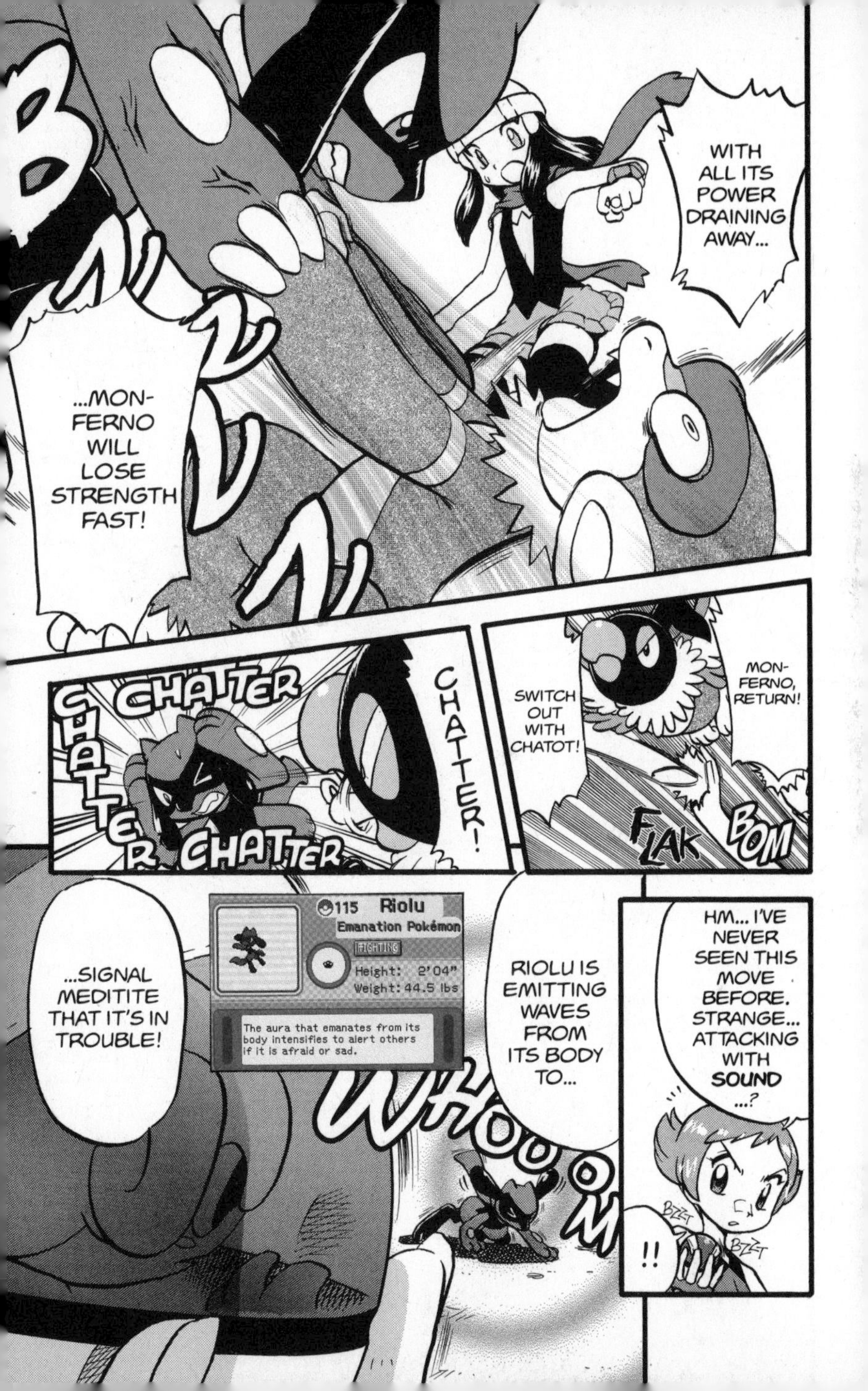
WITH ALL ITS POWER DRAINING AWAY...
...MON-FERNO WILL LOSE STRENGTH FAST!
MON-FERNO, RETURN!
SWITCH OUT WITH CHATOT!
FLAK
BOM
CHATTER!
CHATTER
CHATTER
CHATTER
HM... I'VE NEVER SEEN THIS MOVE BEFORE. STRANGE... ATTACKING WITH **SOUND** ...?
BZZT
BZZT
!!
RIOLU IS EMITTING WAVES FROM ITS BODY TO...
...SIGNAL MEDITITE THAT IT'S IN TROUBLE!
115 Riolu
Emanation Pokémon
FIGHTING
Height: 2'04"
Weight: 44.5 lbs
The aura that emanates from its body intensifies to alert others if it is afraid or sad.
WHOOOOM

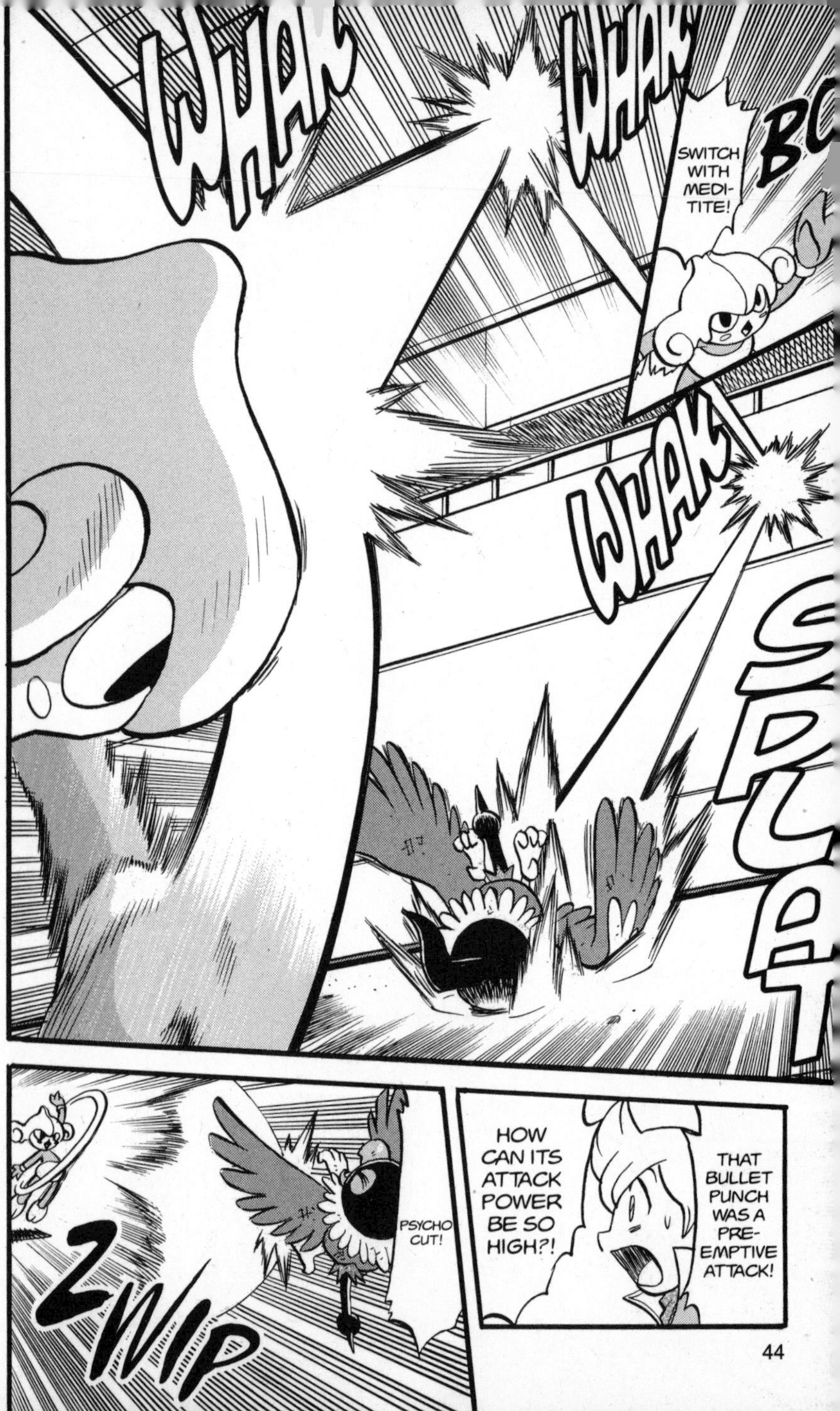
SWITCH WITH MEDI-TITE!
WHAK
WHAK
WHAK
SPLAT
THAT BULLET PUNCH WAS A PRE-EMPTIVE ATTACK!
HOW CAN ITS ATTACK POWER BE SO HIGH?!
PSYCHO CUT!
ZWIP

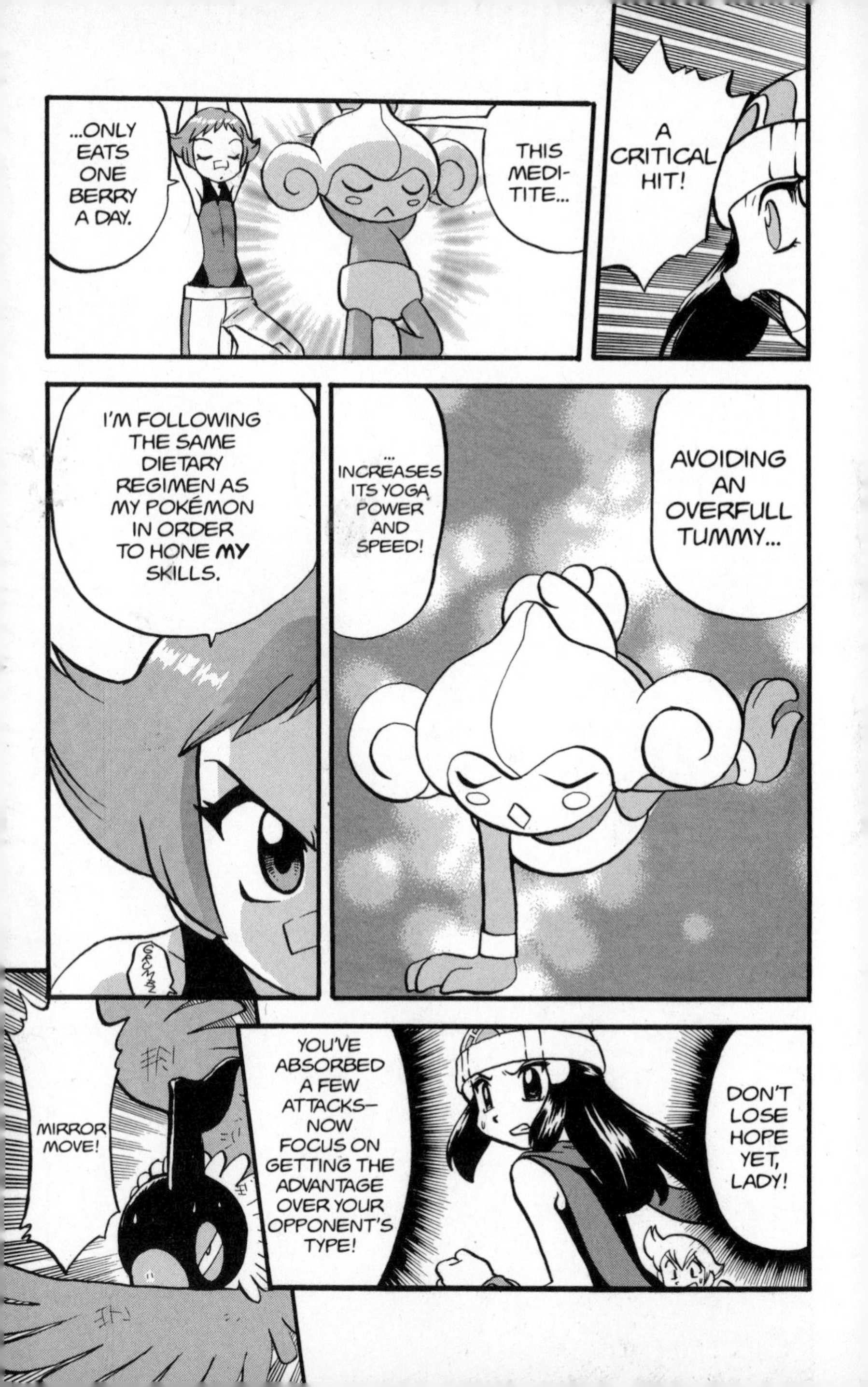
A CRITICAL HIT!
THIS MEDI-TITE...
...ONLY EATS ONE BERRY A DAY.
AVOIDING AN OVERFULL TUMMY...
...INCREASES ITS YOGA POWER AND SPEED!
I'M FOLLOWING THE SAME DIETARY REGIMEN AS MY POKÉMON IN ORDER TO HONE MY SKILLS.
DON'T LOSE HOPE YET, LADY!
YOU'VE ABSORBED A FEW ATTACKS—NOW FOCUS ON GETTING THE ADVANTAGE OVER YOUR OPPONENT'S TYPE!
MIRROR MOVE!

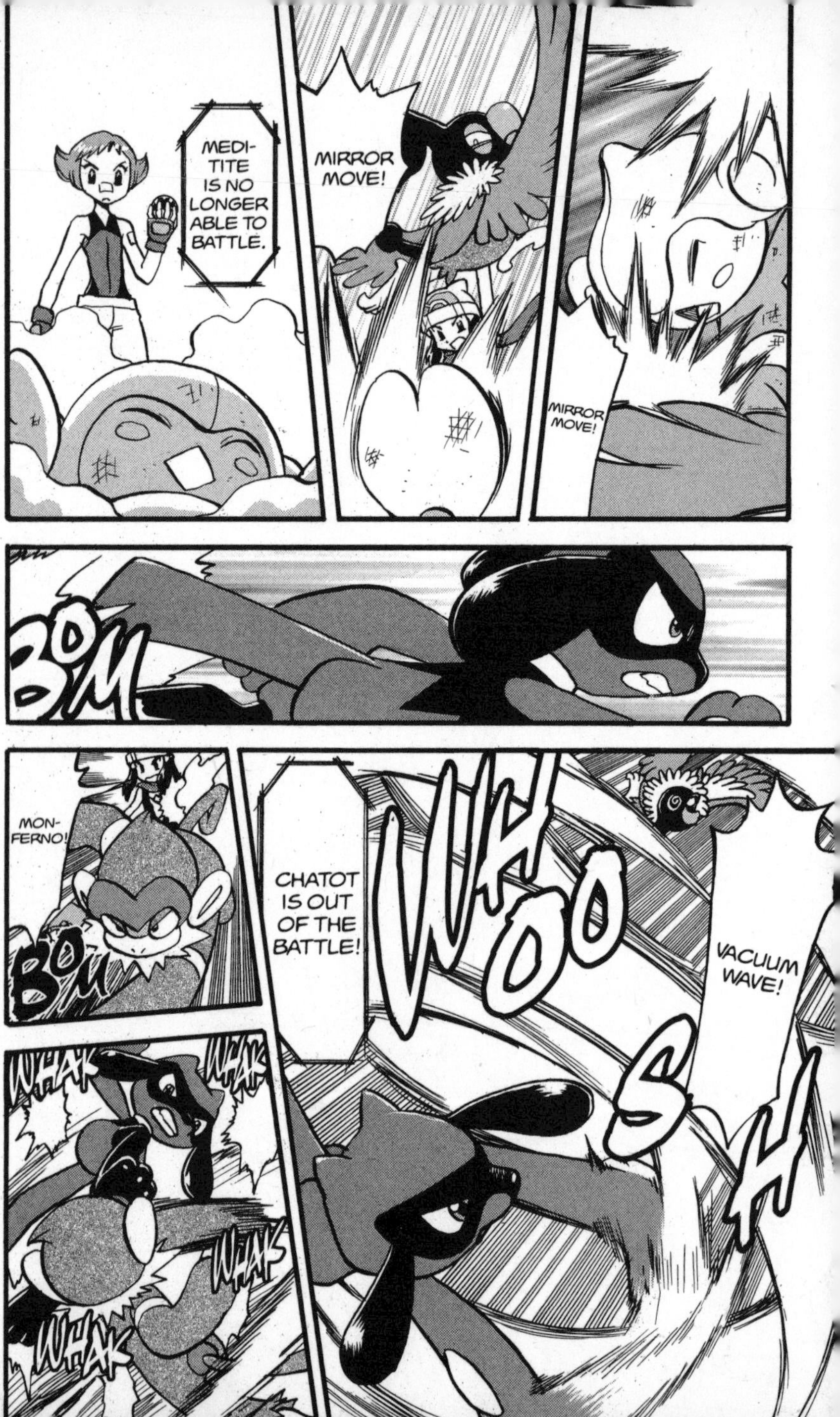
MIRROR MOVE!
MIRROR MOVE!
MEDITITE IS NO LONGER ABLE TO BATTLE.
BOOM
VACUUM WAVE!
WHOOSH
CHATOT IS OUT OF THE BATTLE!
MONFERNO!
BOOM
WHAK
WHAK
WHAK
WHAK

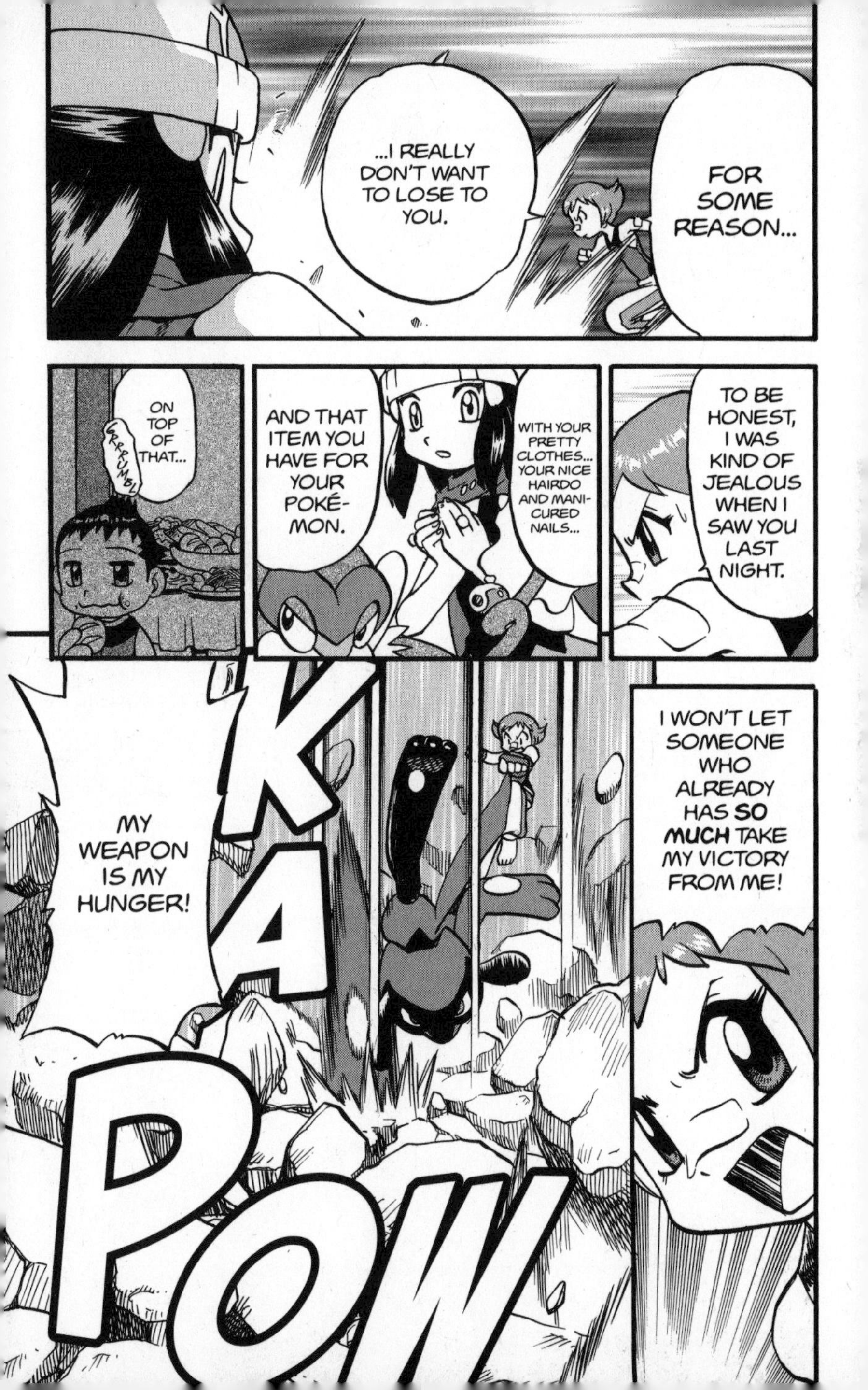
FOR SOME REASON...
...I REALLY DON'T WANT TO LOSE TO YOU.
TO BE HONEST, I WAS KIND OF JEALOUS WHEN I SAW YOU LAST NIGHT.
WITH YOUR PRETTY CLOTHES... YOUR NICE HAIRDO AND MANI-CURED NAILS...
AND THAT ITEM YOU HAVE FOR YOUR POKÉ-MON.
ON TOP OF THAT...
GRRRUMBL
I WON'T LET SOMEONE WHO ALREADY HAS **SO MUCH** TAKE MY VICTORY FROM ME!
KAPOW!
MY WEAPON IS MY HUNGER!

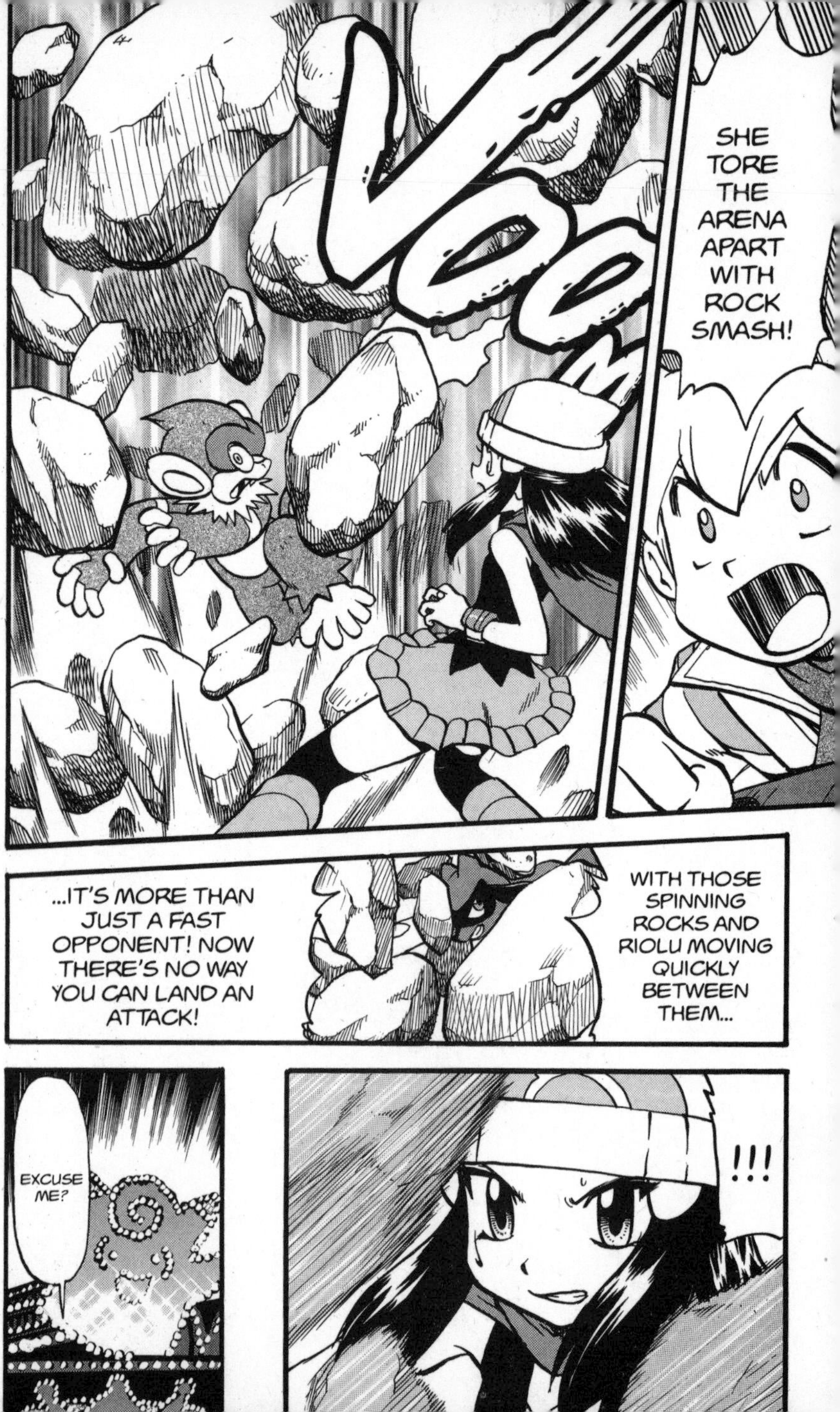
SHE TORE THE ARENA APART WITH ROCK SMASH!
VOOM
WITH THOSE SPINNING ROCKS AND RIOLU MOVING QUICKLY BETWEEN THEM...
...IT'S MORE THAN JUST A FAST OPPONENT! NOW THERE'S NO WAY YOU CAN LAND AN ATTACK!
!!!
EXCUSE ME?

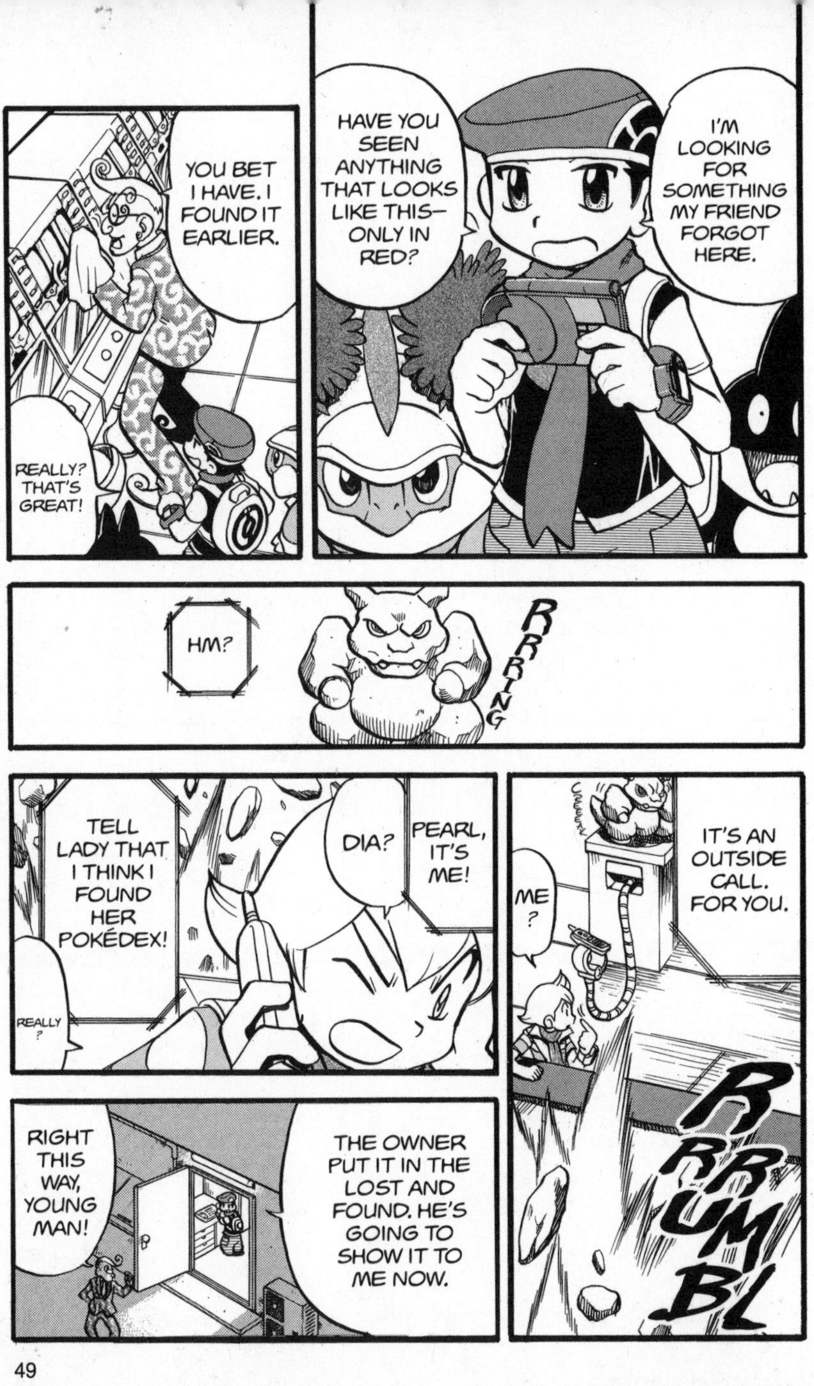
I'M LOOKING FOR SOMETHING MY FRIEND FORGOT HERE.
HAVE YOU SEEN ANYTHING THAT LOOKS LIKE THIS—ONLY IN RED?
YOU BET I HAVE. I FOUND IT EARLIER.
REALLY? THAT'S GREAT!
RRRRING
HM?
IT'S AN OUTSIDE CALL. FOR YOU.
ME?
RRRUMBL
PEARL, IT'S ME!
DIA?
TELL LADY THAT I THINK I FOUND HER POKÉDEX!
REALLY?
THE OWNER PUT IT IN THE LOST AND FOUND. HE'S GOING TO SHOW IT TO ME NOW.
RIGHT THIS WAY, YOUNG MAN!

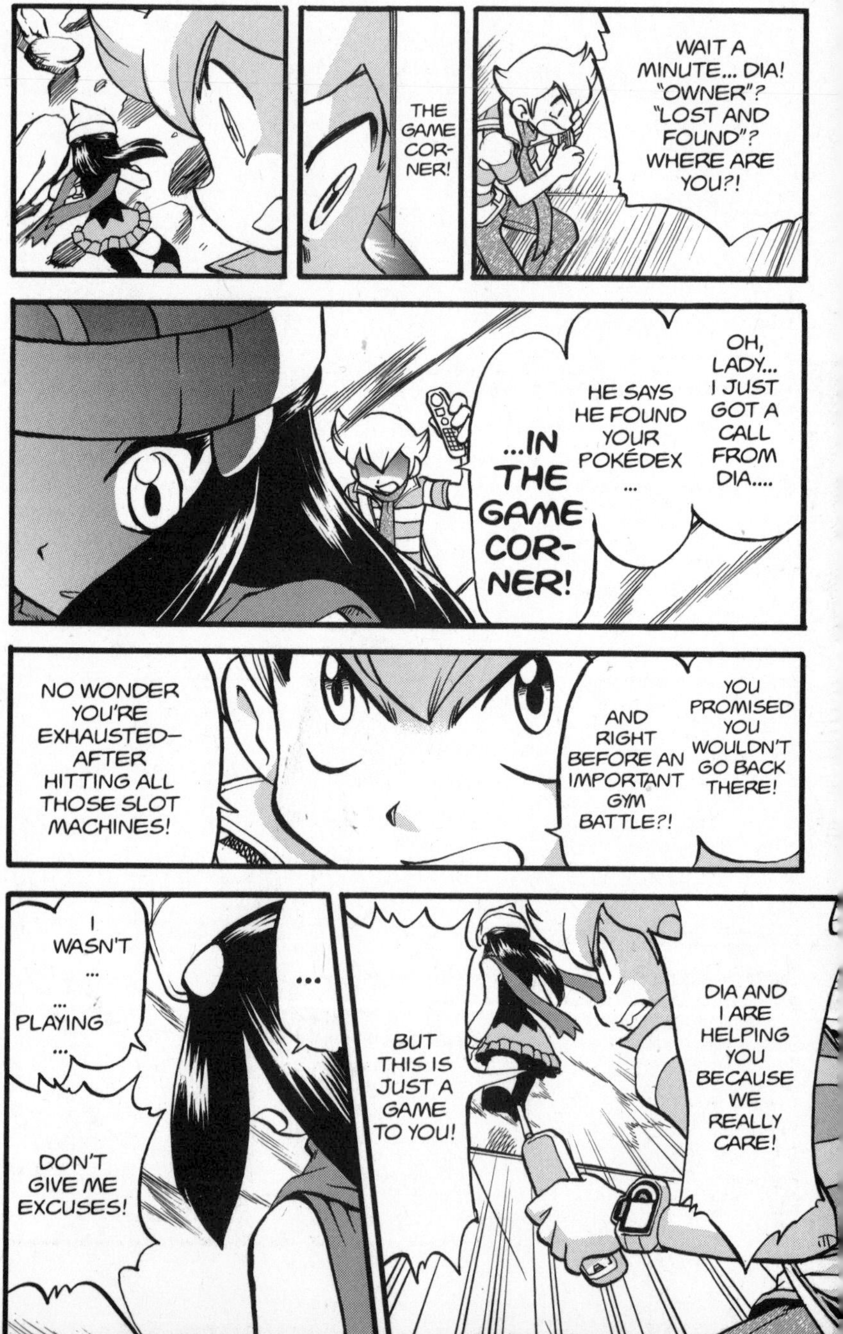
WAIT A MINUTE... DIA! "OWNER"? "LOST AND FOUND"? WHERE ARE YOU?!
THE GAME CORNER!
OH, LADY... I JUST GOT A CALL FROM DIA....
HE SAYS HE FOUND YOUR POKÉDEX ...
...IN THE GAME CORNER!
YOU PROMISED YOU WOULDN'T GO BACK THERE!
AND RIGHT BEFORE AN IMPORTANT GYM BATTLE?!
NO WONDER YOU'RE EXHAUSTED— AFTER HITTING ALL THOSE SLOT MACHINES!
DIA AND I ARE HELPING YOU BECAUSE WE REALLY CARE!
BUT THIS IS JUST A GAME TO YOU!
...
I WASN'T ... ... PLAYING ...
DON'T GIVE ME EXCUSES!

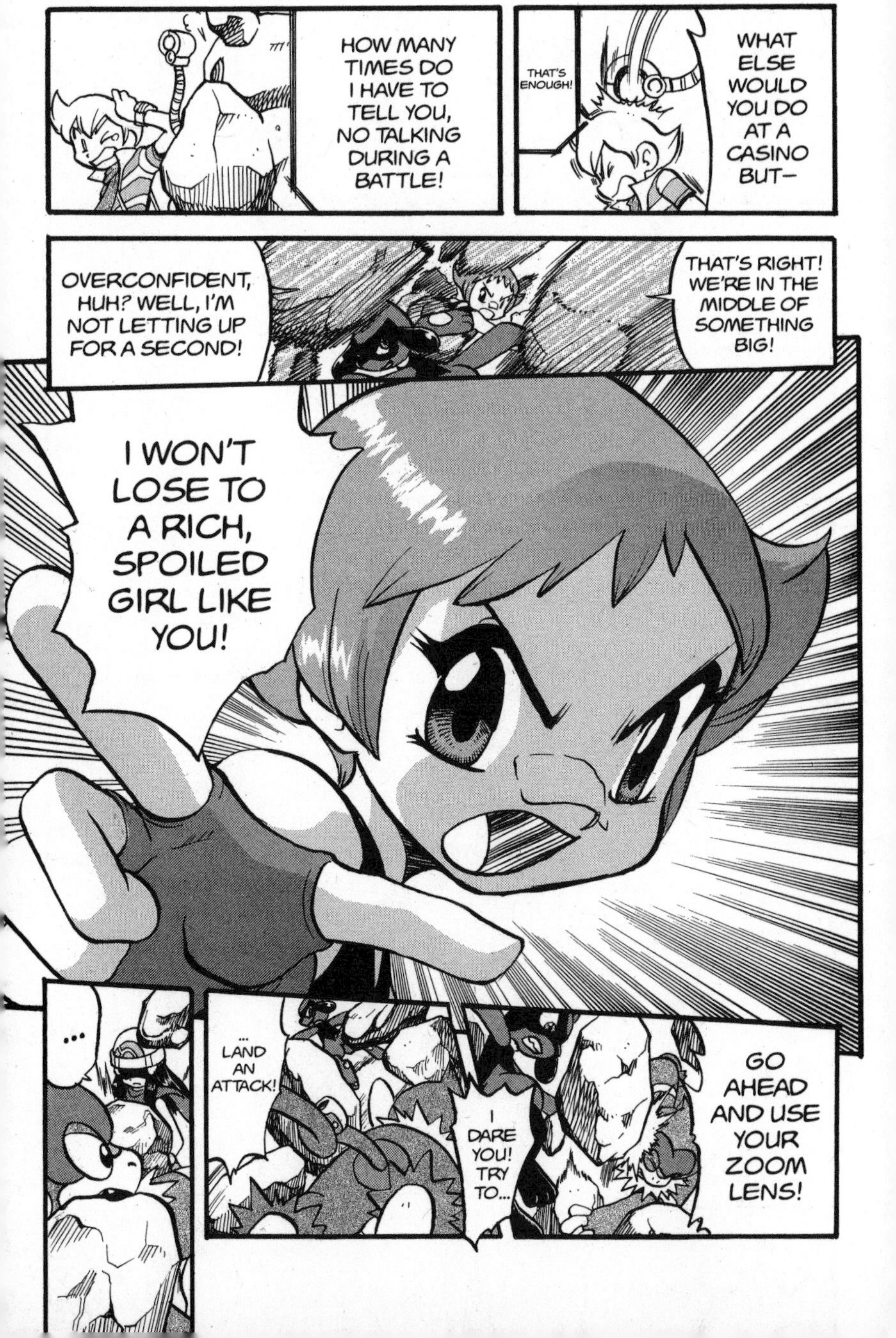
WHAT ELSE WOULD YOU DO AT A CASINO BUT—
THAT'S ENOUGH!
HOW MANY TIMES DO I HAVE TO TELL YOU, NO TALKING DURING A BATTLE!
THAT'S RIGHT! WE'RE IN THE MIDDLE OF SOMETHING BIG!
OVERCONFIDENT, HUH? WELL, I'M NOT LETTING UP FOR A SECOND!
I WON'T LOSE TO A RICH, SPOILED GIRL LIKE YOU!
GO AHEAD AND USE YOUR ZOOM LENS!
I DARE YOU! TRY TO...
... LAND AN ATTACK!
...

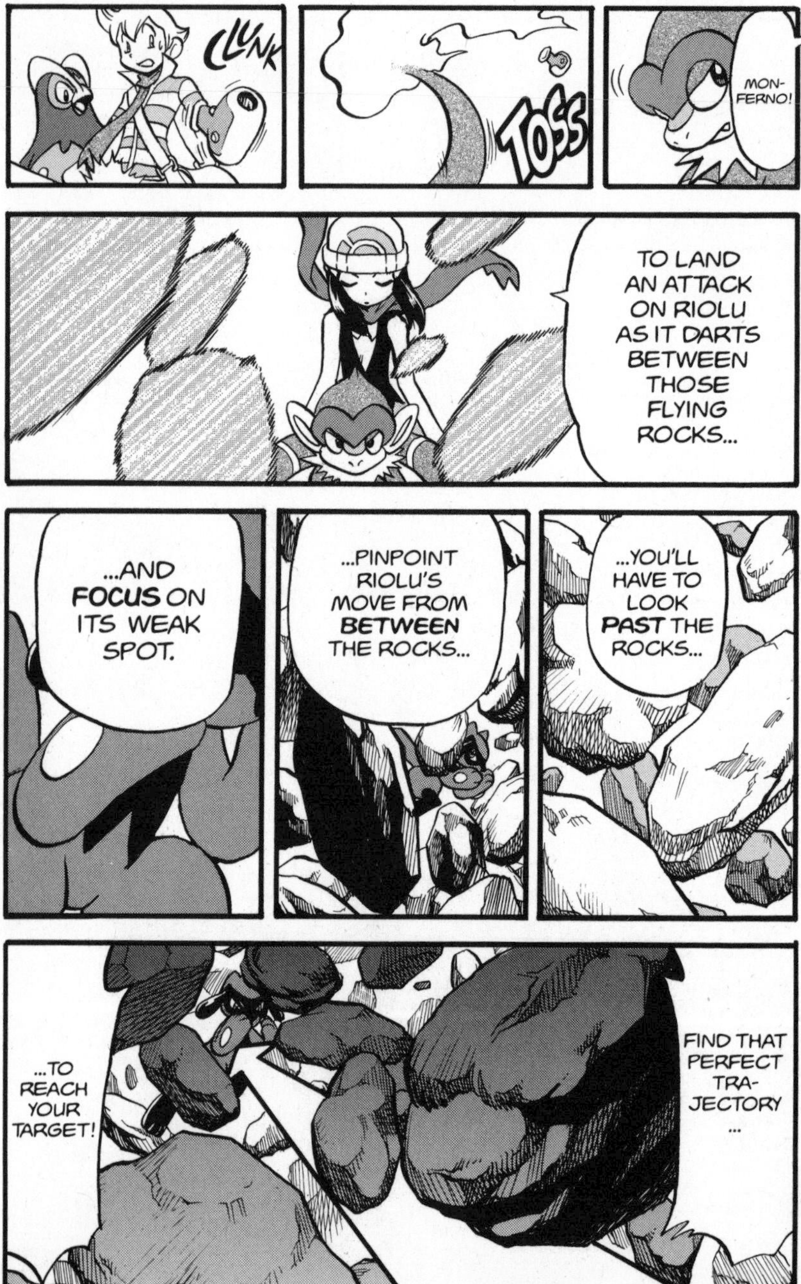
MON-FERNO!
TOSS
CLUNK
TO LAND AN ATTACK ON RIOLU AS IT DARTS BETWEEN THOSE FLYING ROCKS...
...YOU'LL HAVE TO LOOK PAST THE ROCKS...
...PINPOINT RIOLU'S MOVE FROM BETWEEN THE ROCKS...
...AND FOCUS ON ITS WEAK SPOT.
FIND THAT PERFECT TRA-JECTORY ...
...TO REACH YOUR TARGET!

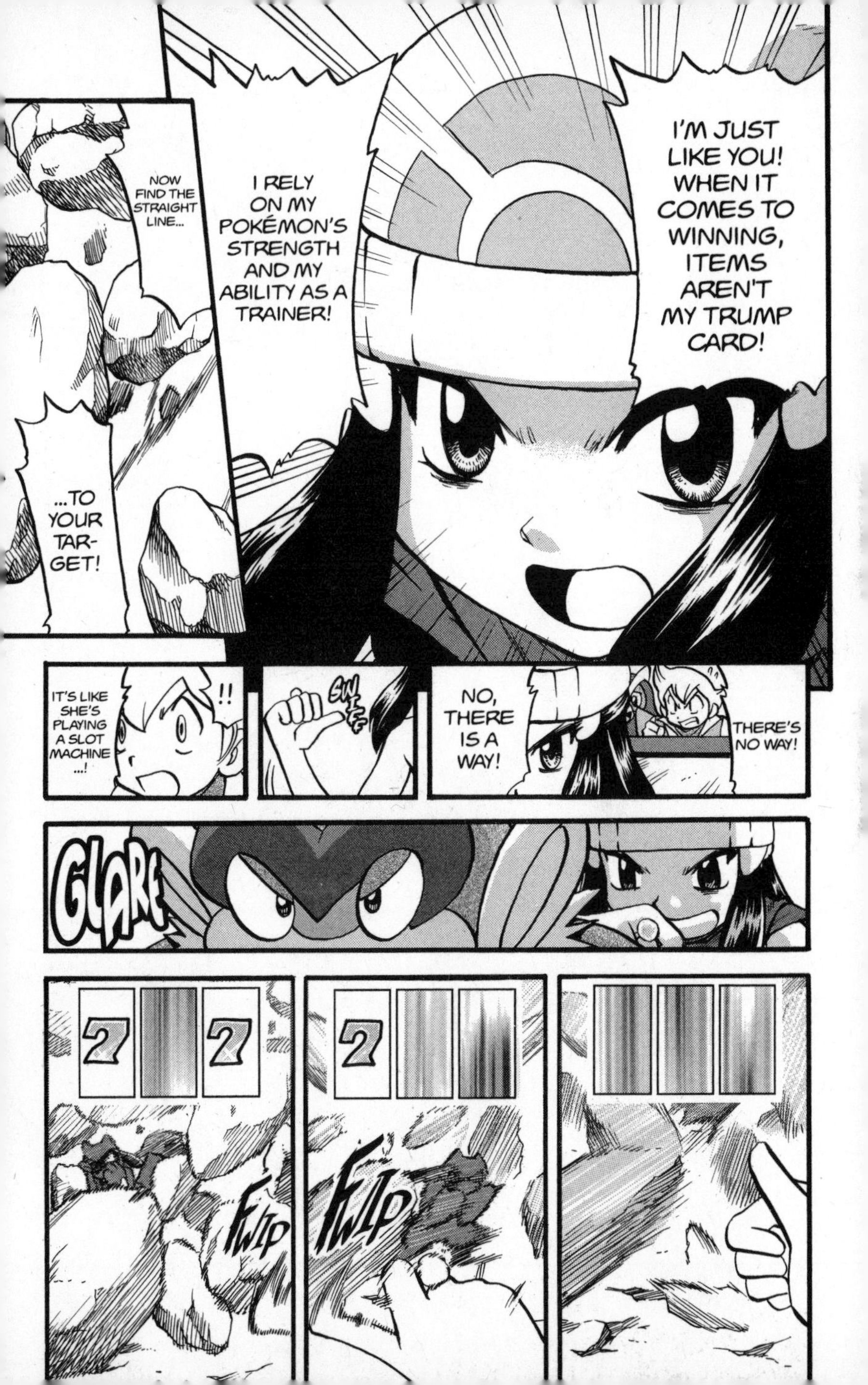
I'M JUST LIKE YOU! WHEN IT COMES TO WINNING, ITEMS AREN'T MY TRUMP CARD!
I RELY ON MY POKÉMON'S STRENGTH AND MY ABILITY AS A TRAINER!
NOW FIND THE STRAIGHT LINE...
...TO YOUR TAR-GET!
THERE'S NO WAY!
NO, THERE IS A WAY!
SWIFF
!!
IT'S LIKE SHE'S PLAYING A SLOT MACHINE ...!
GLARE
FWIP
FWIP

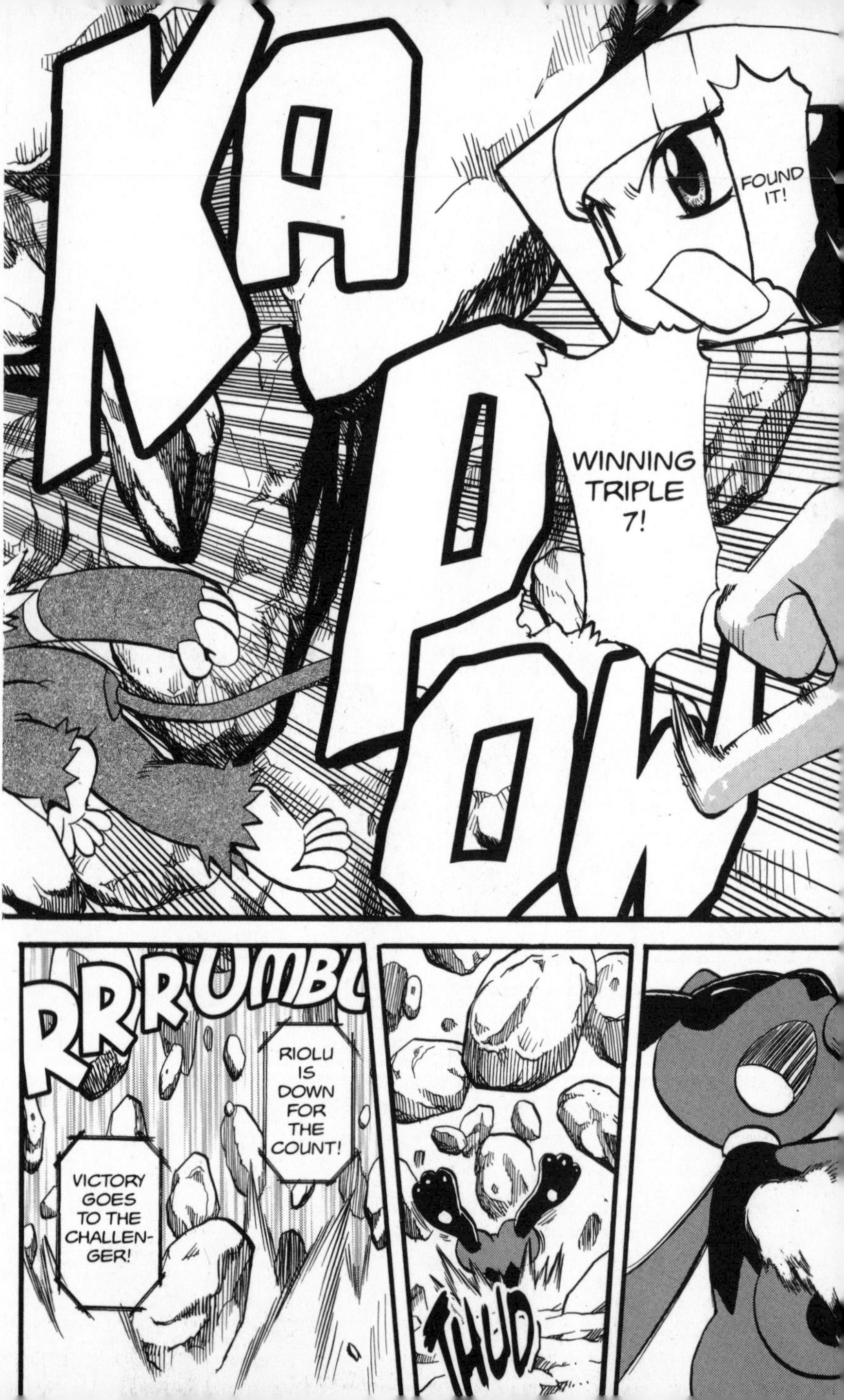
FOUND IT!
KAPOW
WINNING TRIPLE 7!
RIOLU IS DOWN FOR THE COUNT!
THUD
RRRUMBL
VICTORY GOES TO THE CHALLEN-GER!

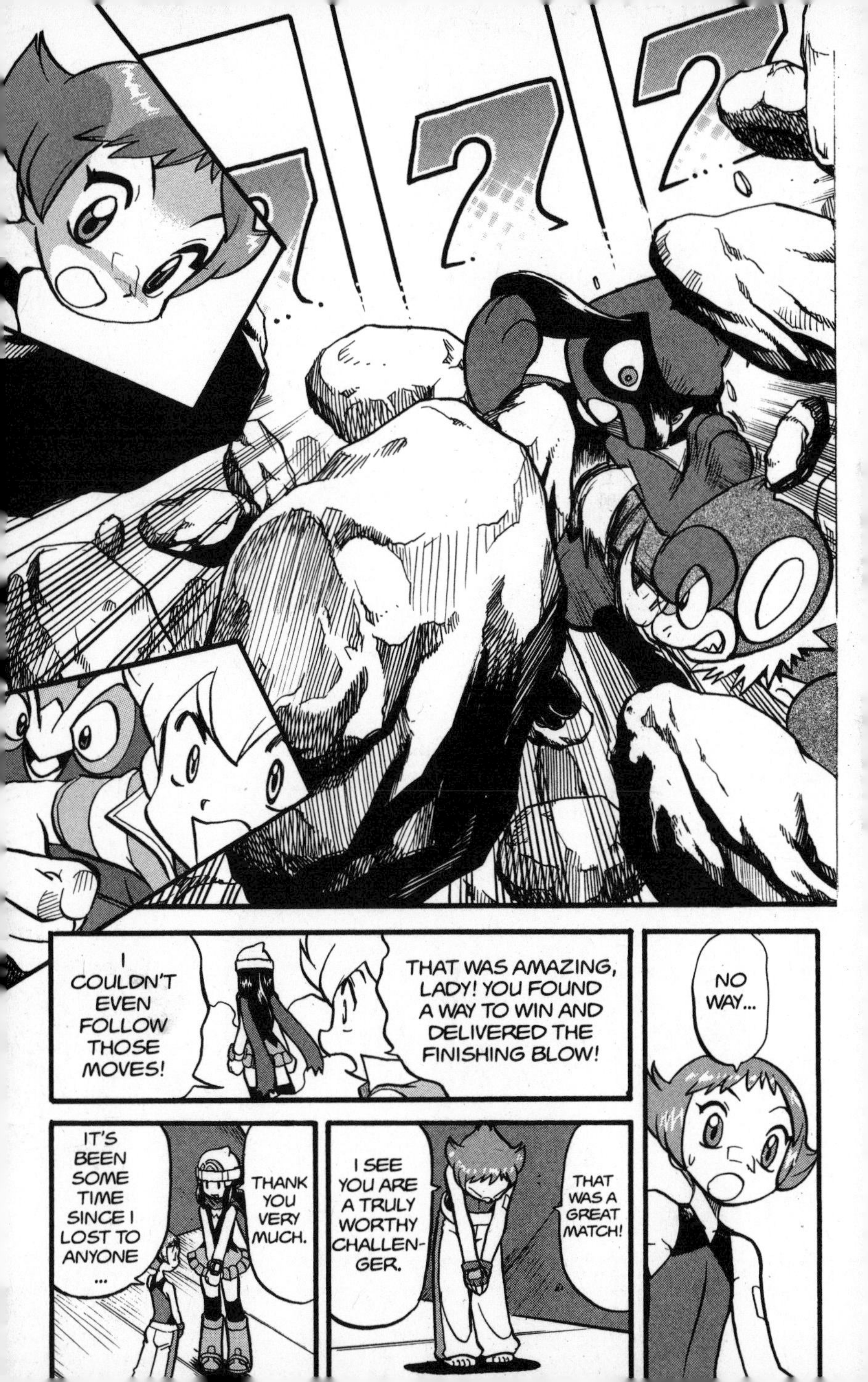
NO WAY...
THAT WAS AMAZING, LADY! YOU FOUND A WAY TO WIN AND DELIVERED THE FINISHING BLOW!
I COULDN'T EVEN FOLLOW THOSE MOVES!
THAT WAS A GREAT MATCH!
I SEE YOU ARE A TRULY WORTHY CHALLEN-GER.
THANK YOU VERY MUCH.
IT'S BEEN SOME TIME SINCE I LOST TO ANYONE ...

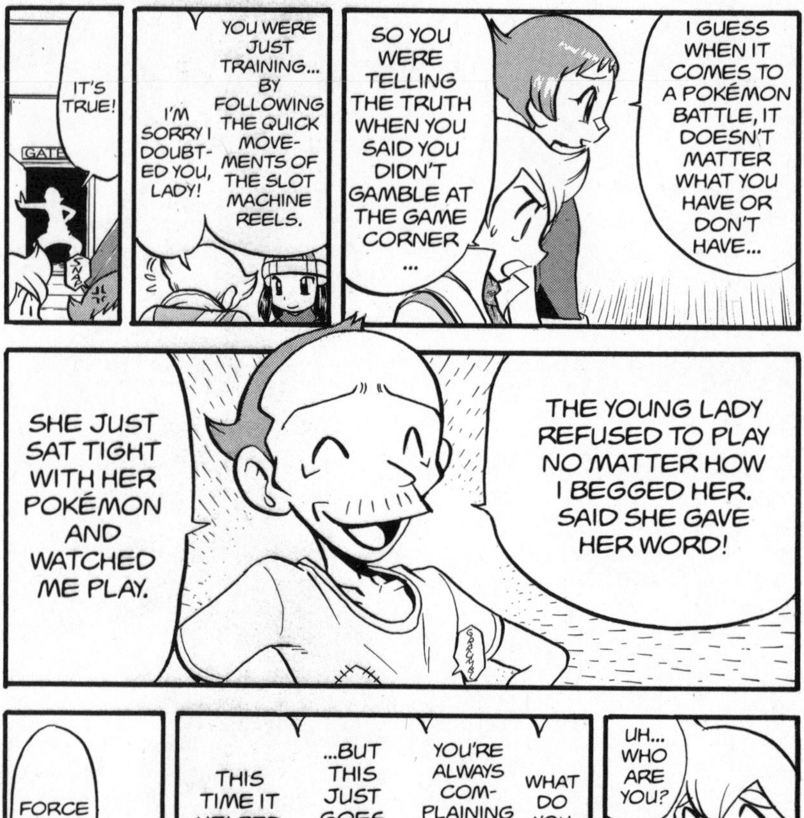
I GUESS WHEN IT COMES TO A POKÉMON BATTLE, IT DOESN'T MATTER WHAT YOU HAVE OR DON'T HAVE...
SO YOU WERE TELLING THE TRUTH WHEN YOU SAID YOU DIDN'T GAMBLE AT THE GAME CORNER ...
YOU WERE JUST TRAINING... BY FOLLOWING THE QUICK MOVEMENTS OF THE SLOT MACHINE REELS.
I'M SORRY I DOUBTED YOU, LADY!
IT'S TRUE!
THE YOUNG LADY REFUSED TO PLAY NO MATTER HOW I BEGGED HER. SAID SHE GAVE HER WORD!
SHE JUST SAT TIGHT WITH HER POKÉMON AND WATCHED ME PLAY.
UH... WHO ARE YOU?
DAD ...
HUH ?!
OH, HELLO, MAYLENE!
WHAT DO YOU KNOW ?
YOU'RE ALWAYS COMPLAINING THAT I WASTE TOO MUCH TIME AT THE GAME CORNER...
...BUT THIS JUST GOES TO SHOW THAT IT'S NOT ALL BAD!
THIS TIME IT HELPED YOU GROW AS A GYM LEADER!
FORCE PALM.
THWACK

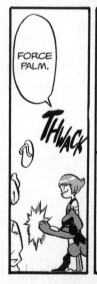

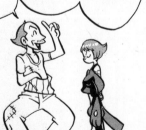

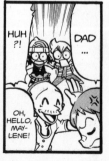

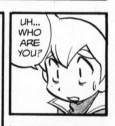

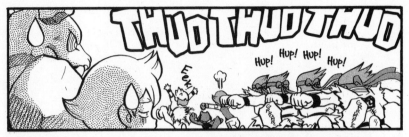

THUD THUD THUD
Hup! Hup! Hup! Hup!
GRUMBLE
GRUMBLE
Eek!
CLIK
I WON...
...THE COBBLE BADGE.
HEY, DIA! LADY JUST DEFEATED MAYLENE!
THAT'S GREAT!
MAY-LENE WAS A REALLY TOUGH OPPO-NENT.
AND WHAT WAS RIOLU...?
Lost and Found
RIOLU WAS REALLY... RIOLU!
LAME!
WOW! THERE SURE IS A LOT OF LOST STUFF IN HERE!
THE OWNER JUST LET ME INTO THIS ROOM...
I WISH HE'D TOLD ME WHERE HE STORED LADY'S POKÉDEX!
NOW WHERE COULD IT BE...?

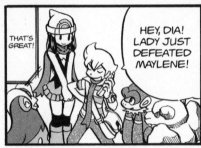

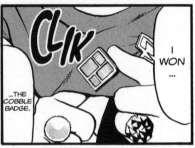

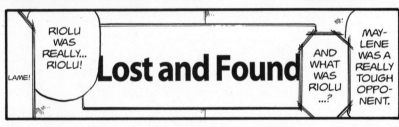

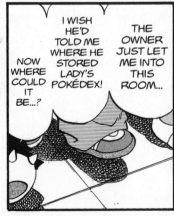

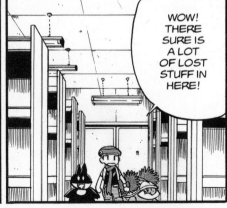

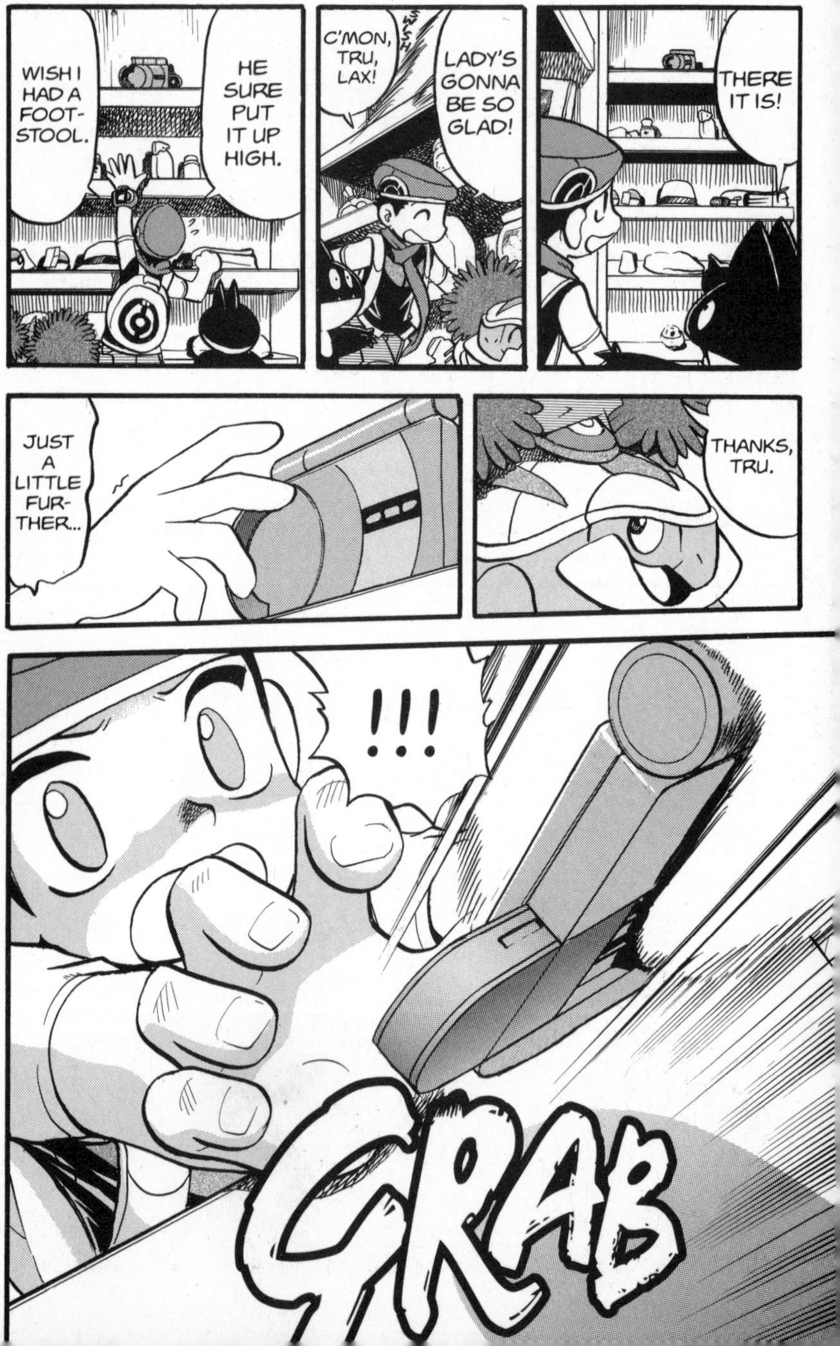
THERE IT IS!
LADY'S GONNA BE SO GLAD!
SWISH
C'MON, TRU, LAX!
HE SURE PUT IT UP HIGH.
WISH I HAD A FOOT-STOOL.
THANKS, TRU.
JUST A LITTLE FUR-THER...
!!!
GRAB

ADVENTURE MAP

Veilstone City ◄

Oreburgh VS Roark Coal Badge	Eterna VS Gardenia Forest Badge	Veilstone VS Maylene Cobble Badge					

DIAMOND

PEARL

▶ TRU

Grotle ♂

LAX

Munchlax ♂

▶ CHIMLER

Monferno ♂

▶ CHATLER

Chatot ♂

▶ PRINPLUP

Prinplup ♀

▶ PONYTA

Ponyta ♂

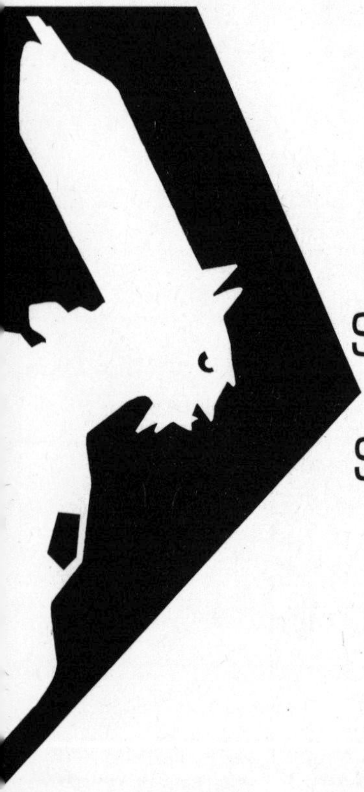

21

Stunning Staravia & Stinky Skuntank I

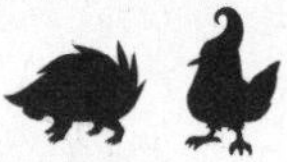

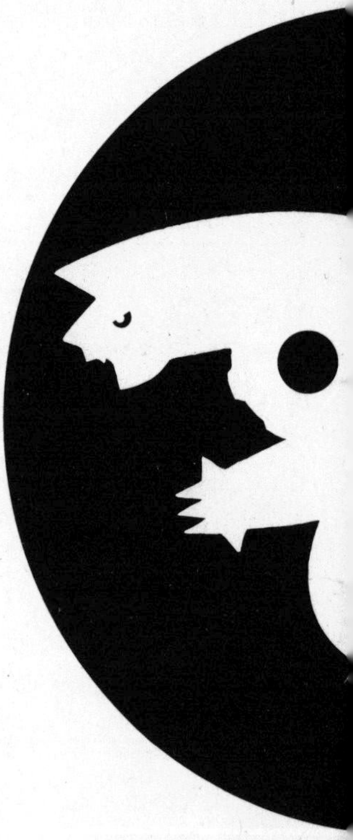

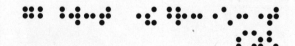

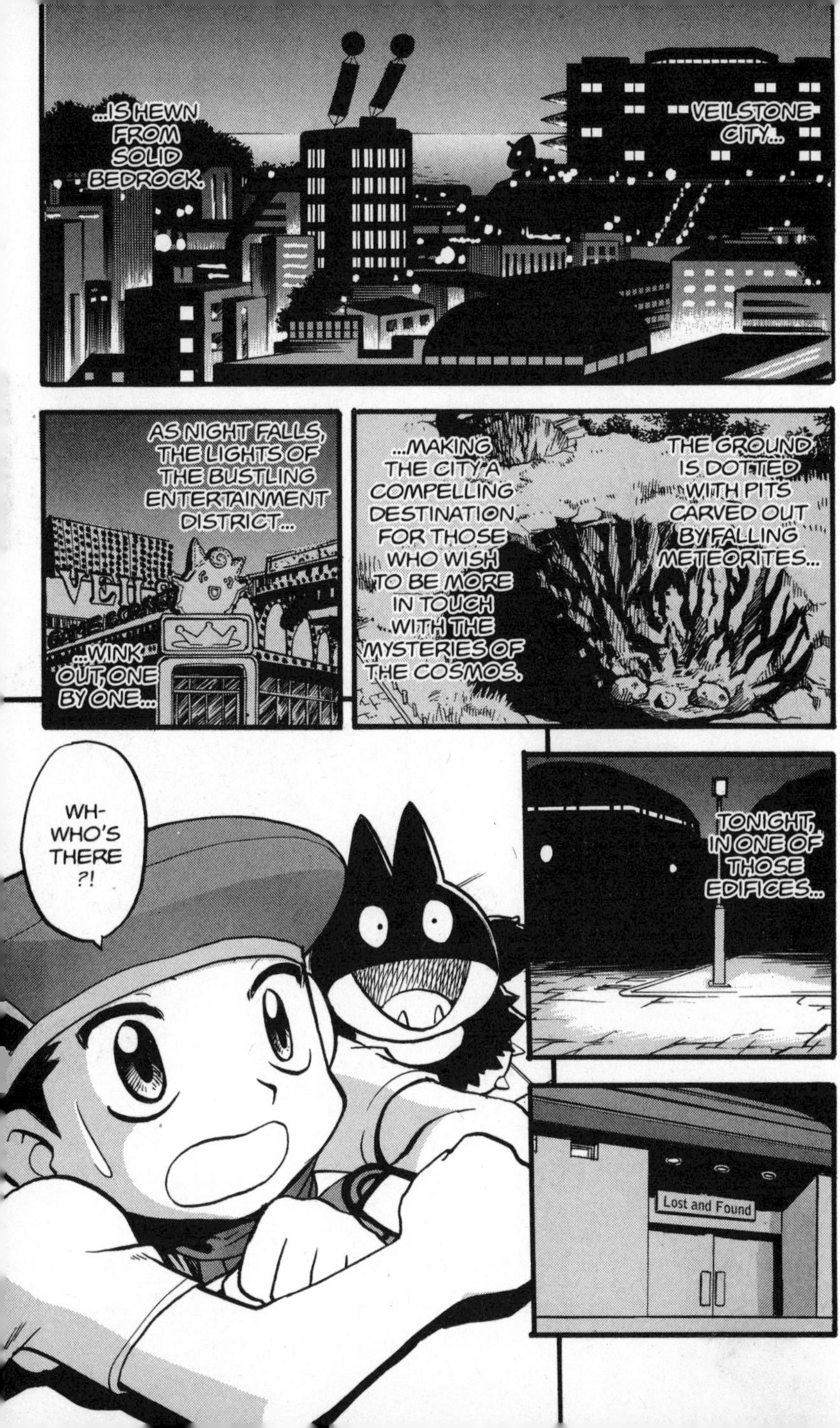
VEILSTONE CITY...
...IS HEWN FROM SOLID BEDROCK.
THE GROUND IS DOTTED WITH PITS CARVED OUT BY FALLING METEORITES...
...MAKING THE CITY A COMPELLING DESTINATION FOR THOSE WHO WISH TO BE MORE IN TOUCH WITH THE MYSTERIES OF THE COSMOS.
AS NIGHT FALLS, THE LIGHTS OF THE BUSTLING ENTERTAINMENT DISTRICT...
...WINK OUT, ONE BY ONE...
TONIGHT, IN ONE OF THOSE EDIFICES...
Lost and Found
WH-WHO'S THERE ?!

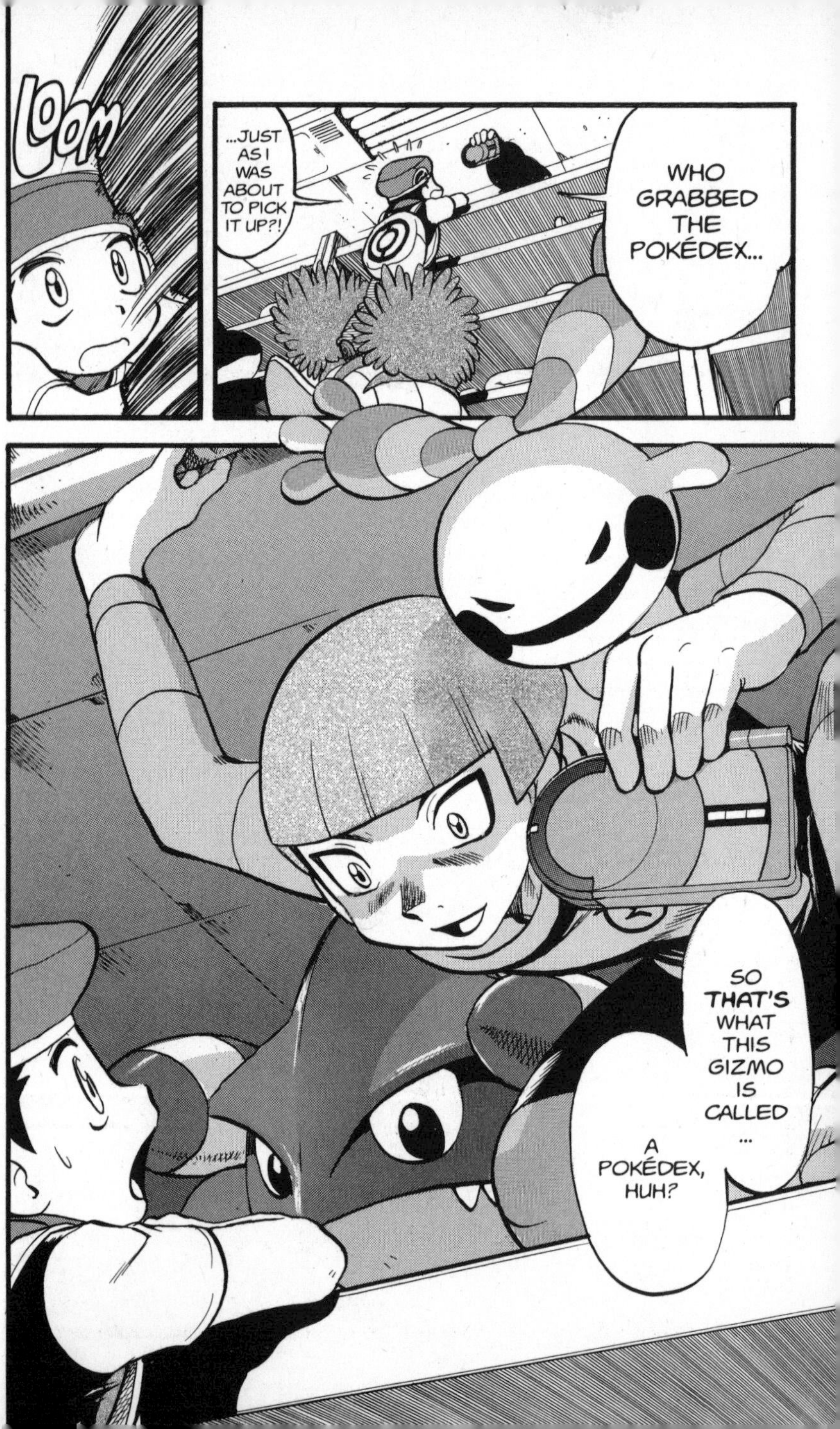
WHO GRABBED THE POKÉDEX...
...JUST AS I WAS ABOUT TO PICK IT UP?!
LOOM
SO **THAT'S** WHAT THIS GIZMO IS CALLED...
A POKÉDEX, HUH?

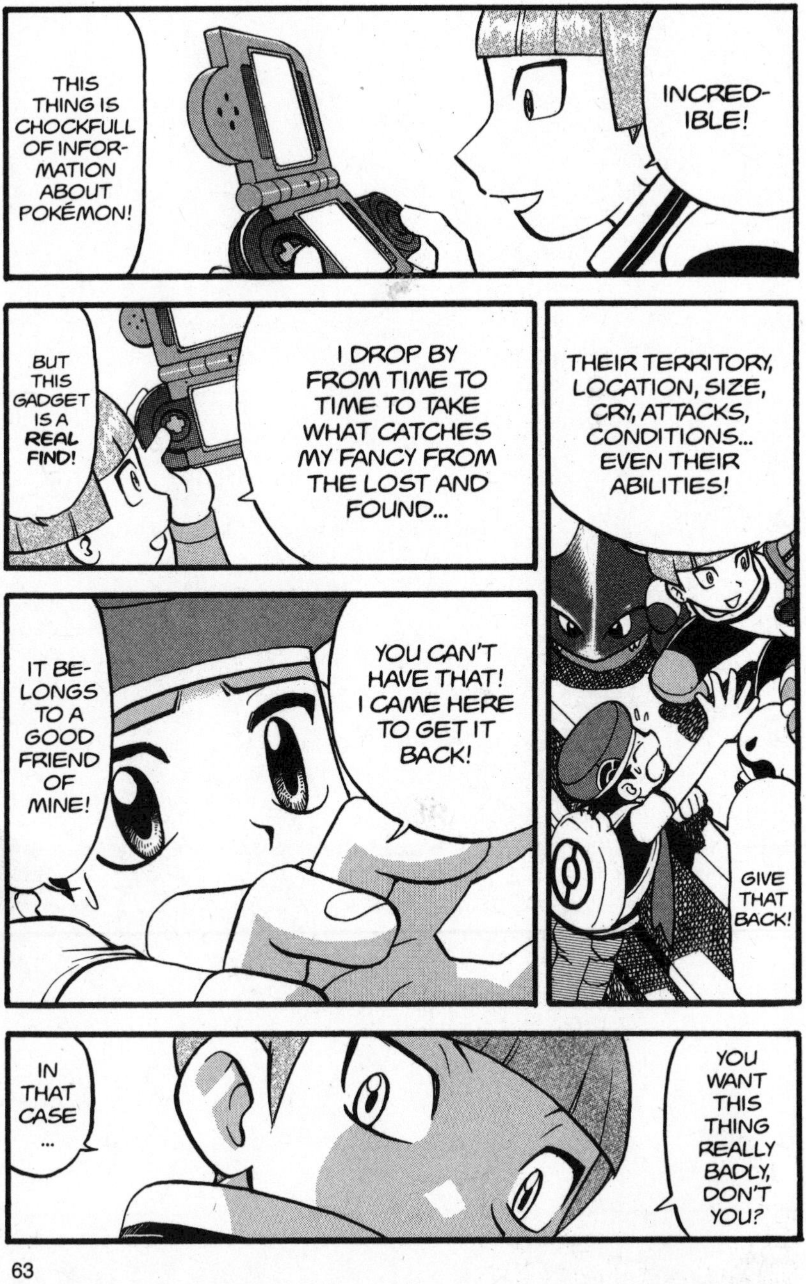
INCREDIBLE!
THIS THING IS CHOCKFULL OF INFORMATION ABOUT POKÉMON!
THEIR TERRITORY, LOCATION, SIZE, CRY, ATTACKS, CONDITIONS... EVEN THEIR ABILITIES!
GIVE THAT BACK!
I DROP BY FROM TIME TO TIME TO TAKE WHAT CATCHES MY FANCY FROM THE LOST AND FOUND...
BUT THIS GADGET IS A **REAL FIND!**
YOU CAN'T HAVE THAT! I CAME HERE TO GET IT BACK!
IT BELONGS TO A GOOD FRIEND OF MINE!
YOU WANT THIS THING REALLY BADLY, DON'T YOU?
IN THAT CASE ...

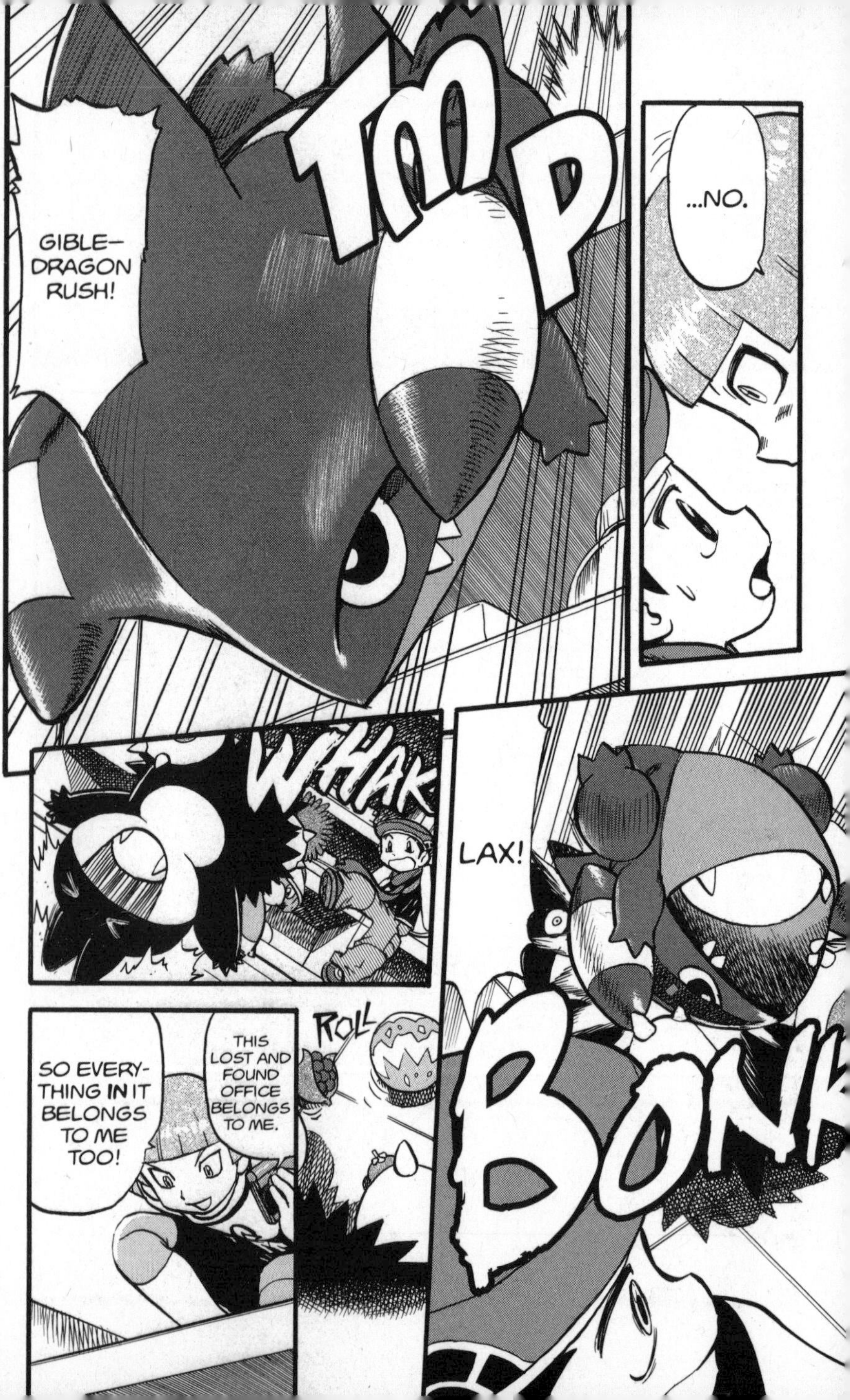
...NO.
TMP
GIBLE— DRAGON RUSH!
LAX!
BONK
WHAK
ROLL
THIS LOST AND FOUND OFFICE BELONGS TO ME.
SO EVERYTHING **IN** IT BELONGS TO ME TOO!

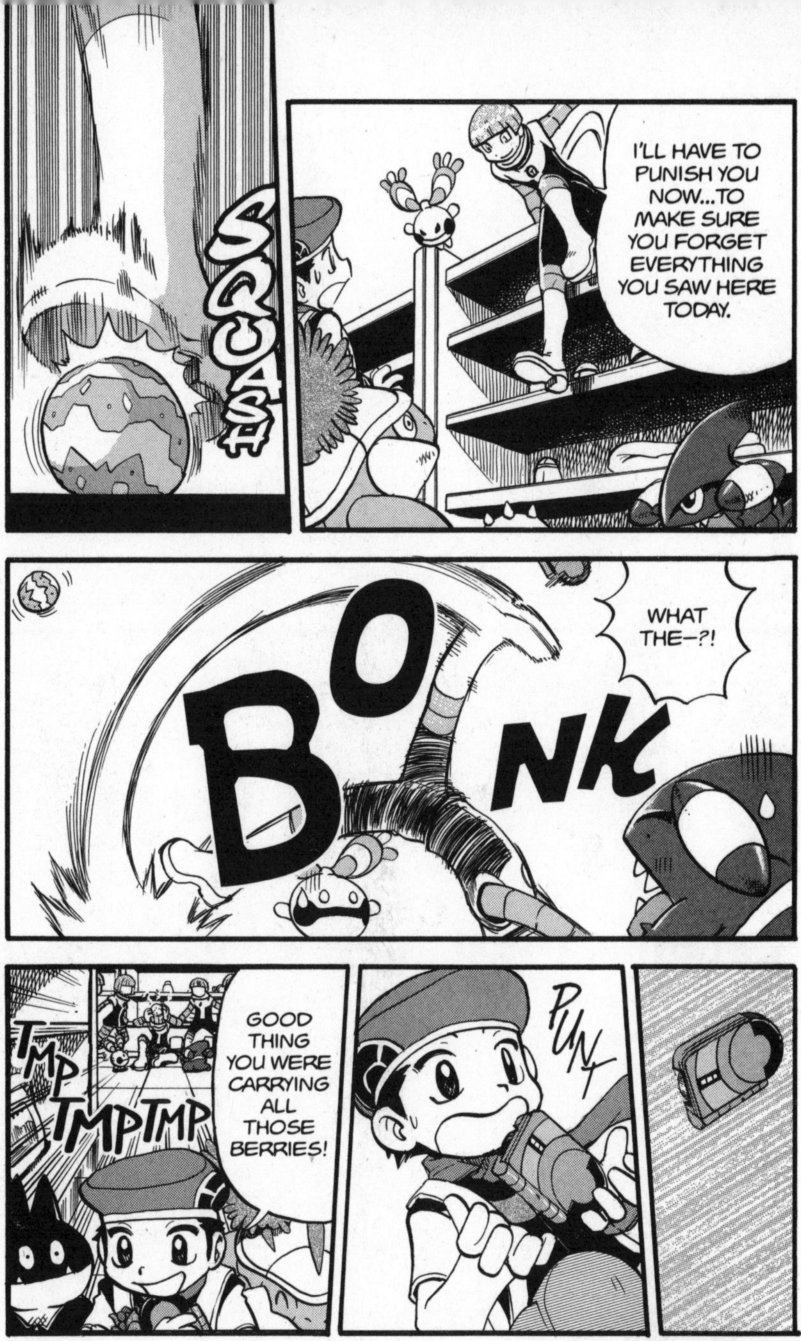
I'LL HAVE TO PUNISH YOU NOW...TO MAKE SURE YOU FORGET EVERYTHING YOU SAW HERE TODAY.
SQUASH
WHAT THE-?!
BONK
GOOD THING YOU WERE CARRYING ALL THOSE BERRIES!
TMP TMPTMP

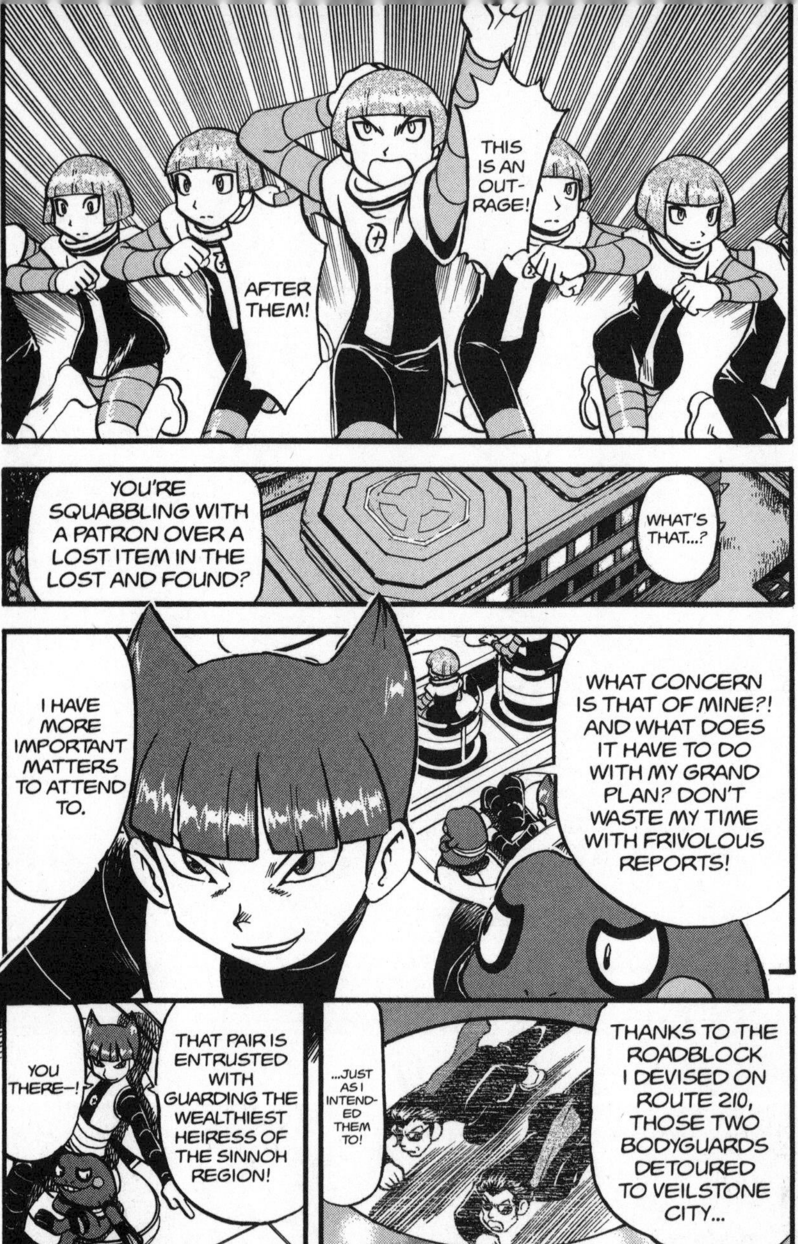
THIS IS AN OUTRAGE!
AFTER THEM!
WHAT'S THAT...?
YOU'RE SQUABBLING WITH A PATRON OVER A LOST ITEM IN THE LOST AND FOUND?
WHAT CONCERN IS THAT OF MINE?! AND WHAT DOES IT HAVE TO DO WITH MY GRAND PLAN? DON'T WASTE MY TIME WITH FRIVOLOUS REPORTS!
I HAVE MORE IMPORTANT MATTERS TO ATTEND TO.
THANKS TO THE ROADBLOCK I DEVISED ON ROUTE 210, THOSE TWO BODYGUARDS DETOURED TO VEILSTONE CITY...
...JUST AS I INTENDED THEM TO!
THAT PAIR IS ENTRUSTED WITH GUARDING THE WEALTHIEST HEIRESS OF THE SINNOH REGION!
YOU THERE—!

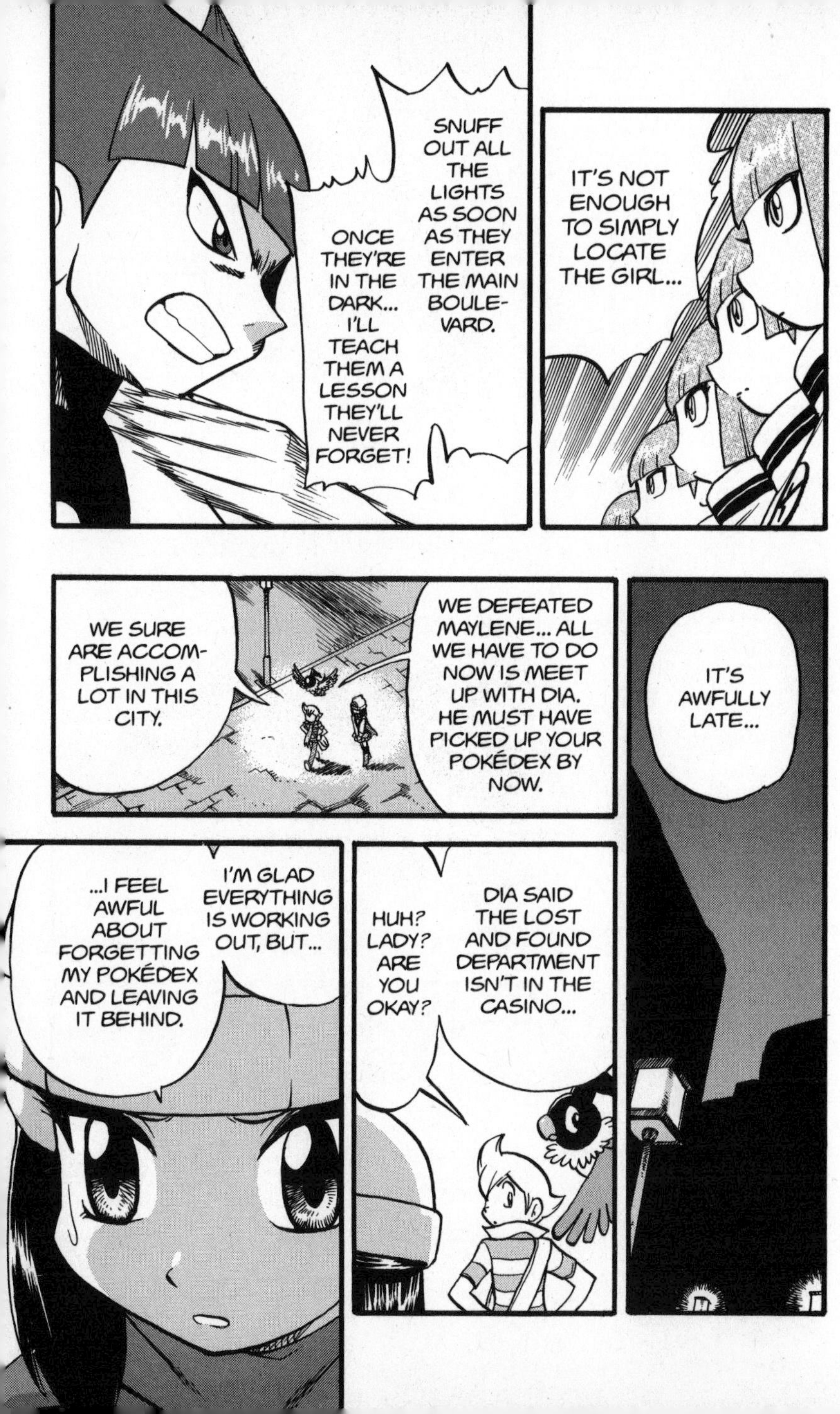
IT'S NOT ENOUGH TO SIMPLY LOCATE THE GIRL...
SNUFF OUT ALL THE LIGHTS AS SOON AS THEY ENTER THE MAIN BOULEVARD.
ONCE THEY'RE IN THE DARK... I'LL TEACH THEM A LESSON THEY'LL NEVER FORGET!
IT'S AWFULLY LATE...
WE DEFEATED MAYLENE... ALL WE HAVE TO DO NOW IS MEET UP WITH DIA. HE MUST HAVE PICKED UP YOUR POKÉDEX BY NOW.
WE SURE ARE ACCOMPLISHING A LOT IN THIS CITY.
DIA SAID THE LOST AND FOUND DEPARTMENT ISN'T IN THE CASINO...
HUH? LADY? ARE YOU OKAY?
I'M GLAD EVERYTHING IS WORKING OUT, BUT...
...I FEEL AWFUL ABOUT FORGETTING MY POKÉDEX AND LEAVING IT BEHIND.

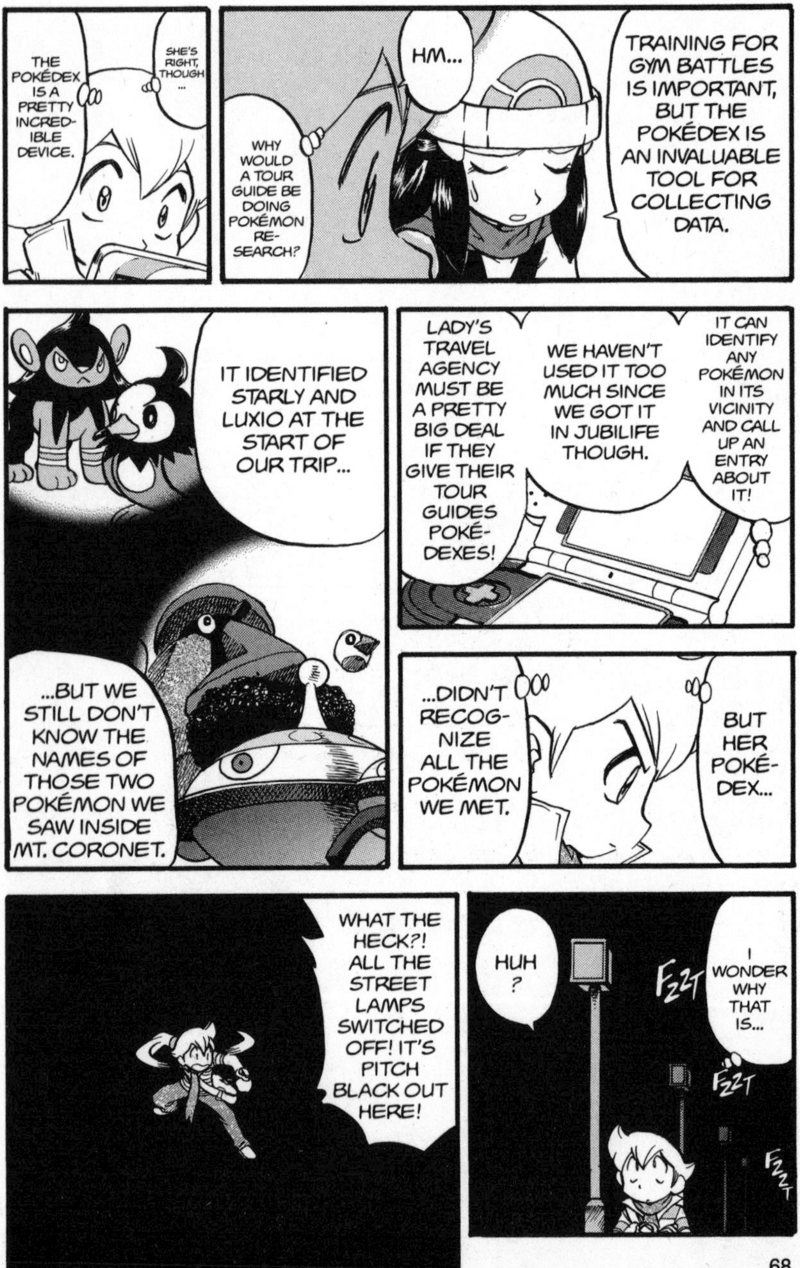
TRAINING FOR GYM BATTLES IS IMPORTANT, BUT THE POKÉDEX IS AN INVALUABLE TOOL FOR COLLECTING DATA.
HM...
WHY WOULD A TOUR GUIDE BE DOING POKÉMON RE-SEARCH?
SHE'S RIGHT, THOUGH...
THE POKÉDEX IS A PRETTY INCRED-IBLE DEVICE.
IT CAN IDENTIFY ANY POKÉMON IN ITS VICINITY AND CALL UP AN ENTRY ABOUT IT!
WE HAVEN'T USED IT TOO MUCH SINCE WE GOT IT IN JUBILIFE THOUGH.
LADY'S TRAVEL AGENCY MUST BE A PRETTY BIG DEAL IF THEY GIVE THEIR TOUR GUIDES POKÉ-DEXES!
BUT HER POKÉ-DEX...
...DIDN'T RECOG-NIZE ALL THE POKÉMON WE MET.
IT IDENTIFIED STARLY AND LUXIO AT THE START OF OUR TRIP...
...BUT WE STILL DON'T KNOW THE NAMES OF THOSE TWO POKÉMON WE SAW INSIDE MT. CORONET.
I WONDER WHY THAT IS...
FZZT
HUH?
FZZT
FZZT
WHAT THE HECK?! ALL THE STREET LAMPS SWITCHED OFF! IT'S PITCH BLACK OUT HERE!

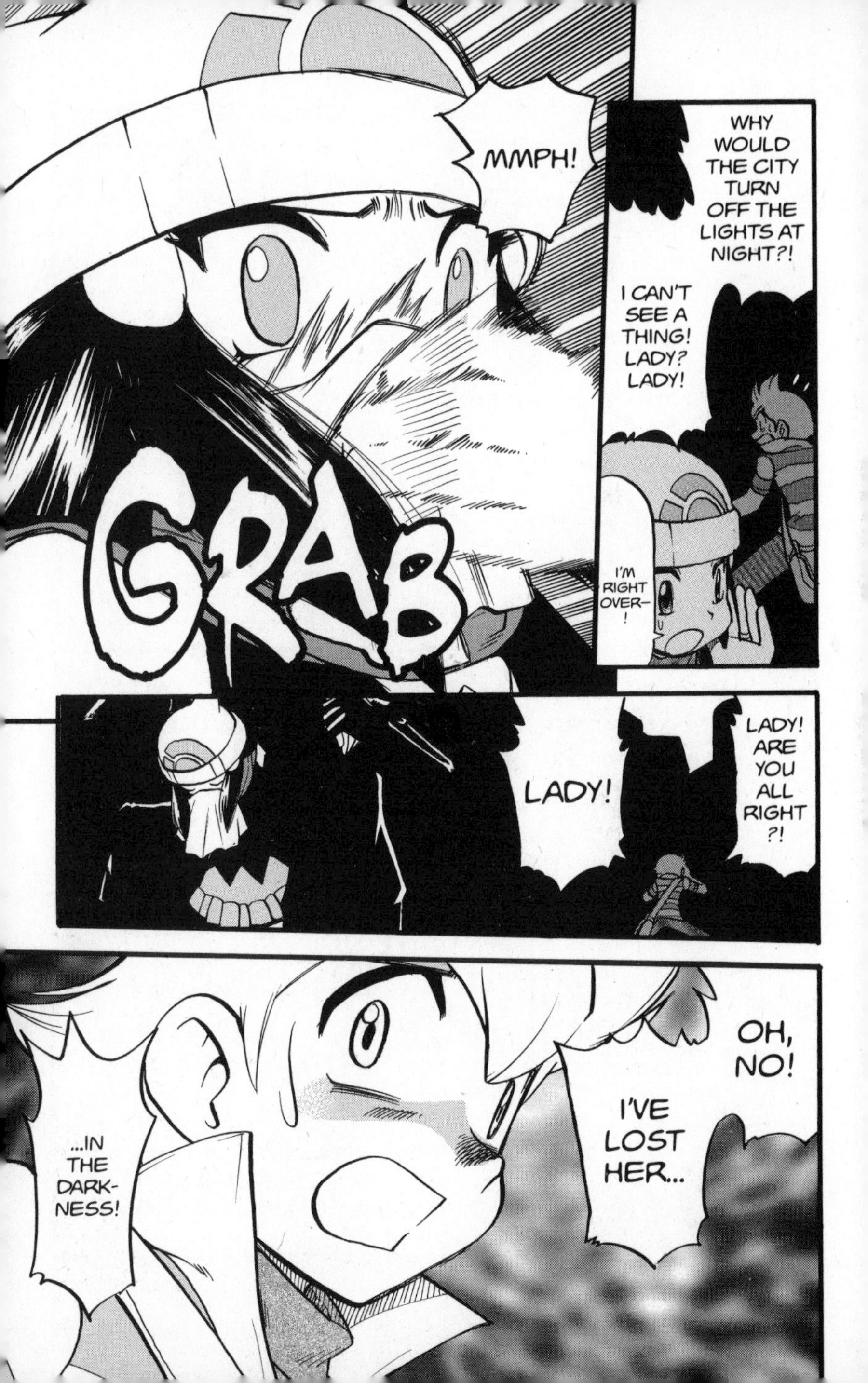

WHY WOULD THE CITY TURN OFF THE LIGHTS AT NIGHT?!
I CAN'T SEE A THING! LADY? LADY!
I'M RIGHT OVER—!
MMPH!
GRAB
LADY! ARE YOU ALL RIGHT?!
LADY!
OH, NO!
I'VE LOST HER...
...IN THE DARKNESS!

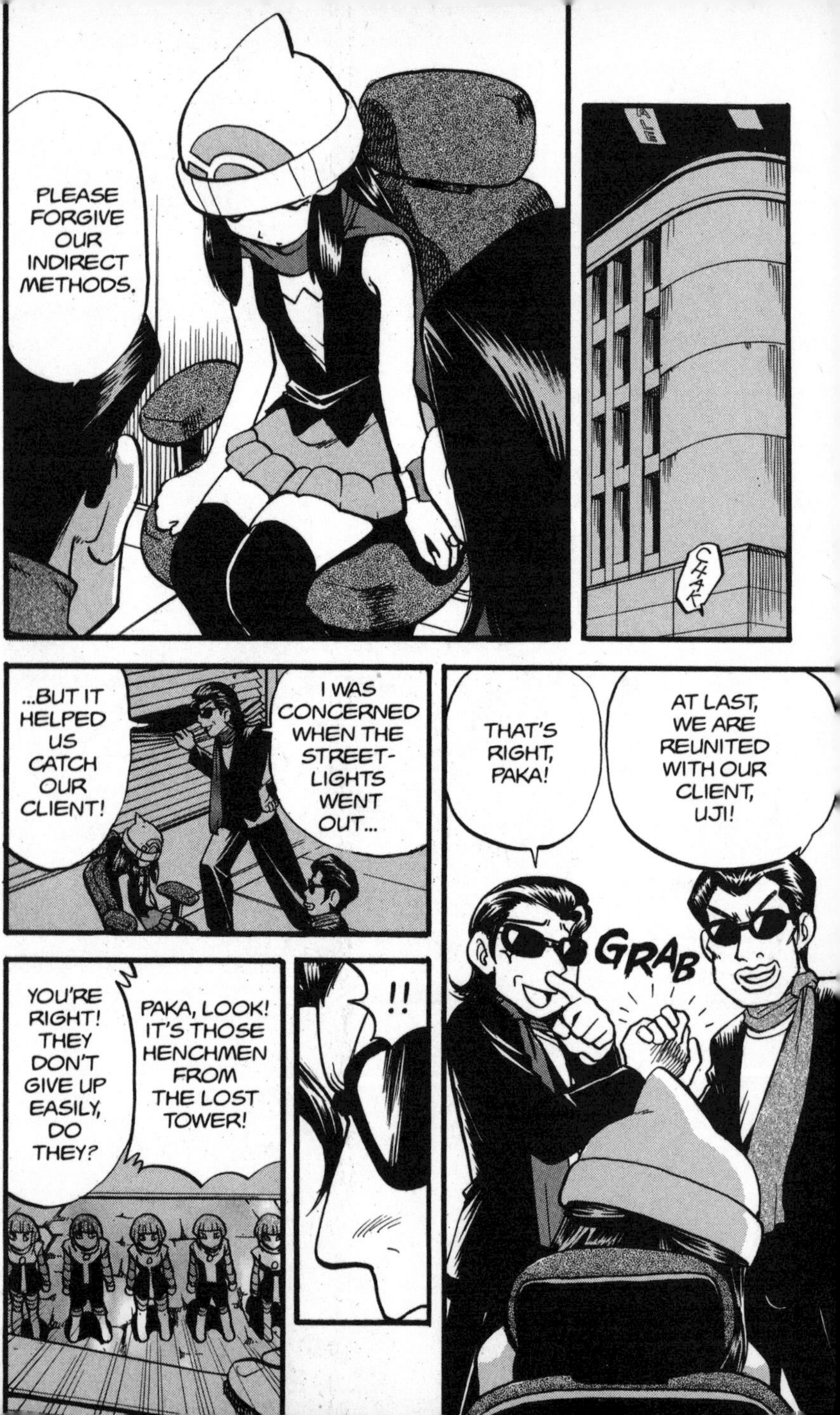
CHAK
PLEASE FORGIVE OUR INDIRECT METHODS.
AT LAST, WE ARE REUNITED WITH OUR CLIENT, UJI!
THAT'S RIGHT, PAKA!
GRAB
I WAS CONCERNED WHEN THE STREET-LIGHTS WENT OUT...
...BUT IT HELPED US CATCH OUR CLIENT!
!!
PAKA, LOOK! IT'S THOSE HENCHMEN FROM THE LOST TOWER!
YOU'RE RIGHT! THEY DON'T GIVE UP EASILY, DO THEY?

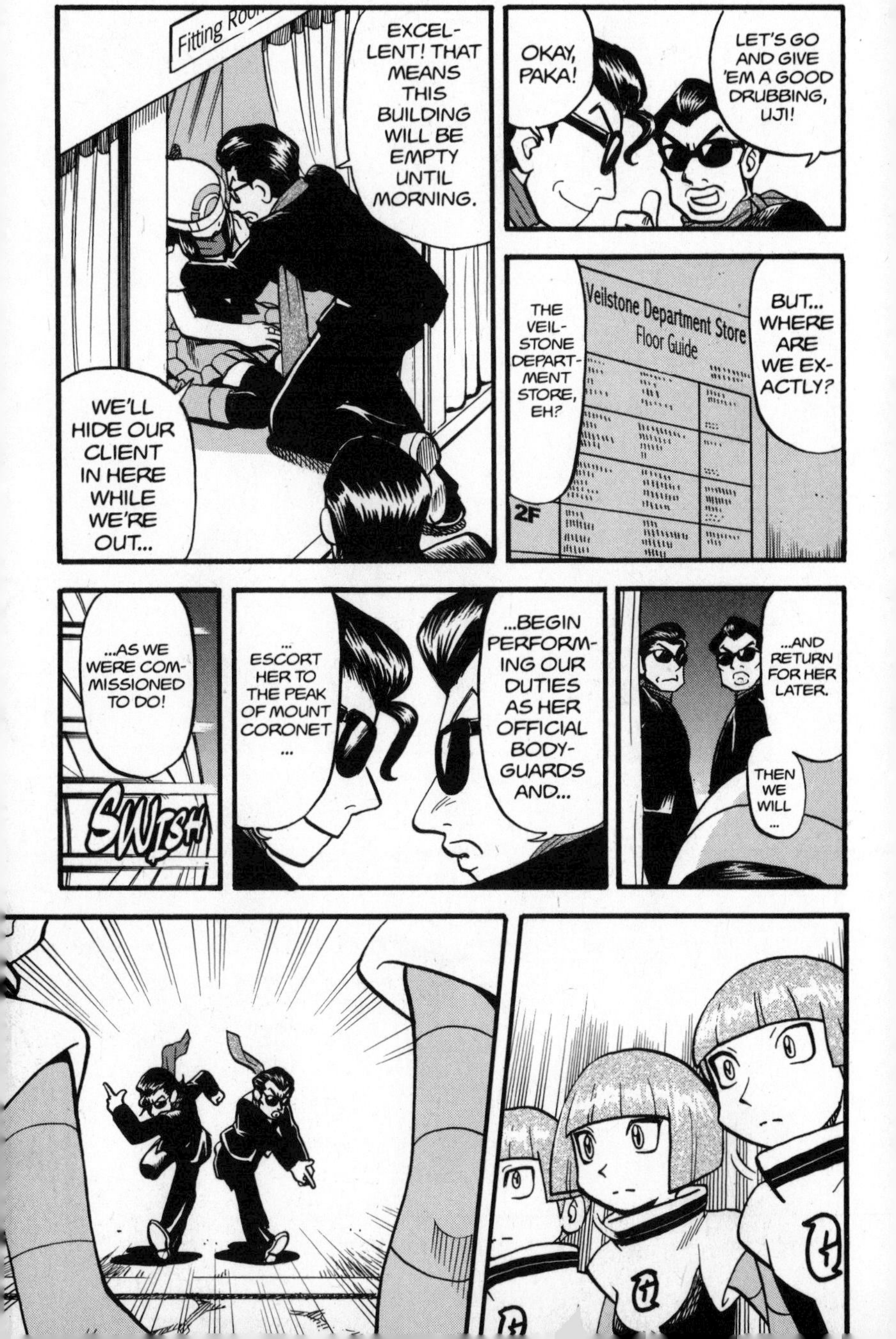
LET'S GO AND GIVE 'EM A GOOD DRUBBING, UJI!
OKAY, PAKA!
BUT... WHERE ARE WE EXACTLY?
Veilstone Department Store Floor Guide
2F
THE VEILSTONE DEPARTMENT STORE, EH?
Fitting Roo
EXCELLENT! THAT MEANS THIS BUILDING WILL BE EMPTY UNTIL MORNING.
WE'LL HIDE OUR CLIENT IN HERE WHILE WE'RE OUT...
...AND RETURN FOR HER LATER.
THEN WE WILL ...
...BEGIN PERFORMING OUR DUTIES AS HER OFFICIAL BODYGUARDS AND...
...ESCORT HER TO THE PEAK OF MOUNT CORONET ...
...AS WE WERE COMMISSIONED TO DO!
SWISH

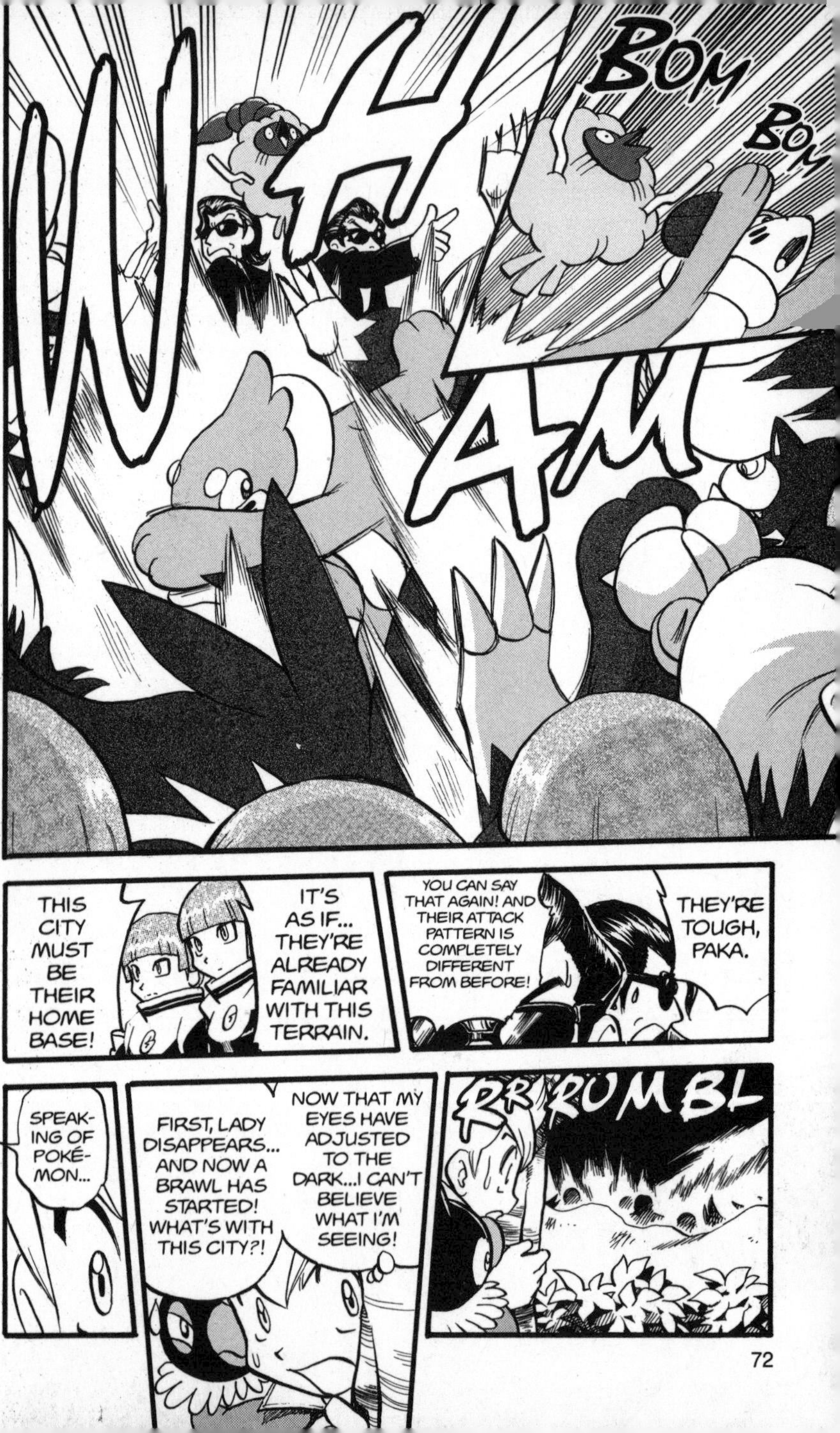
BOM BOM
WHAM
THEY'RE TOUGH, PAKA.
YOU CAN SAY THAT AGAIN! AND THEIR ATTACK PATTERN IS COMPLETELY DIFFERENT FROM BEFORE!
IT'S AS IF... THEY'RE ALREADY FAMILIAR WITH THIS TERRAIN.
THIS CITY MUST BE THEIR HOME BASE!
RRRUMBL
NOW THAT MY EYES HAVE ADJUSTED TO THE DARK...I CAN'T BELIEVE WHAT I'M SEEING!
FIRST, LADY DISAPPEARS... AND NOW A BRAWL HAS STARTED! WHAT'S WITH THIS CITY?!
SPEAKING OF POKÉMON...

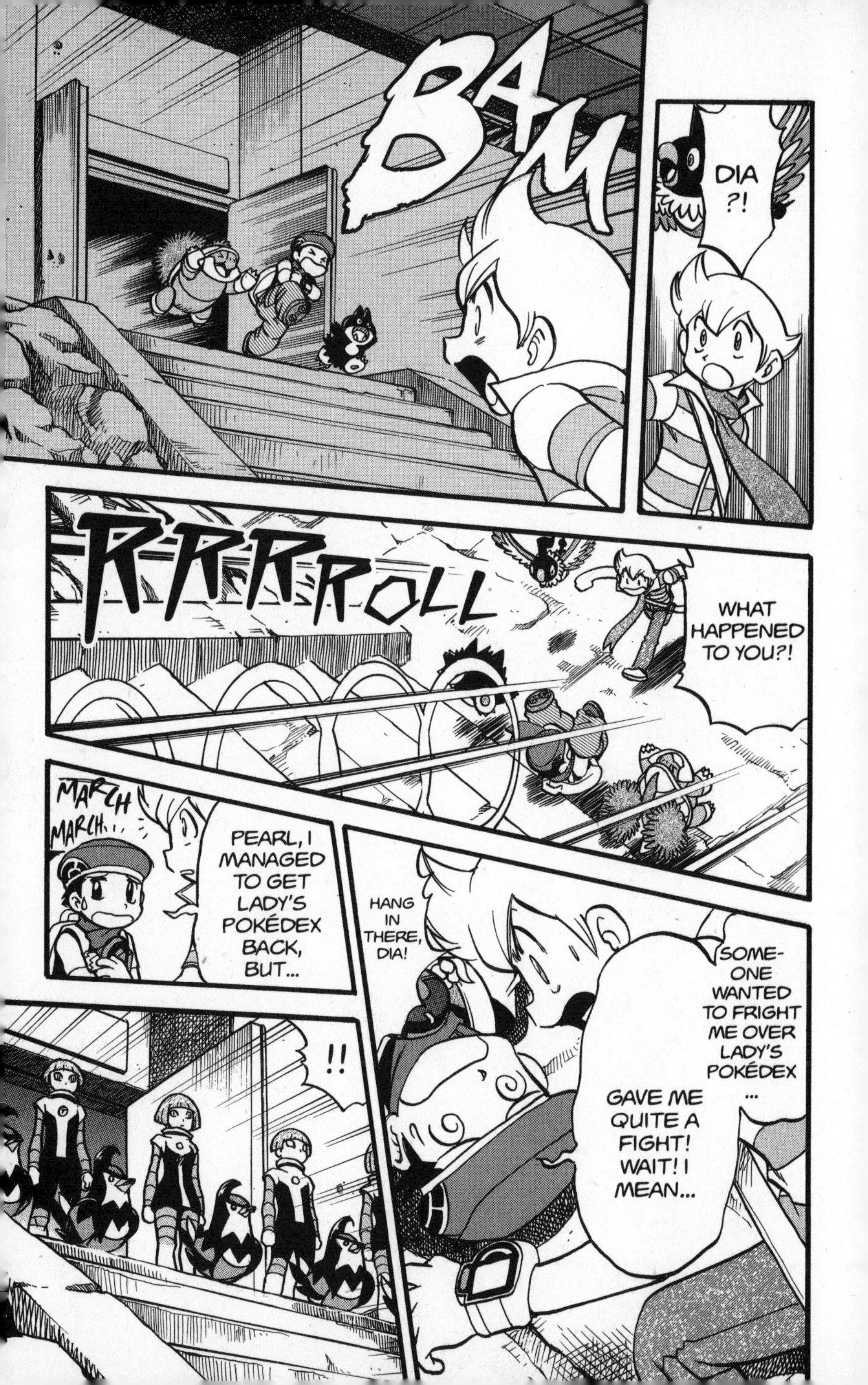
DIA ?!
BAM
RRRROLL
WHAT HAPPENED TO YOU?!
HANG IN THERE, DIA!
SOME-ONE WANTED TO FRIGHT ME OVER LADY'S POKÉDEX ...
GAVE ME QUITE A FIGHT! WAIT! I MEAN...
MARCH MARCH...
PEARL, I MANAGED TO GET LADY'S POKÉDEX BACK, BUT...
!!

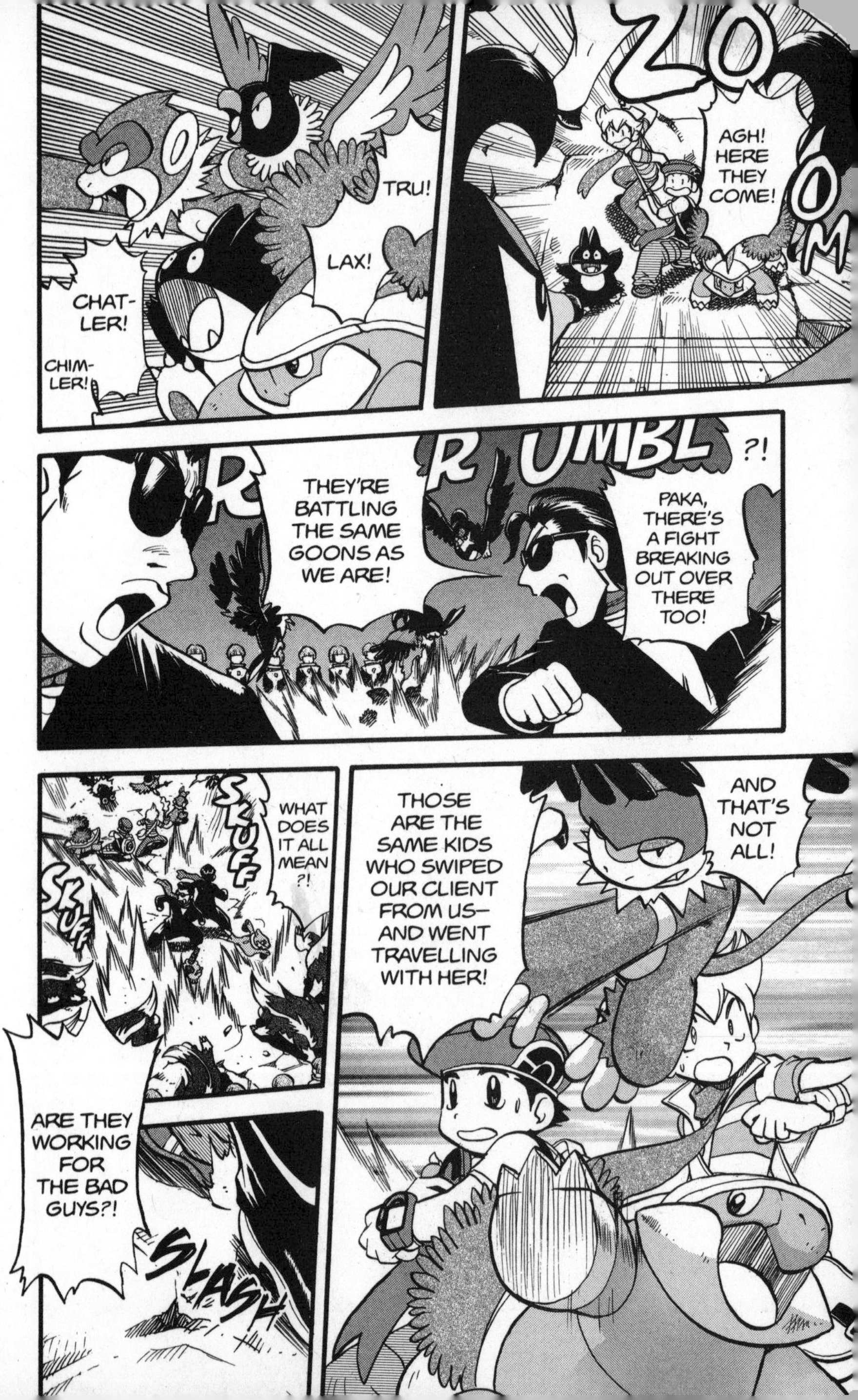

ZOOM
AGH! HERE THEY COME!
TRU!
LAX!
CHAT-LER!
CHIM-LER!
RUMBL
?!
PAKA, THERE'S A FIGHT BREAKING OUT OVER THERE TOO!
THEY'RE BATTLING THE SAME GOONS AS WE ARE!
AND THAT'S NOT ALL!
THOSE ARE THE SAME KIDS WHO SWIPED OUR CLIENT FROM US—AND WENT TRAVELLING WITH HER!
SKUFF
WHAT DOES IT ALL MEAN?!
SKUFF
ARE THEY WORKING FOR THE BAD GUYS?!
SLASH

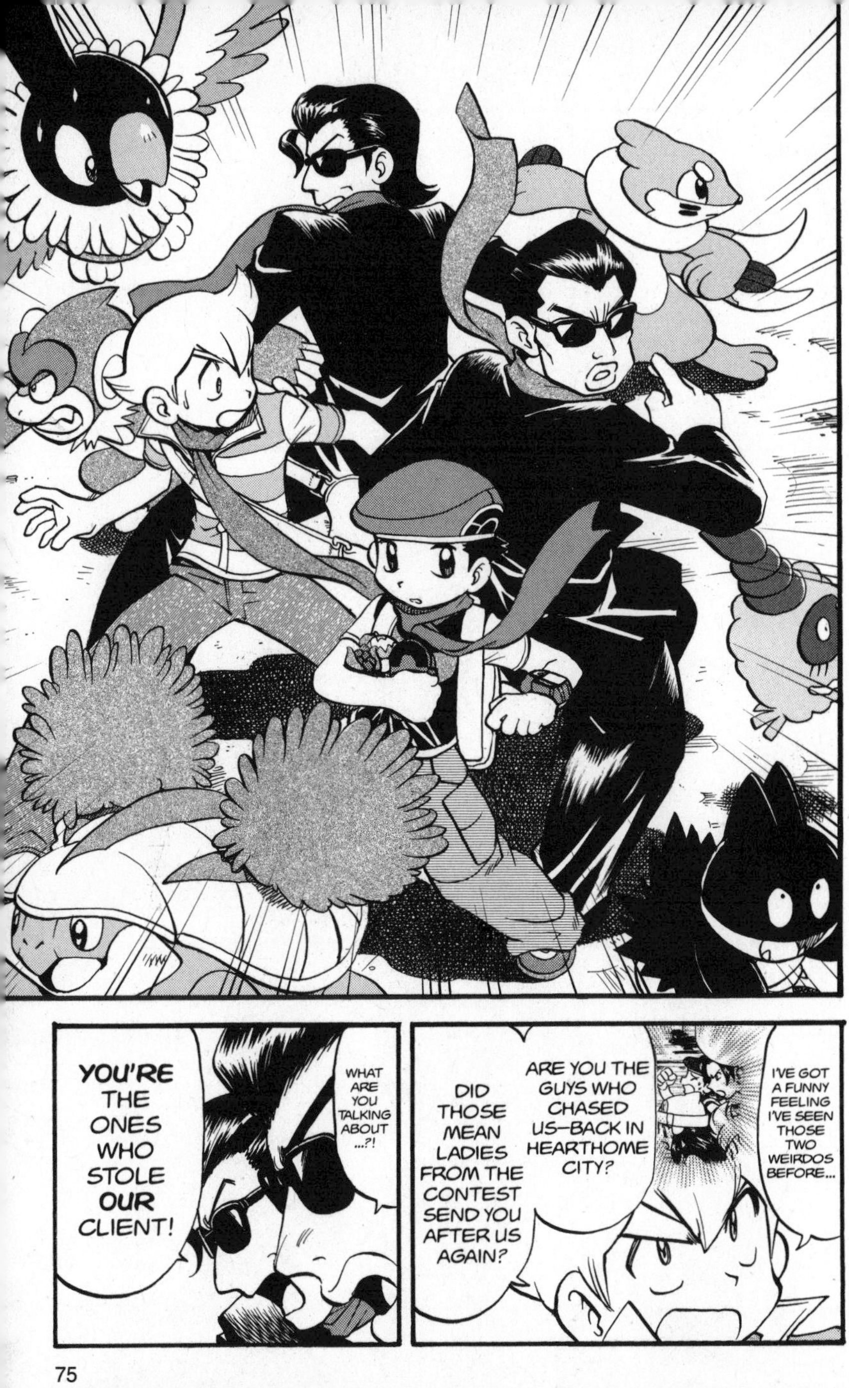
I'VE GOT A FUNNY FEELING I'VE SEEN THOSE TWO WEIRDOS BEFORE...
ARE YOU THE GUYS WHO CHASED US—BACK IN HEARTHOME CITY?
DID THOSE MEAN LADIES FROM THE CONTEST SEND YOU AFTER US AGAIN?
WHAT ARE YOU TALKING ABOUT ...?!
YOU'RE THE ONES WHO STOLE **OUR** CLIENT!

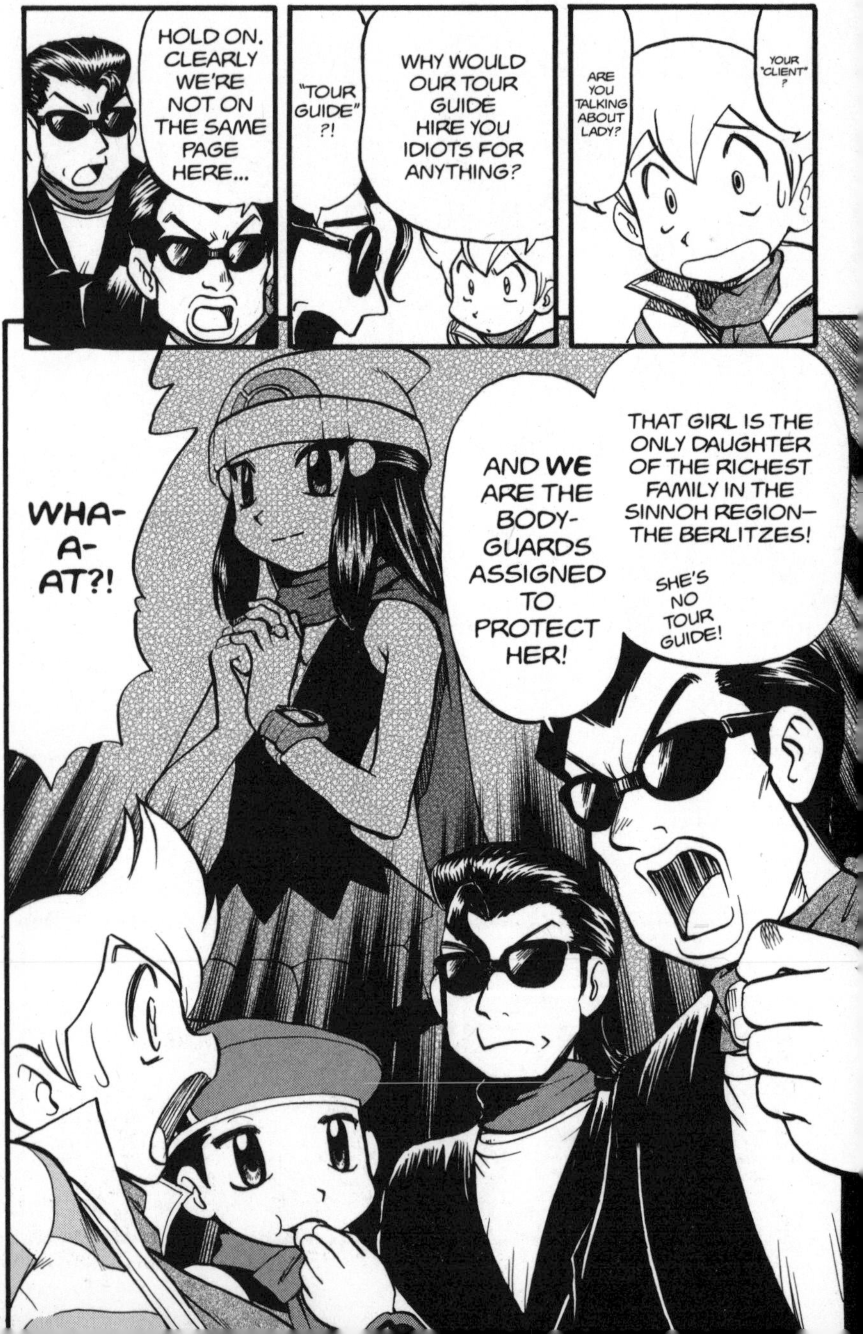

YOUR "CLIENT"?
ARE YOU TALKING ABOUT LADY?
WHY WOULD OUR TOUR GUIDE HIRE YOU IDIOTS FOR ANYTHING?
"TOUR GUIDE"?!
HOLD ON. CLEARLY WE'RE NOT ON THE SAME PAGE HERE...
THAT GIRL IS THE ONLY DAUGHTER OF THE RICHEST FAMILY IN THE SINNOH REGION—THE BERLITZES!
SHE'S NO TOUR GUIDE!
AND WE ARE THE BODY-GUARDS ASSIGNED TO PROTECT HER!
WHA-A-AT?!

ADVENTURE MAP

Veilstone City ◀

Oreburgh VS Roark Coal Badge	Eterna VS Gardenia Forest Badge	Veilstone VS Maylene Cobble Badge					

DIAMOND

PEARL

▶ TRU
Grotle ♂

▶ LAX
Munchlax ♂

▶ CHIMLER
Monferno ♂

▶ CHATLER
Chatot ♂

▶ PRINPLUP
Prinplup ♀

▶ PONYTA
Ponyta ♂

22

Stunning
Staravia &
Stinky
Skuntank 2

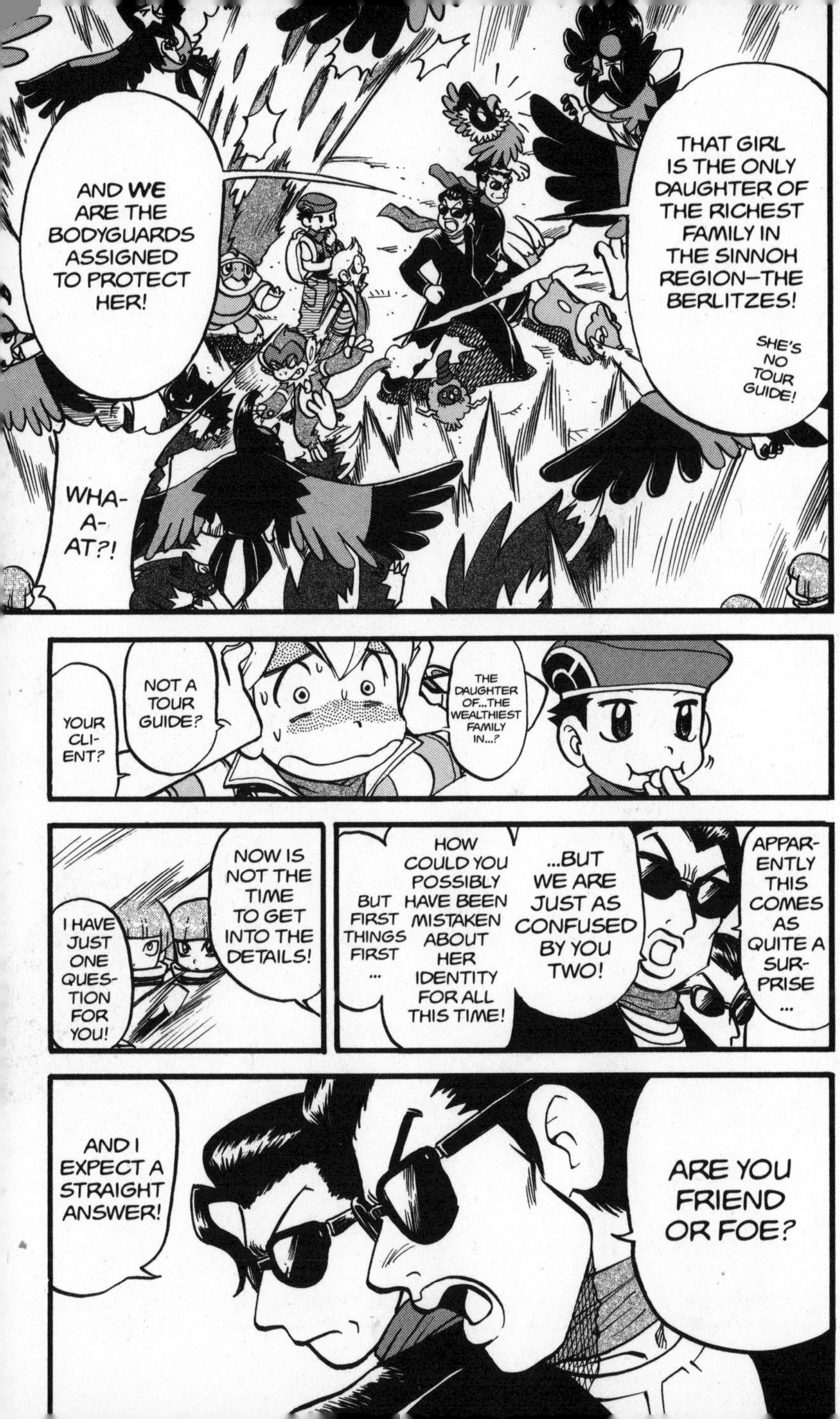
THAT GIRL IS THE ONLY DAUGHTER OF THE RICHEST FAMILY IN THE SINNOH REGION—THE BERLITZES!
SHE'S NO TOUR GUIDE!
AND WE ARE THE BODYGUARDS ASSIGNED TO PROTECT HER!
WHA-A-AT?!
THE DAUGHTER OF...THE WEALTHIEST FAMILY IN...?
NOT A TOUR GUIDE?
YOUR CLIENT?
APPARENTLY THIS COMES AS QUITE A SURPRISE...
...BUT WE ARE JUST AS CONFUSED BY YOU TWO!
HOW COULD YOU POSSIBLY HAVE BEEN MISTAKEN ABOUT HER IDENTITY FOR ALL THIS TIME!
BUT FIRST THINGS FIRST...
NOW IS NOT THE TIME TO GET INTO THE DETAILS!
I HAVE JUST ONE QUESTION FOR YOU!
ARE YOU FRIEND OR FOE?
AND I EXPECT A STRAIGHT ANSWER!

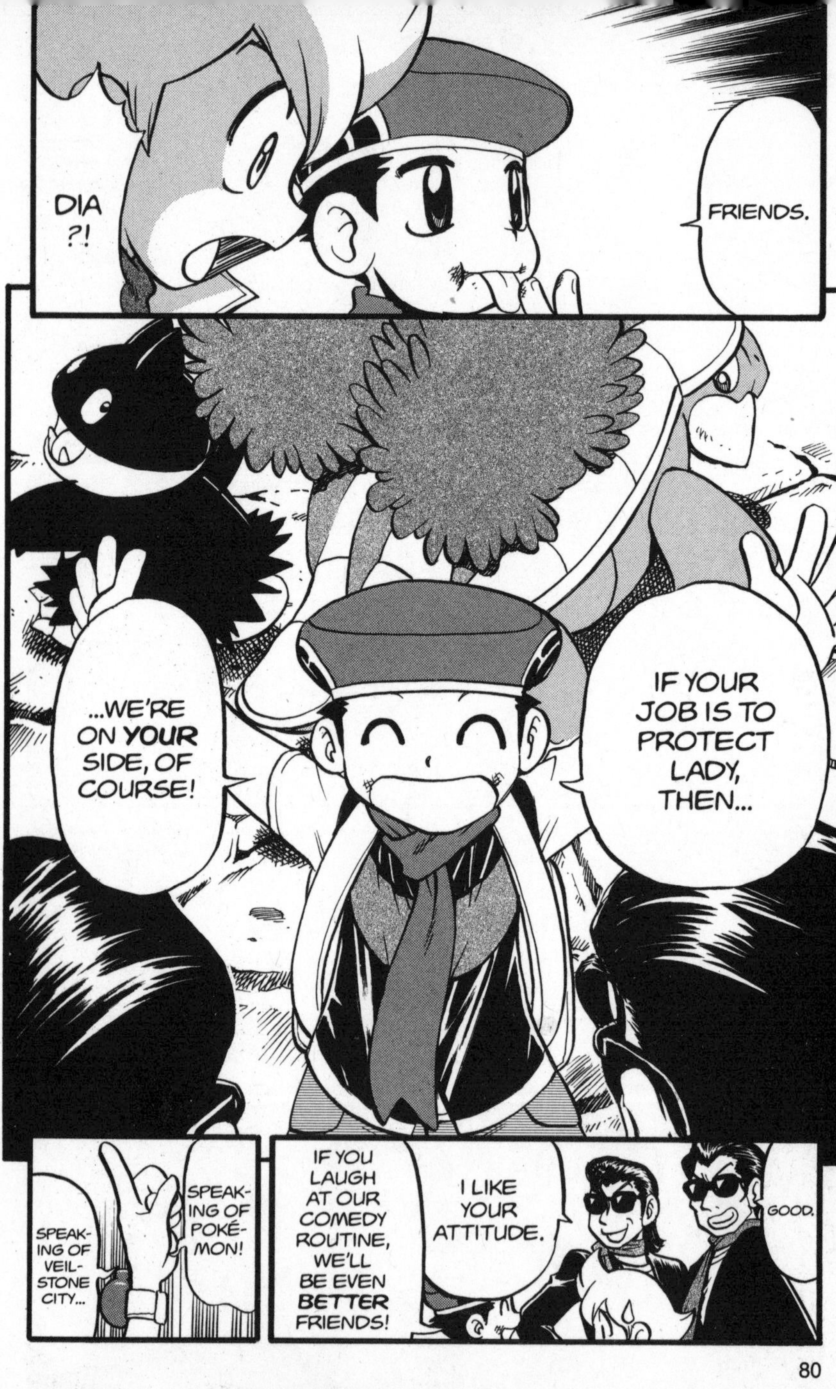
FRIENDS.
DIA ?!
IF YOUR JOB IS TO PROTECT LADY, THEN...
...WE'RE ON **YOUR** SIDE, OF COURSE!
GOOD.
I LIKE YOUR ATTITUDE.
IF YOU LAUGH AT OUR COMEDY ROUTINE, WE'LL BE EVEN **BETTER** FRIENDS!
SPEAK-ING OF POKÉ-MON!
SPEAK-ING OF VEIL-STONE CITY...

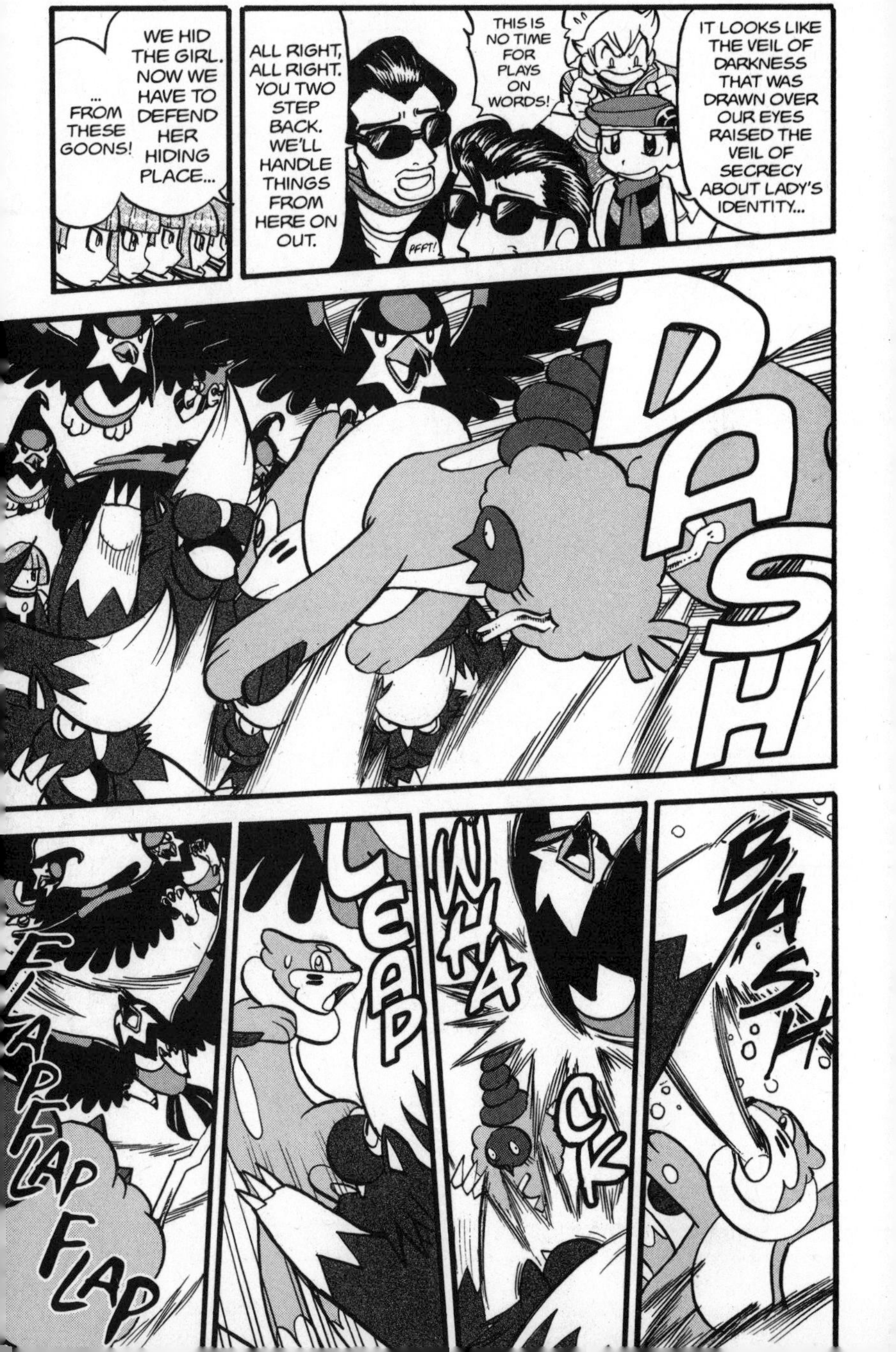
IT LOOKS LIKE THE VEIL OF DARKNESS THAT WAS DRAWN OVER OUR EYES RAISED THE VEIL OF SECRECY ABOUT LADY'S IDENTITY...
THIS IS NO TIME FOR PLAYS ON WORDS!
PFFT!
ALL RIGHT, ALL RIGHT. YOU TWO STEP BACK. WE'LL HANDLE THINGS FROM HERE ON OUT.
WE HID THE GIRL. NOW WE HAVE TO DEFEND HER HIDING PLACE...
... FROM THESE GOONS!
DASH
BASH
WHA
CK
LEAP
FLAP FLAP FLAP

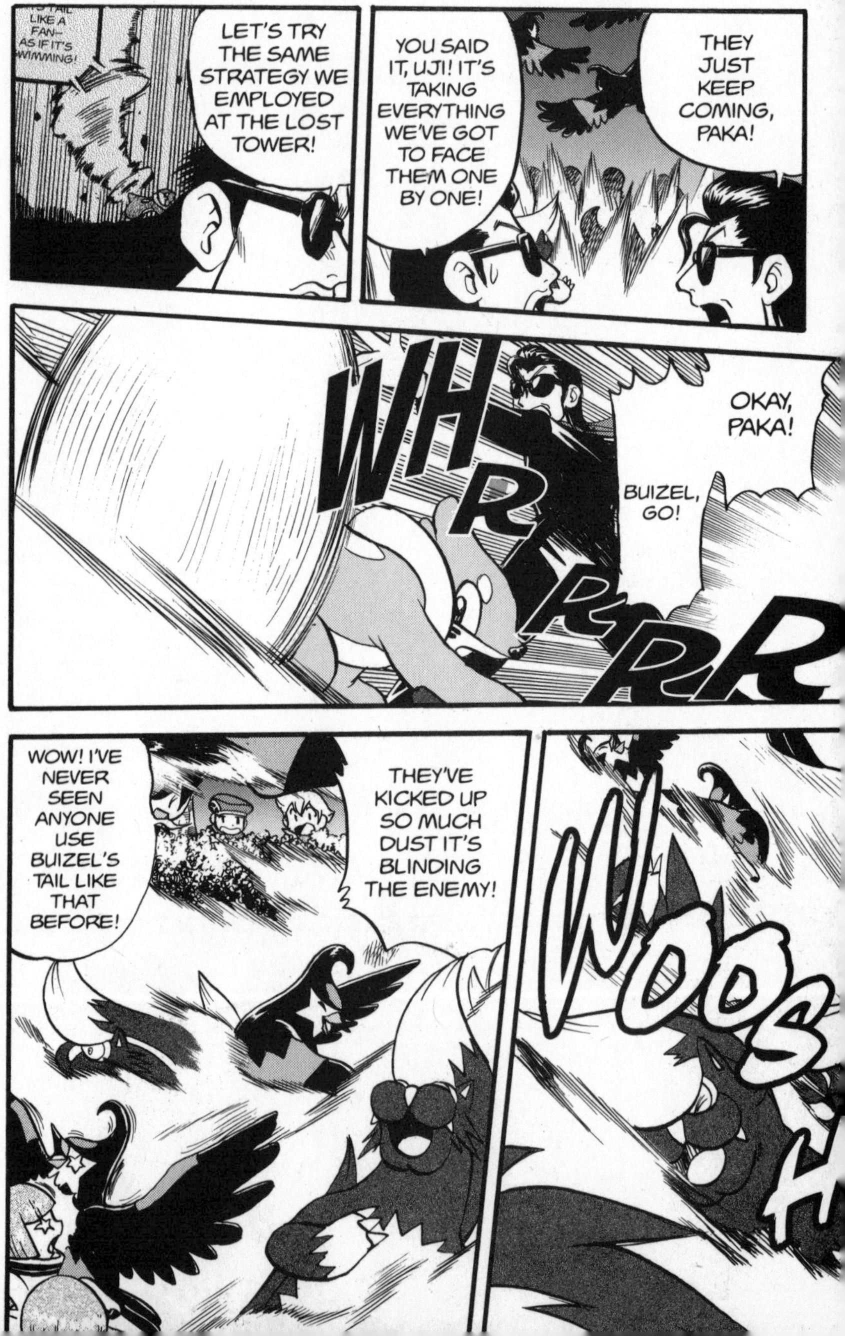
THEY JUST KEEP COMING, PAKA!
YOU SAID IT, UJI! IT'S TAKING EVERYTHING WE'VE GOT TO FACE THEM ONE BY ONE!
LET'S TRY THE SAME STRATEGY WE EMPLOYED AT THE LOST TOWER!
LIKE A FAN— AS IF IT'S WIMMING!
OKAY, PAKA!
BUIZEL, GO!
WHRRRRR
WOOS
THEY'VE KICKED UP SO MUCH DUST IT'S BLINDING THE ENEMY!
WOW! I'VE NEVER SEEN ANYONE USE BUIZEL'S TAIL LIKE THAT BEFORE!

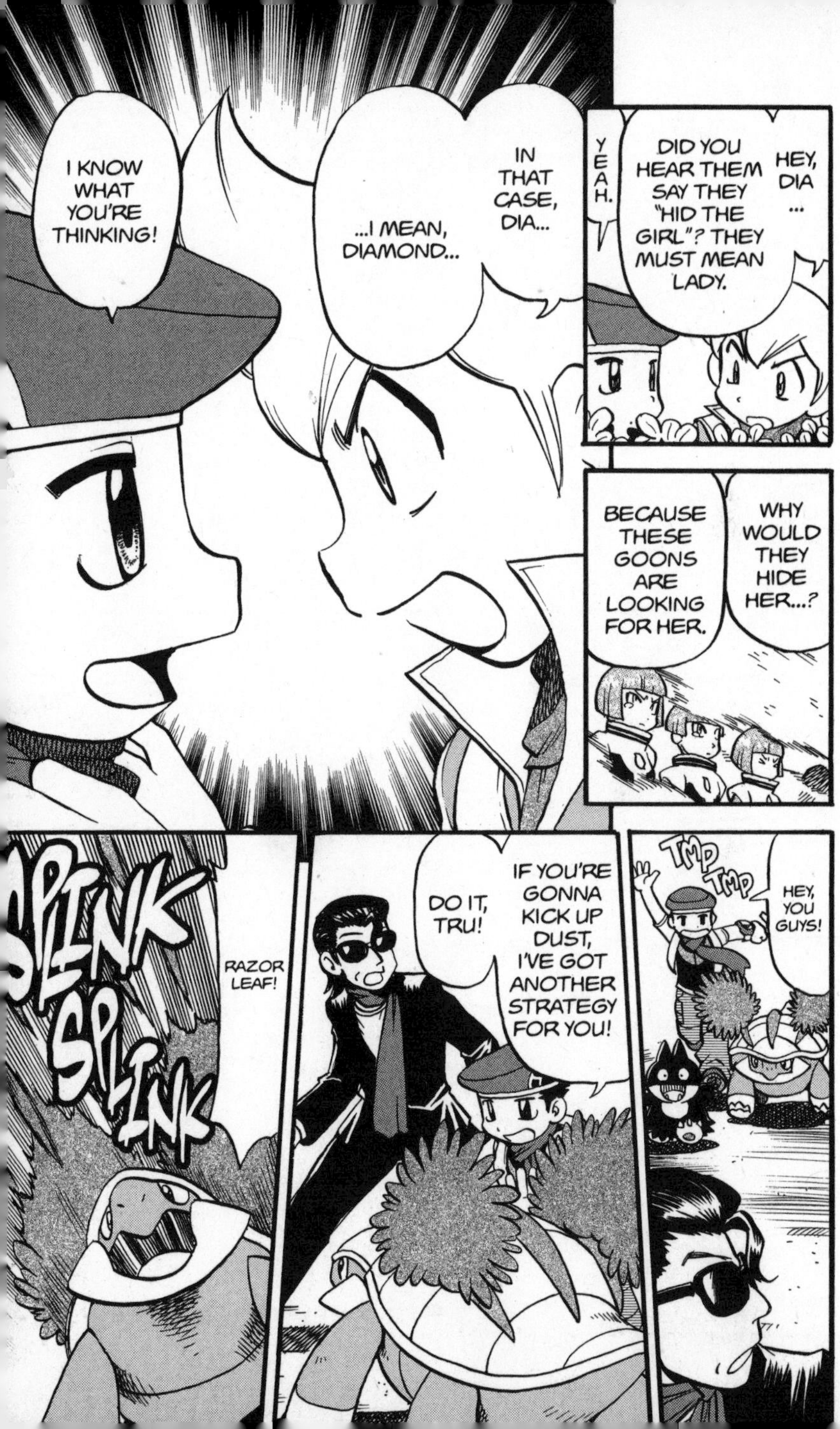
HEY, DIA...
DID YOU HEAR THEM SAY THEY "HID THE GIRL"? THEY MUST MEAN LADY.
YEAH.
WHY WOULD THEY HIDE HER...?
BECAUSE THESE GOONS ARE LOOKING FOR HER.
IN THAT CASE, DIA...
...I MEAN, DIAMOND...
I KNOW WHAT YOU'RE THINKING!
TMP TMP
HEY, YOU GUYS!
IF YOU'RE GONNA KICK UP DUST, I'VE GOT ANOTHER STRATEGY FOR YOU!
DO IT, TRU!
RAZOR LEAF!
SPLINK SPLINK

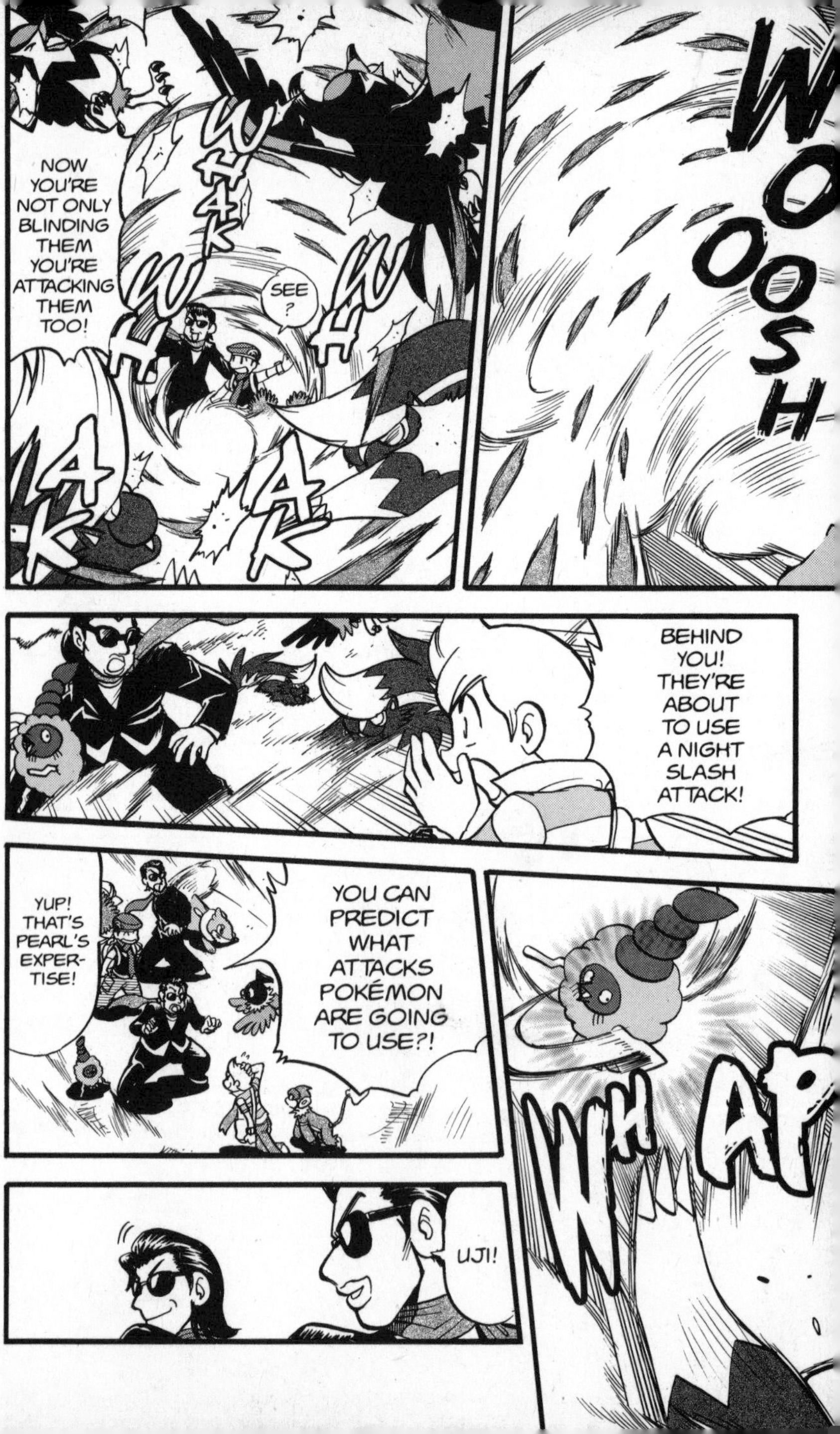
WOOOOSH
WHAK
NOW YOU'RE NOT ONLY BLINDING THEM YOU'RE ATTACKING THEM TOO!
SEE?
WHAK
WHAK
BEHIND YOU! THEY'RE ABOUT TO USE A NIGHT SLASH ATTACK!
WHAP
YOU CAN PREDICT WHAT ATTACKS POKÉMON ARE GOING TO USE?!
YUP! THAT'S PEARL'S EXPER-TISE!
UJI!

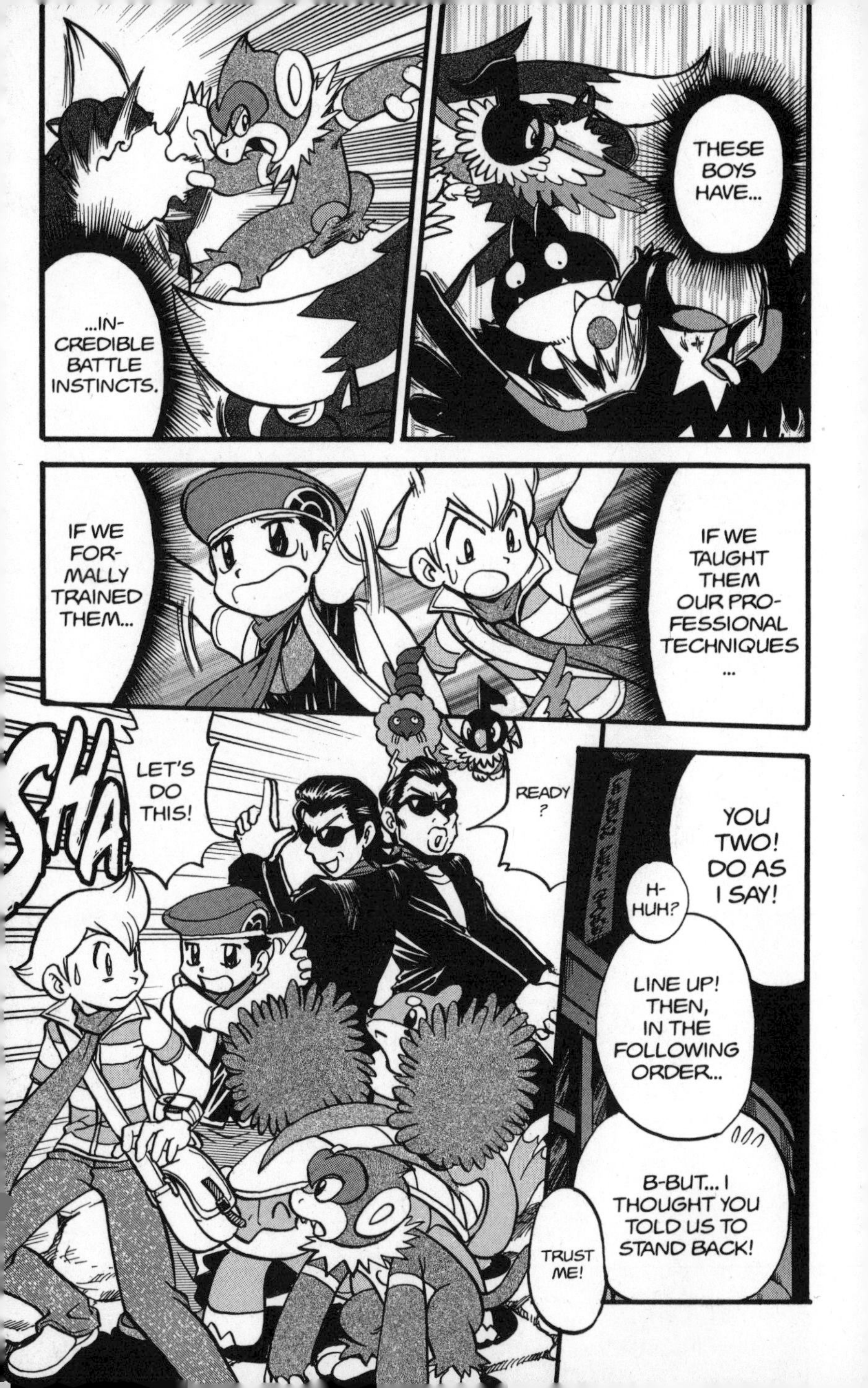
THESE BOYS HAVE...
...IN-CREDIBLE BATTLE INSTINCTS.
IF WE TAUGHT THEM OUR PRO-FESSIONAL TECHNIQUES...
IF WE FOR-MALLY TRAINED THEM...
YOU TWO! DO AS I SAY!
H-HUH?
LINE UP! THEN, IN THE FOLLOWING ORDER...
B-BUT... I THOUGHT YOU TOLD US TO STAND BACK!
TRUST ME!
READY?
LET'S DO THIS!
SHA

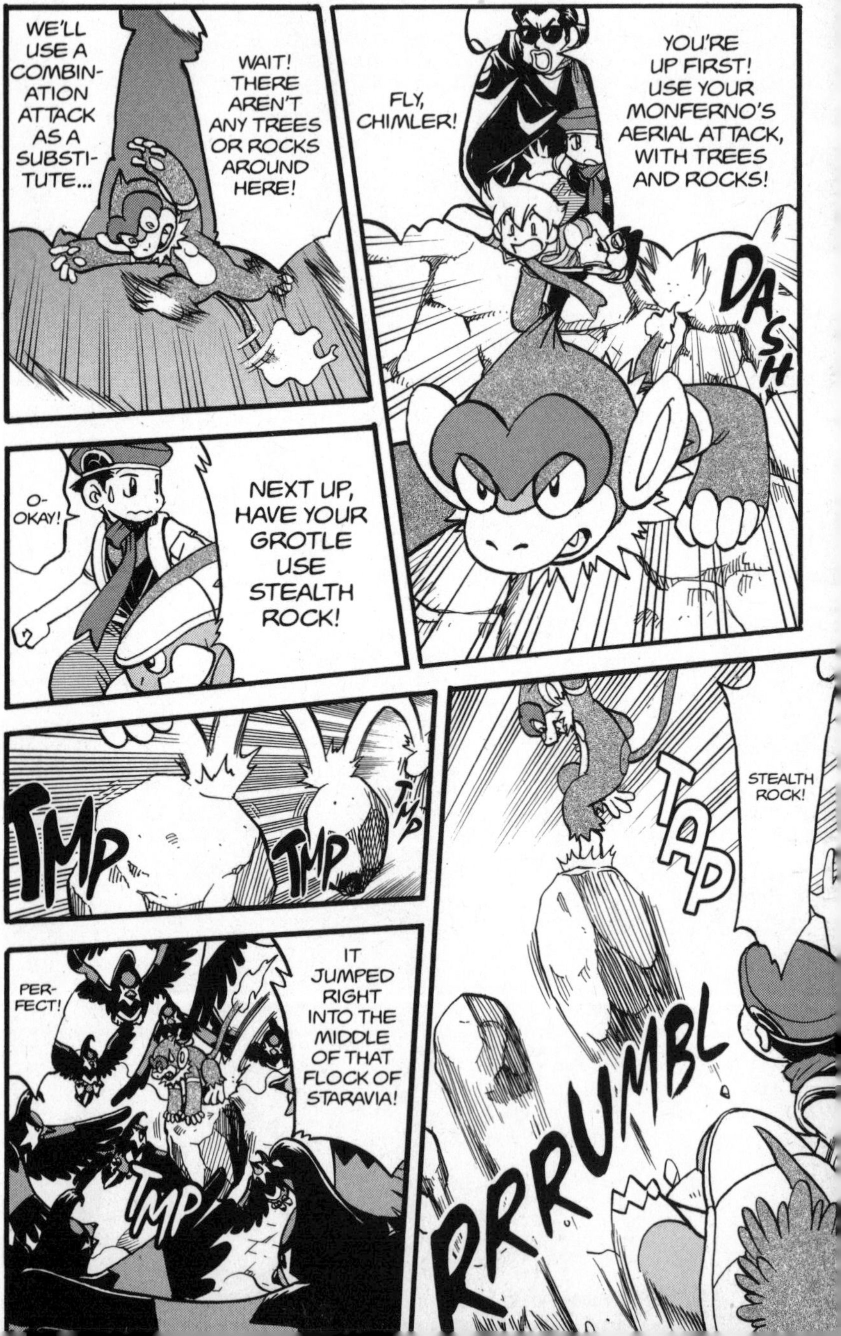
YOU'RE UP FIRST! USE YOUR MONFERNO'S AERIAL ATTACK, WITH TREES AND ROCKS!
FLY, CHIMLER!
DASH
WAIT! THERE AREN'T ANY TREES OR ROCKS AROUND HERE!
WE'LL USE A COMBIN-ATION ATTACK AS A SUBSTI-TUTE...
NEXT UP, HAVE YOUR GROTLE USE STEALTH ROCK!
O-OKAY!
STEALTH ROCK!
TAP
RRRUMBL
TMP
TMP
TMP
IT JUMPED RIGHT INTO THE MIDDLE OF THAT FLOCK OF STARAVIA!
PER-FECT!
TMP

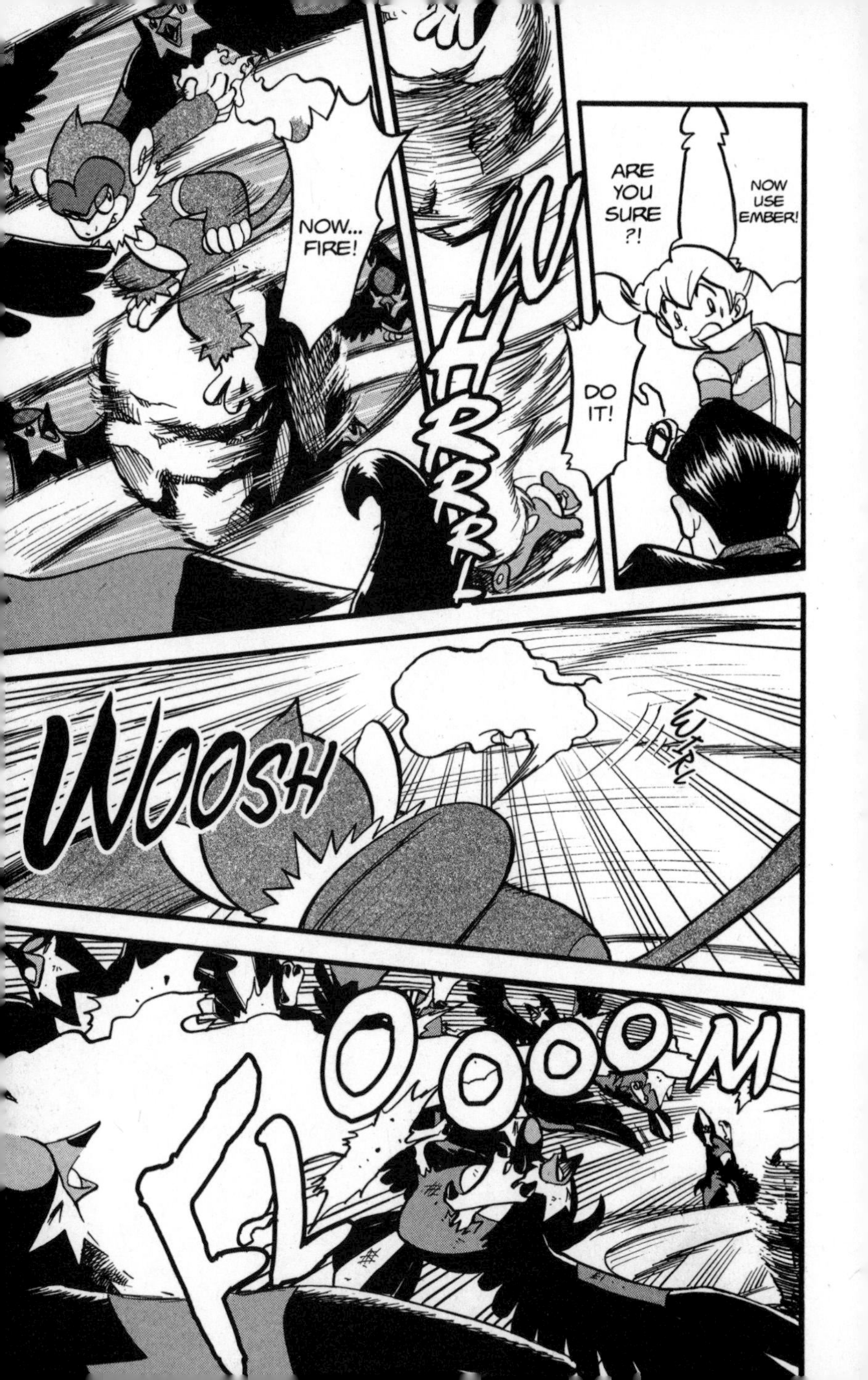
NOW USE EMBER!
ARE YOU SURE ?!
DO IT!
WHIRRRL
NOW... FIRE!
TWIRL
WOOSH
OOOOM

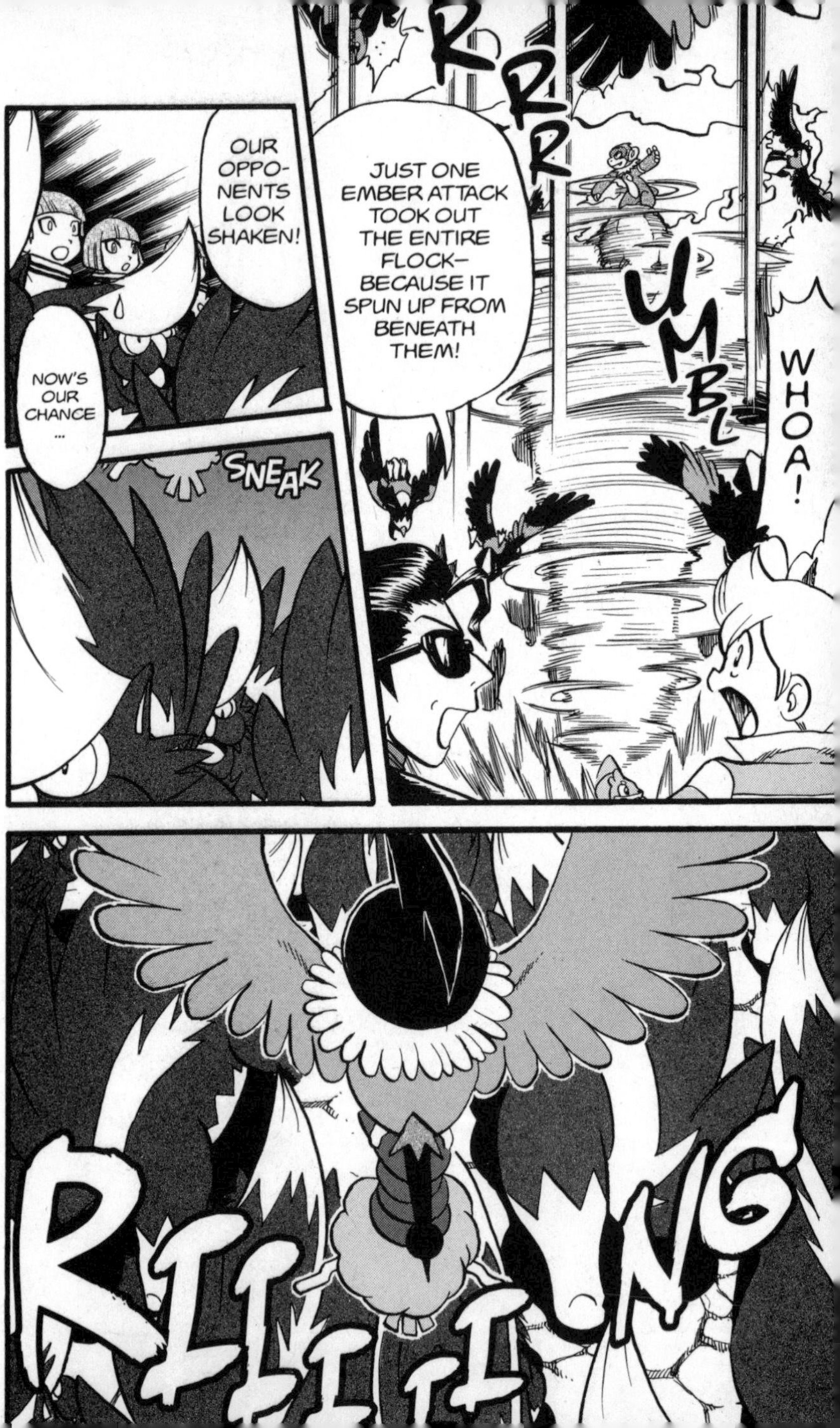
RRRUMBL
WHOA!
JUST ONE EMBER ATTACK TOOK OUT THE ENTIRE FLOCK— BECAUSE IT SPUN UP FROM BENEATH THEM!
OUR OPPONENTS LOOK SHAKEN!
NOW'S OUR CHANCE ...
SNEAK
RIIIIING

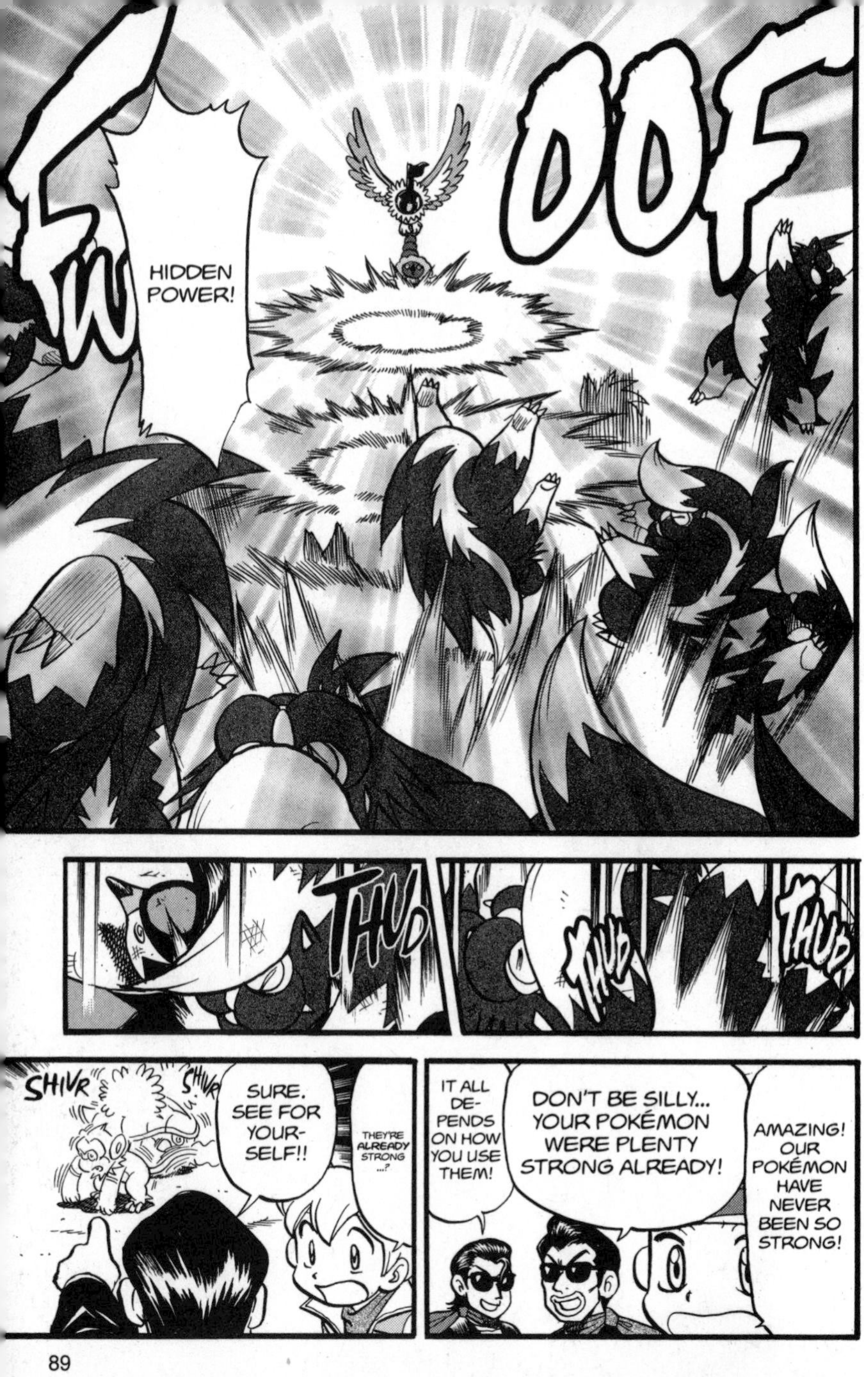
FWOOF
HIDDEN POWER!
THUD
THUD
THUD
AMAZING! OUR POKÉMON HAVE NEVER BEEN SO STRONG!
DON'T BE SILLY... YOUR POKÉMON WERE PLENTY STRONG ALREADY!
IT ALL DE-PENDS ON HOW YOU USE THEM!
THEY'RE ALREADY STRONG ...?
SURE. SEE FOR YOUR-SELF!!
SHIVR
SHIVR

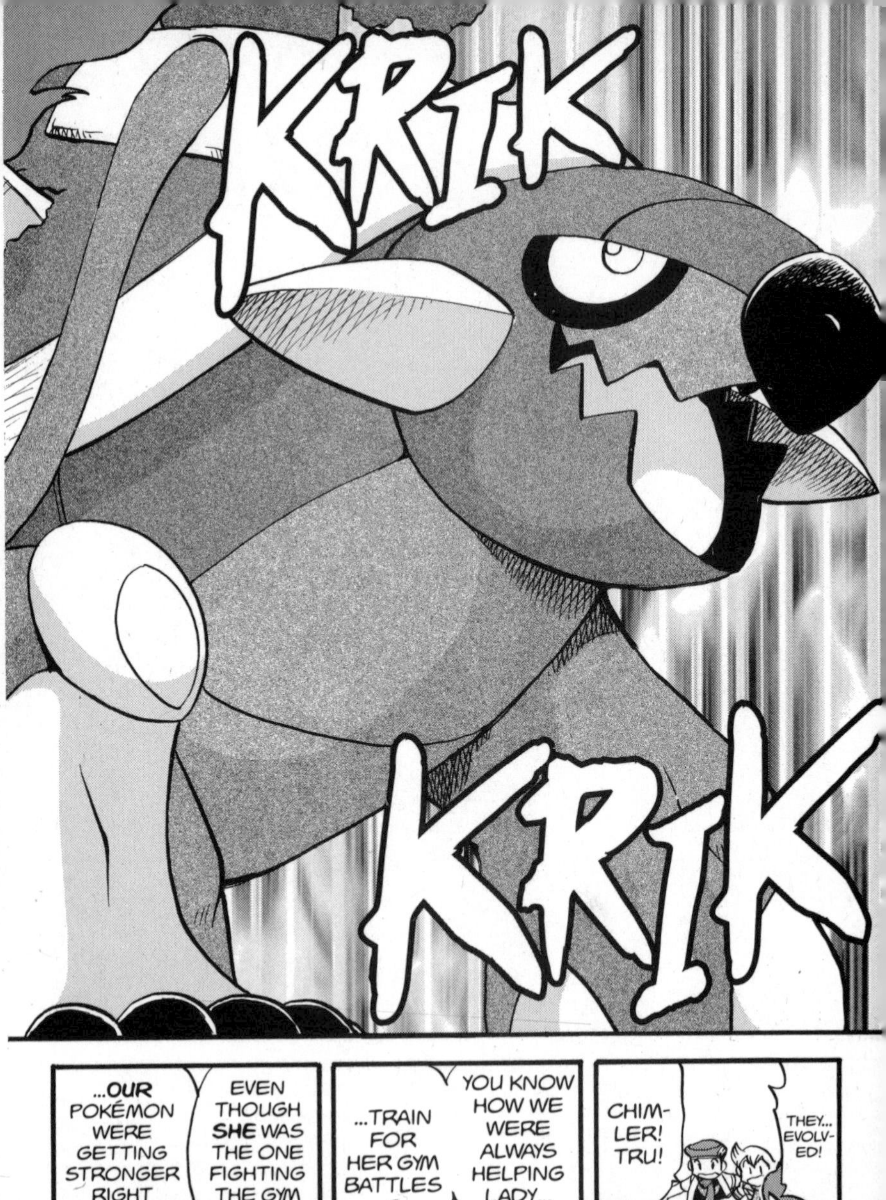
KRIK
KRIK
THEY... EVOLV-ED!
CHIM-LER! TRU!
YOU KNOW HOW WE WERE ALWAYS HELPING LADY...
...TRAIN FOR HER GYM BATTLES?
EVEN THOUGH **SHE** WAS THE ONE FIGHTING THE GYM BATTLES...
...**OUR** POKÉMON WERE GETTING STRONGER RIGHT ALONGSIDE HERS!

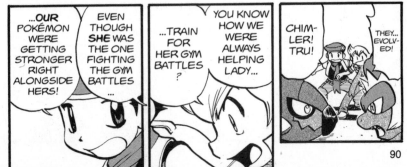

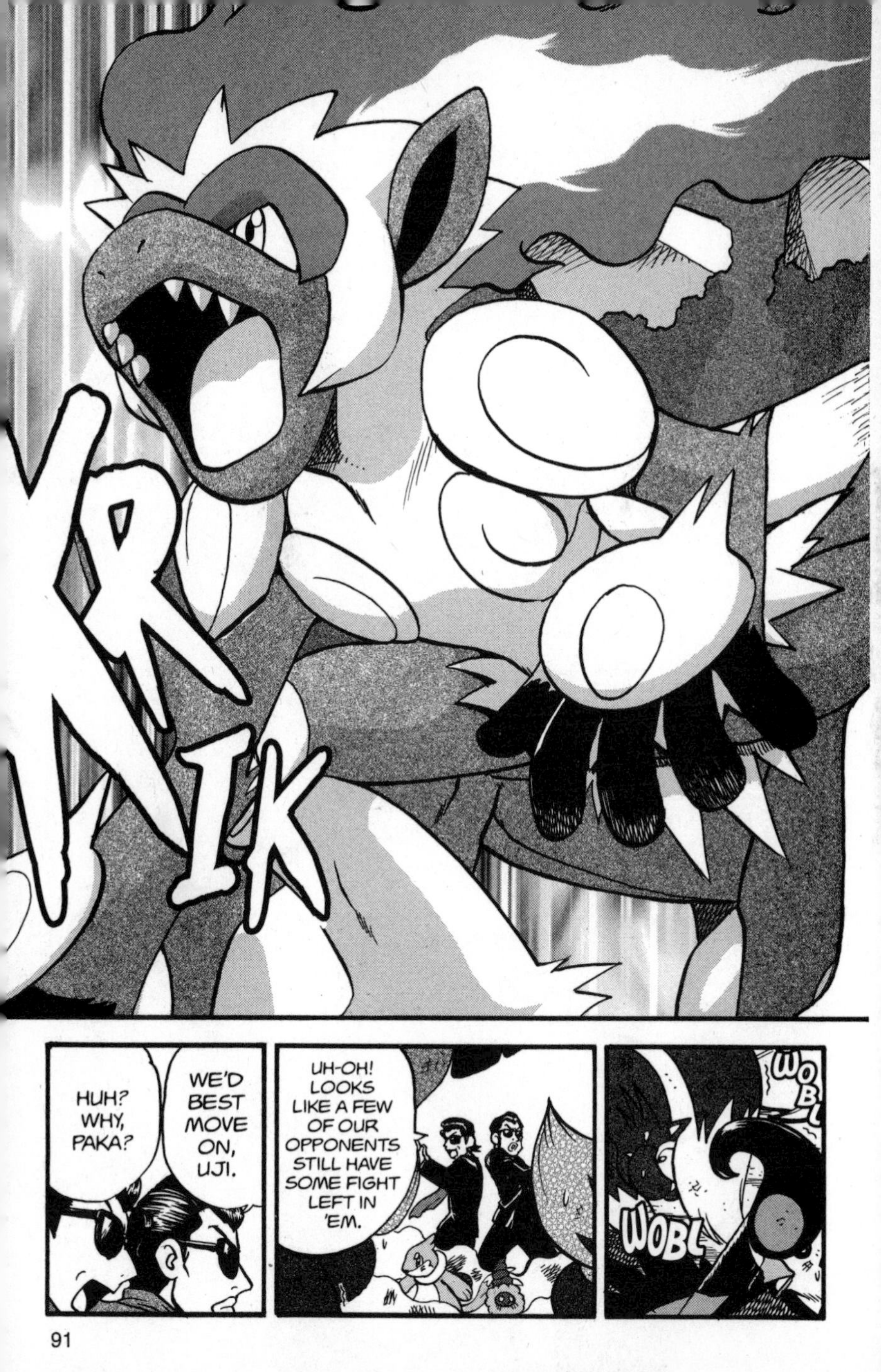
KRIK
WOBL
WOBL
UH-OH! LOOKS LIKE A FEW OF OUR OPPONENTS STILL HAVE SOME FIGHT LEFT IN 'EM.
WE'D BEST MOVE ON, UJI.
HUH? WHY, PAKA?

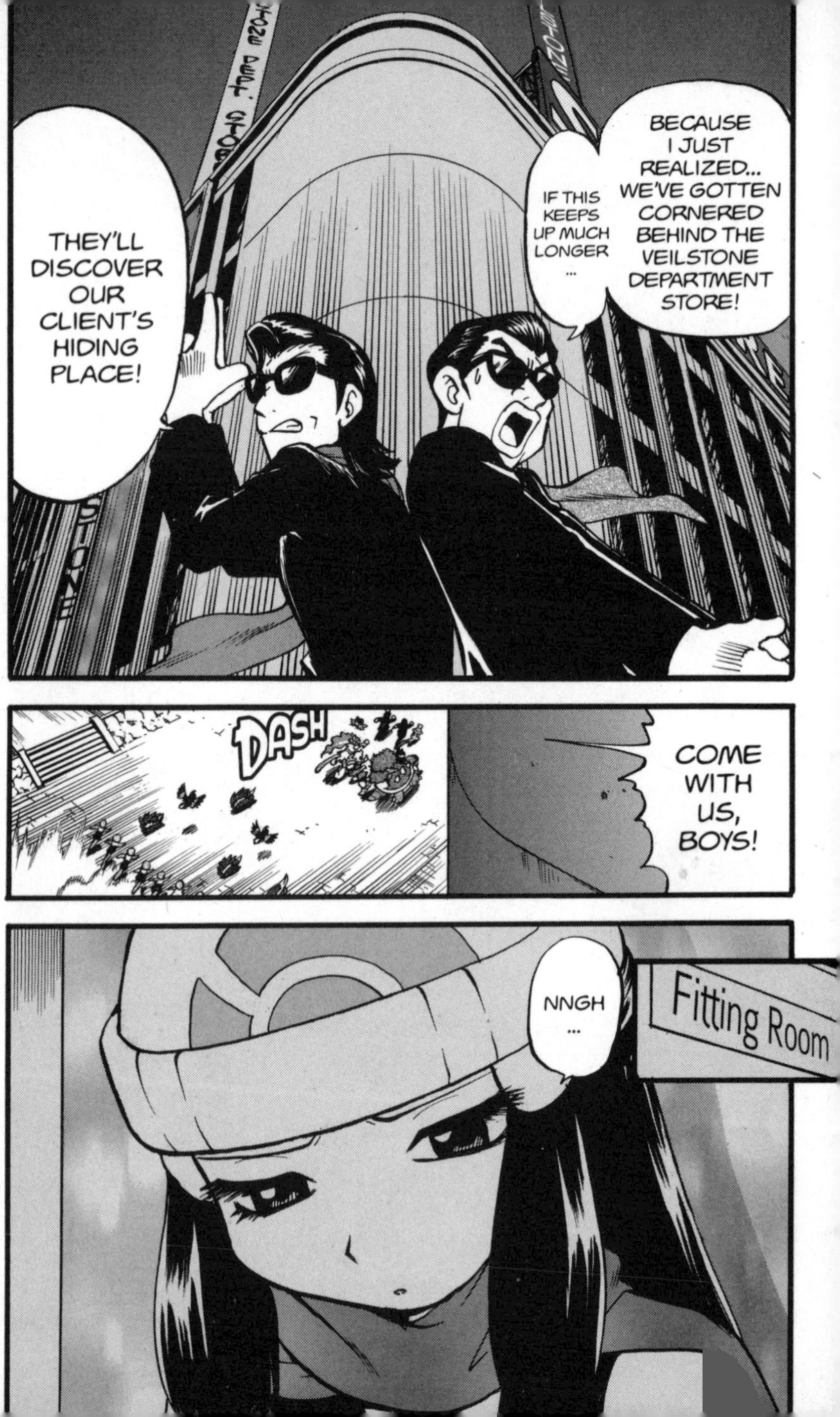
BECAUSE I JUST REALIZED... WE'VE GOTTEN CORNERED BEHIND THE VEILSTONE DEPARTMENT STORE!
IF THIS KEEPS UP MUCH LONGER ...
THEY'LL DISCOVER OUR CLIENT'S HIDING PLACE!
COME WITH US, BOYS!
DASH
Fitting Room
NNGH ...

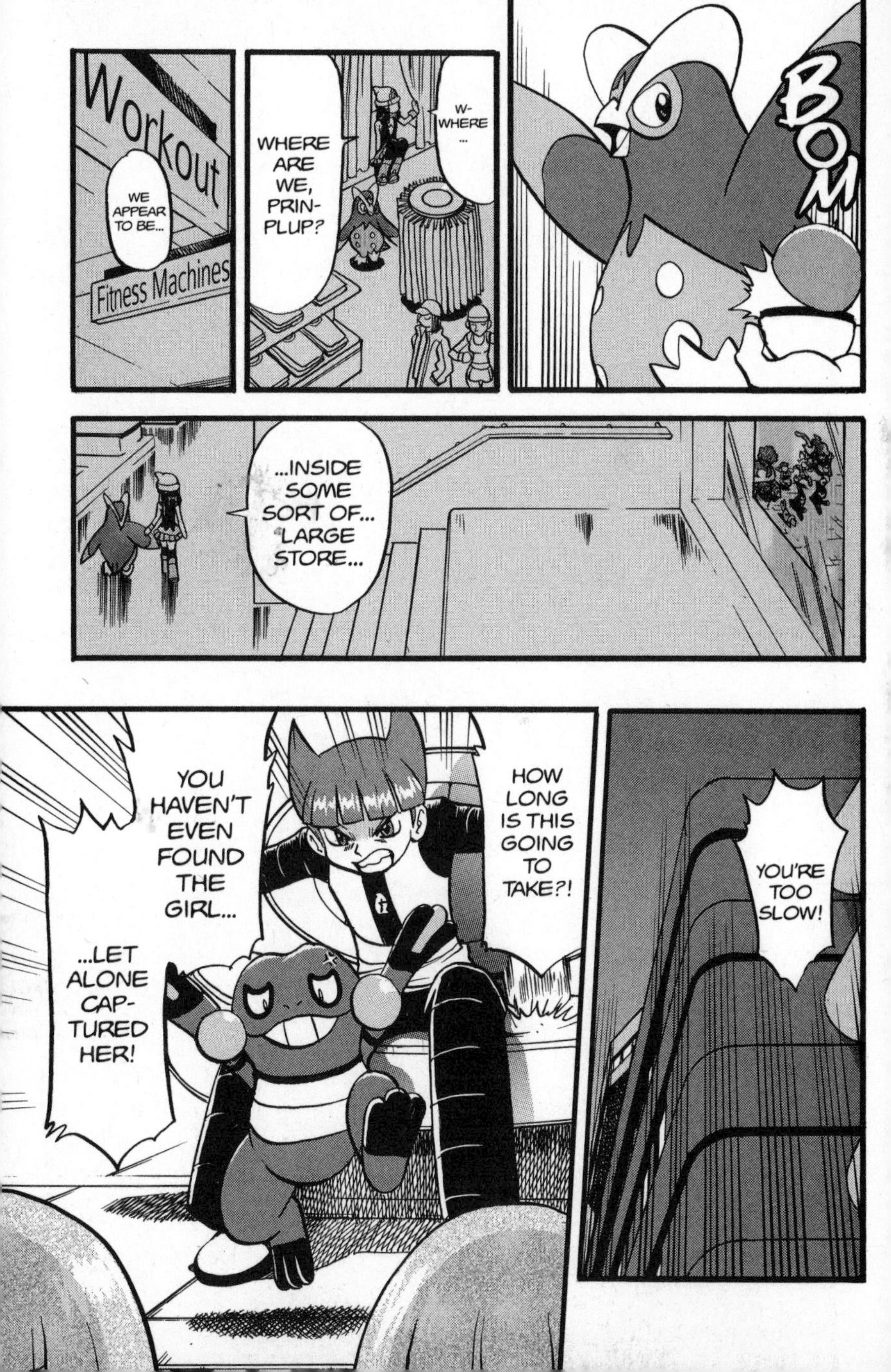
BOM
W-WHERE...
WHERE ARE WE, PRINPLUP?
Workout
WE APPEAR TO BE...
Fitness Machines
...INSIDE SOME SORT OF... LARGE STORE...
YOU'RE TOO SLOW!
HOW LONG IS THIS GOING TO TAKE?!
YOU HAVEN'T EVEN FOUND THE GIRL...
...LET ALONE CAPTURED HER!

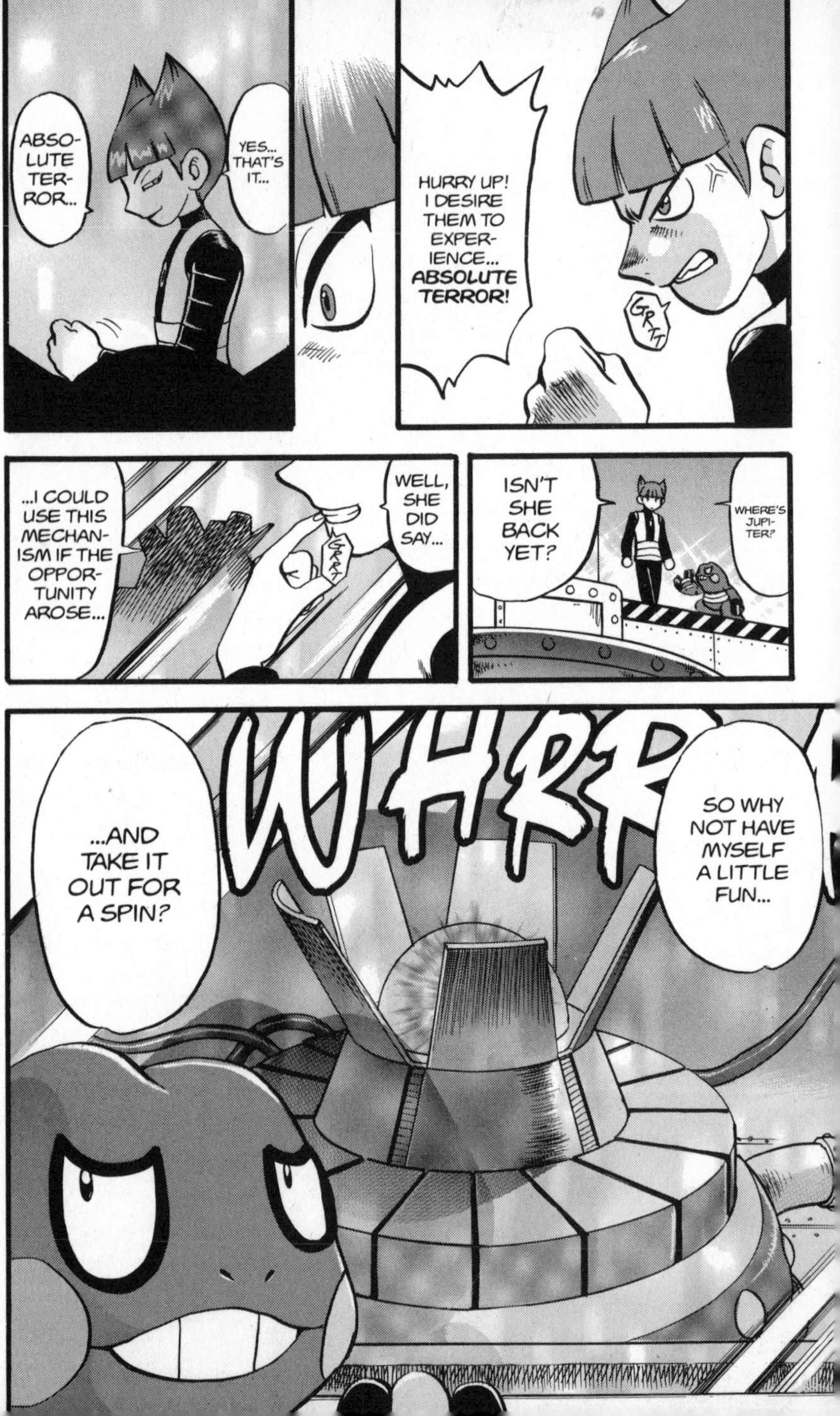
HURRY UP! I DESIRE THEM TO EXPERIENCE... **ABSOLUTE TERROR!**
YES... THAT'S IT...
ABSOLUTE TERROR...
WHERE'S JUPITER?
ISN'T SHE BACK YET?
WELL, SHE DID SAY...
...I COULD USE THIS MECHANISM IF THE OPPORTUNITY AROSE...
WHRR
SO WHY NOT HAVE MYSELF A LITTLE FUN...
...AND TAKE IT OUT FOR A SPIN?

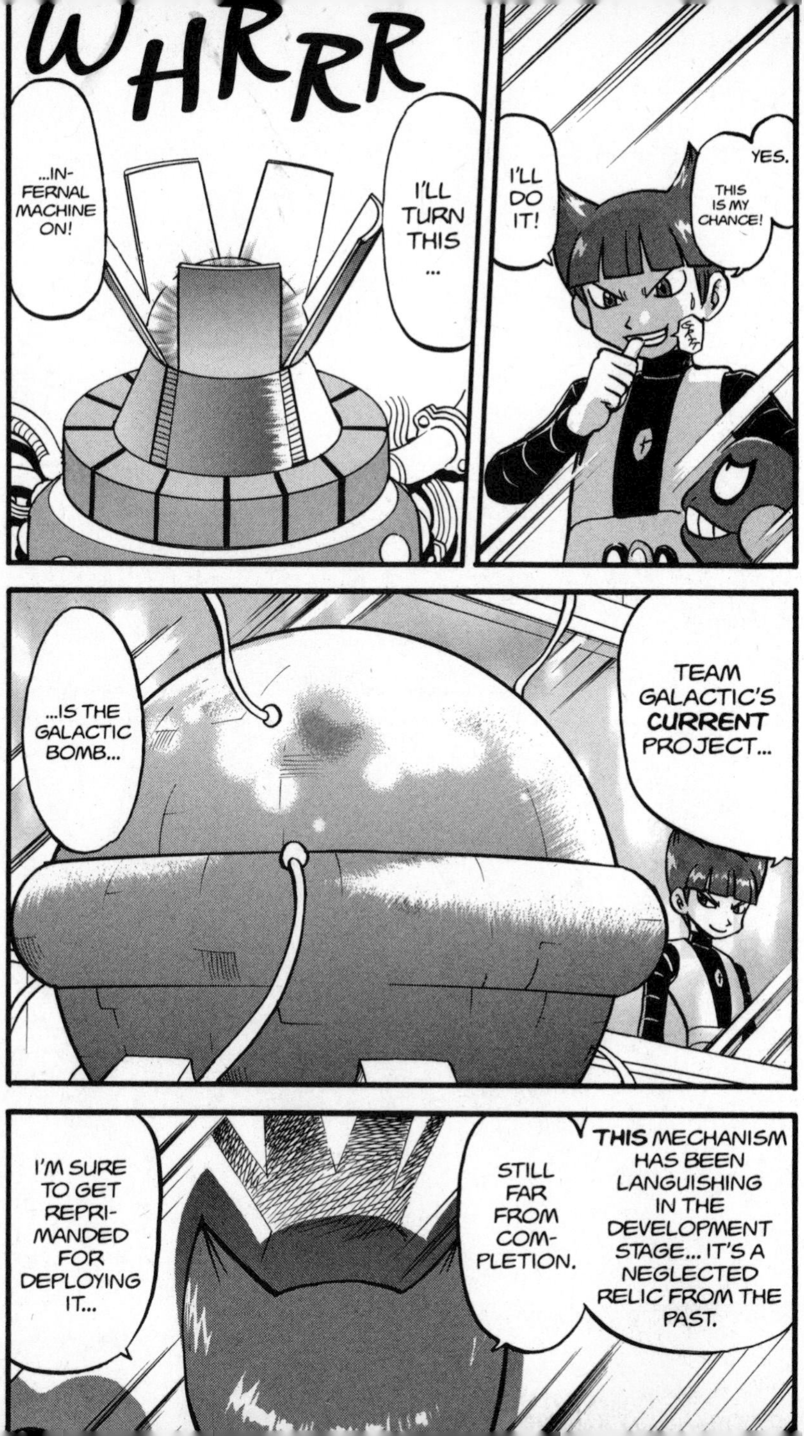
YES.
THIS IS MY CHANCE!
I'LL DO IT!
WHRRR
I'LL TURN THIS ...
...IN-FERNAL MACHINE ON!
TEAM GALACTIC'S **CURRENT** PROJECT...
...IS THE GALACTIC BOMB...
THIS MECHANISM HAS BEEN LANGUISHING IN THE DEVELOPMENT STAGE... IT'S A NEGLECTED RELIC FROM THE PAST.
STILL FAR FROM COM-PLETION.
I'M SURE TO GET REPRI-MANDED FOR DEPLOYING IT...

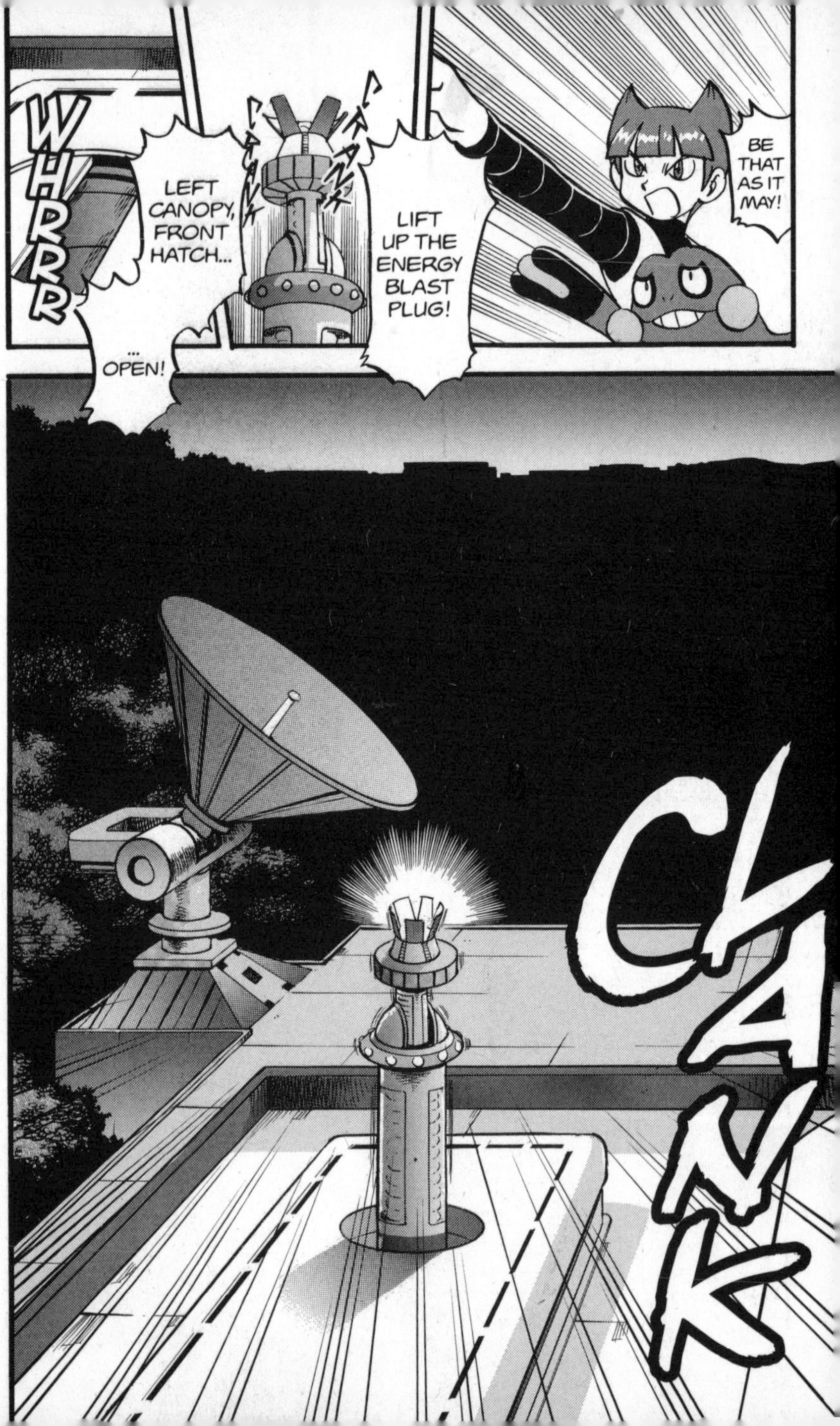
BE THAT AS IT MAY!
LIFT UP THE ENERGY BLAST PLUG!
CRANK
CRANK
LEFT CANOPY, FRONT HATCH...
WHRRR
...OPEN!
CLANK

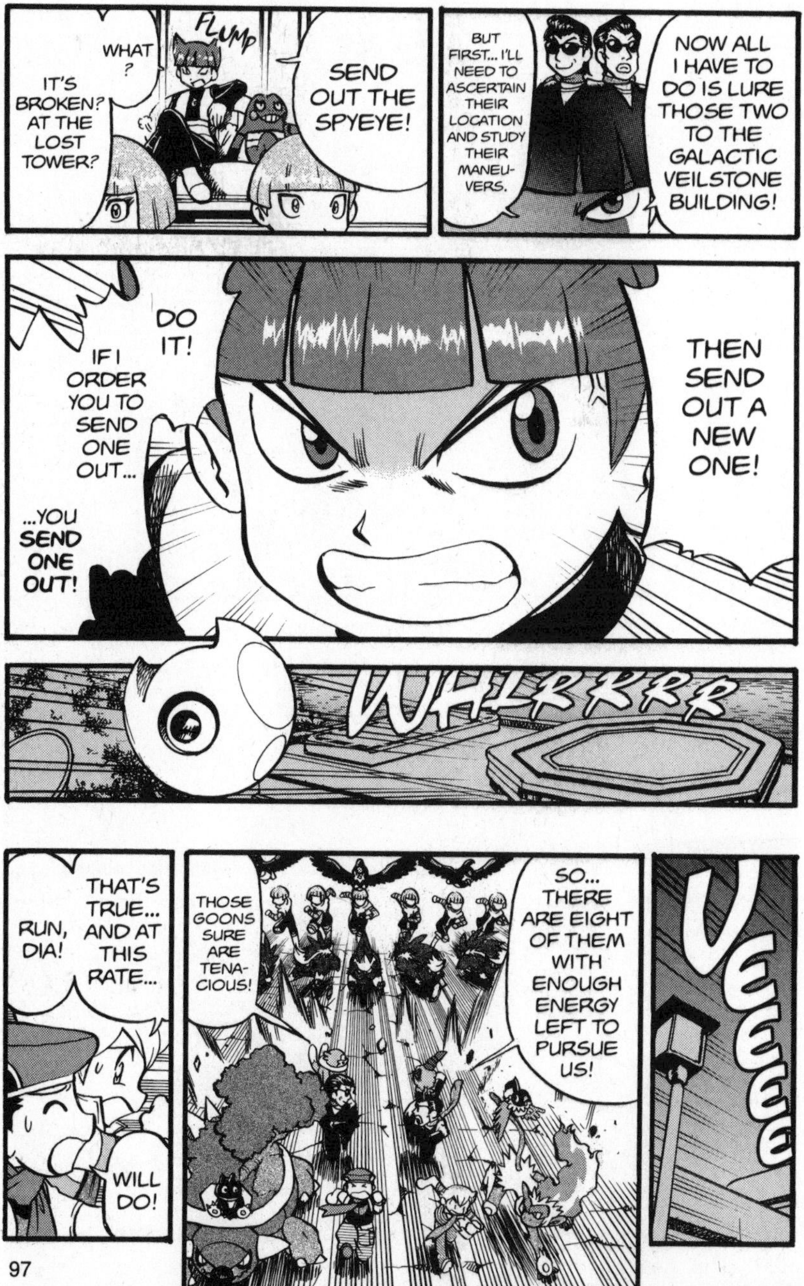
NOW ALL I HAVE TO DO IS LURE THOSE TWO TO THE GALACTIC VEILSTONE BUILDING!
BUT FIRST... I'LL NEED TO ASCERTAIN THEIR LOCATION AND STUDY THEIR MANEU-VERS.
SEND OUT THE SPYEYE!
FLUMP
WHAT?
IT'S BROKEN? AT THE LOST TOWER?
THEN SEND OUT A NEW ONE!
DO IT!
IF I ORDER YOU TO SEND ONE OUT...
...YOU SEND ONE OUT!
WHIRRRR
VEEEE
SO... THERE ARE EIGHT OF THEM WITH ENOUGH ENERGY LEFT TO PURSUE US!
THOSE GOONS SURE ARE TENA-CIOUS!
THAT'S TRUE... AND AT THIS RATE...
RUN, DIA!
WILL DO!

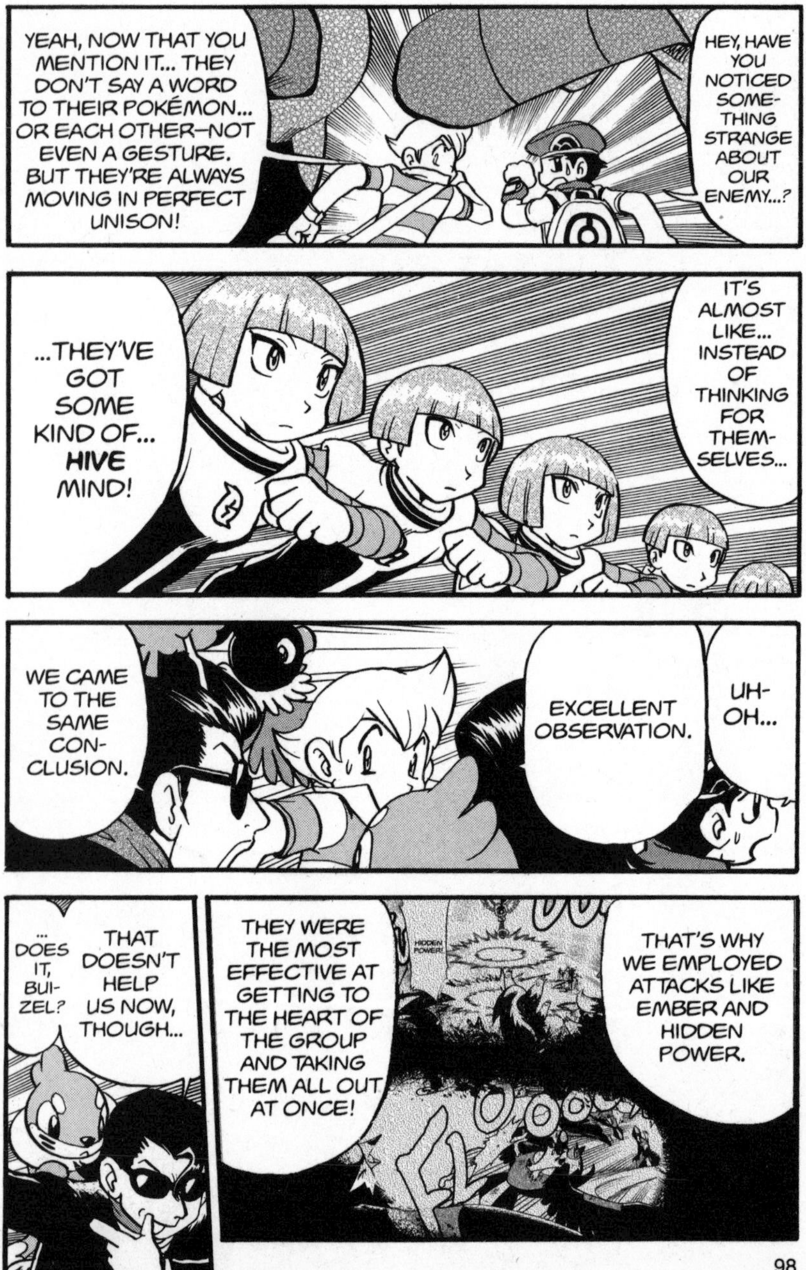
HEY, HAVE YOU NOTICED SOMETHING STRANGE ABOUT OUR ENEMY...?
YEAH, NOW THAT YOU MENTION IT... THEY DON'T SAY A WORD TO THEIR POKÉMON... OR EACH OTHER—NOT EVEN A GESTURE. BUT THEY'RE ALWAYS MOVING IN PERFECT UNISON!
IT'S ALMOST LIKE... INSTEAD OF THINKING FOR THEMSELVES...
...THEY'VE GOT SOME KIND OF... **HIVE** MIND!
UH-OH...
EXCELLENT OBSERVATION.
WE CAME TO THE SAME CONCLUSION.
THAT'S WHY WE EMPLOYED ATTACKS LIKE EMBER AND HIDDEN POWER.
HIDDEN POWER!
THEY WERE THE MOST EFFECTIVE AT GETTING TO THE HEART OF THE GROUP AND TAKING THEM ALL OUT AT ONCE!
THAT DOESN'T HELP US NOW, THOUGH...
...DOES IT, BUIZEL?

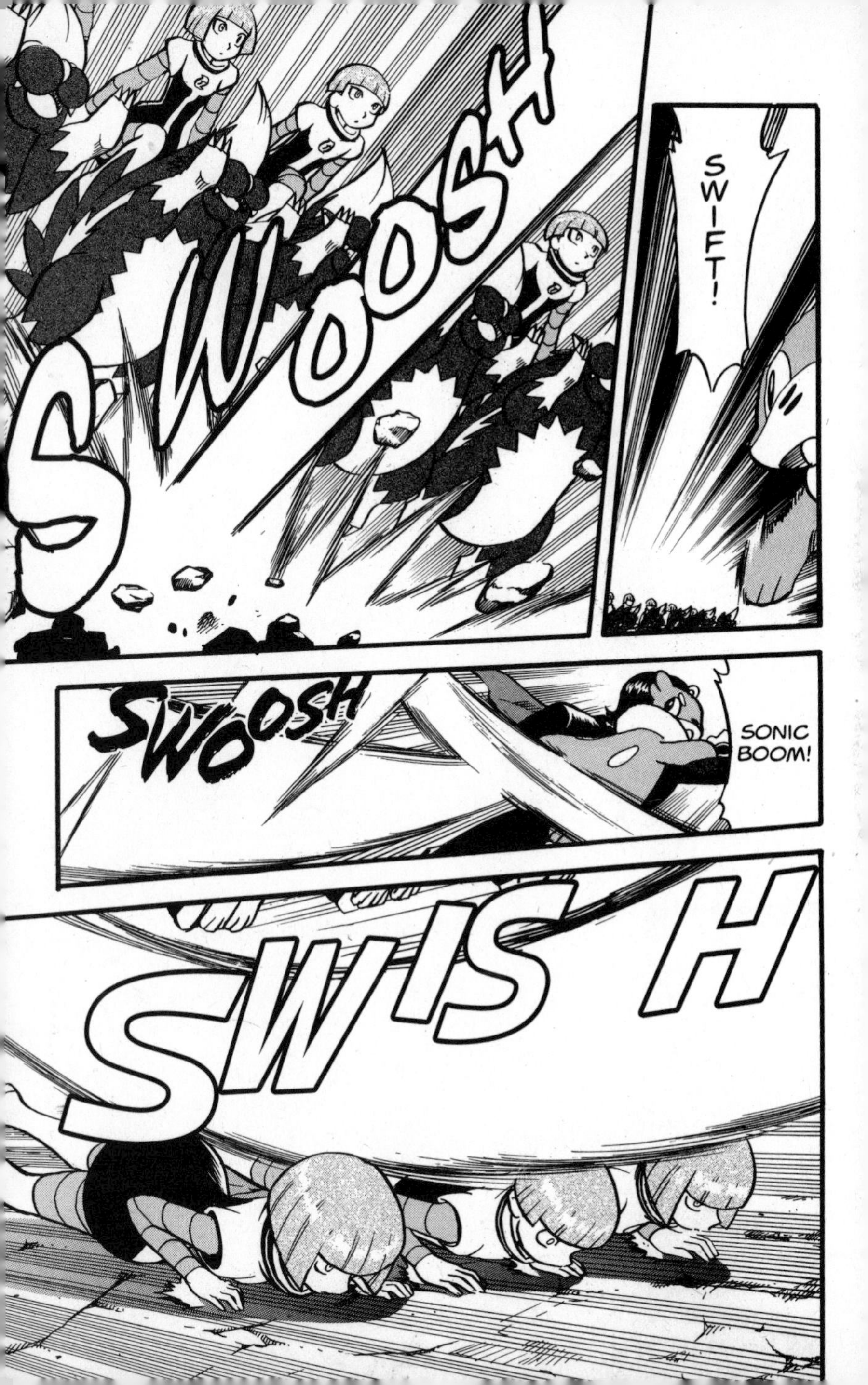
SWIFT!
SWOOSH
SONIC BOOM!
SWOOSH
SWISH

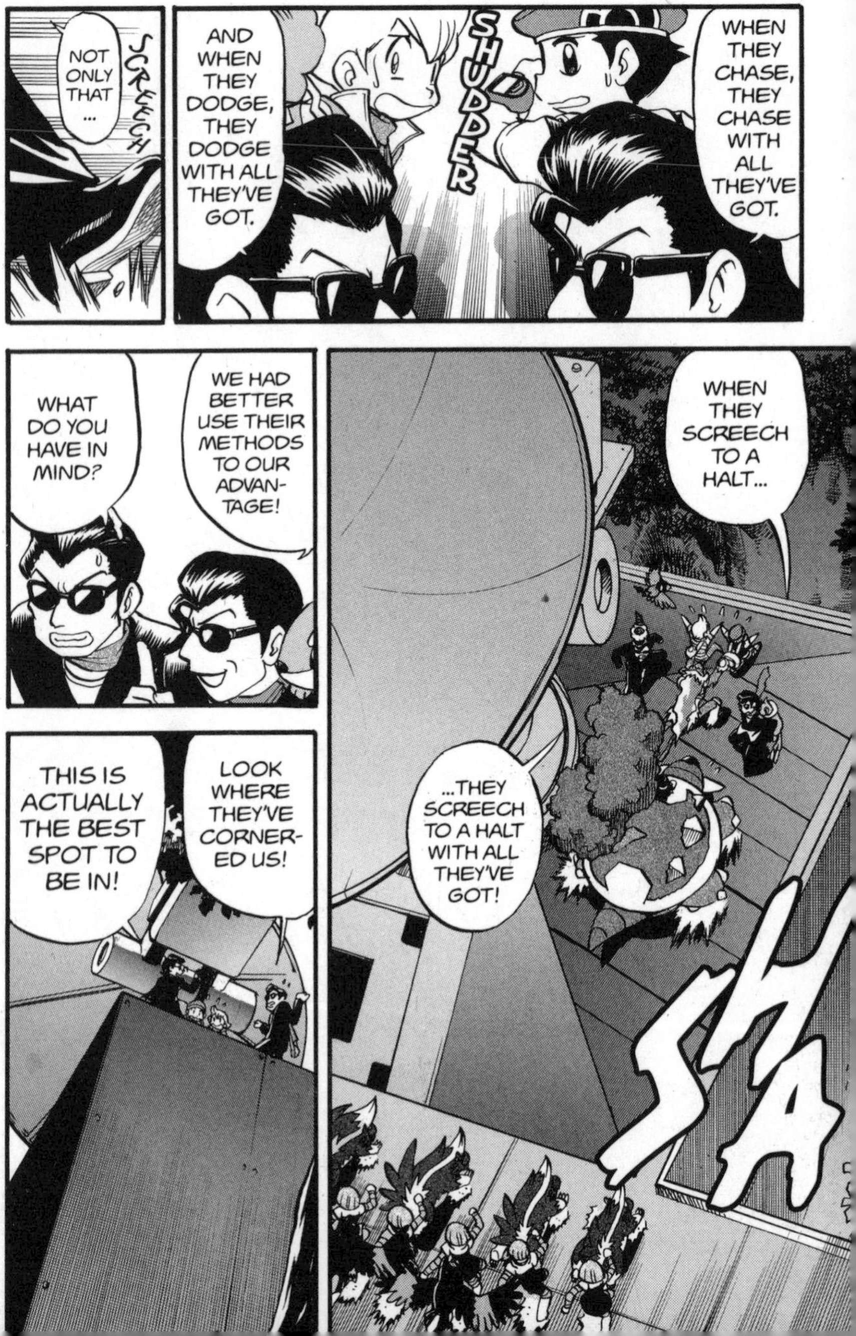
WHEN THEY CHASE, THEY CHASE WITH ALL THEY'VE GOT.
SHUDDER
AND WHEN THEY DODGE, THEY DODGE WITH ALL THEY'VE GOT.
SCREECH
NOT ONLY THAT ...
WHEN THEY SCREECH TO A HALT...
...THEY SCREECH TO A HALT WITH ALL THEY'VE GOT!
SHA
WE HAD BETTER USE THEIR METHODS TO OUR ADVAN-TAGE!
WHAT DO YOU HAVE IN MIND?
LOOK WHERE THEY'VE CORNER-ED US!
THIS IS ACTUALLY THE BEST SPOT TO BE IN!

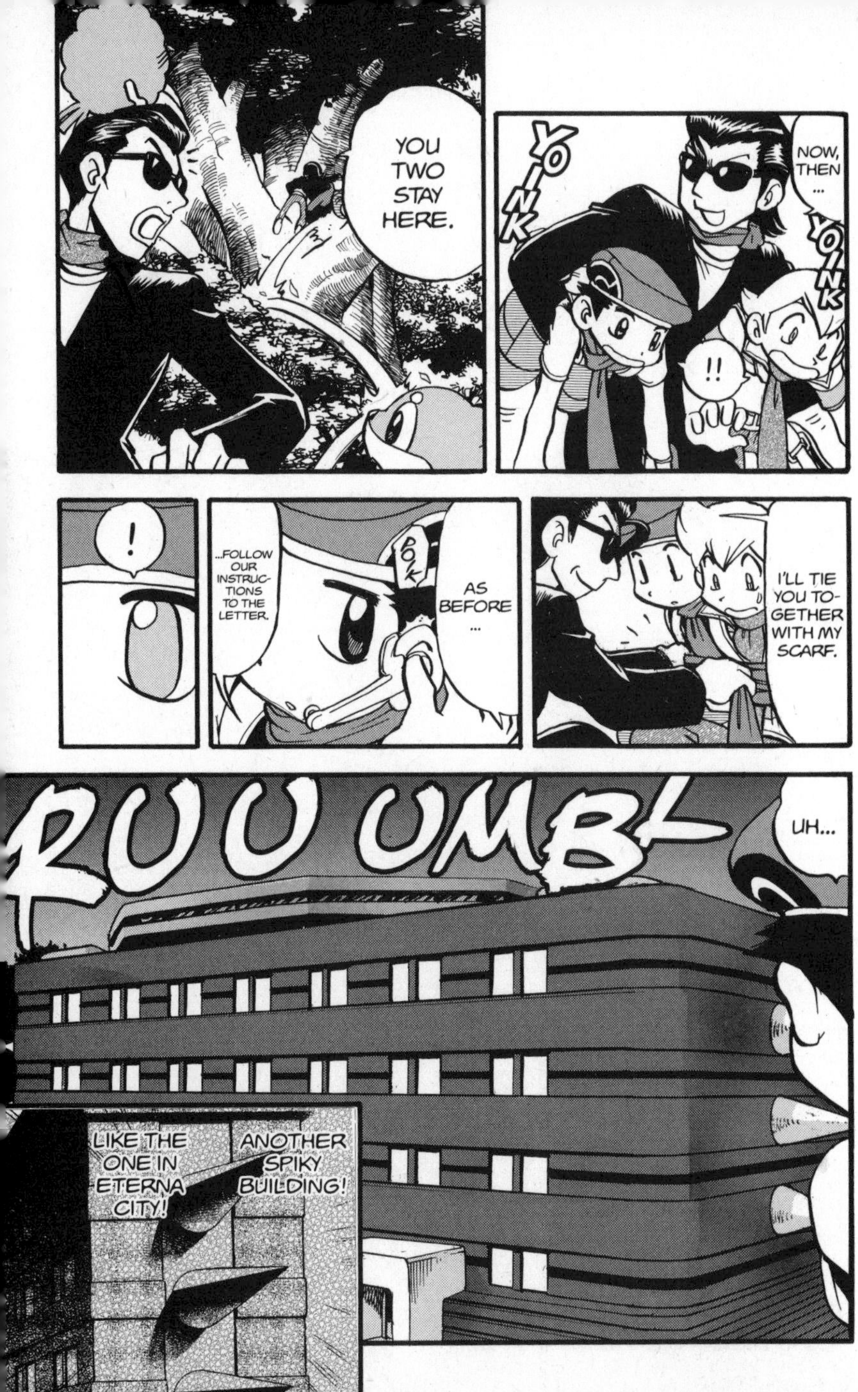

NOW, THEN ...
YOINK
YOINK
!!
YOU TWO STAY HERE.
I'LL TIE YOU TOGETHER WITH MY SCARF.
AS BEFORE ...
POK
...FOLLOW OUR INSTRUCTIONS TO THE LETTER.
!
UH...
RUUUMB
ANOTHER SPIKY BUILDING!
LIKE THE ONE IN ETERNA CITY!

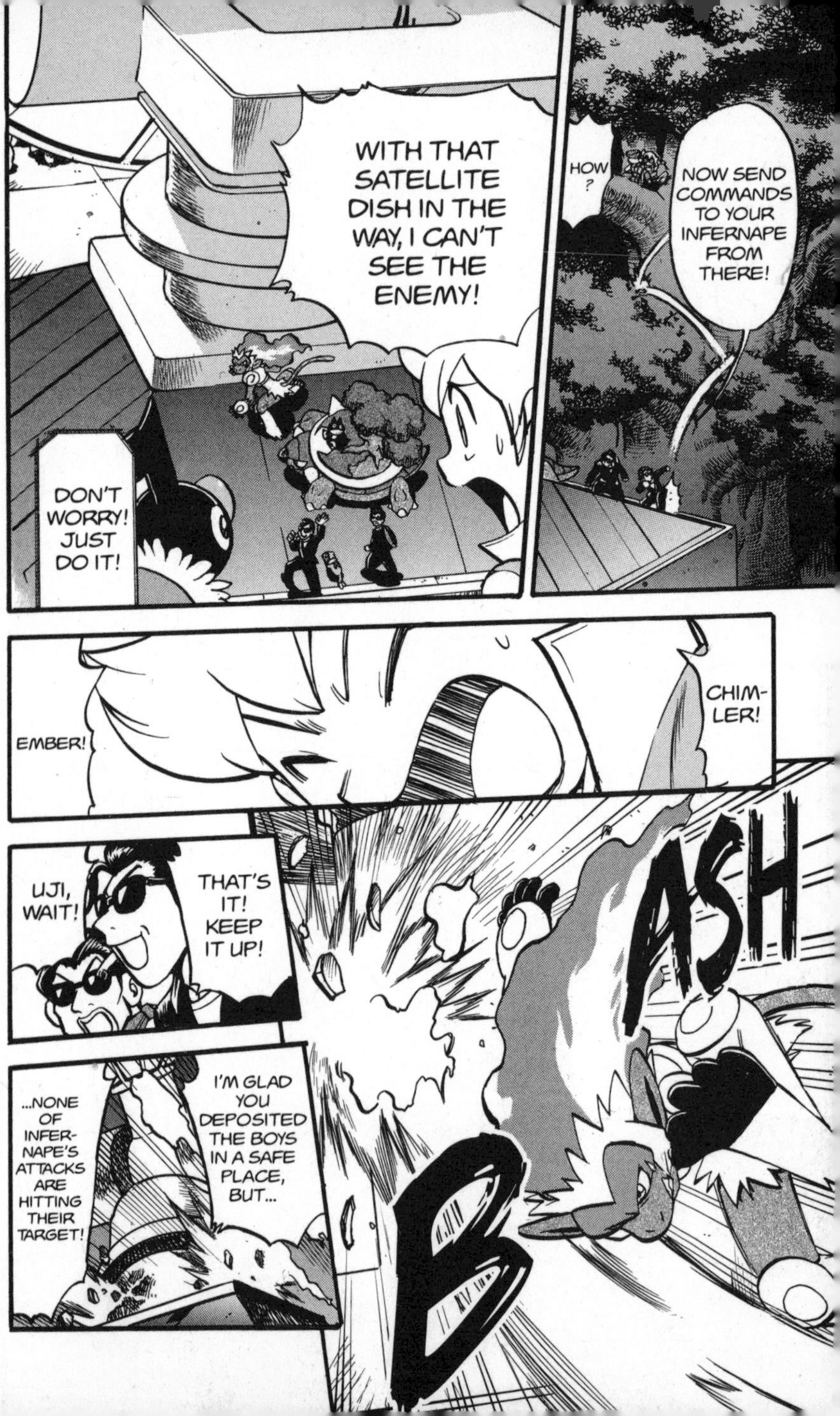
NOW SEND COMMANDS TO YOUR INFERNAPE FROM THERE!
HOW?
WITH THAT SATELLITE DISH IN THE WAY, I CAN'T SEE THE ENEMY!
DON'T WORRY! JUST DO IT!
CHIMLER!
EMBER!
BASH
THAT'S IT! KEEP IT UP!
UJI, WAIT!
I'M GLAD YOU DEPOSITED THE BOYS IN A SAFE PLACE, BUT...
...NONE OF INFERNAPE'S ATTACKS ARE HITTING THEIR TARGET!

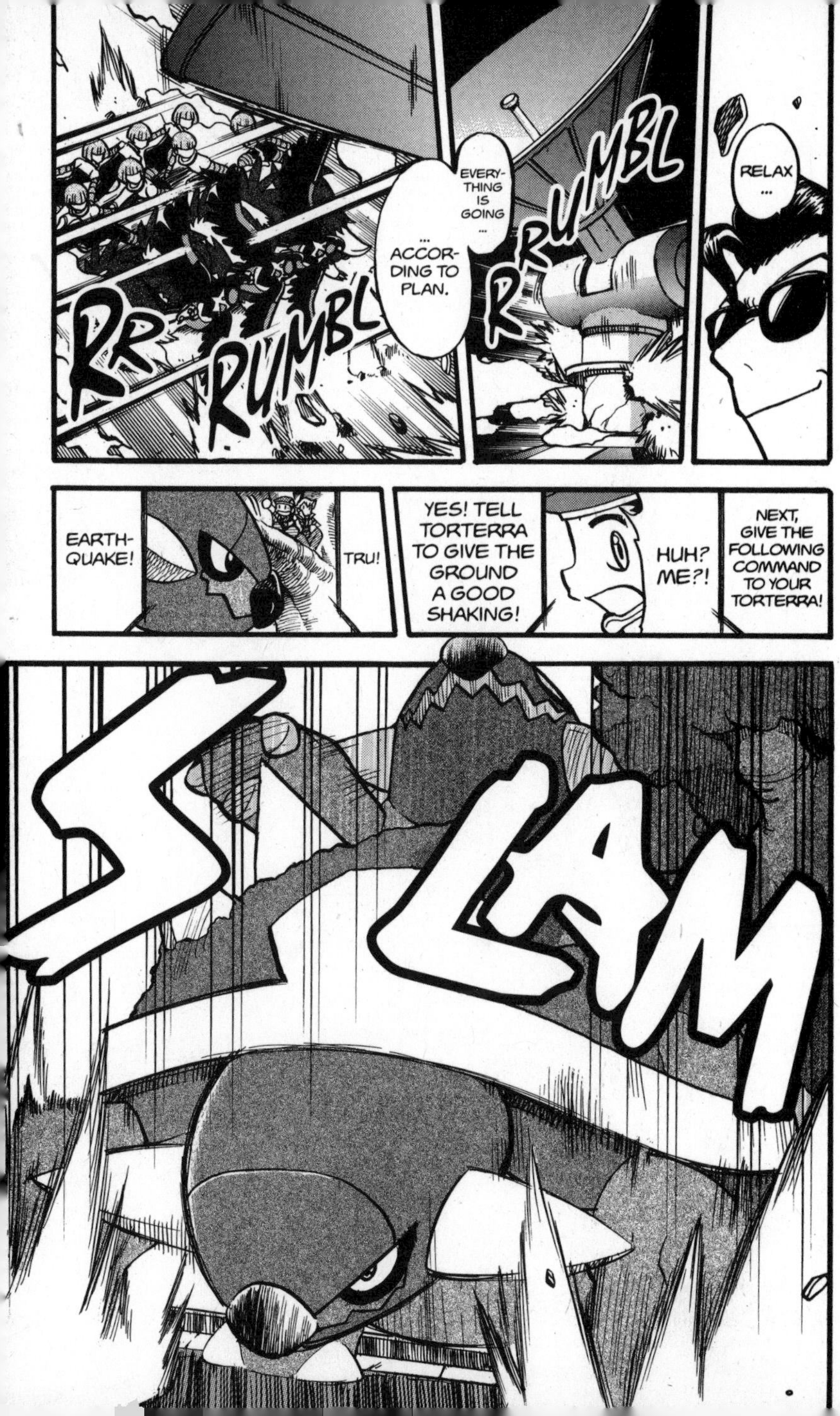
RELAX ...
EVERY-THING IS GOING ... ... ACCORDING TO PLAN.
RRUMBL
RRUMBL
NEXT, GIVE THE FOLLOWING COMMAND TO YOUR TORTERRA!
HUH? ME?!
YES! TELL TORTERRA TO GIVE THE GROUND A GOOD SHAKING!
TRU!
EARTH-QUAKE!
SLAM

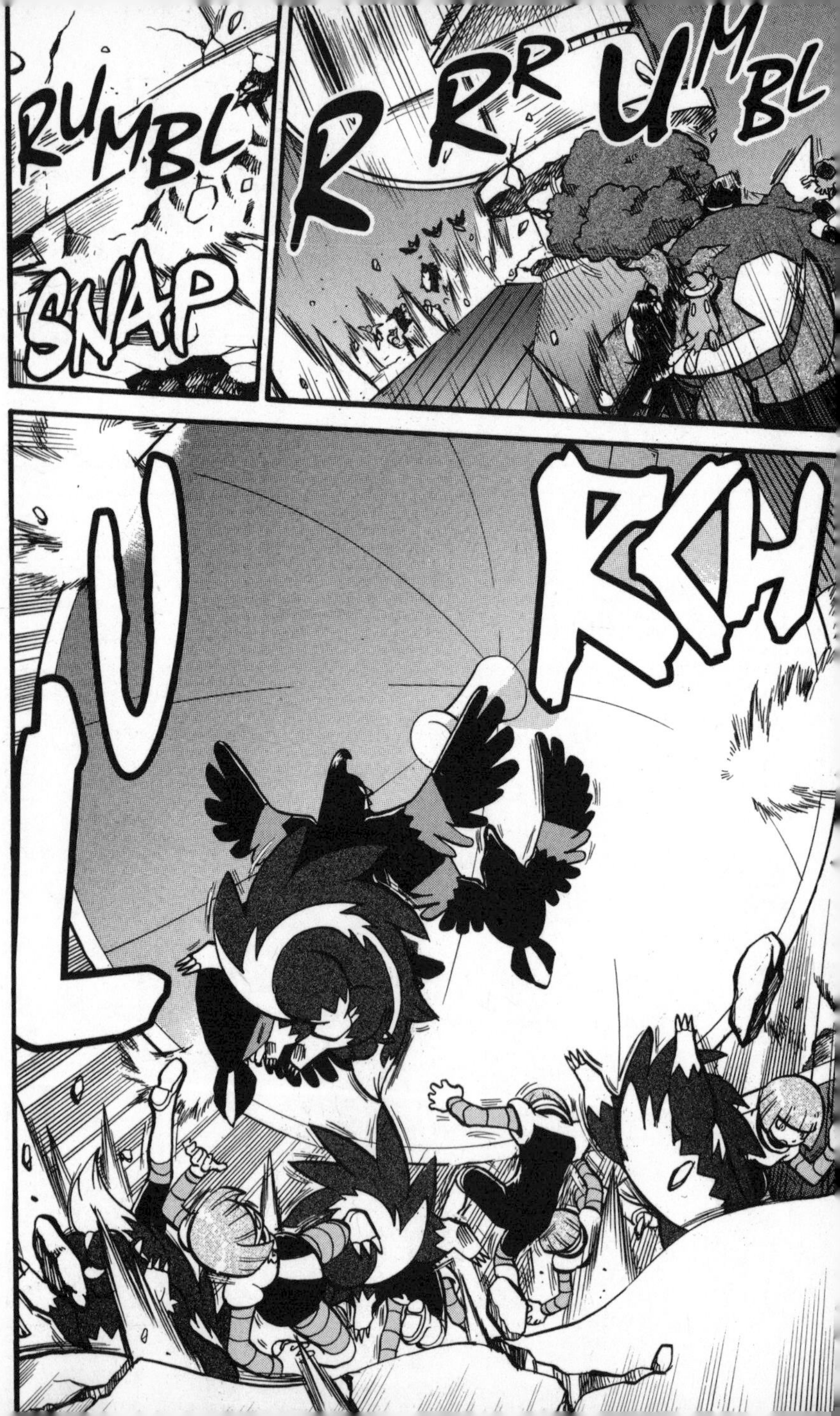
RRRUMBL
RUMBL
SNAP
LURCH

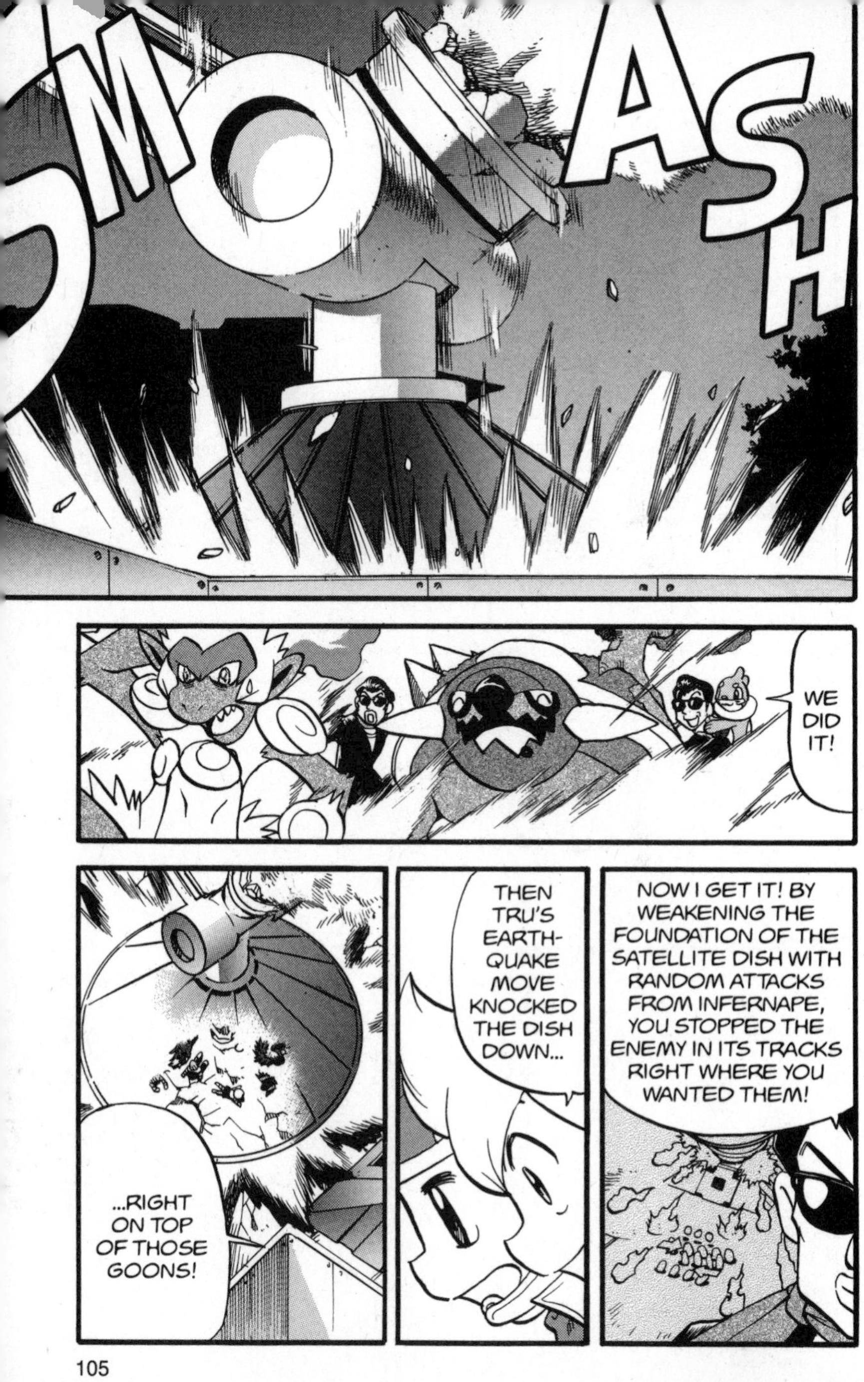
SMASH
WE DID IT!
NOW I GET IT! BY WEAKENING THE FOUNDATION OF THE SATELLITE DISH WITH RANDOM ATTACKS FROM INFERNAPE, YOU STOPPED THE ENEMY IN ITS TRACKS RIGHT WHERE YOU WANTED THEM!
THEN TRU'S EARTH-QUAKE MOVE KNOCKED THE DISH DOWN...
...RIGHT ON TOP OF THOSE GOONS!

THAT WAS LAME. IF YOU'RE GOING TO MAKE PUNS ABOUT FOOD, WHY DON'T YOU SAY YOU'VE NEVER SERVED A **SATELLITE DISH** BEFORE.

I DON'T THINK A **CAKE** MADE OF **EARTH** WOULD TASTE VERY GOOD...

AND IT'S ALL THANKS TO THE POWER OF YOUR POKÉMON!

WE RAN THE RISK OF THE EARTHQUAKE ATTACK HURTING US TOO—BUT IT WAS WORTH IT!

COME ON. LET'S GO RETRIEVE OUR CLIENT NOW AND HAVE A GOOD TALK TOGETHER.

HA HA HA!

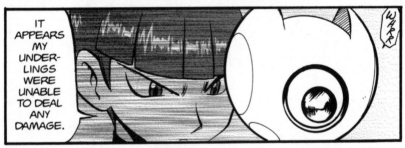

IT APPEARS MY UNDER-LINGS WERE UNABLE TO DEAL ANY DAMAGE.

...LURE MY TARGETS WITHIN RANGE OF MY DEVICE.

AT LEAST THEY WERE ABLE TO...

BUT THEY'VE ACCOM-PLISHED MORE THAN ENOUGH.

KL-KKLK

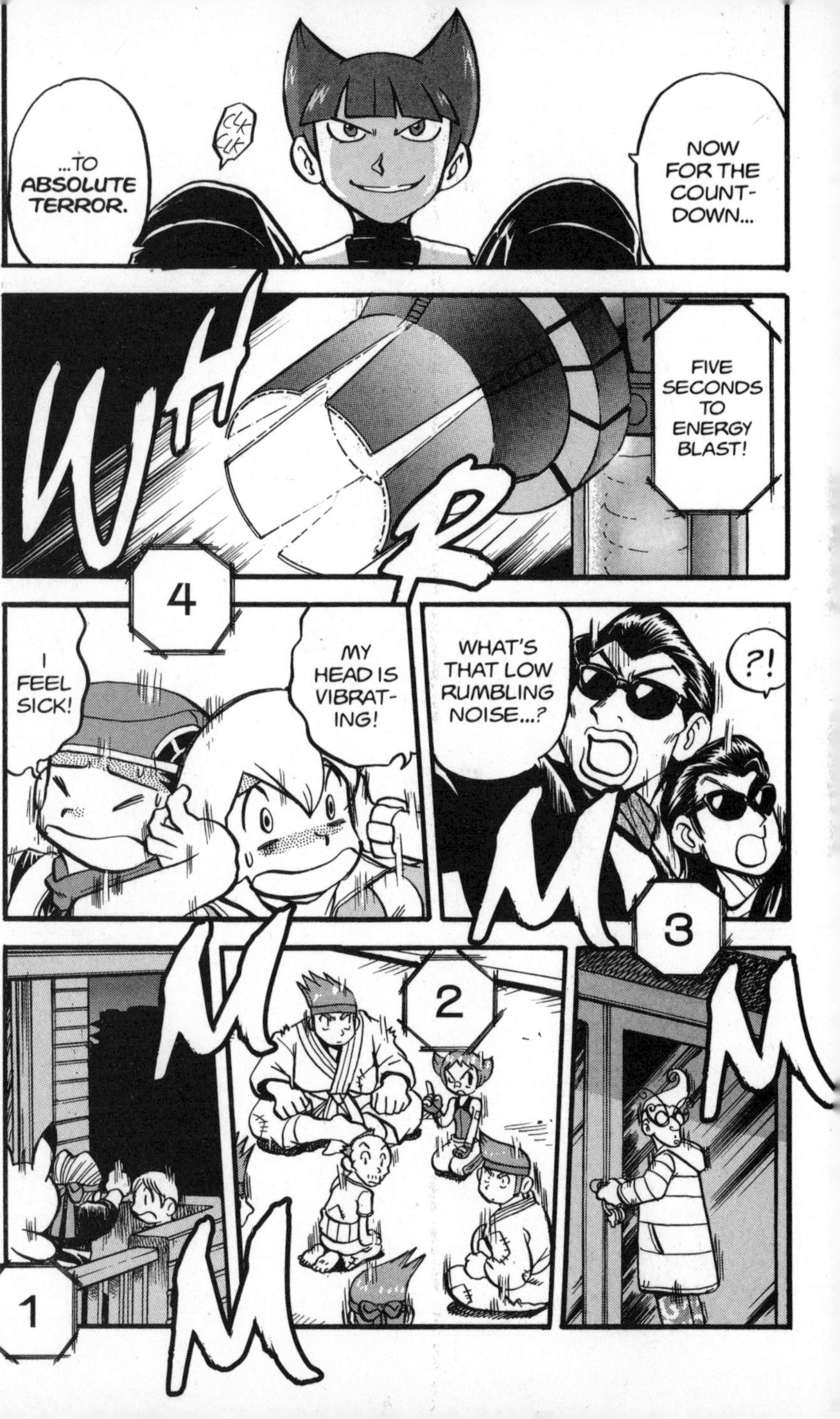

NOW FOR THE COUNT-DOWN...
CLK CLK
...TO ABSOLUTE TERROR.
FIVE SECONDS TO ENERGY BLAST!
WHR
4
?!
WHAT'S THAT LOW RUMBLING NOISE...?
MY HEAD IS VIBRATING!
I FEEL SICK!
MMMMM
3
2
1

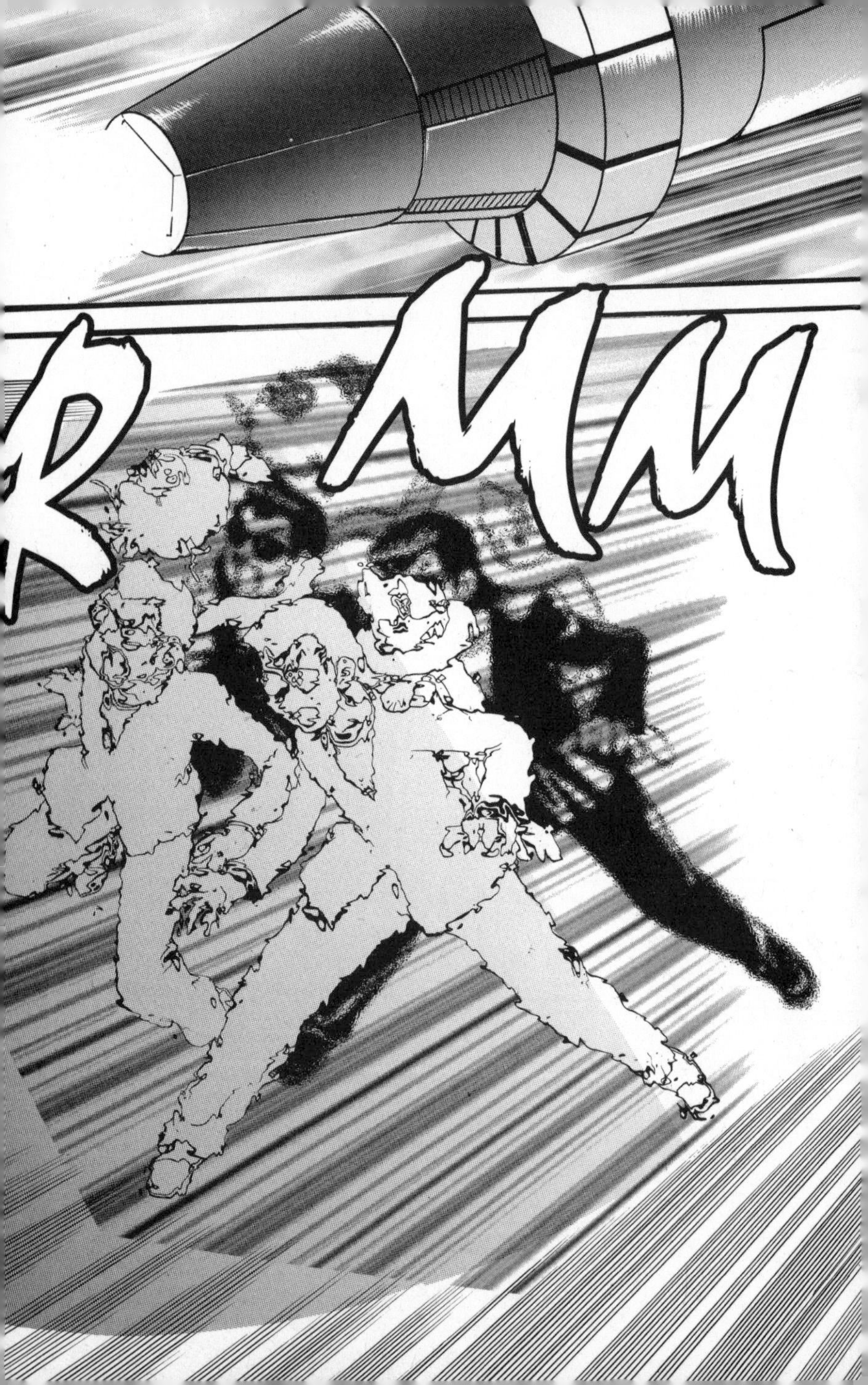
RMM

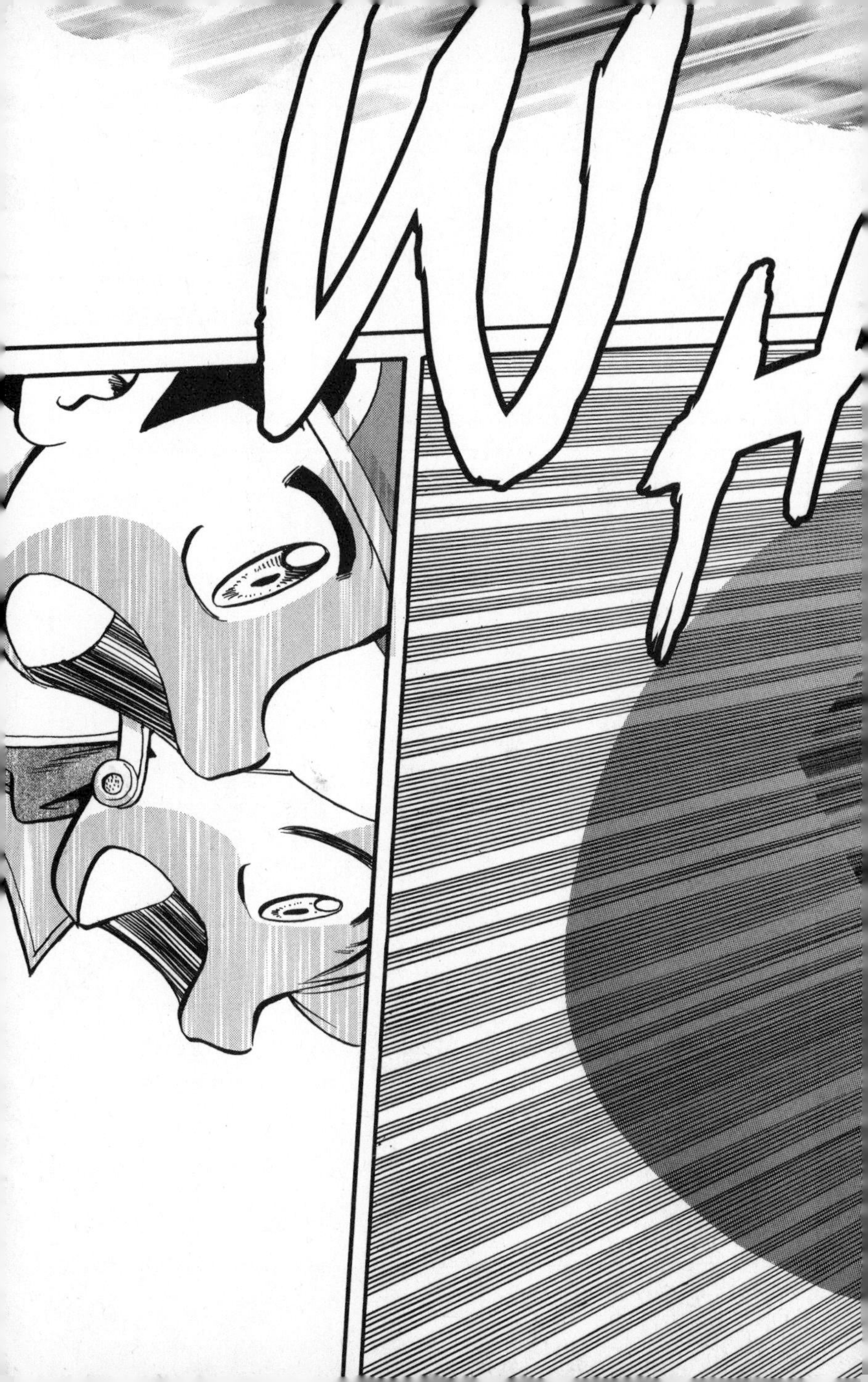
WH

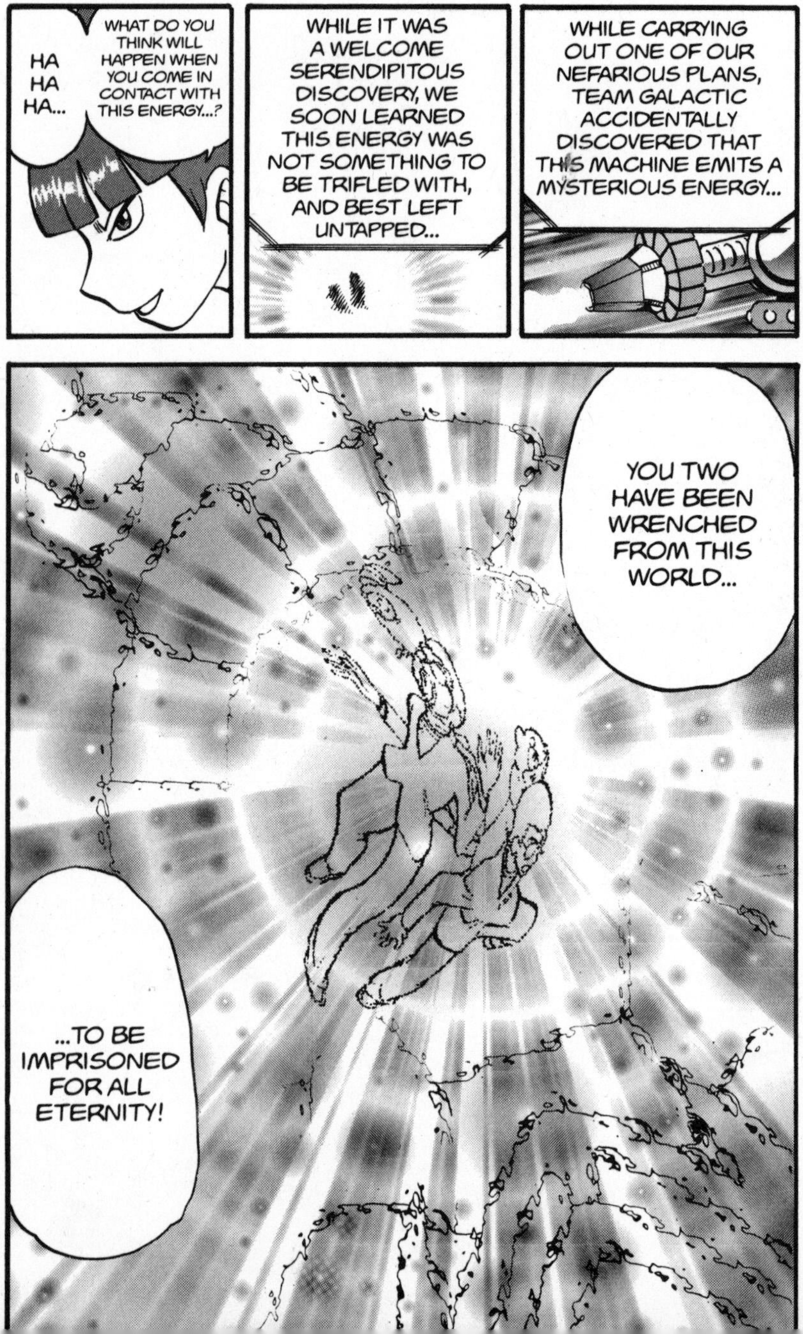
WHILE CARRYING OUT ONE OF OUR NEFARIOUS PLANS, TEAM GALACTIC ACCIDENTALLY DISCOVERED THAT THIS MACHINE EMITS A MYSTERIOUS ENERGY...
WHILE IT WAS A WELCOME SERENDIPITOUS DISCOVERY, WE SOON LEARNED THIS ENERGY WAS NOT SOMETHING TO BE TRIFLED WITH, AND BEST LEFT UNTAPPED...
WHAT DO YOU THINK WILL HAPPEN WHEN YOU COME IN CONTACT WITH THIS ENERGY...?
HA HA HA...
YOU TWO HAVE BEEN WRENCHED FROM THIS WORLD...
...TO BE IMPRISONED FOR ALL ETERNITY!

23

Great
Gible

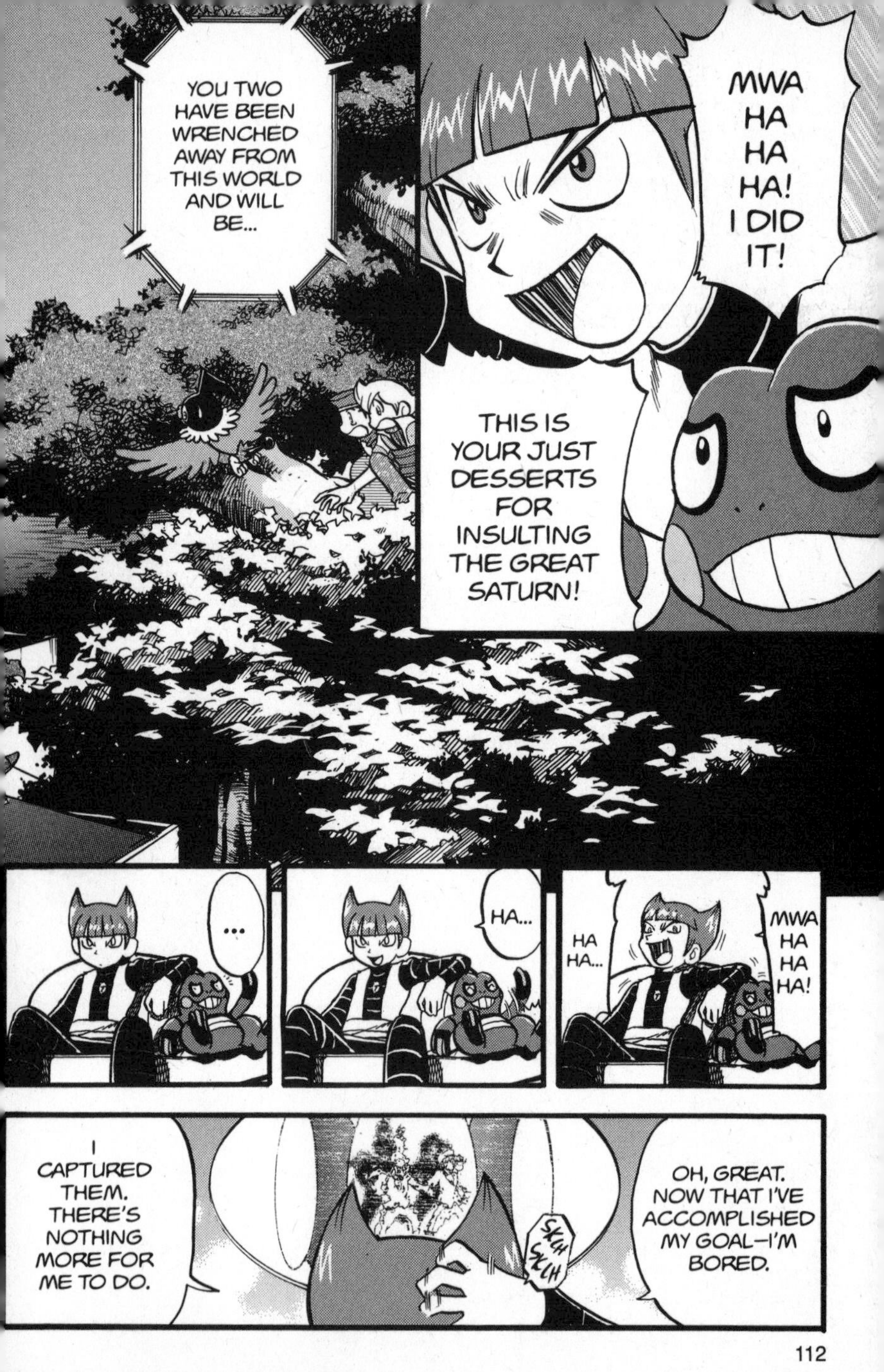
MWA HA HA HA! I DID IT!
THIS IS YOUR JUST DESSERTS FOR INSULTING THE GREAT SATURN!
YOU TWO HAVE BEEN WRENCHED AWAY FROM THIS WORLD AND WILL BE...
MWA HA HA HA!
HA HA...
HA...
...
OH, GREAT. NOW THAT I'VE ACCOMPLISHED MY GOAL—I'M BORED.
SKCH SKCH
I CAPTURED THEM. THERE'S NOTHING MORE FOR ME TO DO.

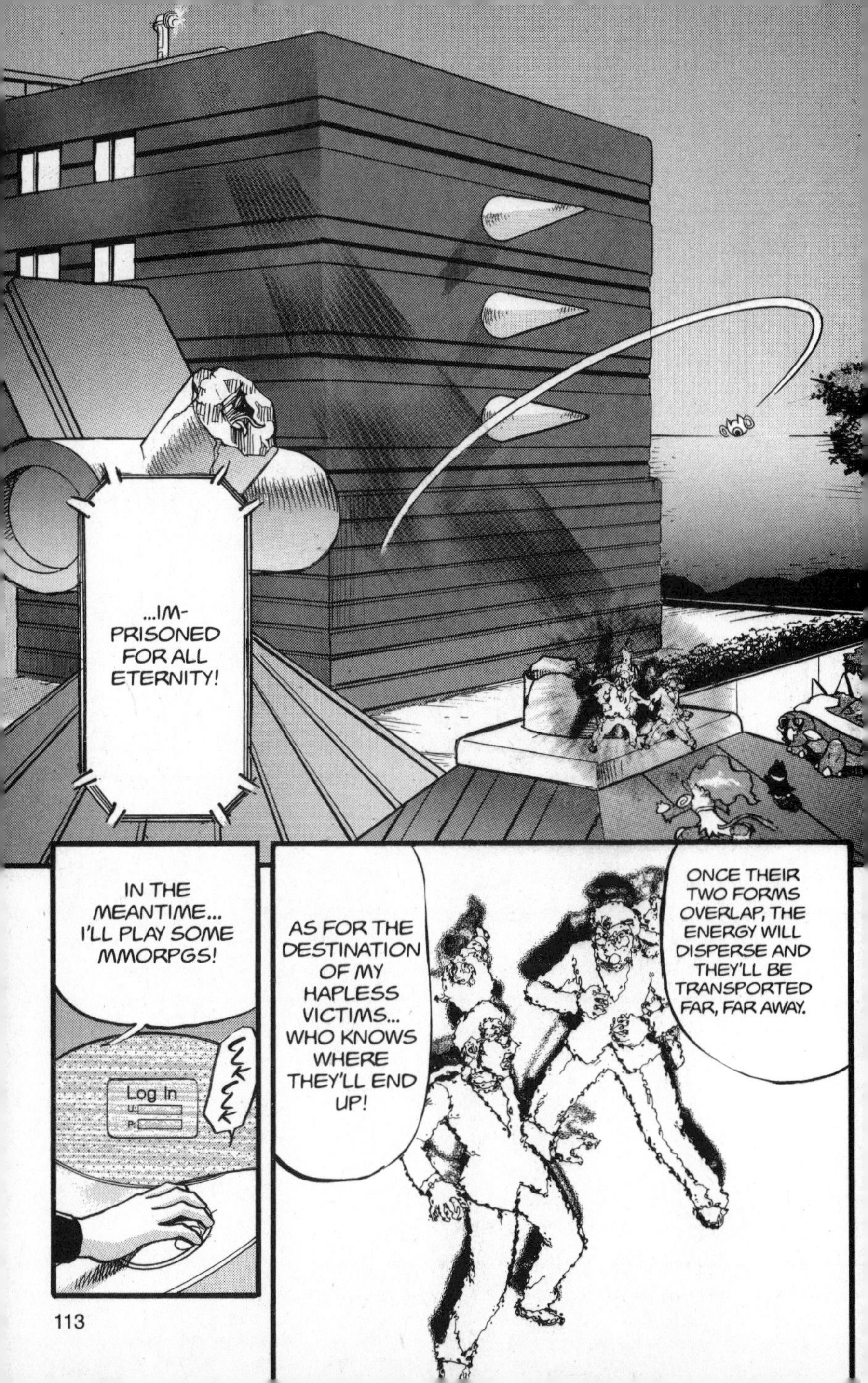
...IM-PRISONED FOR ALL ETERNITY!
ONCE THEIR TWO FORMS OVERLAP, THE ENERGY WILL DISPERSE AND THEY'LL BE TRANSPORTED FAR, FAR AWAY.
AS FOR THE DESTINATION OF MY HAPLESS VICTIMS... WHO KNOWS WHERE THEY'LL END UP!
IN THE MEANTIME... I'LL PLAY SOME MMORPGS!
CLK CLK
Log In
U:
P:

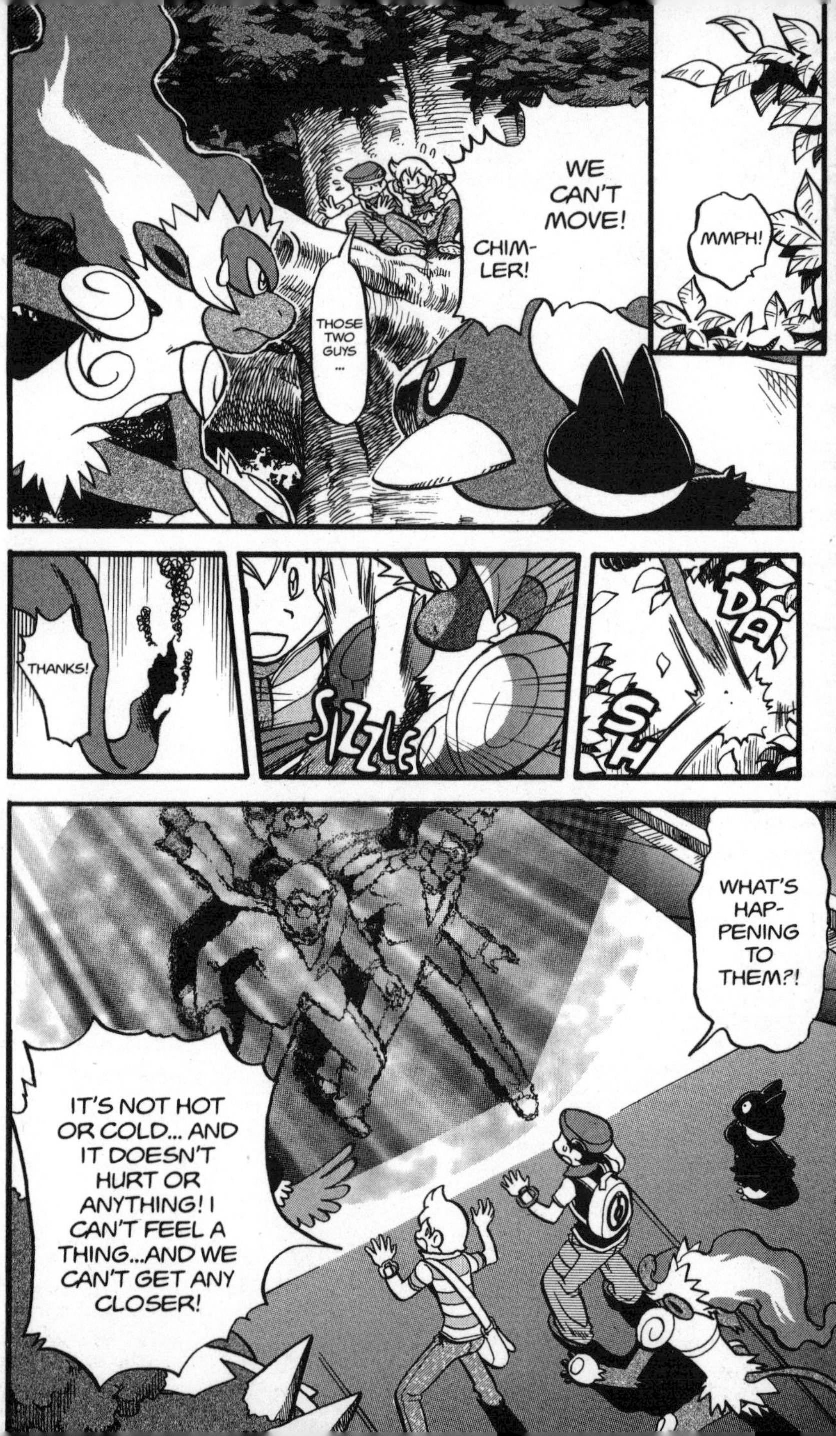
MMPH!
WE CAN'T MOVE!
CHIM-LER!
THOSE TWO GUYS ...
DA
SH
SIZZLE
THANKS!
WHAT'S HAP-PENING TO THEM?!
IT'S NOT HOT OR COLD... AND IT DOESN'T HURT OR ANYTHING! I CAN'T FEEL A THING...AND WE CAN'T GET ANY CLOSER!

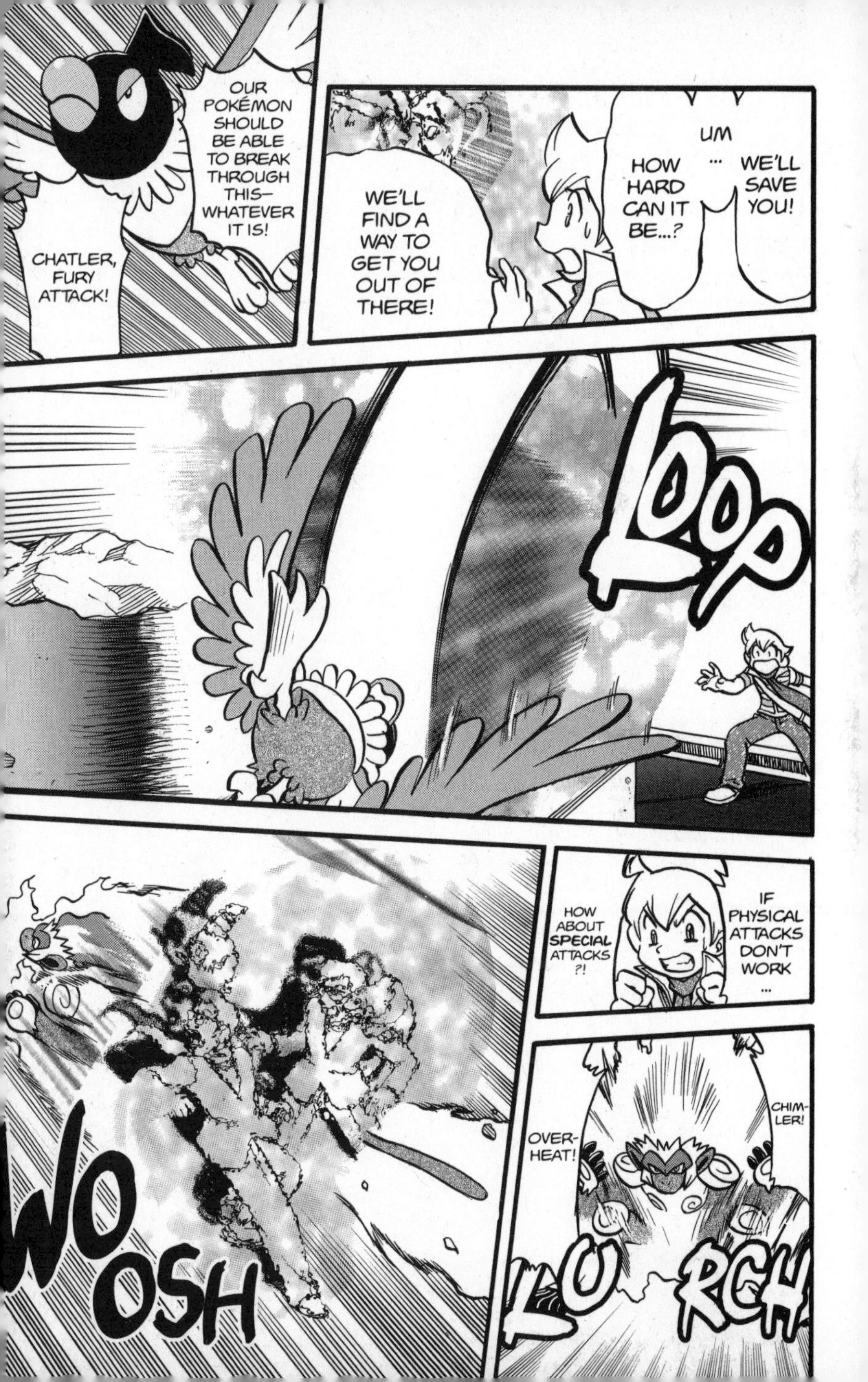
WE'LL SAVE YOU!
UM...
HOW HARD CAN IT BE...?
WE'LL FIND A WAY TO GET YOU OUT OF THERE!
OUR POKÉMON SHOULD BE ABLE TO BREAK THROUGH THIS—WHATEVER IT IS!
CHATLER, FURY ATTACK!
LOOP
IF PHYSICAL ATTACKS DON'T WORK ...
HOW ABOUT **SPECIAL** ATTACKS?!
CHIMLER!
OVERHEAT!
LURCH
WOOSH

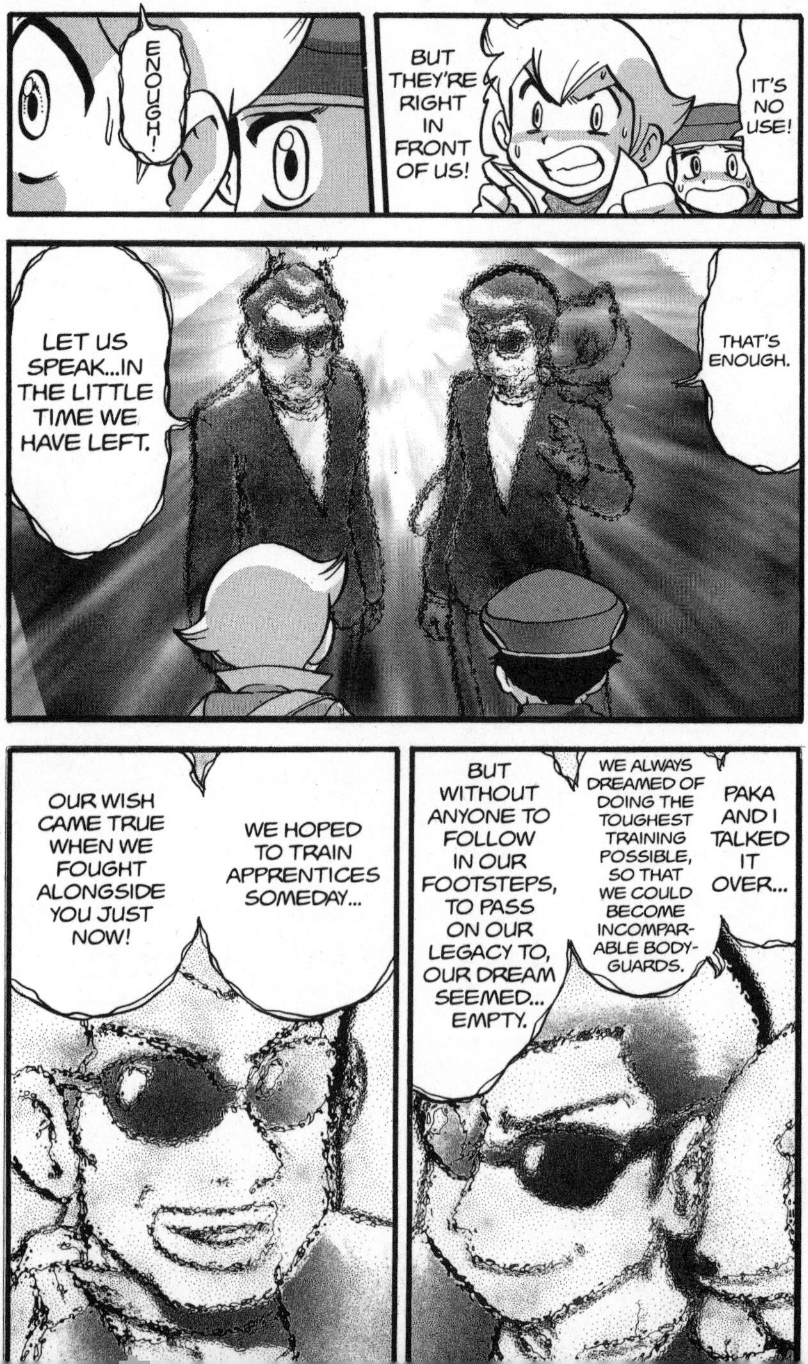
IT'S NO USE!
BUT THEY'RE RIGHT IN FRONT OF US!
ENOUGH!
THAT'S ENOUGH.
LET US SPEAK...IN THE LITTLE TIME WE HAVE LEFT.
PAKA AND I TALKED IT OVER...
WE ALWAYS DREAMED OF DOING THE TOUGHEST TRAINING POSSIBLE, SO THAT WE COULD BECOME INCOMPARABLE BODYGUARDS.
BUT WITHOUT ANYONE TO FOLLOW IN OUR FOOTSTEPS, TO PASS ON OUR LEGACY TO, OUR DREAM SEEMED... EMPTY.
WE HOPED TO TRAIN APPRENTICES SOMEDAY...
OUR WISH CAME TRUE WHEN WE FOUGHT ALONGSIDE YOU JUST NOW!

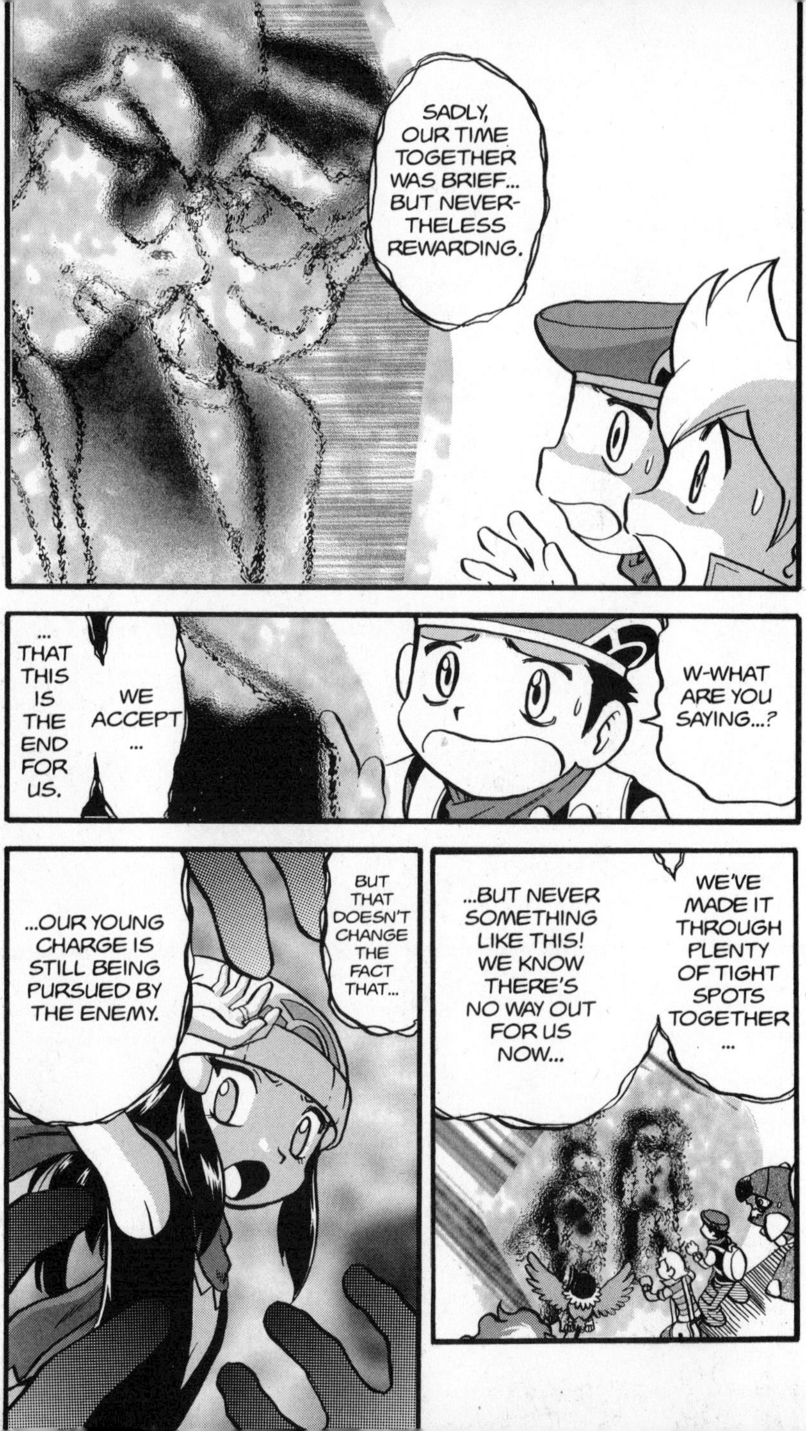
SADLY, OUR TIME TOGETHER WAS BRIEF... BUT NEVER-THELESS REWARDING.
W-WHAT ARE YOU SAYING...?
WE ACCEPT...
...THAT THIS IS THE END FOR US.
WE'VE MADE IT THROUGH PLENTY OF TIGHT SPOTS TOGETHER...
...BUT NEVER SOMETHING LIKE THIS! WE KNOW THERE'S NO WAY OUT FOR US NOW...
BUT THAT DOESN'T CHANGE THE FACT THAT...
...OUR YOUNG CHARGE IS STILL BEING PURSUED BY THE ENEMY.

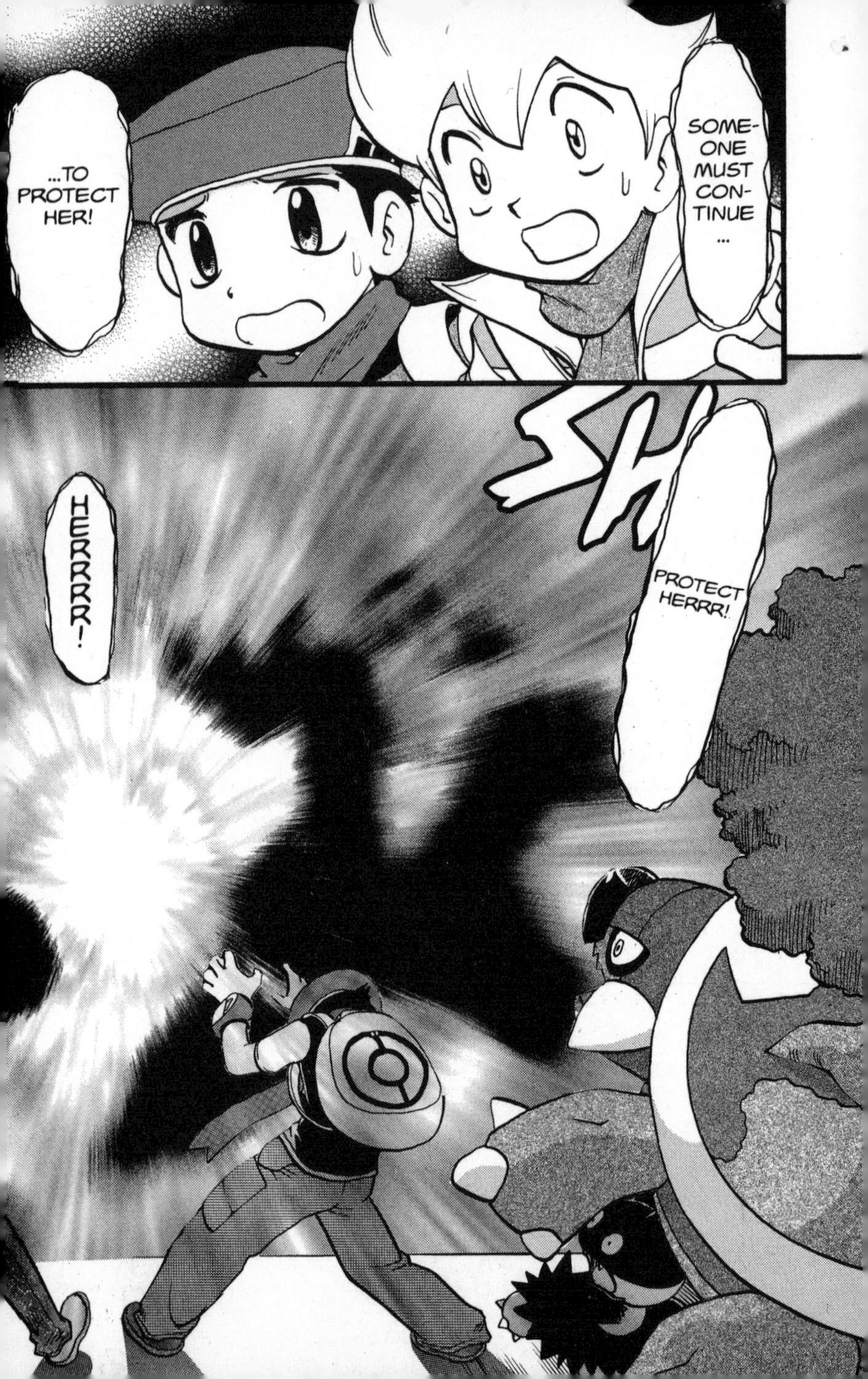
SOME-ONE MUST CON-TINUE...
...TO PROTECT HER!
SH
PROTECT HERRR!
HERRRR!

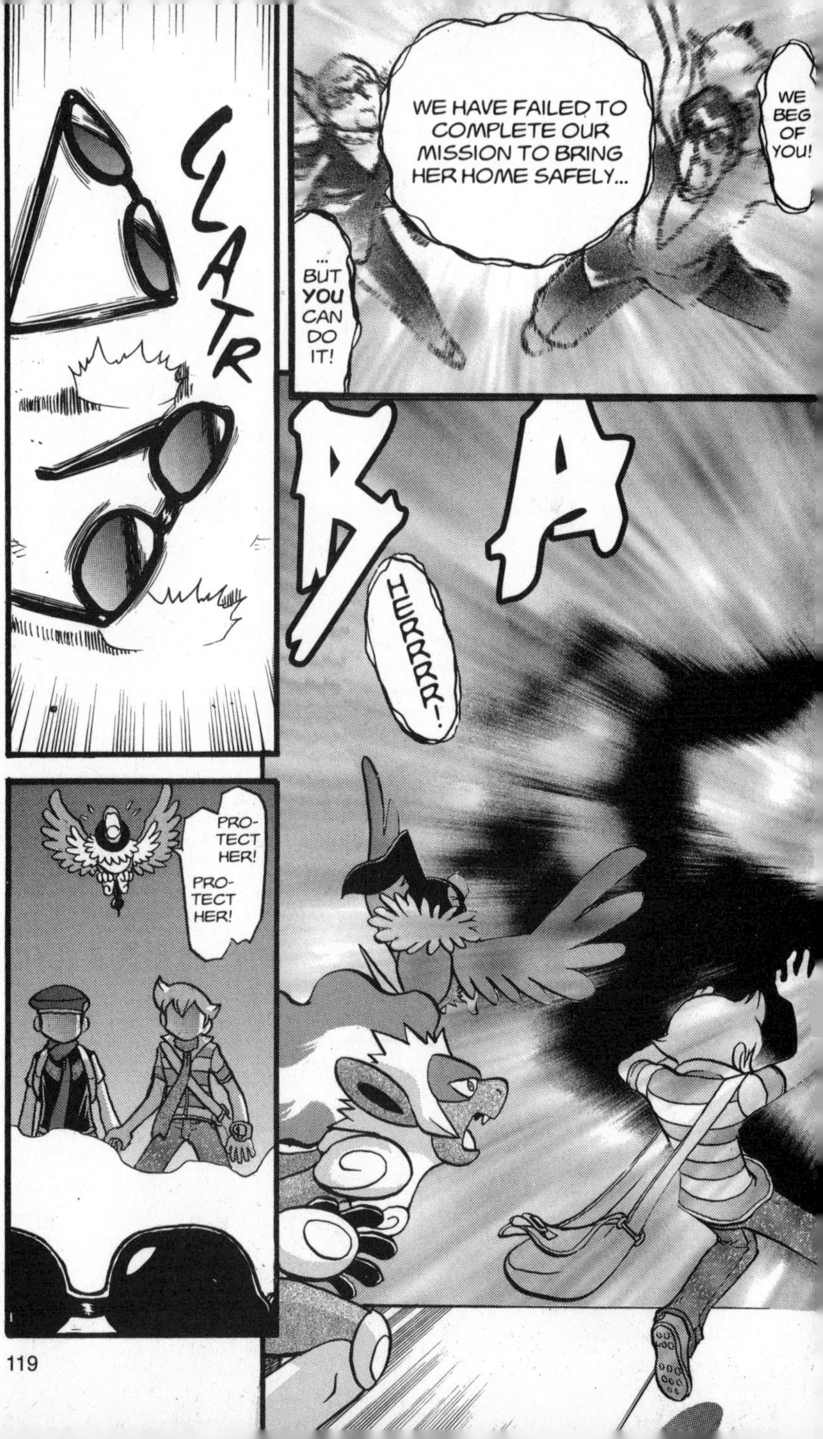
WE HAVE FAILED TO COMPLETE OUR MISSION TO BRING HER HOME SAFELY...
WE BEG OF YOU!
...BUT YOU CAN DO IT!
CLATR
BA
HERRRRR!
PROTECT HER!
PROTECT HER!

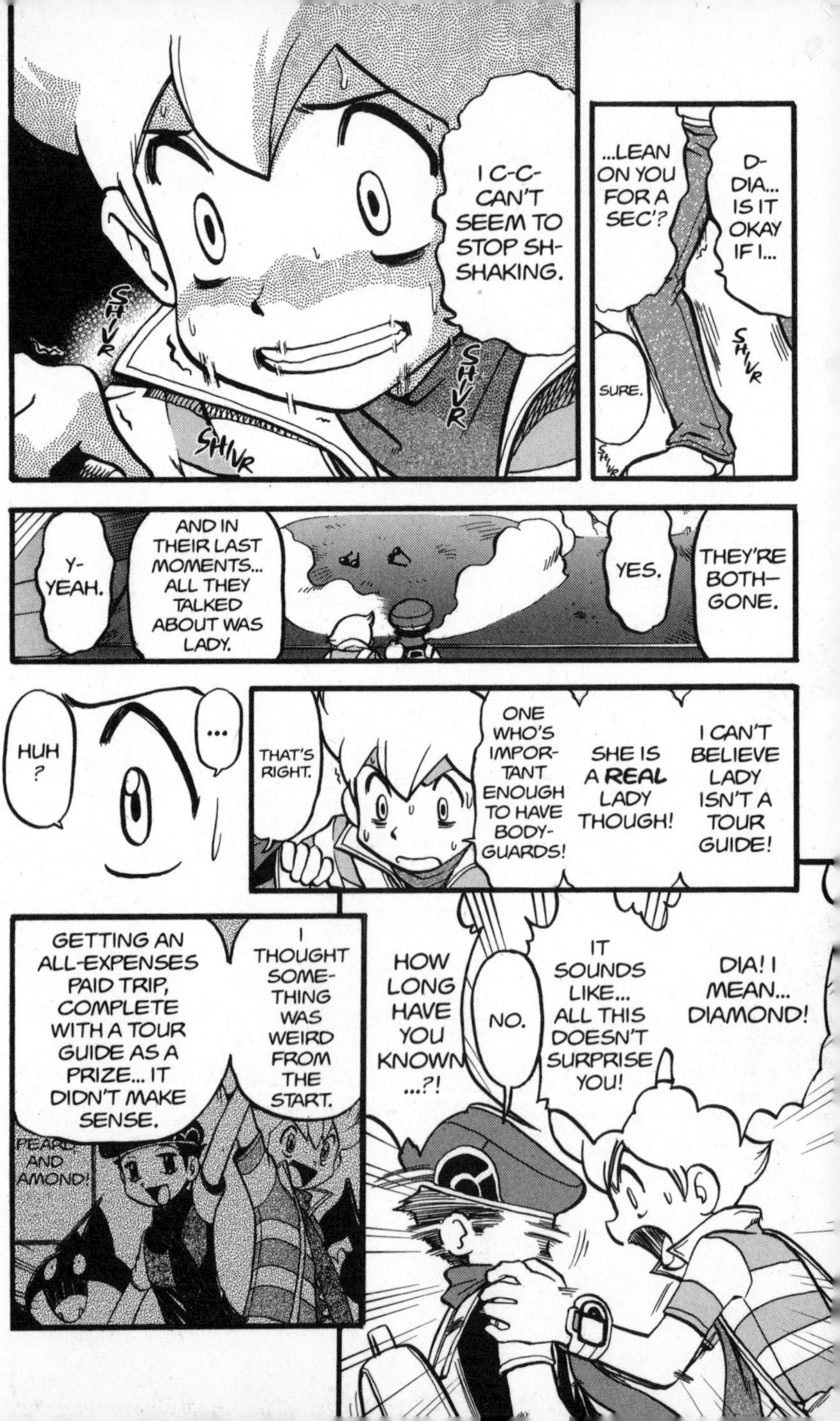
D-DIA... IS IT OKAY IF I...
...LEAN ON YOU FOR A SEC'?
SHIVR
SURE.
SHIVR
I C-C-CAN'T SEEM TO STOP SH-SHAKING.
SHIVR
SHIVR
SHIVR
THEY'RE BOTH—GONE.
YES.
AND IN THEIR LAST MOMENTS... ALL THEY TALKED ABOUT WAS LADY.
Y-YEAH.
I CAN'T BELIEVE LADY ISN'T A TOUR GUIDE!
SHE IS A **REAL** LADY THOUGH!
ONE WHO'S IMPORTANT ENOUGH TO HAVE BODYGUARDS!
THAT'S RIGHT.
...
HUH?
DIA! I MEAN... DIAMOND!
IT SOUNDS LIKE... ALL THIS DOESN'T SURPRISE YOU!
NO.
HOW LONG HAVE YOU KNOWN...?!
I THOUGHT SOMETHING WAS WEIRD FROM THE START.
GETTING AN ALL-EXPENSES PAID TRIP, COMPLETE WITH A TOUR GUIDE AS A PRIZE... IT DIDN'T MAKE SENSE.
PEARL AND AMOND!

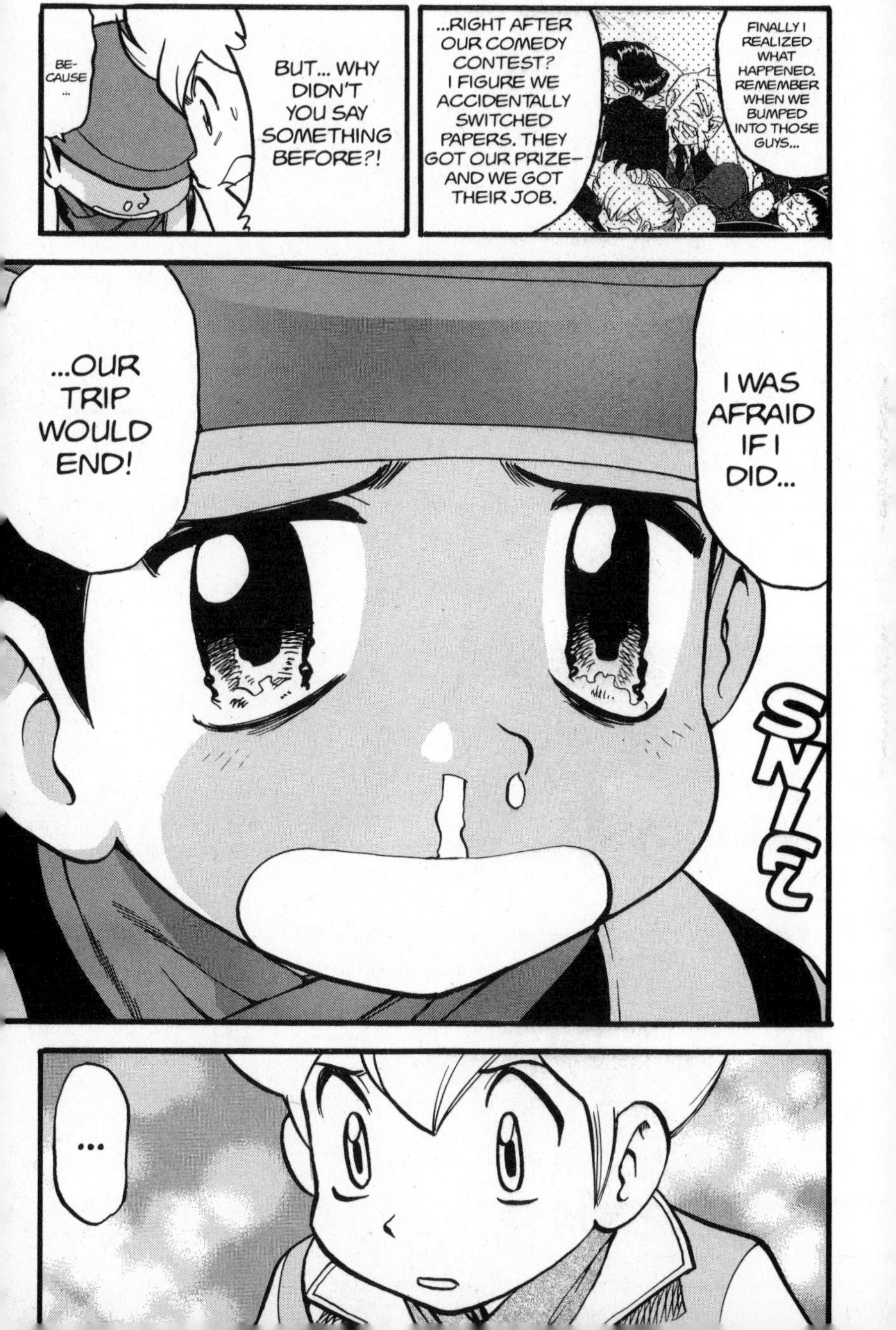
FINALLY I REALIZED WHAT HAPPENED. REMEMBER WHEN WE BUMPED INTO THOSE GUYS...
...RIGHT AFTER OUR COMEDY CONTEST? I FIGURE WE ACCIDENTALLY SWITCHED PAPERS. THEY GOT OUR PRIZE— AND WE GOT THEIR JOB.
BUT... WHY DIDN'T YOU SAY SOMETHING BEFORE?!
BE-CAUSE ...
I WAS AFRAID IF I DID...
...OUR TRIP WOULD END!
SNIFF
...

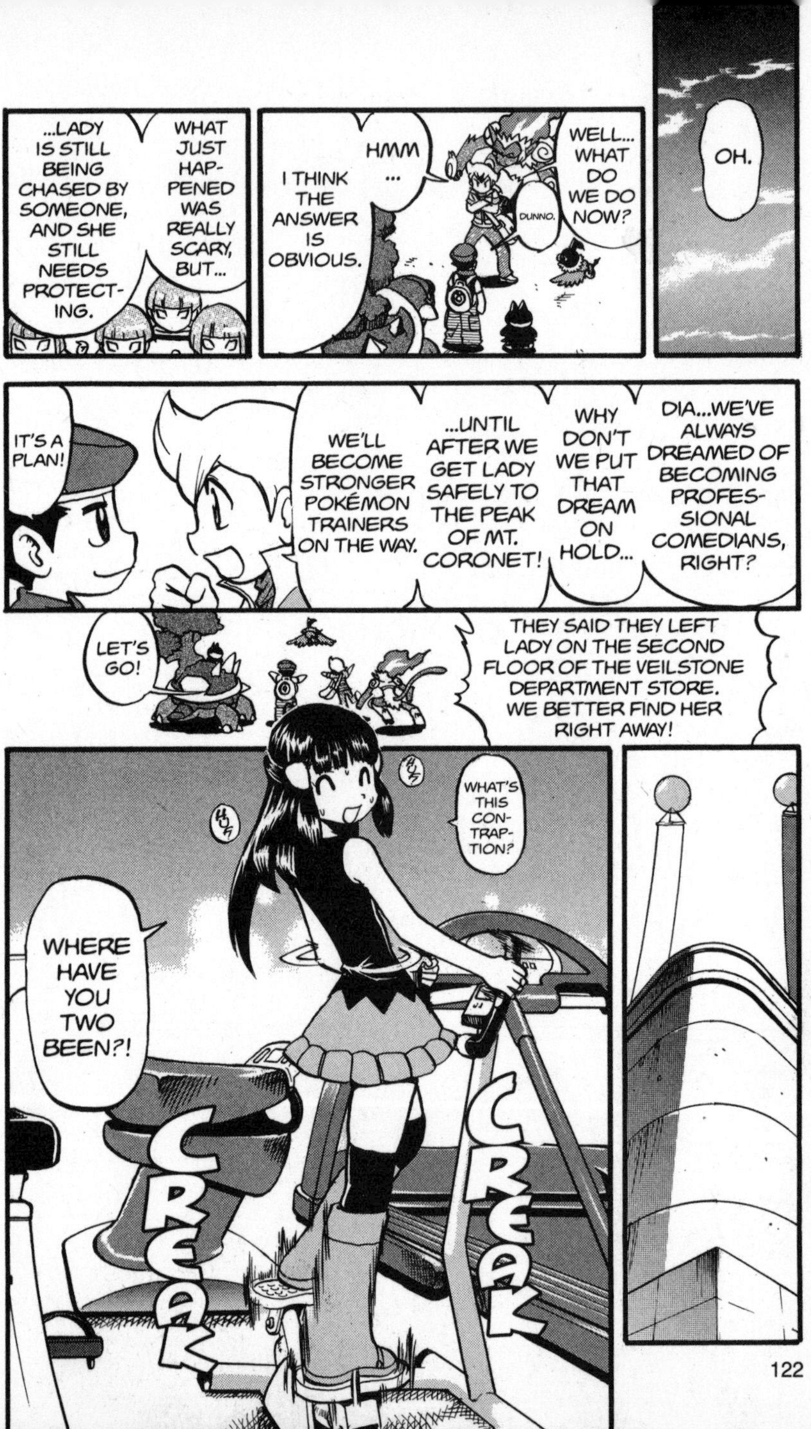
OH.
WELL... WHAT DO WE DO NOW?
DUNNO.
HMM...
I THINK THE ANSWER IS OBVIOUS.
WHAT JUST HAPPENED WAS REALLY SCARY, BUT...
...LADY IS STILL BEING CHASED BY SOMEONE, AND SHE STILL NEEDS PROTECTING.
DIA...WE'VE ALWAYS DREAMED OF BECOMING PROFESSIONAL COMEDIANS, RIGHT?
WHY DON'T WE PUT THAT DREAM ON HOLD...
...UNTIL AFTER WE GET LADY SAFELY TO THE PEAK OF MT. CORONET!
WE'LL BECOME STRONGER POKÉMON TRAINERS ON THE WAY.
IT'S A PLAN!
THEY SAID THEY LEFT LADY ON THE SECOND FLOOR OF THE VEILSTONE DEPARTMENT STORE. WE BETTER FIND HER RIGHT AWAY!
LET'S GO!
WHAT'S THIS CONTRAPTION?
WHERE HAVE YOU TWO BEEN?!
CREAK
CREAK

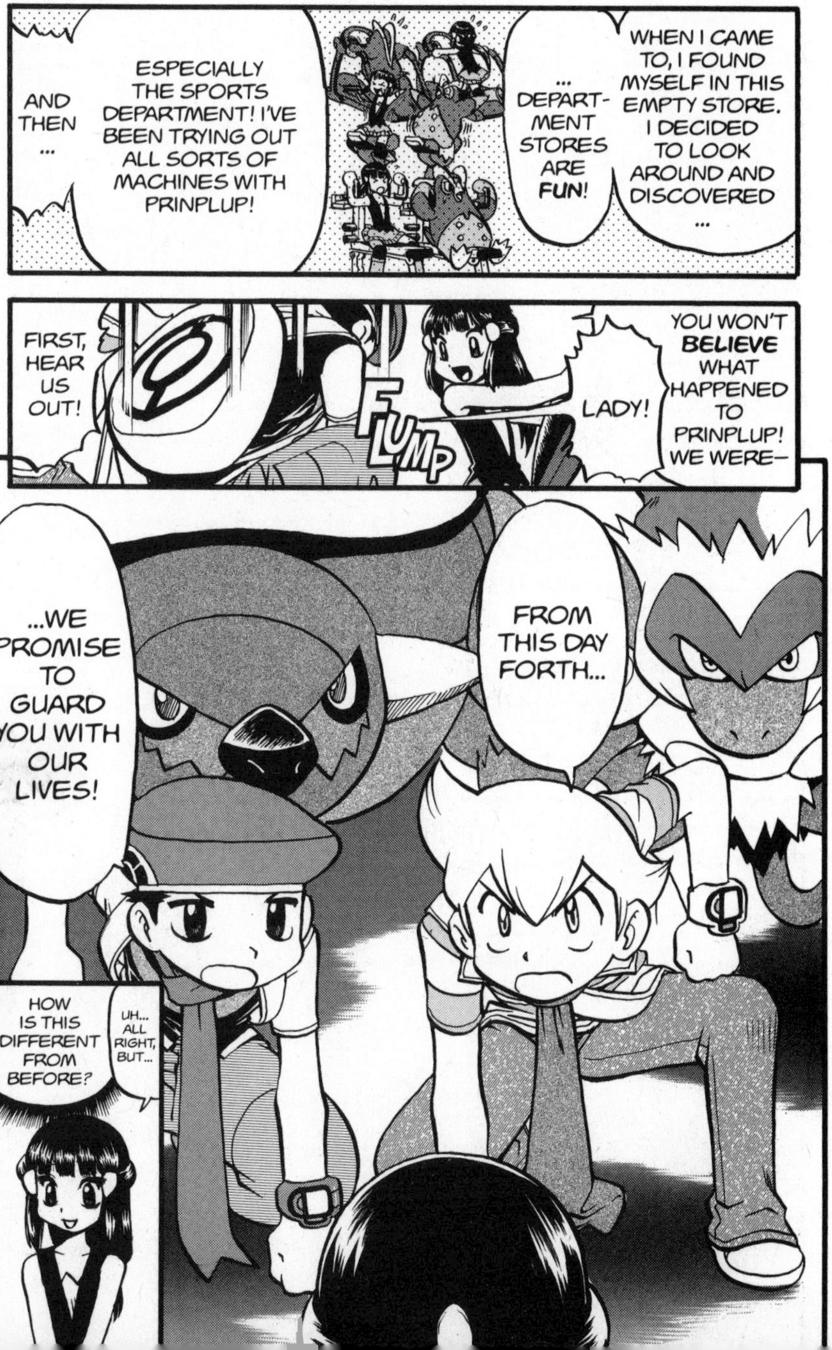
WHEN I CAME TO, I FOUND MYSELF IN THIS EMPTY STORE. I DECIDED TO LOOK AROUND AND DISCOVERED ...
... DEPARTMENT STORES ARE **FUN**!
ESPECIALLY THE SPORTS DEPARTMENT! I'VE BEEN TRYING OUT ALL SORTS OF MACHINES WITH PRINPLUP!
AND THEN ...
YOU WON'T **BELIEVE** WHAT HAPPENED TO PRINPLUP! WE WERE—
LADY!
FLUMP
FIRST, HEAR US OUT!
FROM THIS DAY FORTH...
...WE PROMISE TO GUARD YOU WITH OUR LIVES!
UH... ALL RIGHT, BUT...
HOW IS THIS DIFFERENT FROM BEFORE?

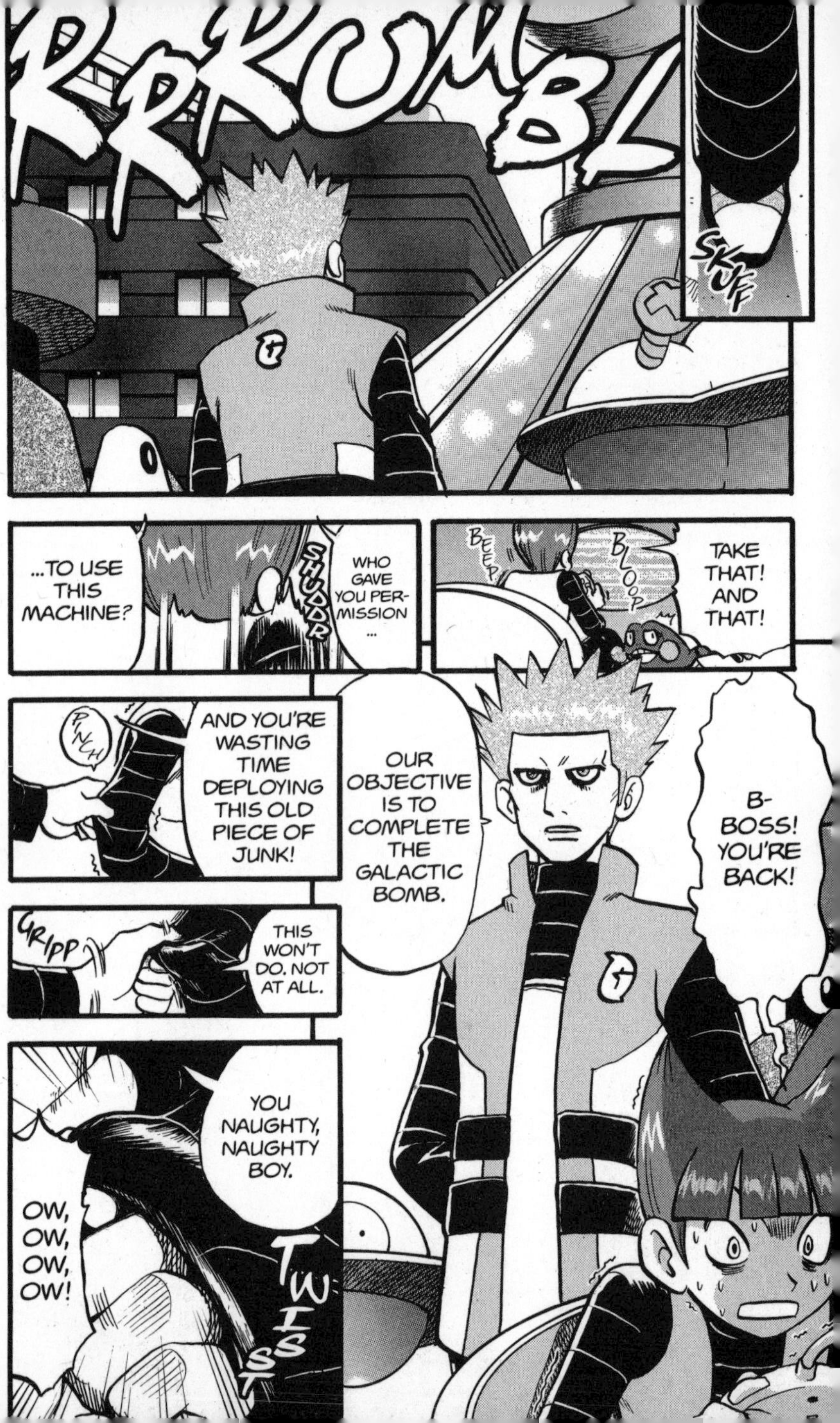
SKUFF
RRKUMBL
BEEP
BLOOP
TAKE THAT! AND THAT!
WHO GAVE YOU PERMISSION...
SHUDDR
...TO USE THIS MACHINE?
B-BOSS! YOU'RE BACK!
OUR OBJECTIVE IS TO COMPLETE THE GALACTIC BOMB.
AND YOU'RE WASTING TIME DEPLOYING THIS OLD PIECE OF JUNK!
PINCH
THIS WON'T DO. NOT AT ALL.
GRIPP
YOU NAUGHTY, NAUGHTY BOY.
TWISST
OW, OW, OW, OW!

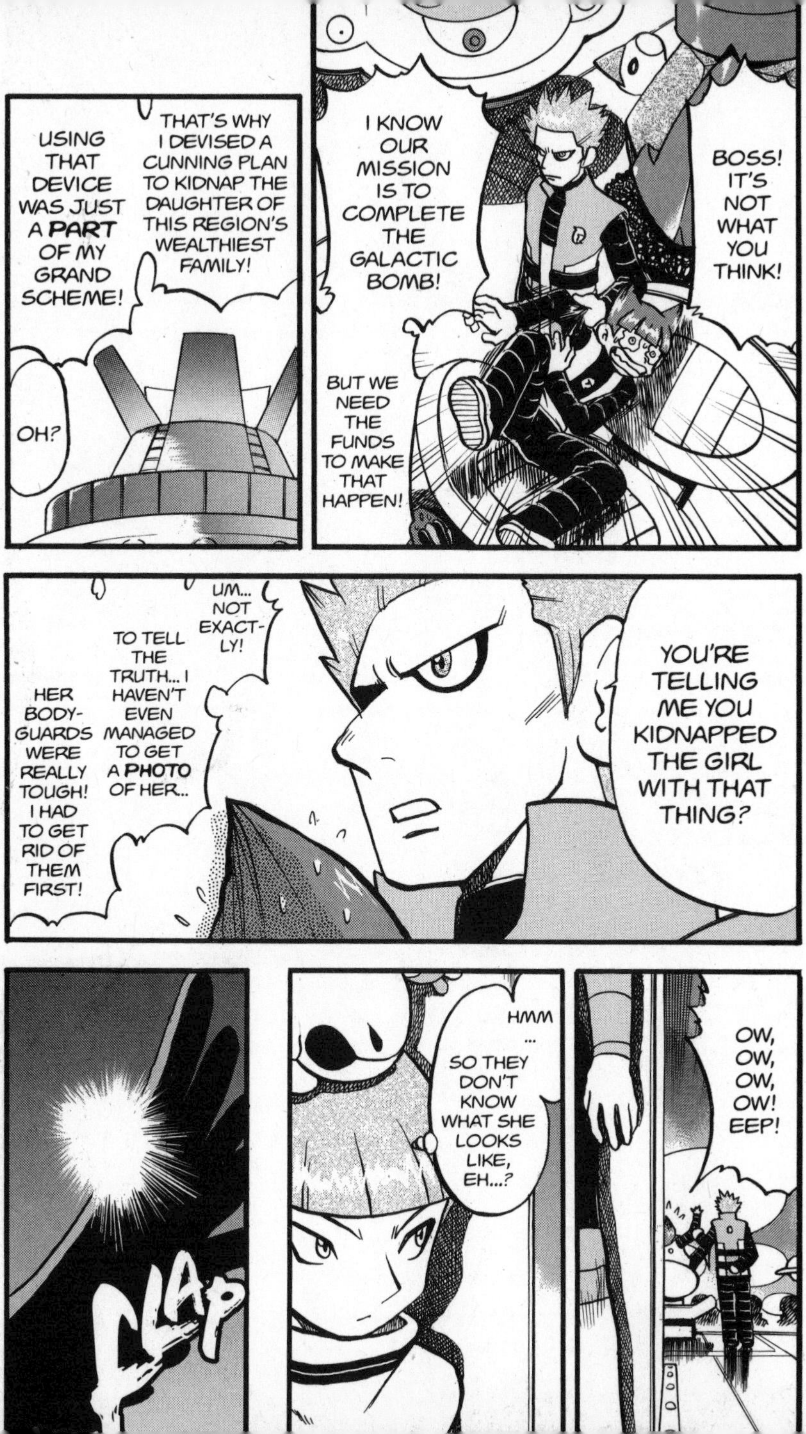
BOSS! IT'S NOT WHAT YOU THINK!
I KNOW OUR MISSION IS TO COMPLETE THE GALACTIC BOMB!
BUT WE NEED THE FUNDS TO MAKE THAT HAPPEN!
THAT'S WHY I DEVISED A CUNNING PLAN TO KIDNAP THE DAUGHTER OF THIS REGION'S WEALTHIEST FAMILY!
USING THAT DEVICE WAS JUST A **PART** OF MY GRAND SCHEME!
OH?
YOU'RE TELLING ME YOU KIDNAPPED THE GIRL WITH THAT THING?
UM... NOT EXACT-LY!
TO TELL THE TRUTH... I HAVEN'T EVEN MANAGED TO GET A **PHOTO** OF HER...
HER BODY-GUARDS WERE REALLY TOUGH! I HAD TO GET RID OF THEM FIRST!
OW, OW, OW, OW! EEP!
HMM...
SO THEY DON'T KNOW WHAT SHE LOOKS LIKE, EH...?
CLAP

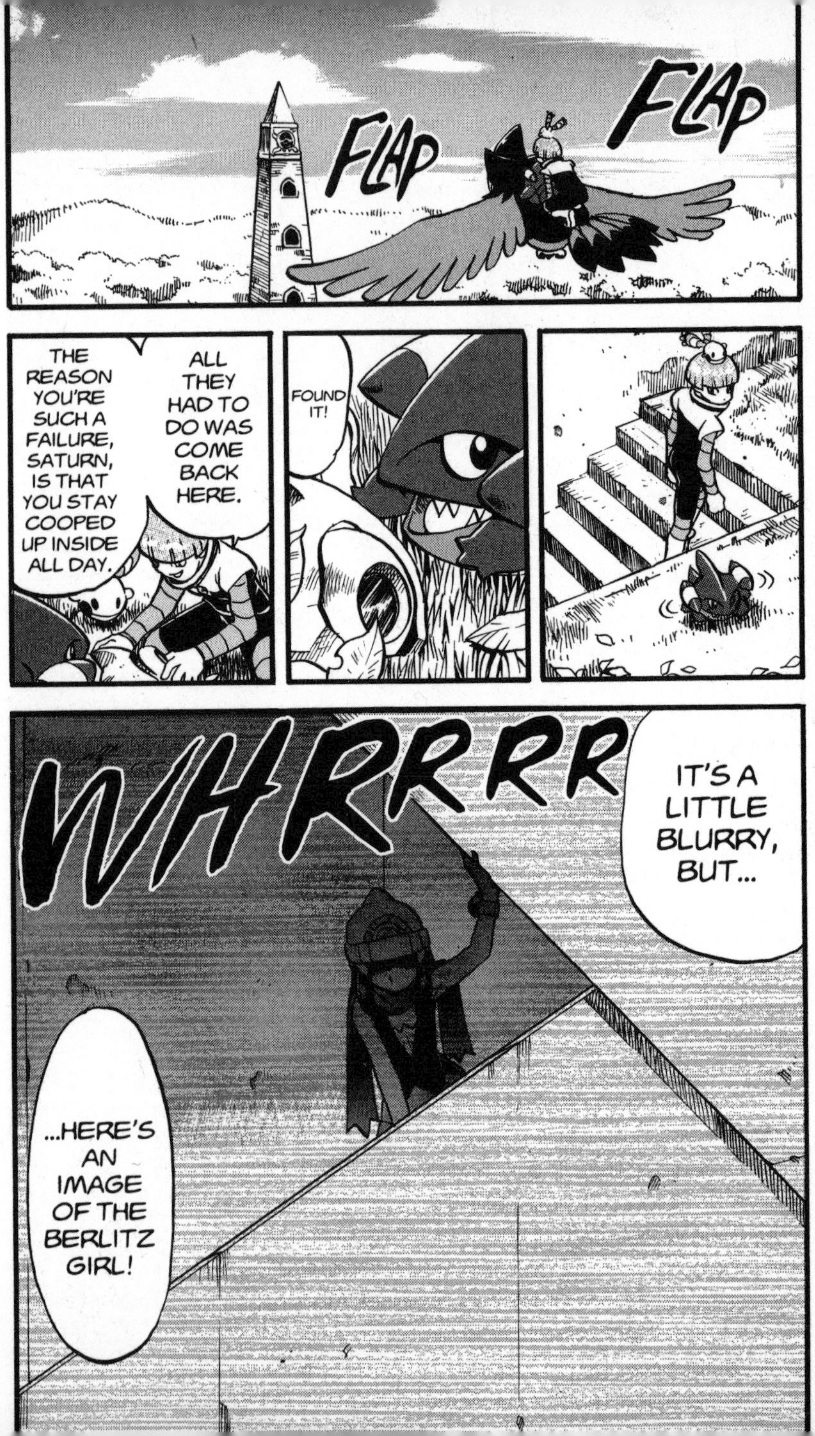
FLAP
FLAP
FOUND IT!
ALL THEY HAD TO DO WAS COME BACK HERE.
THE REASON YOU'RE SUCH A FAILURE, SATURN, IS THAT YOU STAY COOPED UP INSIDE ALL DAY.
WHRRRRR
IT'S A LITTLE BLURRY, BUT...
...HERE'S AN IMAGE OF THE BERLITZ GIRL!

◇ ADVENTURE MAP ○

Route 214 ◀

Oreburgh VS Roark Coal Badge	Eterna VS Gardenia Forest Badge	Veilstone VS Maylene Cobble Badge					

LADY

DIAMOND

▶ TRU
Torterra ♂

▶ LAX
Munchlax ♂

PEARL

▶ CHIMLER
Infernape ♂

▶ CHATLER
Chatot ♂

▶EMPOLEON
Empoleon ♀

▶ PONYTA
Ponyta ♂

24

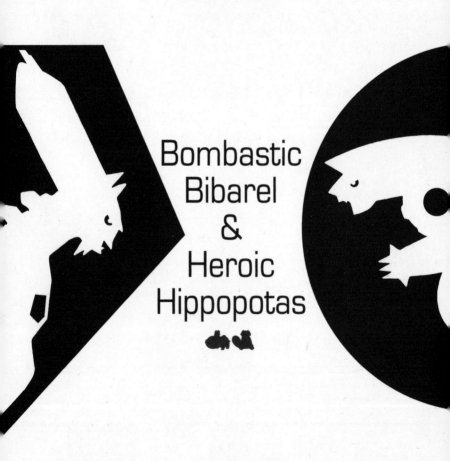

Bombastic
Bibarel
&
Heroic
Hippopotas

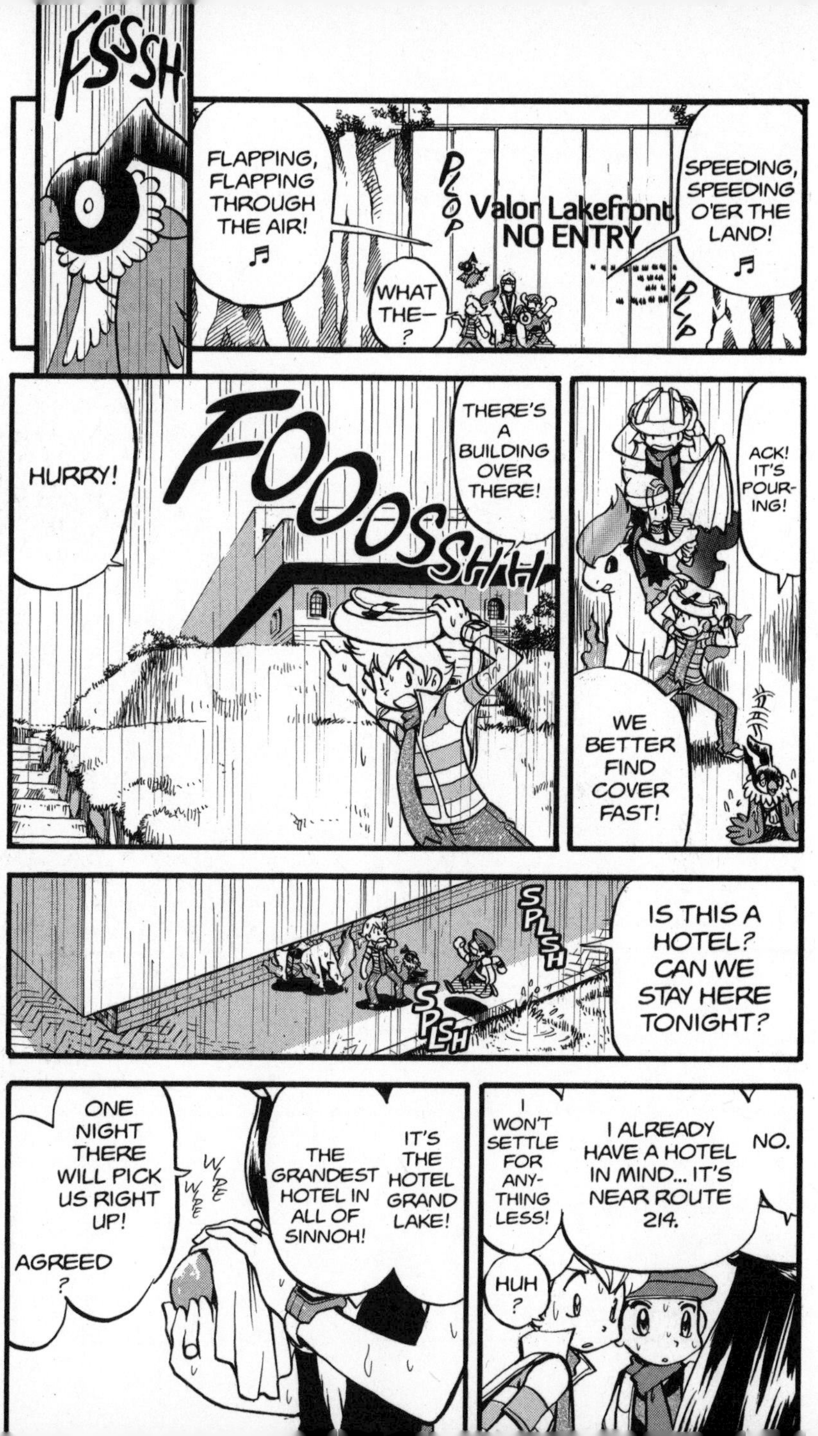
SPEEDING, SPEEDING O'ER THE LAND! ♬
PLIP
Valor Lakefront NO ENTRY
PLOP
FLAPPING, FLAPPING THROUGH THE AIR! ♬
WHAT THE—?
FSSSH
ACK! IT'S POURING!
WE BETTER FIND COVER FAST!
THERE'S A BUILDING OVER THERE!
FOOOSSHHH
HURRY!
IS THIS A HOTEL? CAN WE STAY HERE TONIGHT?
SPLSH
SPLSH
NO.
I ALREADY HAVE A HOTEL IN MIND... IT'S NEAR ROUTE 214.
I WON'T SETTLE FOR ANYTHING LESS!
HUH?
IT'S THE HOTEL GRAND LAKE!
THE GRANDEST HOTEL IN ALL OF SINNOH!
WIPE WIPE
ONE NIGHT THERE WILL PICK US RIGHT UP!
AGREED?

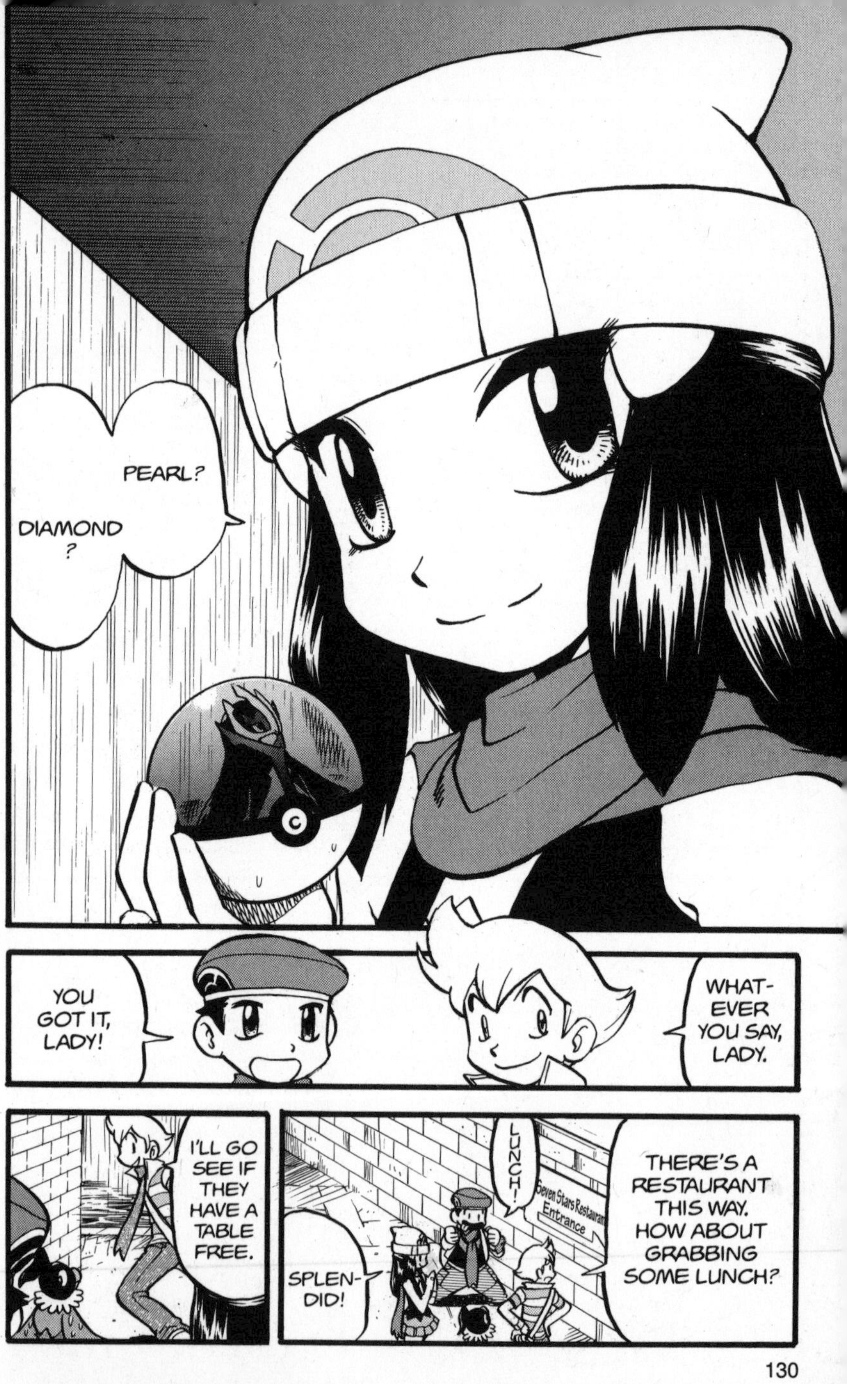
PEARL? DIAMOND?
WHATEVER YOU SAY, LADY.
YOU GOT IT, LADY!
THERE'S A RESTAURANT THIS WAY. HOW ABOUT GRABBING SOME LUNCH?
LUNCH!
Seven Stars Restaurant Entrance
SPLENDID!
I'LL GO SEE IF THEY HAVE A TABLE FREE.

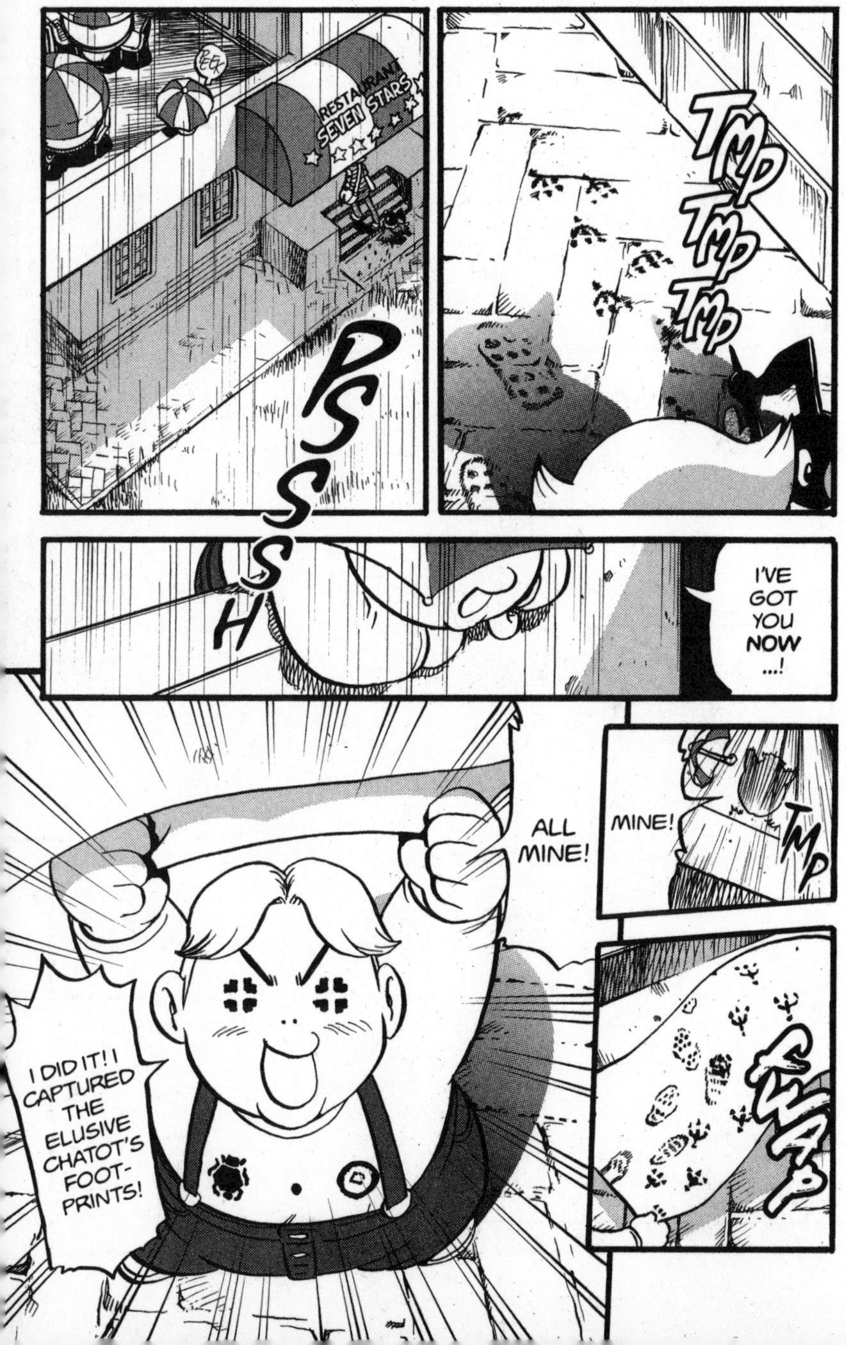
TMP TMP TMP
PEEK
RESTAURANT SEVEN STARS
PSSSH
I'VE GOT YOU NOW ...!
MINE!
TMP
FWAP
ALL MINE!
I DID IT! I CAPTURED THE ELUSIVE CHATOT'S FOOT-PRINTS!

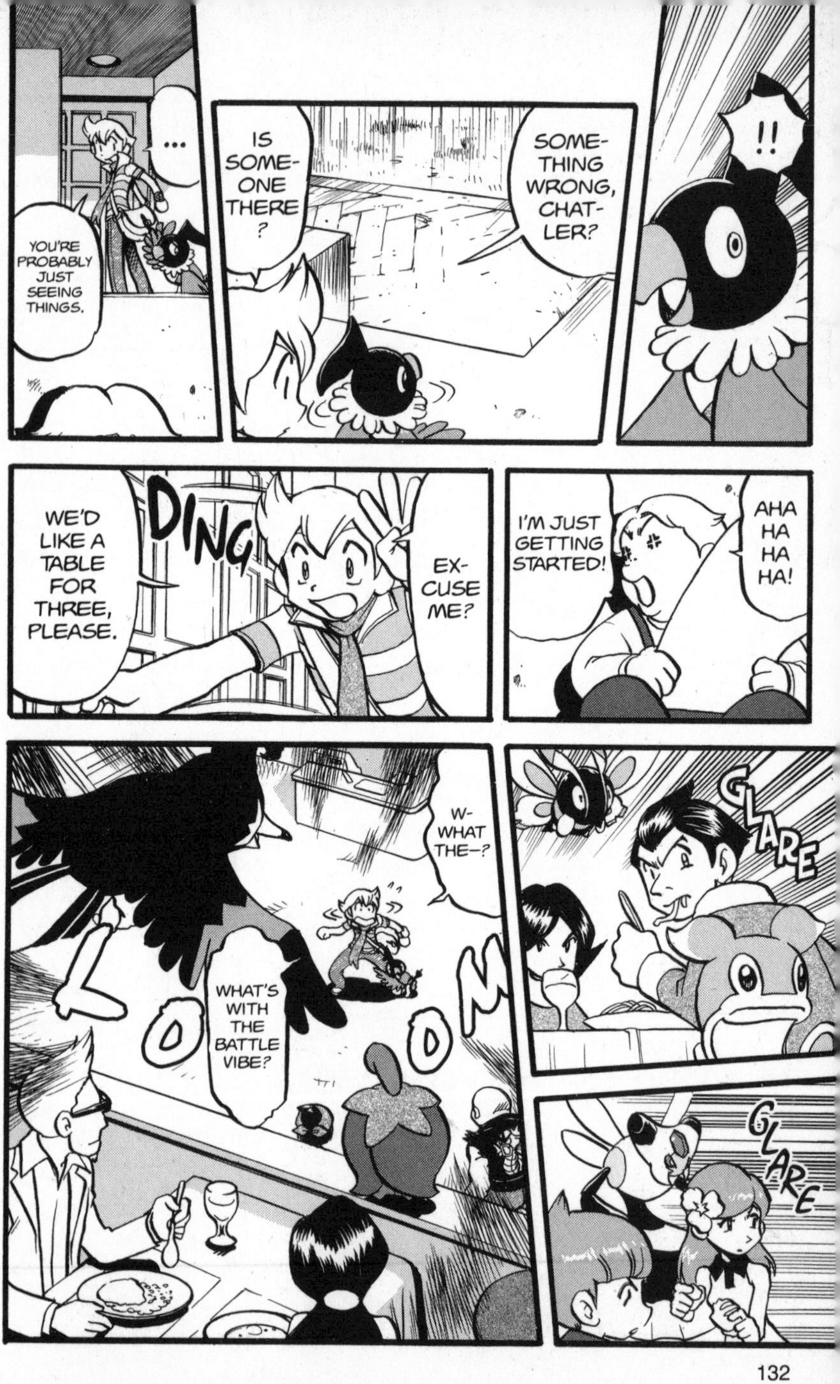
!!
SOME-THING WRONG, CHATLER?
IS SOMEONE THERE?
...
YOU'RE PROBABLY JUST SEEING THINGS.
AHA HA HA HA!
I'M JUST GETTING STARTED!
DING
WE'D LIKE A TABLE FOR THREE, PLEASE.
EX-CUSE ME?
GLARE
GLARE
W-WHAT THE-?
WHAT'S WITH THE BATTLE VIBE?

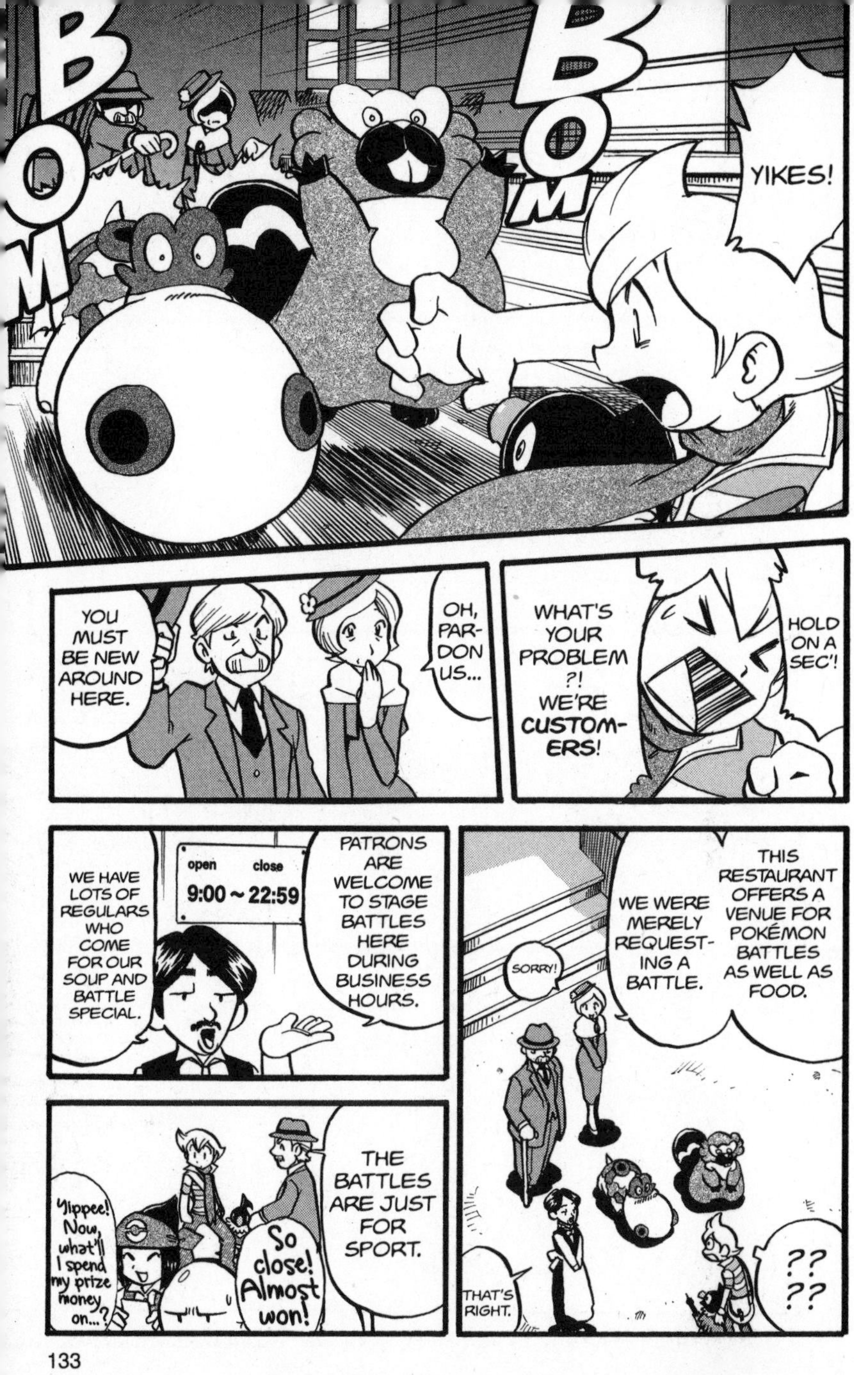
BOOM
BOOM
YIKES!
HOLD ON A SEC'!
WHAT'S YOUR PROBLEM?! WE'RE CUSTOMERS!
OH, PARDON US...
YOU MUST BE NEW AROUND HERE.
THIS RESTAURANT OFFERS A VENUE FOR POKÉMON BATTLES AS WELL AS FOOD.
WE WERE MERELY REQUESTING A BATTLE.
SORRY!
????
THAT'S RIGHT.
open close
9:00 ~ 22:59
PATRONS ARE WELCOME TO STAGE BATTLES HERE DURING BUSINESS HOURS.
WE HAVE LOTS OF REGULARS WHO COME FOR OUR SOUP AND BATTLE SPECIAL.
THE BATTLES ARE JUST FOR SPORT.
So close! Almost won!
Yippee! Now, what'll I spend my prize money on...?

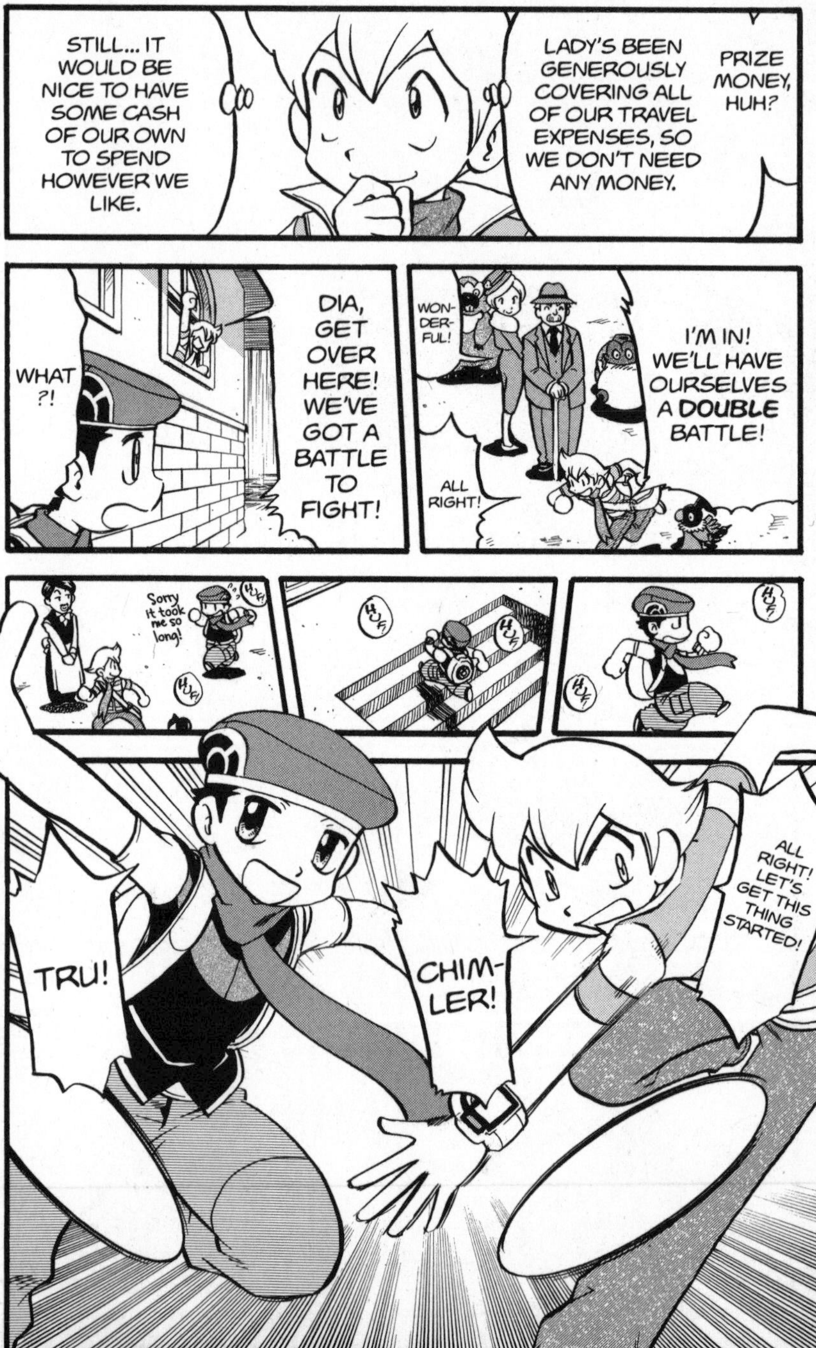
PRIZE MONEY, HUH?
LADY'S BEEN GENEROUSLY COVERING ALL OF OUR TRAVEL EXPENSES, SO WE DON'T NEED ANY MONEY.
STILL... IT WOULD BE NICE TO HAVE SOME CASH OF OUR OWN TO SPEND HOWEVER WE LIKE.
I'M IN! WE'LL HAVE OURSELVES A **DOUBLE** BATTLE!
WON-DER-FUL!
ALL RIGHT!
DIA, GET OVER HERE! WE'VE GOT A BATTLE TO FIGHT!
WHAT?!
HUF!
HUF!
HUF!
HUF!
HUF!
Sorry it took me so long!
HUF!
ALL RIGHT! LET'S GET THIS THING STARTED!
CHIM-LER!
TRU!

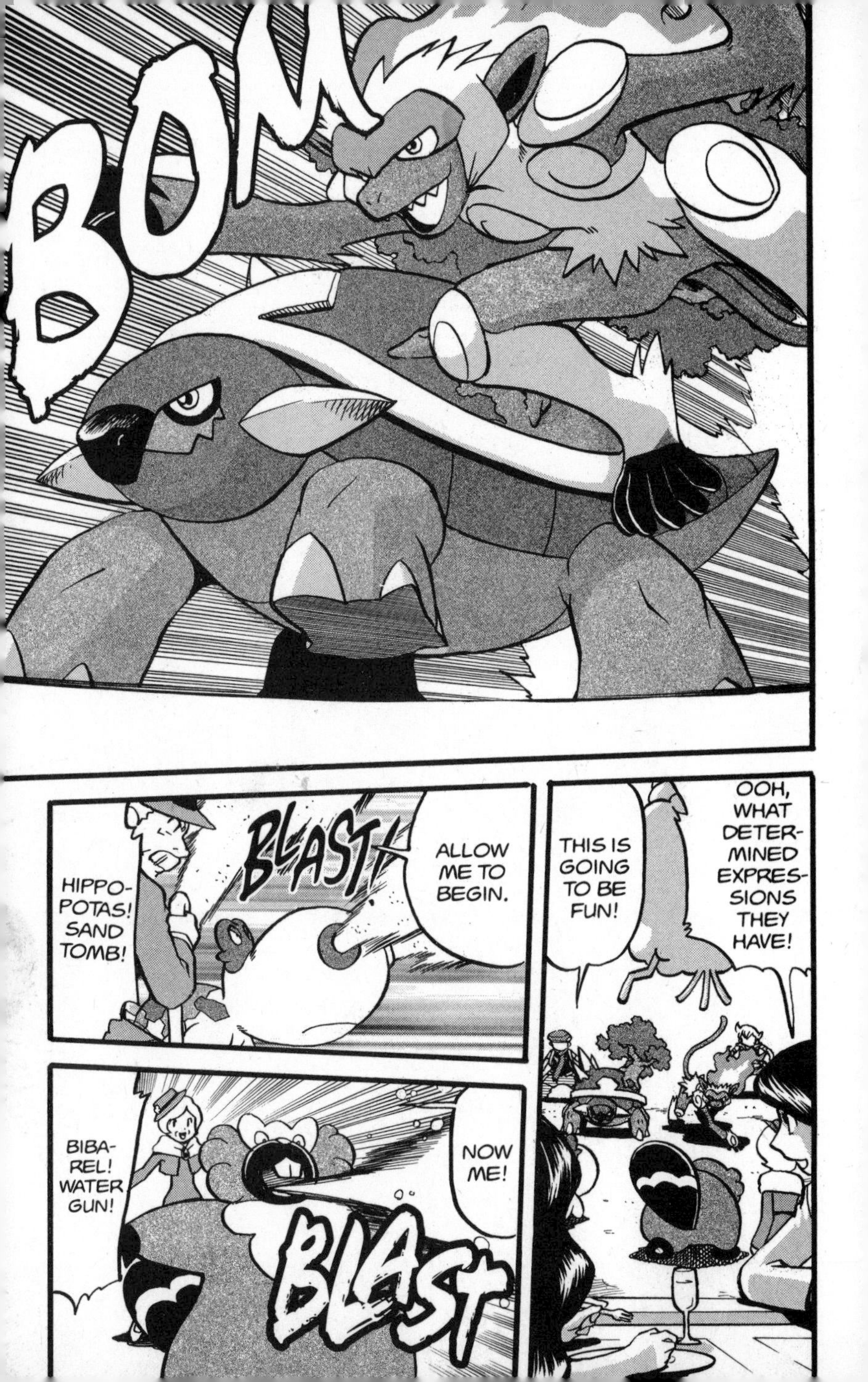
BOM
OOH, WHAT DETER-MINED EXPRES-SIONS THEY HAVE!
THIS IS GOING TO BE FUN!
ALLOW ME TO BEGIN.
BLAST!
HIPPO-POTAS! SAND TOMB!
NOW ME!
BIBA-REL! WATER GUN!
BLAST

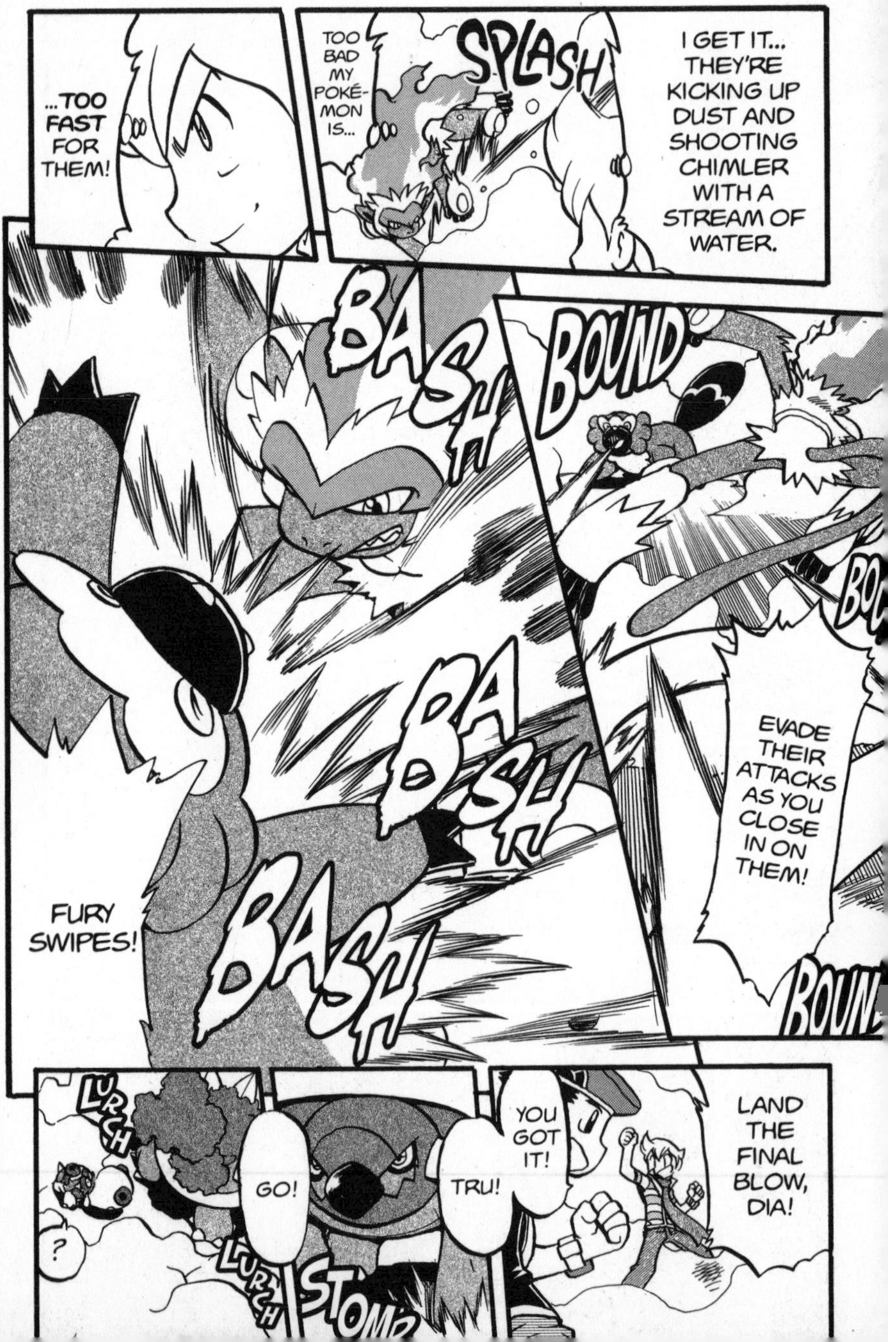
I GET IT... THEY'RE KICKING UP DUST AND SHOOTING CHIMLER WITH A STREAM OF WATER.
SPLASH
TOO BAD MY POKÉMON IS...
...TOO FAST FOR THEM!
BOUND
EVADE THEIR ATTACKS AS YOU CLOSE IN ON THEM!
BASH
BASH
BASH
FURY SWIPES!
LAND THE FINAL BLOW, DIA!
YOU GOT IT!
TRU!
GO!
LURCH
?
LURCH
STOMP

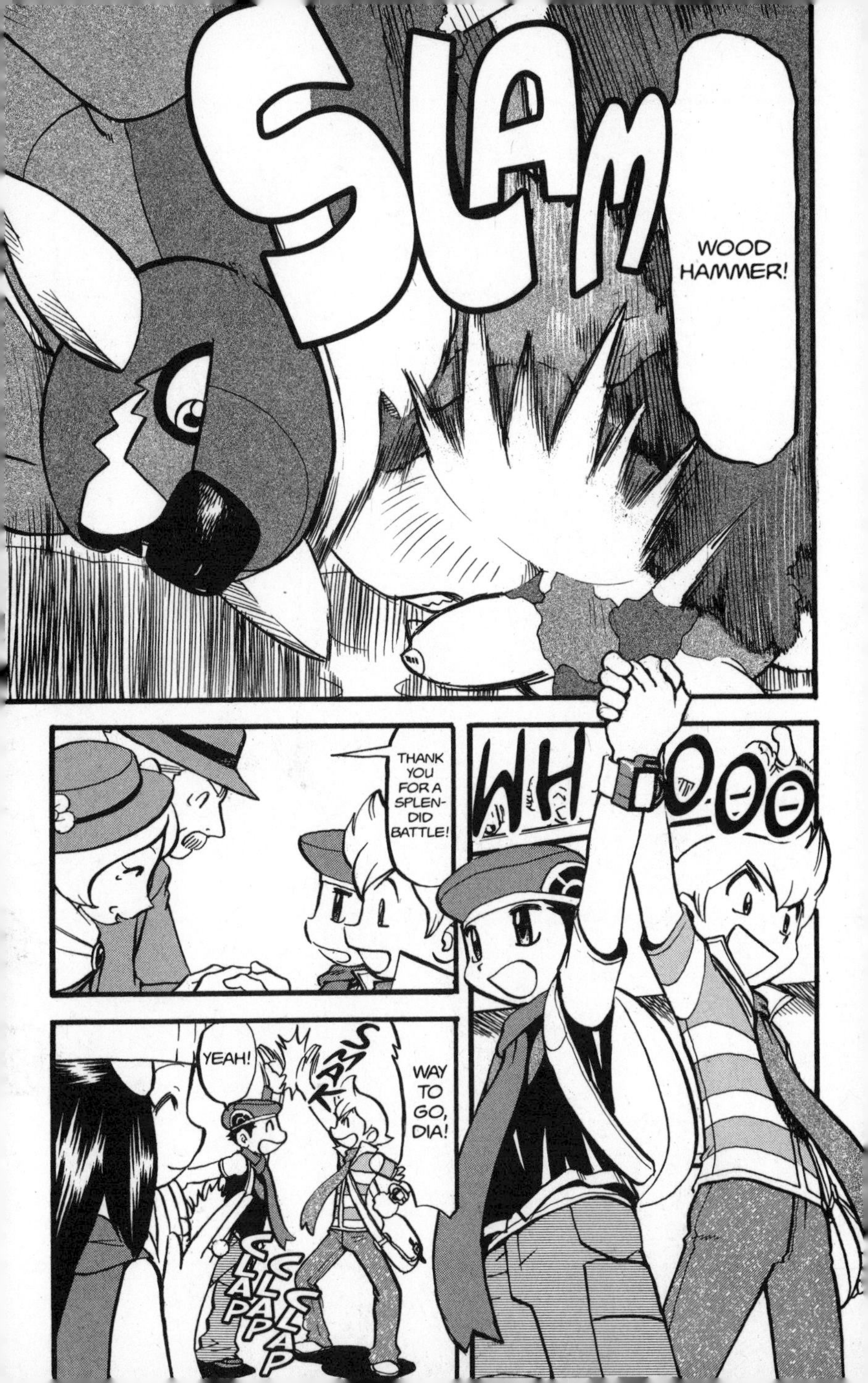
SLAM
WOOD HAMMER!
WHOOOO
THANK YOU FOR A SPLEN-DID BATTLE!
WAY TO GO, DIA!
SMAK
YEAH!
CLAP CLAP CLAP

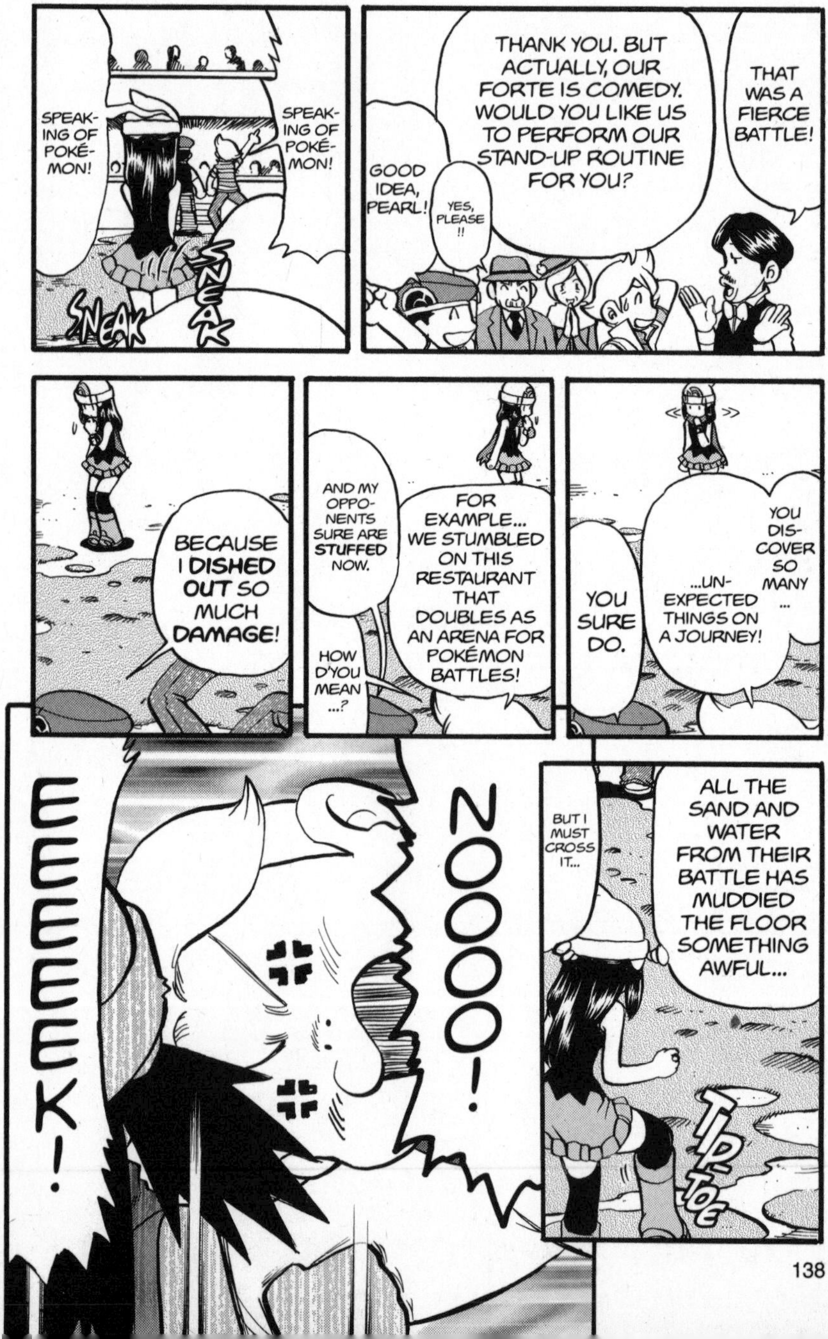
THAT WAS A FIERCE BATTLE!
THANK YOU. BUT ACTUALLY, OUR FORTE IS COMEDY. WOULD YOU LIKE US TO PERFORM OUR STAND-UP ROUTINE FOR YOU?
YES, PLEASE!!
GOOD IDEA, PEARL!
SPEAKING OF POKÉMON!
SPEAKING OF POKÉMON!
SNEAK
SNEAK
YOU DISCOVER SO MANY...
...UNEXPECTED THINGS ON A JOURNEY!
YOU SURE DO.
FOR EXAMPLE... WE STUMBLED ON THIS RESTAURANT THAT DOUBLES AS AN ARENA FOR POKÉMON BATTLES!
AND MY OPPONENTS SURE ARE STUFFED NOW.
HOW D'YOU MEAN...?
BECAUSE I DISHED OUT SO MUCH DAMAGE!
ALL THE SAND AND WATER FROM THEIR BATTLE HAS MUDDIED THE FLOOR SOMETHING AWFUL...
BUT I MUST CROSS IT...
TIP-TOE
NOOOO!
EEEEEEK!

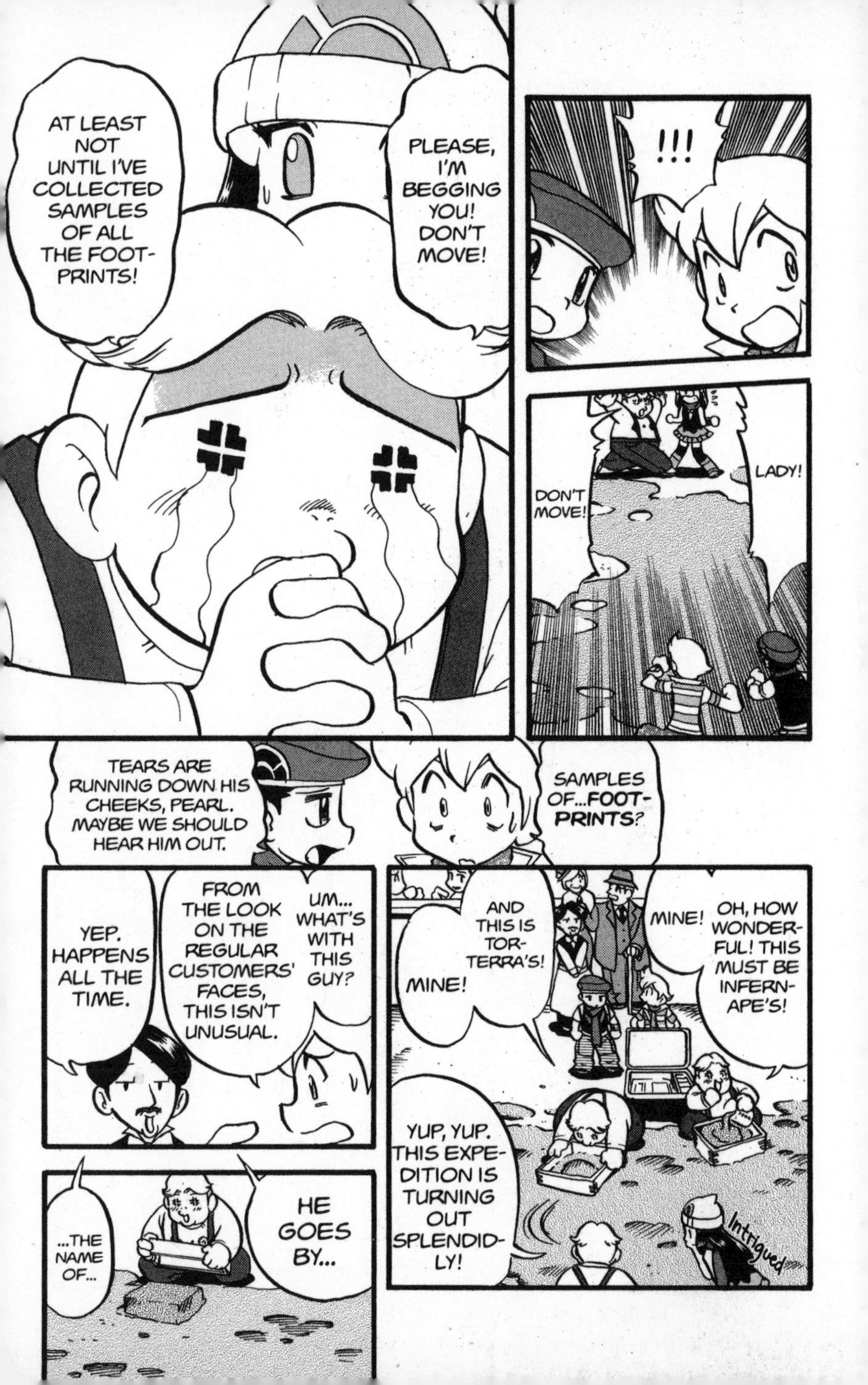
!!!
LADY!
DON'T MOVE!
PLEASE, I'M BEGGING YOU! DON'T MOVE!
AT LEAST NOT UNTIL I'VE COLLECTED SAMPLES OF ALL THE FOOT-PRINTS!
SAMPLES OF...FOOT-PRINTS?
TEARS ARE RUNNING DOWN HIS CHEEKS, PEARL. MAYBE WE SHOULD HEAR HIM OUT.
OH, HOW WONDER-FUL! THIS MUST BE INFERN-APE'S!
MINE!
AND THIS IS TOR-TERRA'S!
MINE!
YUP, YUP. THIS EXPE-DITION IS TURNING OUT SPLENDID-LY!
Intrigued
UM... WHAT'S WITH THIS GUY?
FROM THE LOOK ON THE REGULAR CUSTOMERS' FACES, THIS ISN'T UNUSUAL.
YEP. HAPPENS ALL THE TIME.
HE GOES BY...
...THE NAME OF...

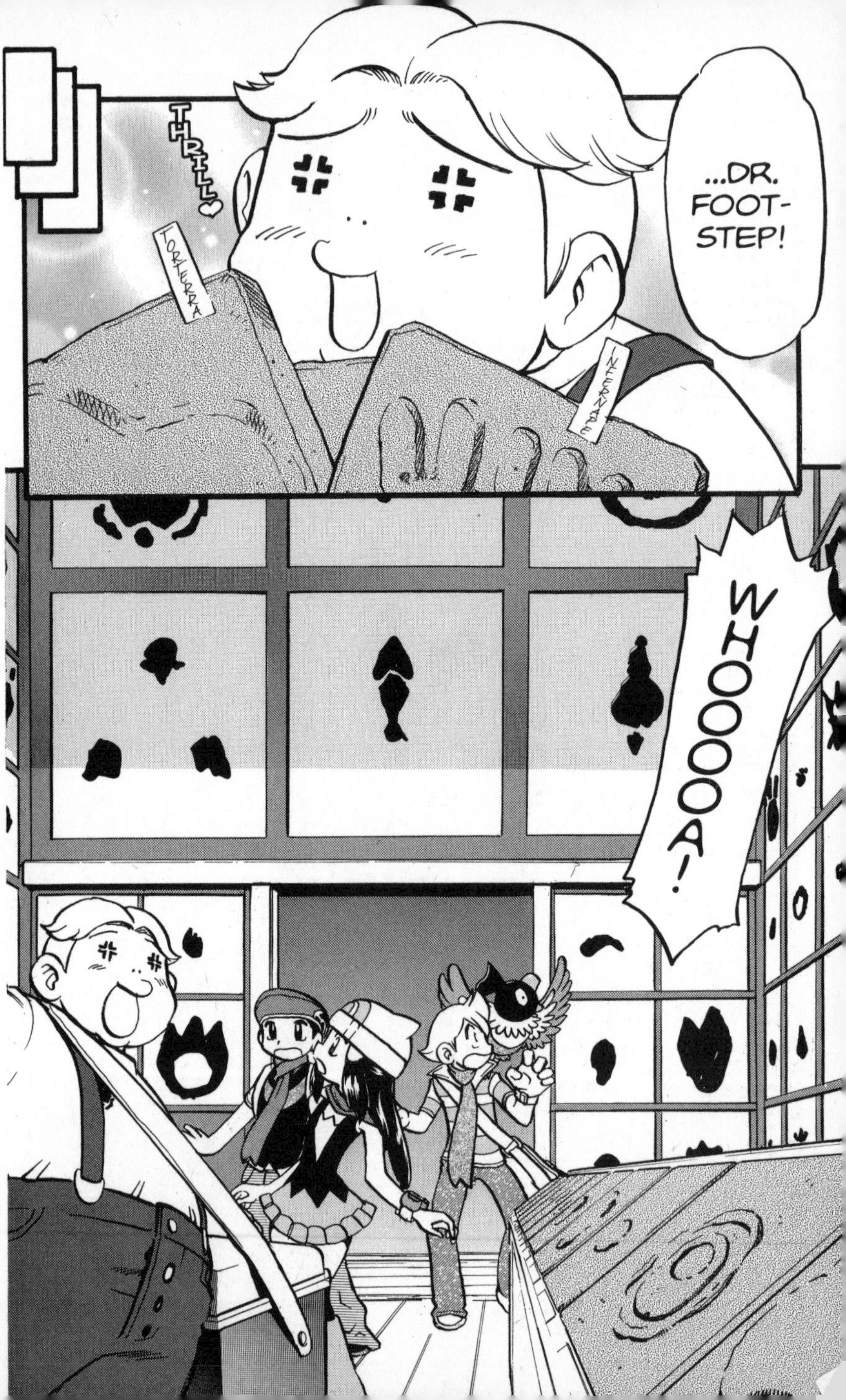
...DR. FOOT-
STEP!
THRILL♡
TORTERRA
INFERNAPE
WHOOOOOA!

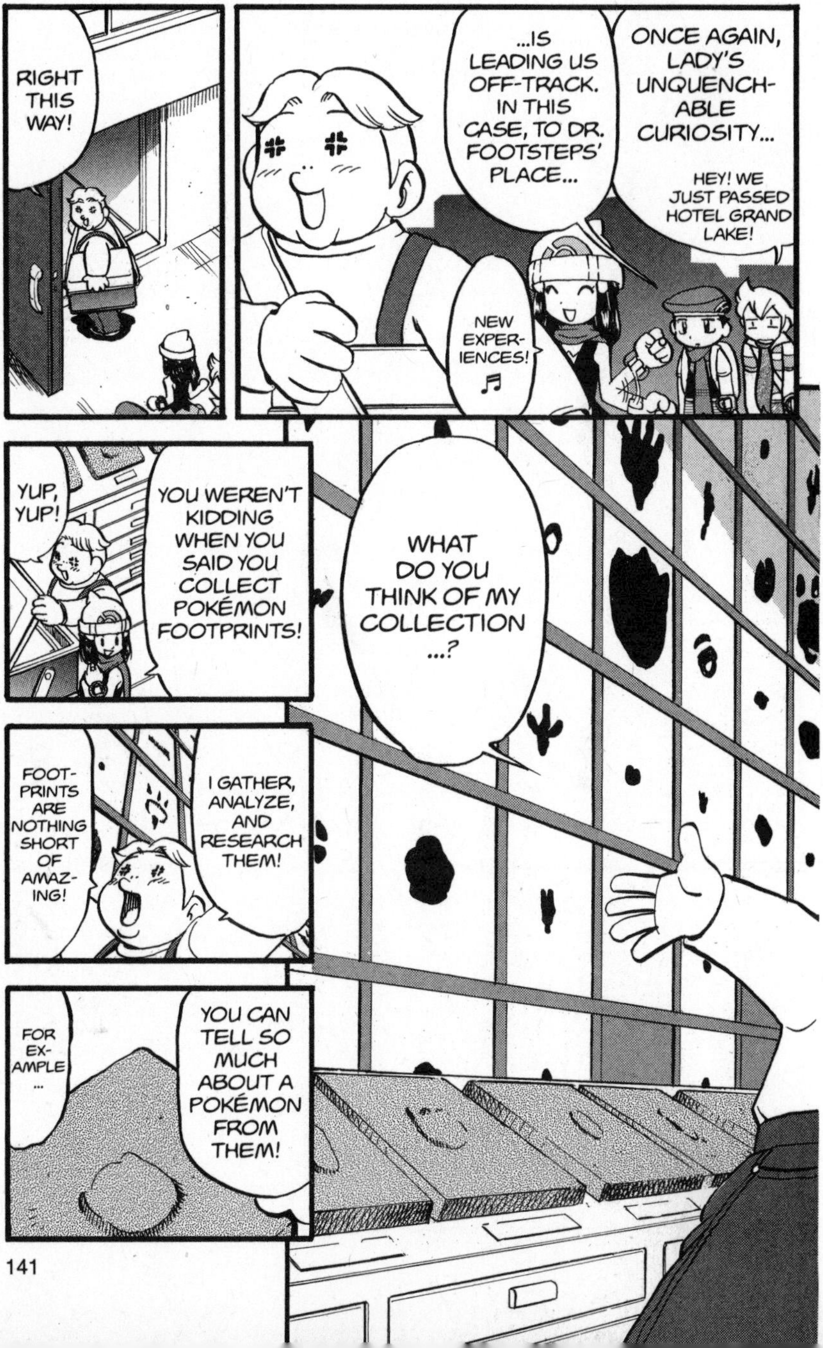

ONCE AGAIN, LADY'S UNQUENCH-ABLE CURIOSITY...
...IS LEADING US OFF-TRACK. IN THIS CASE, TO DR. FOOTSTEPS' PLACE...
HEY! WE JUST PASSED HOTEL GRAND LAKE!
NEW EXPER-IENCES! ♪
RIGHT THIS WAY!
WHAT DO YOU THINK OF MY COLLECTION ...?
YOU WEREN'T KIDDING WHEN YOU SAID YOU COLLECT POKÉMON FOOTPRINTS!
YUP, YUP!
I GATHER, ANALYZE, AND RESEARCH THEM!
FOOT-PRINTS ARE NOTHING SHORT OF AMAZ-ING!
YOU CAN TELL SO MUCH ABOUT A POKÉMON FROM THEM!
FOR EX-AMPLE ...

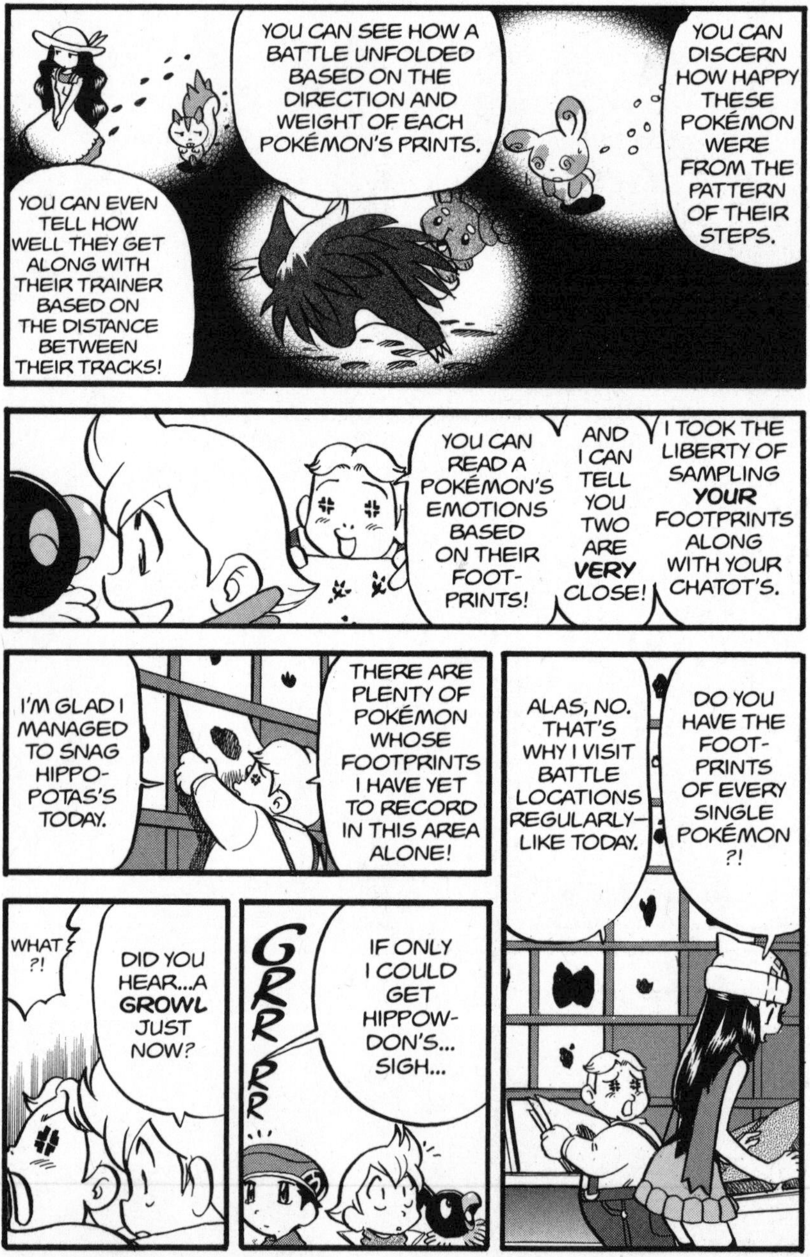
YOU CAN DISCERN HOW HAPPY THESE POKÉMON WERE FROM THE PATTERN OF THEIR STEPS.
YOU CAN SEE HOW A BATTLE UNFOLDED BASED ON THE DIRECTION AND WEIGHT OF EACH POKÉMON'S PRINTS.
YOU CAN EVEN TELL HOW WELL THEY GET ALONG WITH THEIR TRAINER BASED ON THE DISTANCE BETWEEN THEIR TRACKS!
I TOOK THE LIBERTY OF SAMPLING **YOUR** FOOTPRINTS ALONG WITH YOUR CHATOT'S.
AND I CAN TELL YOU TWO ARE **VERY** CLOSE!
YOU CAN READ A POKÉMON'S EMOTIONS BASED ON THEIR FOOT-PRINTS!
DO YOU HAVE THE FOOT-PRINTS OF EVERY SINGLE POKÉMON ?!
ALAS, NO. THAT'S WHY I VISIT BATTLE LOCATIONS REGULARLY—LIKE TODAY.
THERE ARE PLENTY OF POKÉMON WHOSE FOOTPRINTS I HAVE YET TO RECORD IN THIS AREA ALONE!
I'M GLAD I MANAGED TO SNAG HIPPO-POTAS'S TODAY.
IF ONLY I COULD GET HIPPOW-DON'S... SIGH...
GRRRRR
DID YOU HEAR...A **GROWL** JUST NOW?
WHAT ?!

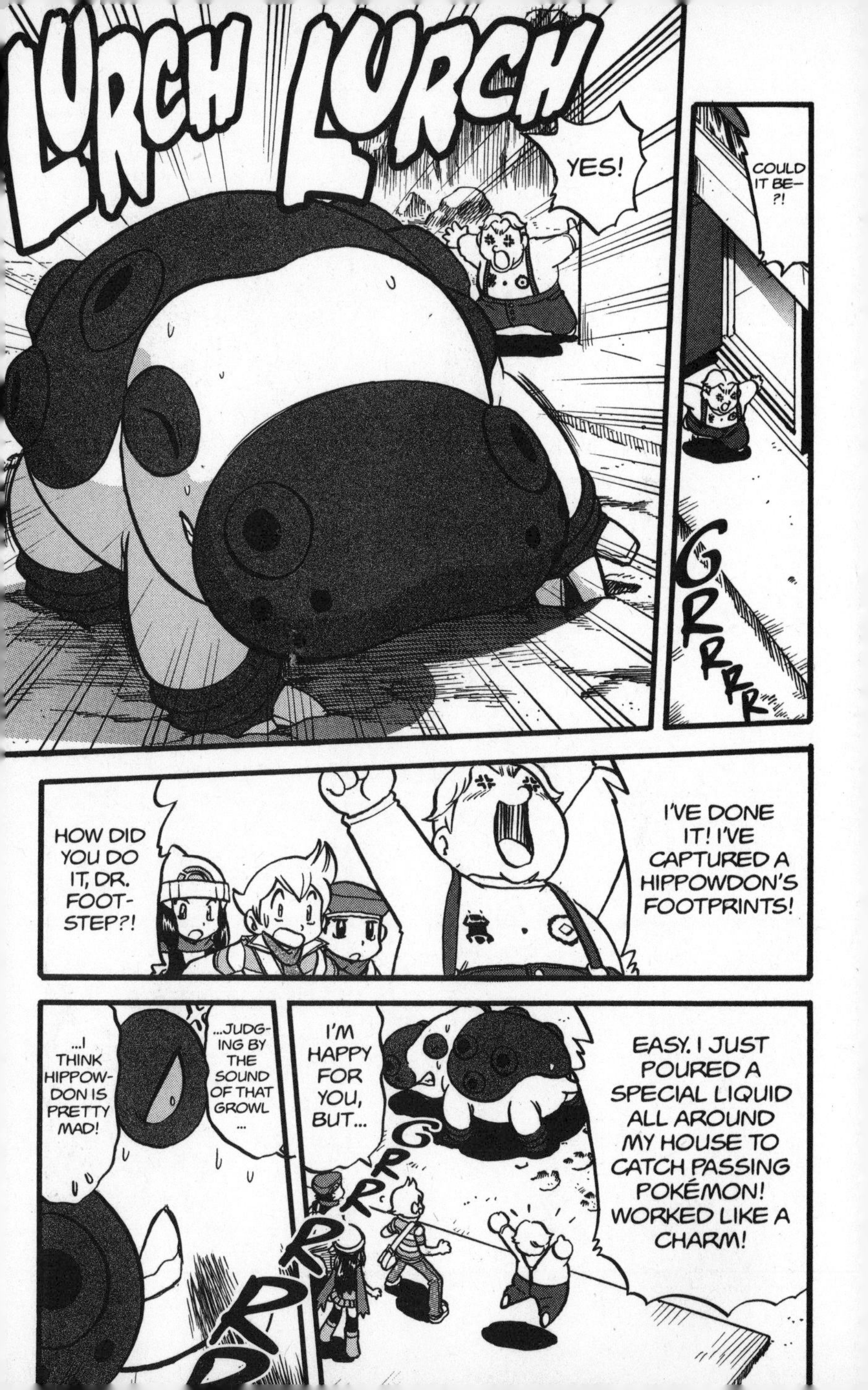
COULD IT BE—?!
GRRRR
LURCH LURCH
YES!
I'VE DONE IT! I'VE CAPTURED A HIPPOWDON'S FOOTPRINTS!
HOW DID YOU DO IT, DR. FOOT-STEP?!
EASY. I JUST POURED A SPECIAL LIQUID ALL AROUND MY HOUSE TO CATCH PASSING POKÉMON! WORKED LIKE A CHARM!
I'M HAPPY FOR YOU, BUT...
GRRR
...JUDG-ING BY THE SOUND OF THAT GROWL ...
...I THINK HIPPOW-DON IS PRETTY MAD!
RRRR

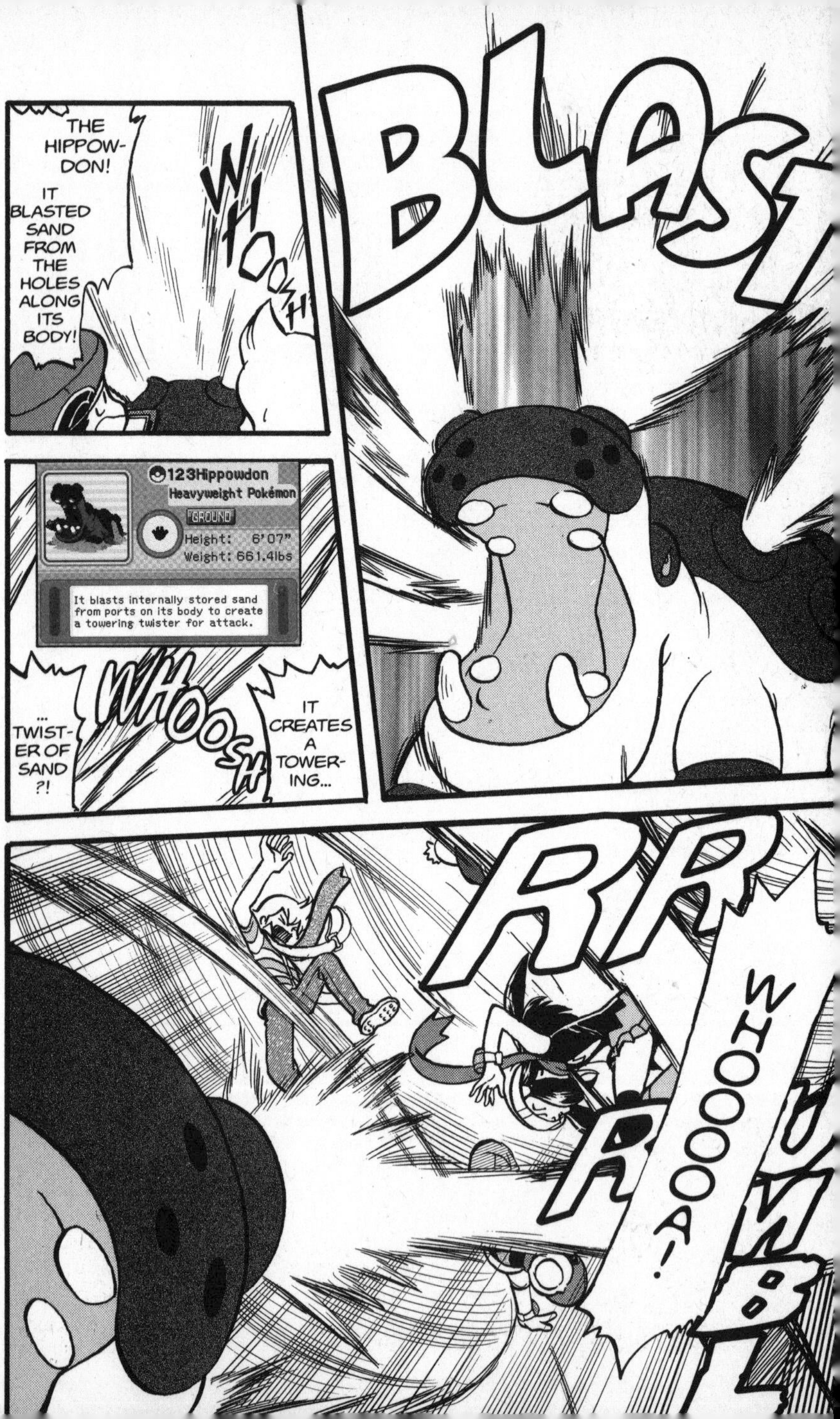
BLAS
THE HIPPOWDON!
IT BLASTED SAND FROM THE HOLES ALONG ITS BODY!
WHOOSH
123 Hippowdon
Heavyweight Pokémon
GROUND
Height: 6'07"
Weight: 661.4lbs
It blasts internally stored sand from ports on its body to create a towering twister for attack.
IT CREATES A TOWERING...
WHOOSH
...TWISTER OF SAND?!
WHOOOOA!
RRAA

ADVENTURE MAP

▶ Valor Lakefront ◀

Oreburgh VS Roark Coal Badge	Eterna VS Gardenia Forest Badge	Veilstone VS Maylene Cobble Badge					

LADY

DIAMOND

PEARL

▶ TRU
Torterra ♂

▶ LAX
Munchlax ♂

▶ CHIMLER
Infernape ♂

▶ CHATLER
Chatot ♂

▶ EMPOLEON
Empoleon ♀

▶ PONYTA
Ponyta ♂

25

Dramatic
Drapion
&
Crafty
Kricketune I

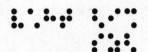

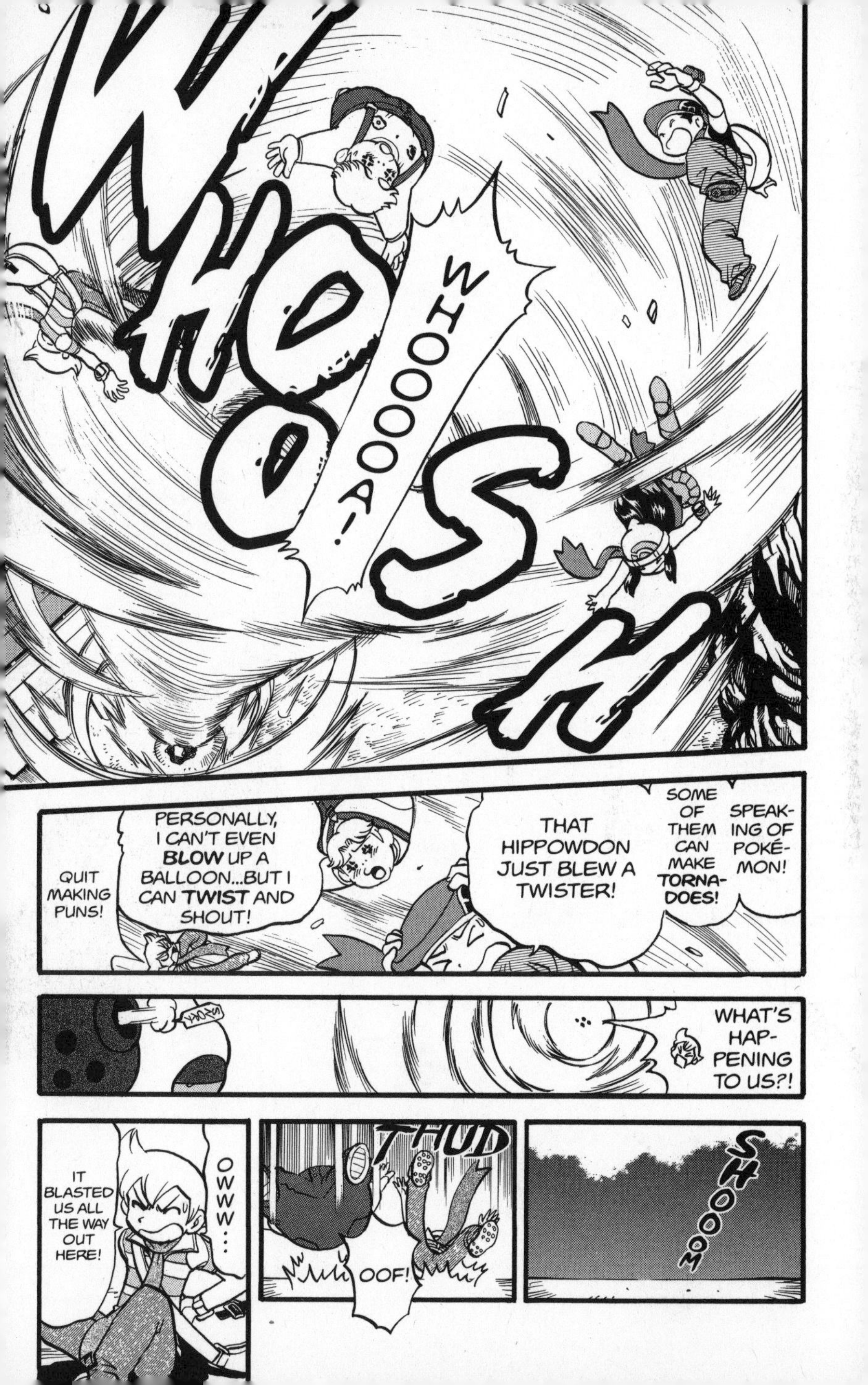
WHOOSH
WHOOOOOA-!
SPEAKING OF POKÉMON!
SOME OF THEM CAN MAKE TORNADOES!
THAT HIPPOWDON JUST BLEW A TWISTER!
PERSONALLY, I CAN'T EVEN BLOW UP A BALLOON...BUT I CAN TWIST AND SHOUT!
QUIT MAKING PUNS!
WHAT'S HAPPENING TO US?!
SHOOOOM
THUD
OOF!
OWWW...
IT BLASTED US ALL THE WAY OUT HERE!

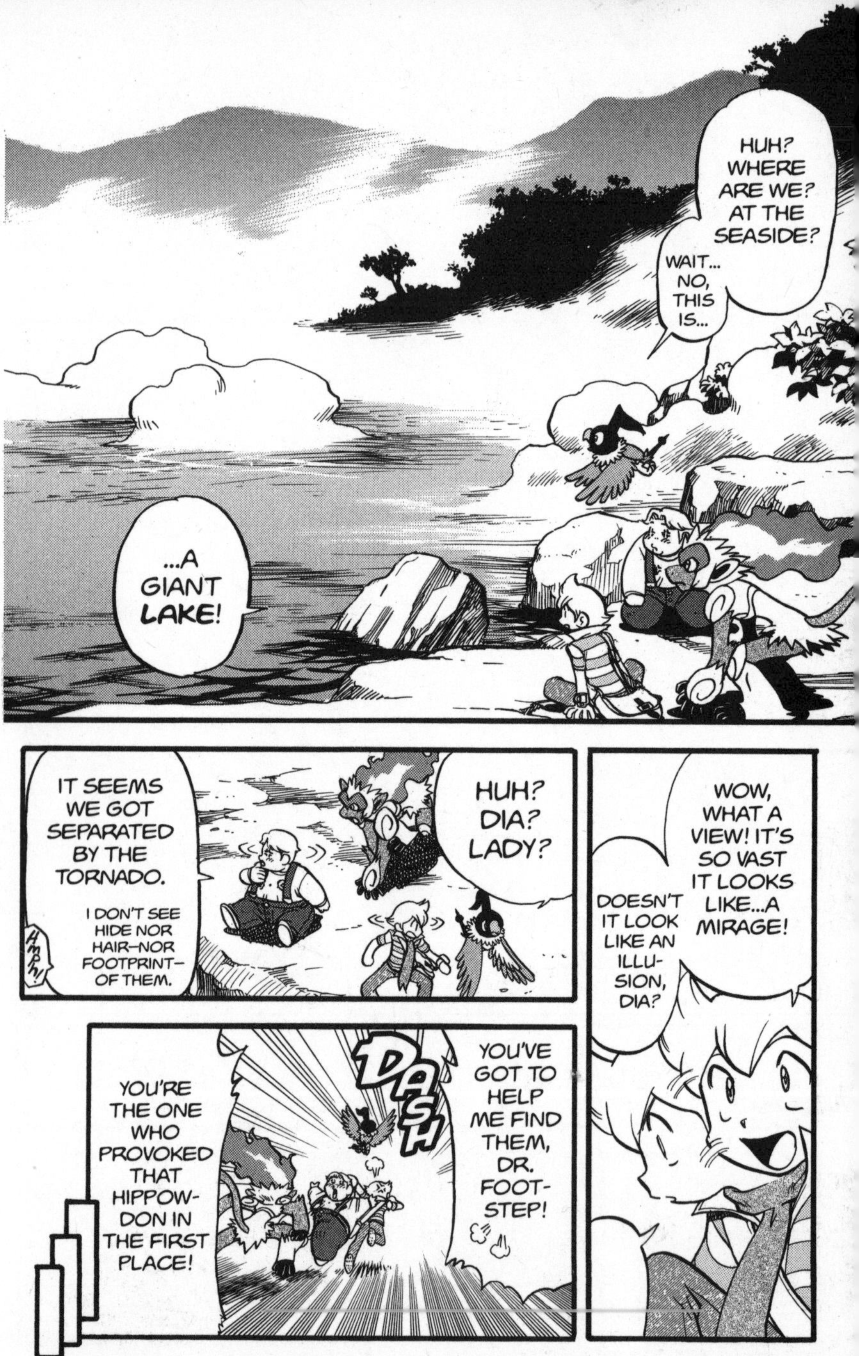
HUH? WHERE ARE WE? AT THE SEASIDE?
WAIT... NO, THIS IS...
...A GIANT LAKE!
WOW, WHAT A VIEW! IT'S SO VAST IT LOOKS LIKE...A MIRAGE!
DOESN'T IT LOOK LIKE AN ILLUSION, DIA?
HUH? DIA? LADY?
IT SEEMS WE GOT SEPARATED BY THE TORNADO.
I DON'T SEE HIDE NOR HAIR—NOR FOOTPRINT—OF THEM.
HMPH!
DASH
YOU'VE GOT TO HELP ME FIND THEM, DR. FOOTSTEP!
YOU'RE THE ONE WHO PROVOKED THAT HIPPOWDON IN THE FIRST PLACE!

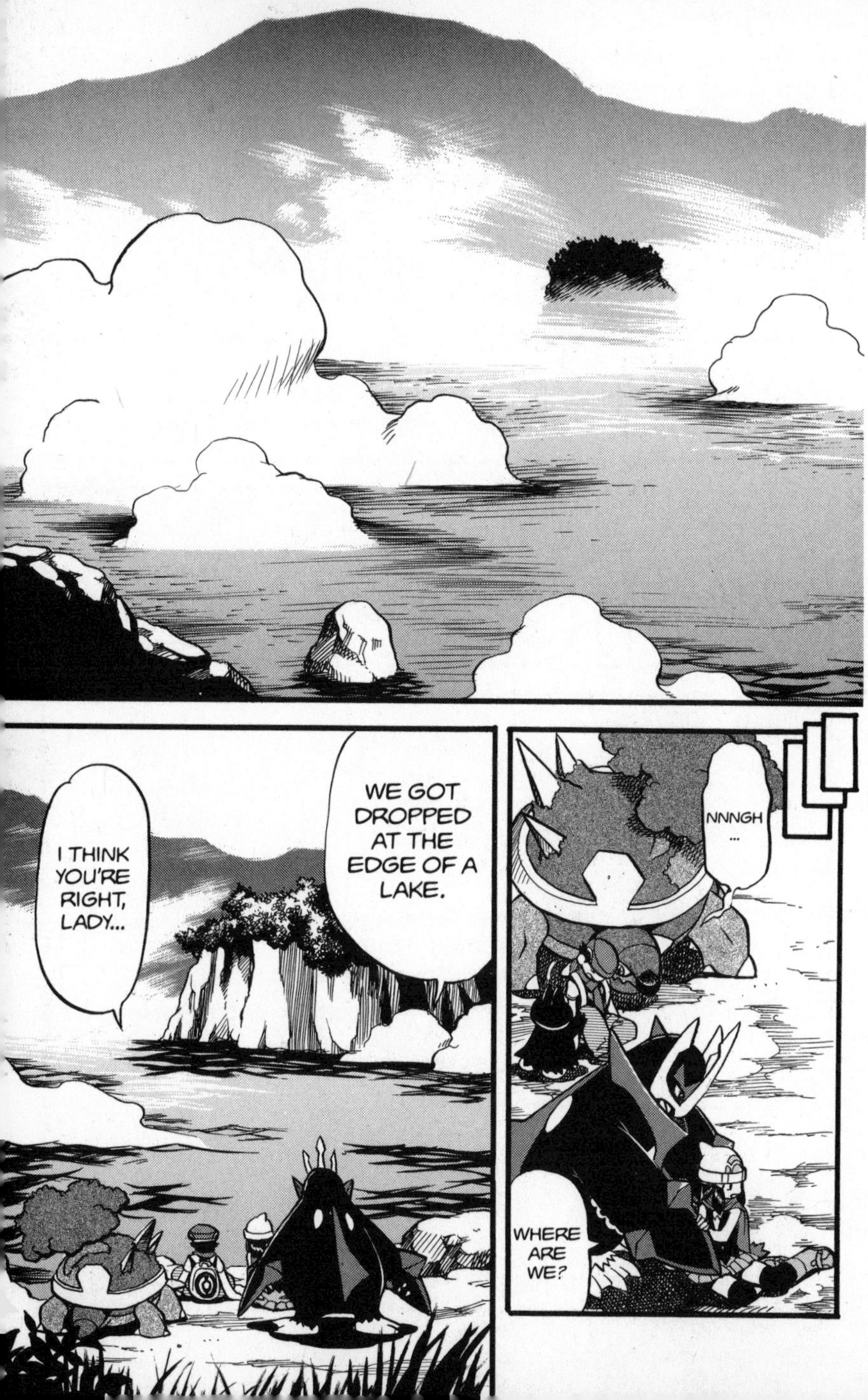
NNNGH ...
WHERE ARE WE?
WE GOT DROPPED AT THE EDGE OF A LAKE.
I THINK YOU'RE RIGHT, LADY...

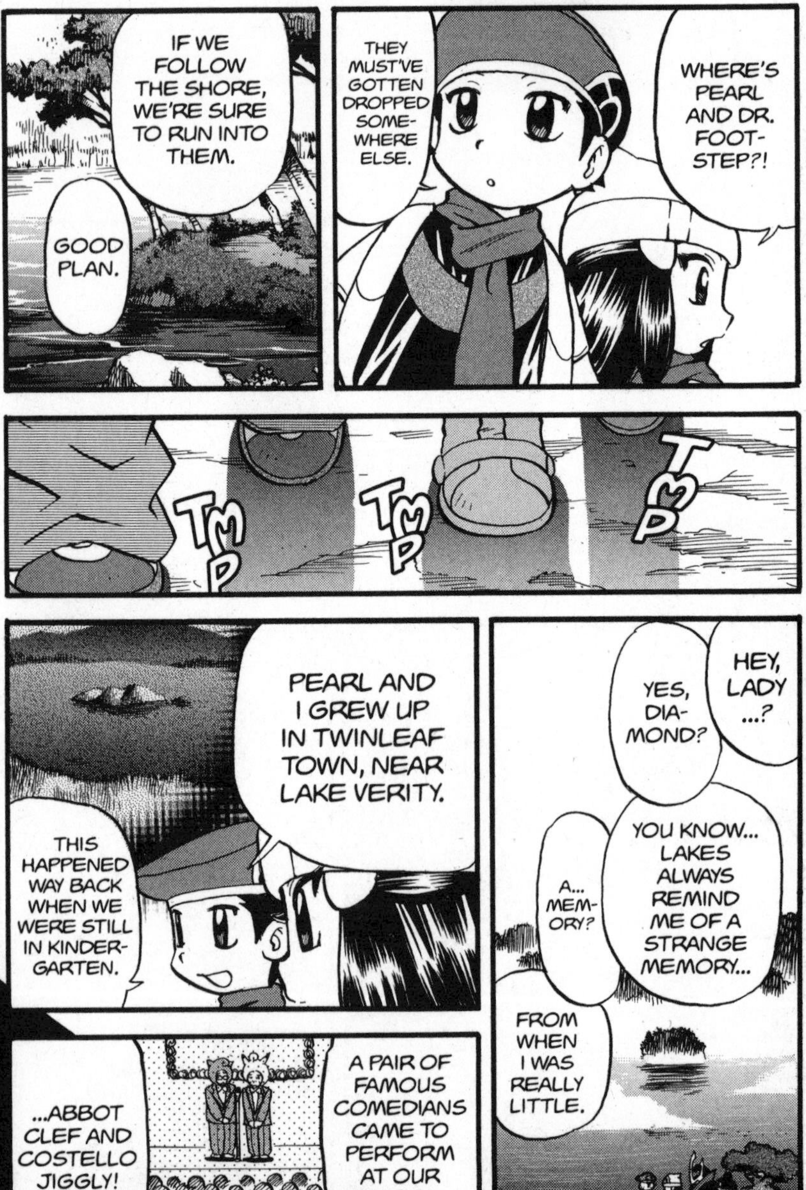
WHERE'S PEARL AND DR. FOOTSTEP?!
THEY MUST'VE GOTTEN DROPPED SOMEWHERE ELSE.
IF WE FOLLOW THE SHORE, WE'RE SURE TO RUN INTO THEM.
GOOD PLAN.
TMP
TMP
TMP
HEY, LADY ...?
YES, DIAMOND?
YOU KNOW... LAKES ALWAYS REMIND ME OF A STRANGE MEMORY...
A... MEMORY?
FROM WHEN I WAS REALLY LITTLE.
PEARL AND I GREW UP IN TWINLEAF TOWN, NEAR LAKE VERITY.
THIS HAPPENED WAY BACK WHEN WE WERE STILL IN KINDERGARTEN.
A PAIR OF FAMOUS COMEDIANS CAME TO PERFORM AT OUR SCHOOL...
...ABBOT CLEF AND COSTELLO JIGGLY!

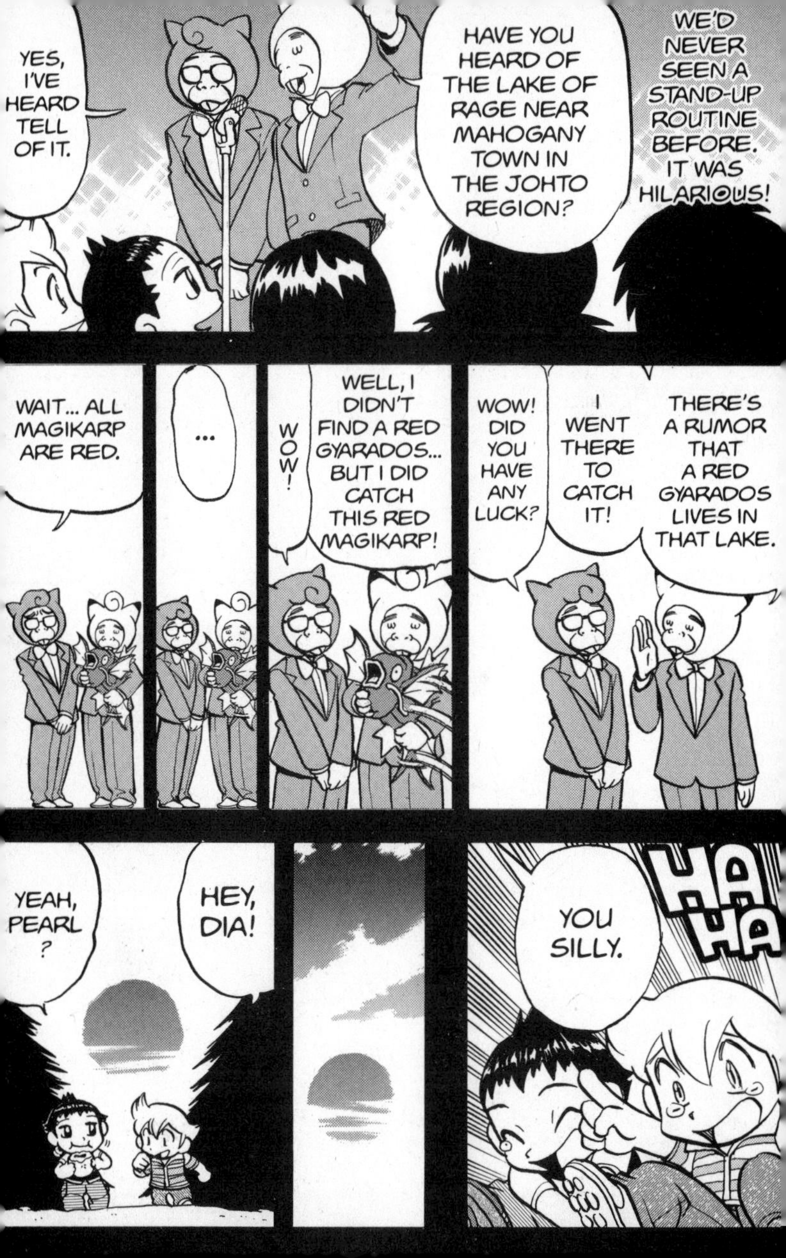
WE'D NEVER SEEN A STAND-UP ROUTINE BEFORE. IT WAS HILARIOUS!
HAVE YOU HEARD OF THE LAKE OF RAGE NEAR MAHOGANY TOWN IN THE JOHTO REGION?
YES, I'VE HEARD TELL OF IT.
THERE'S A RUMOR THAT A RED GYARADOS LIVES IN THAT LAKE.
I WENT THERE TO CATCH IT!
WOW! DID YOU HAVE ANY LUCK?
WELL, I DIDN'T FIND A RED GYARADOS... BUT I DID CATCH THIS RED MAGIKARP!
WOW!
...
WAIT... ALL MAGIKARP ARE RED.
HA HA
YOU SILLY.
HEY, DIA!
YEAH, PEARL?

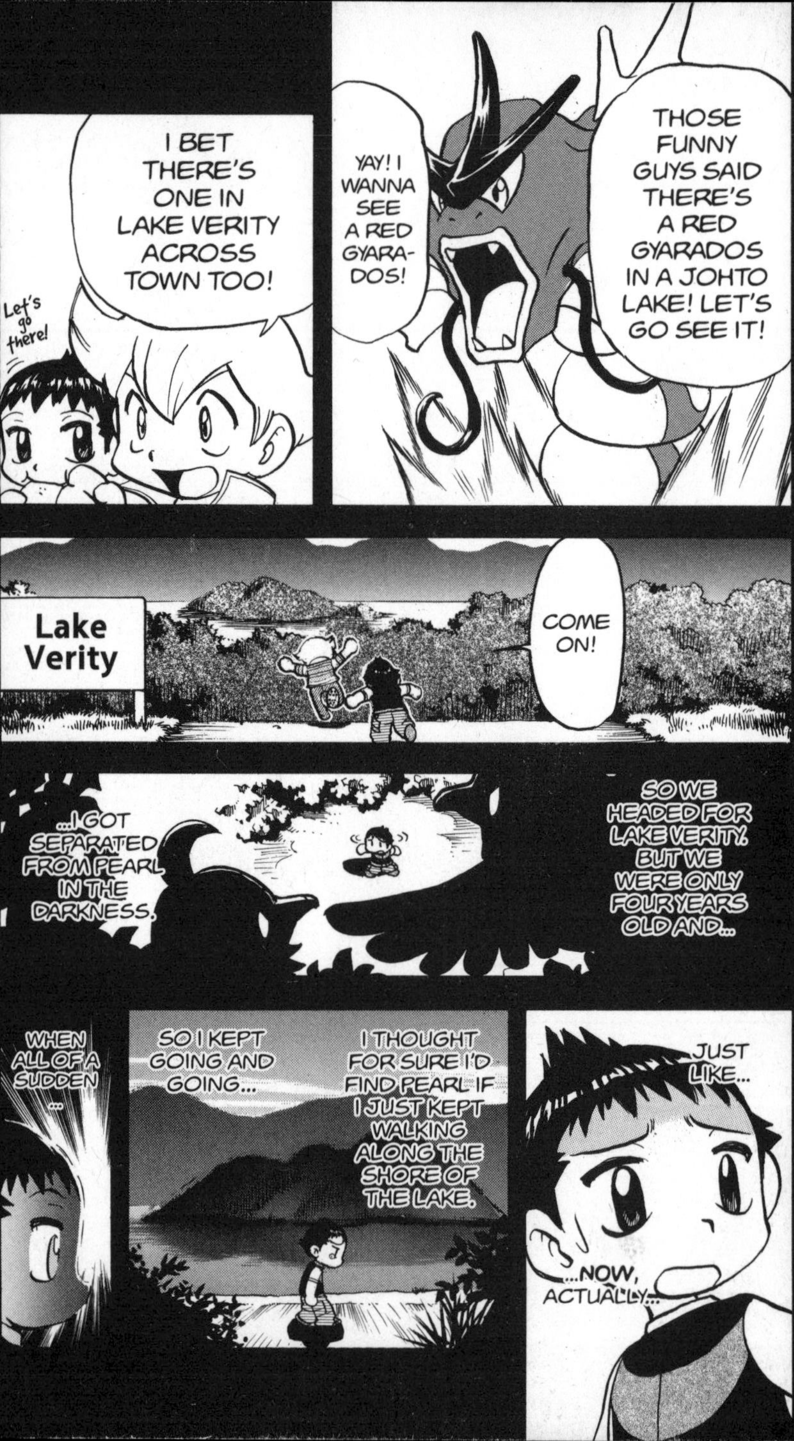
THOSE FUNNY GUYS SAID THERE'S A RED GYARADOS IN A JOHTO LAKE! LET'S GO SEE IT!
YAY! I WANNA SEE A RED GYARA-DOS!
I BET THERE'S ONE IN LAKE VERITY ACROSS TOWN TOO!
Let's go there!
COME ON!
Lake Verity
SO WE HEADED FOR LAKE VERITY. BUT WE WERE ONLY FOUR YEARS OLD AND...
...I GOT SEPARATED FROM PEARL IN THE DARKNESS.
JUST LIKE...
...NOW, ACTUALLY...
I THOUGHT FOR SURE I'D FIND PEARL IF I JUST KEPT WALKING ALONG THE SHORE OF THE LAKE.
SO I KEPT GOING AND GOING...
WHEN ALL OF A SUDDEN...

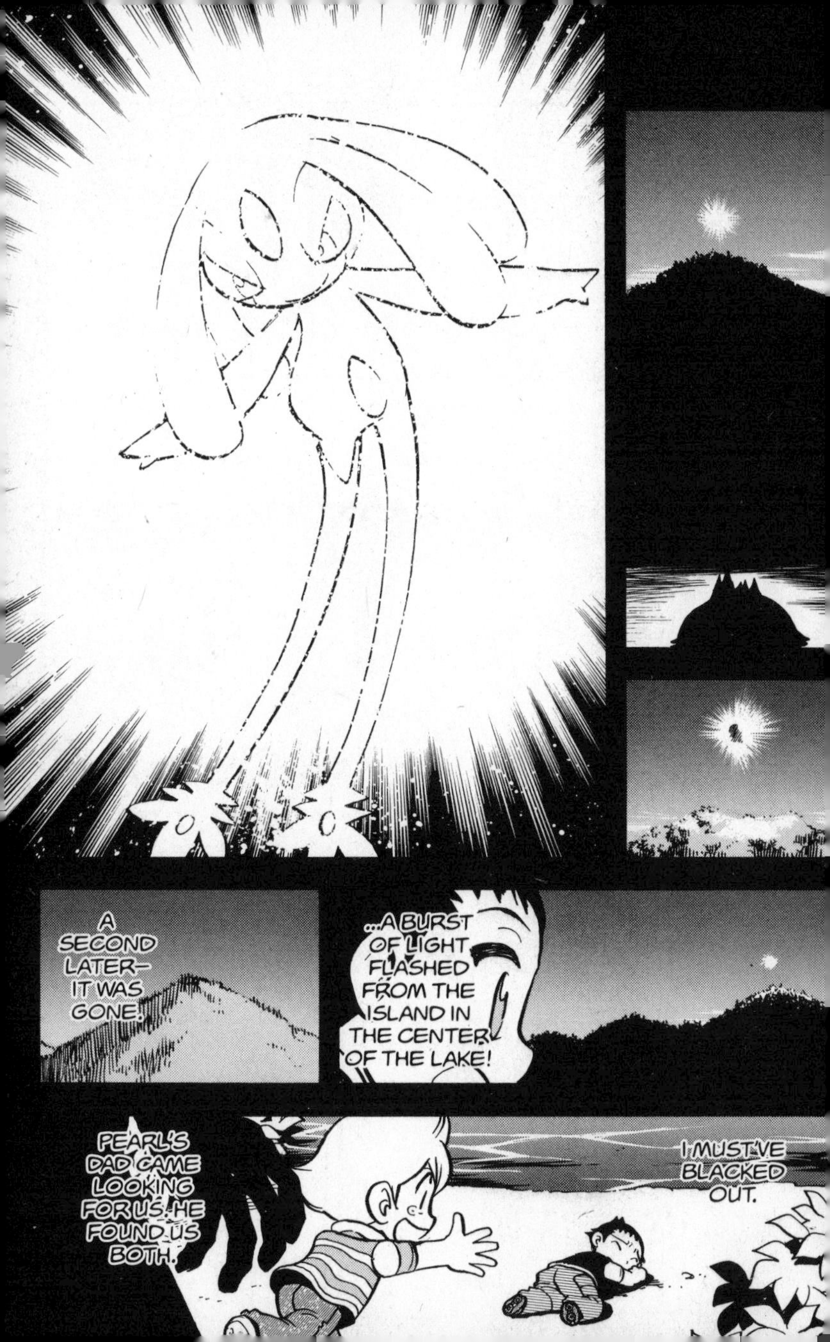
...A BURST OF LIGHT FLASHED FROM THE ISLAND IN THE CENTER OF THE LAKE!
A SECOND LATER— IT WAS GONE!
I MUST'VE BLACKED OUT.
PEARL'S DAD CAME LOOKING FOR US. HE FOUND US BOTH.

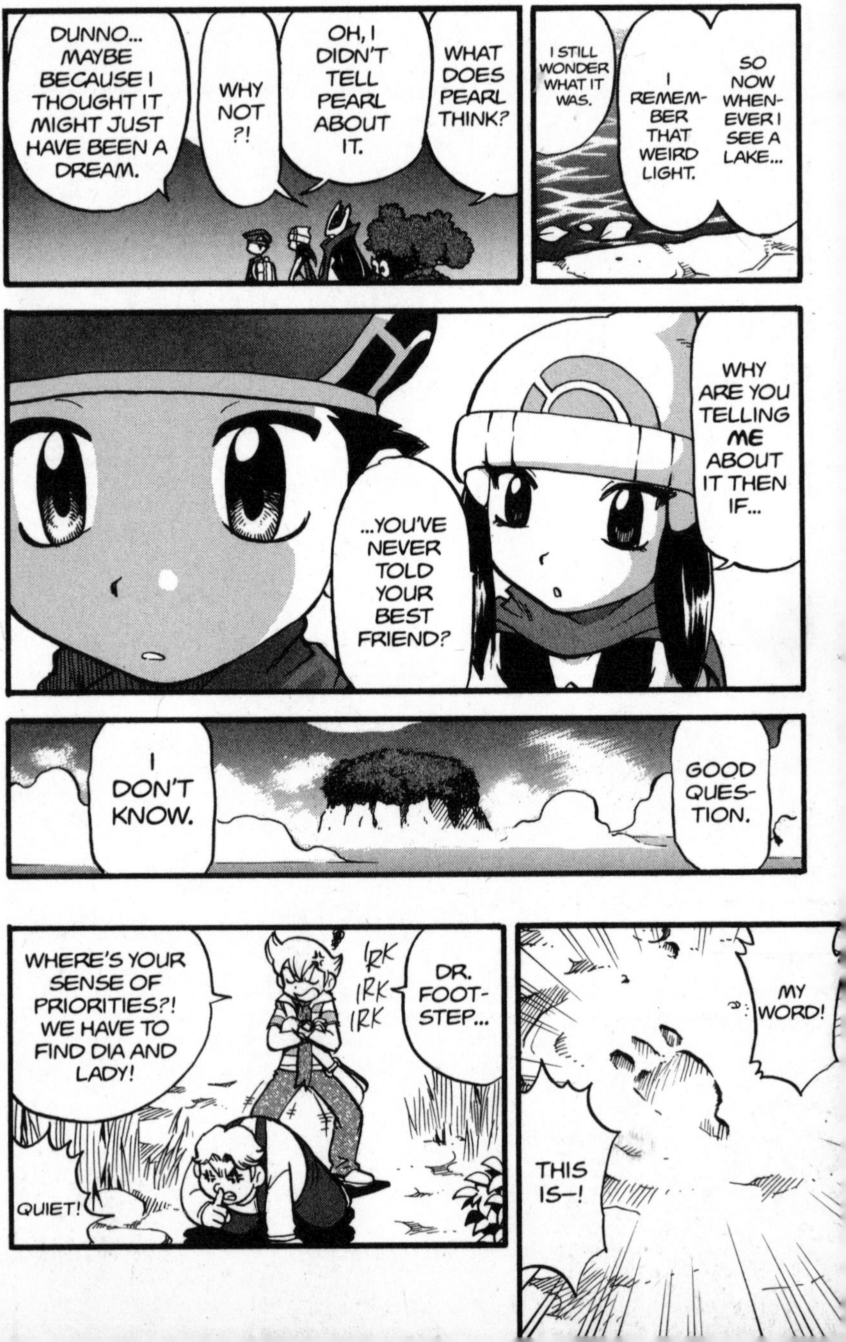
SO NOW WHENEVER I SEE A LAKE...
I REMEMBER THAT WEIRD LIGHT.
I STILL WONDER WHAT IT WAS.
WHAT DOES PEARL THINK?
OH, I DIDN'T TELL PEARL ABOUT IT.
WHY NOT?!
DUNNO... MAYBE BECAUSE I THOUGHT IT MIGHT JUST HAVE BEEN A DREAM.
WHY ARE YOU TELLING **ME** ABOUT IT THEN IF...
...YOU'VE NEVER TOLD YOUR BEST FRIEND?
GOOD QUESTION.
I DON'T KNOW.
MY WORD!
THIS IS—!
DR. FOOTSTEP...
IRK IRK IRK
WHERE'S YOUR SENSE OF PRIORITIES?! WE HAVE TO FIND DIA AND LADY!
QUIET!

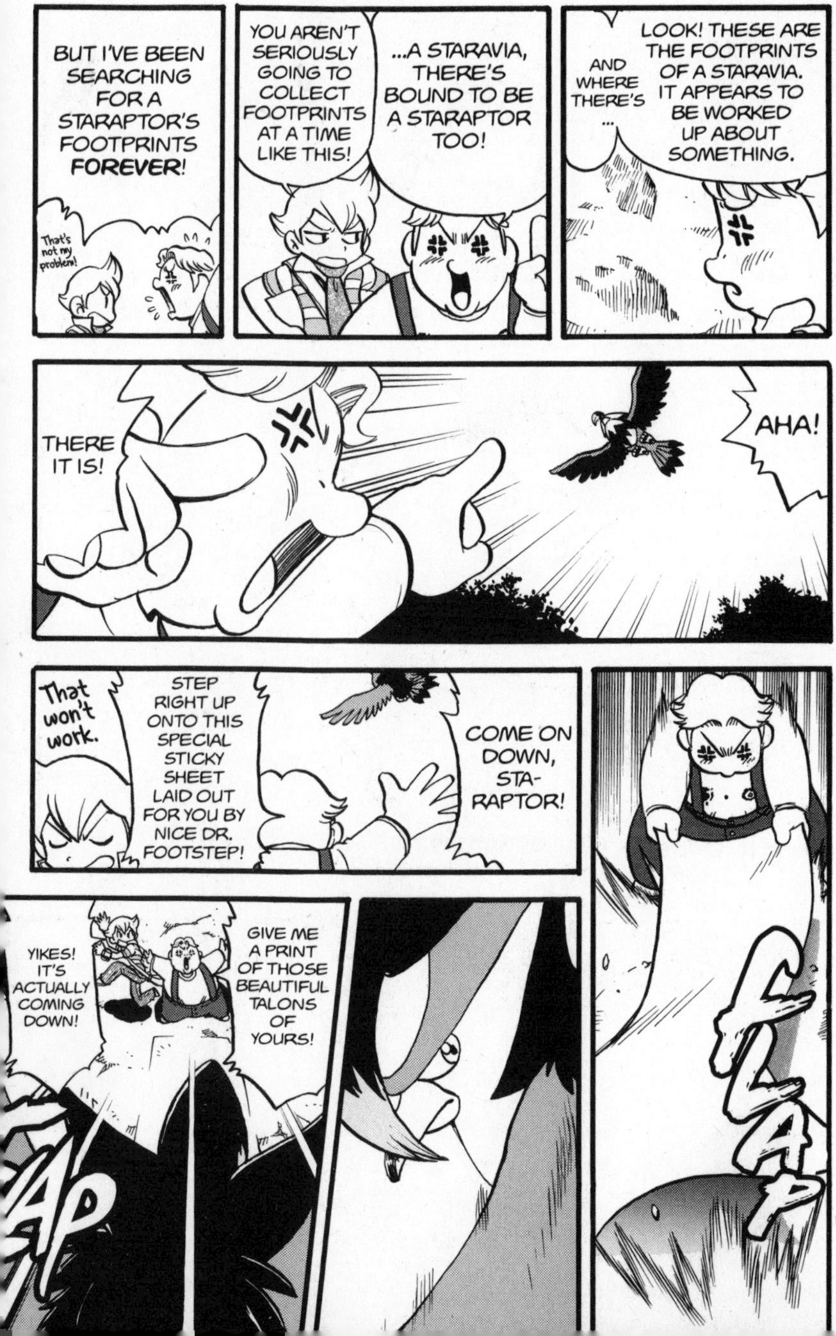
LOOK! THESE ARE THE FOOTPRINTS OF A STARAVIA. IT APPEARS TO BE WORKED UP ABOUT SOMETHING.
AND WHERE THERE'S ...
...A STARAVIA, THERE'S BOUND TO BE A STARAPTOR TOO!
YOU AREN'T SERIOUSLY GOING TO COLLECT FOOTPRINTS AT A TIME LIKE THIS!
BUT I'VE BEEN SEARCHING FOR A STARAPTOR'S FOOTPRINTS FOREVER!
That's not my problem!
AHA!
THERE IT IS!
CLAP
COME ON DOWN, STA-RAPTOR!
STEP RIGHT UP ONTO THIS SPECIAL STICKY SHEET LAID OUT FOR YOU BY NICE DR. FOOTSTEP!
That won't work.
GIVE ME A PRINT OF THOSE BEAUTIFUL TALONS OF YOURS!
YIKES! IT'S ACTUALLY COMING DOWN!

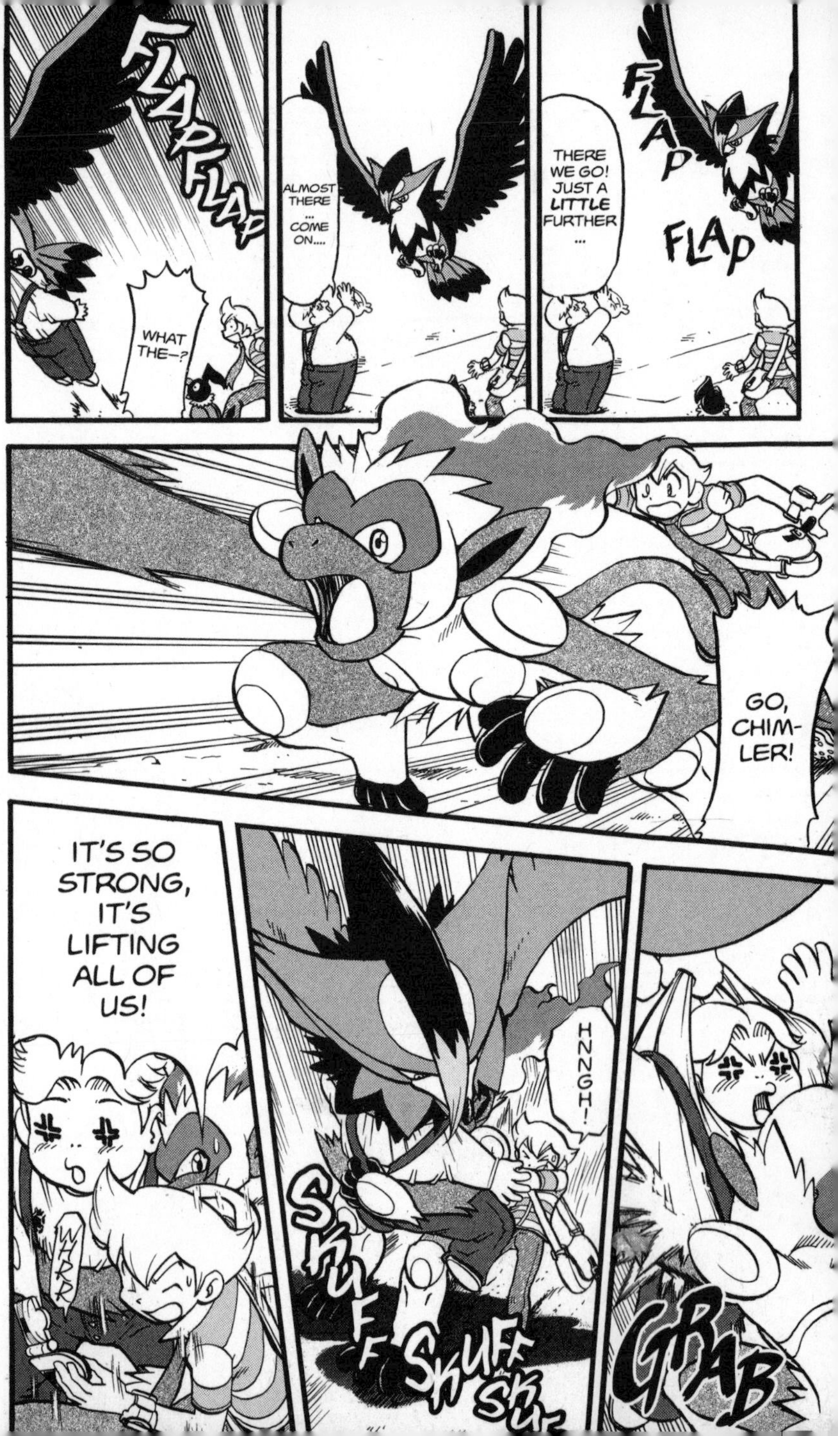
THERE WE GO! JUST A LITTLE FURTHER ...
FLAP
FLAP
ALMOST THERE ... COME ON....
FLAPFLAP
WHAT THE—?
GO, CHIMLER!
GRAB
HNNGH!
SKUFF
SKUFF
IT'S SO STRONG, IT'S LIFTING ALL OF US!
WHRR

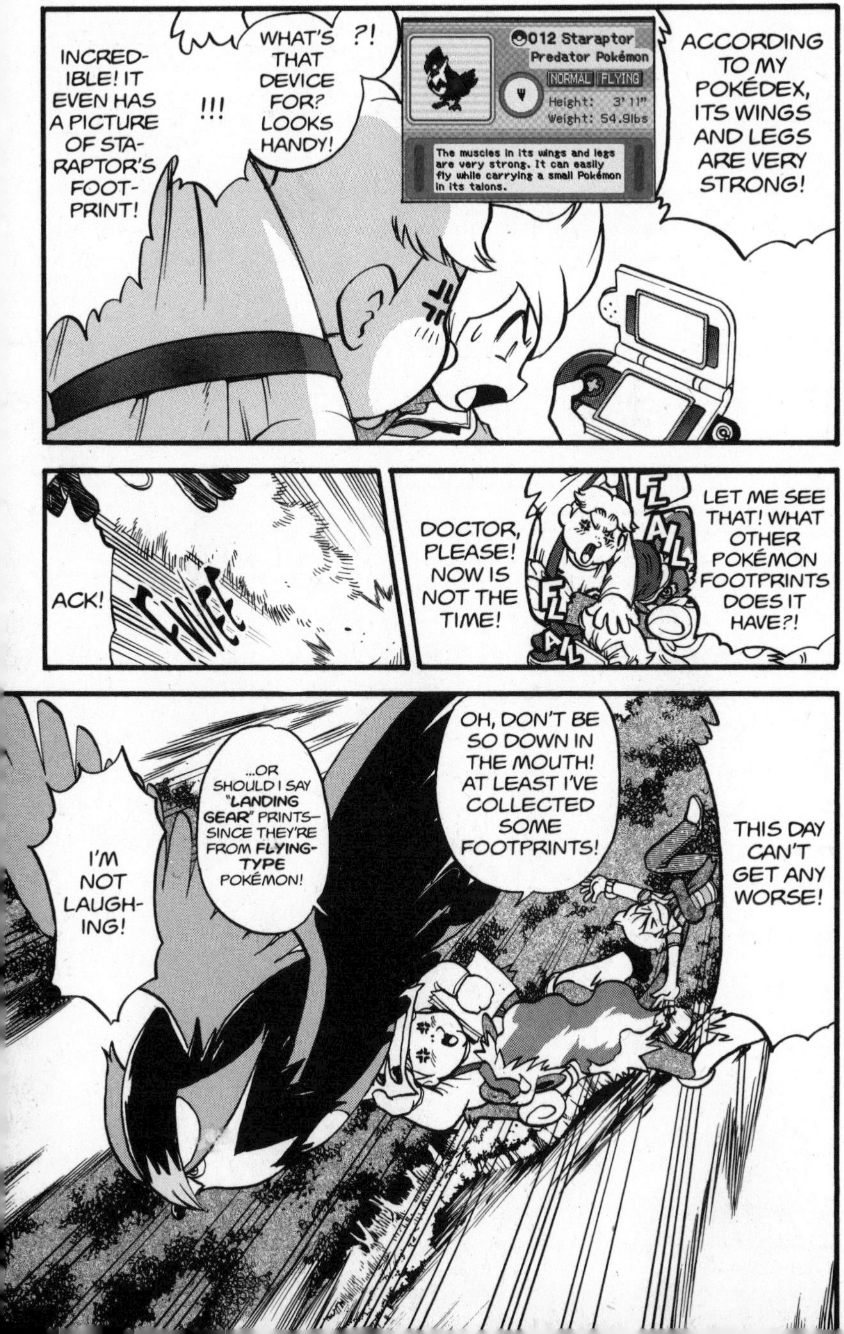
ACCORDING TO MY POKÉDEX, ITS WINGS AND LEGS ARE VERY STRONG!
012 Staraptor
Predator Pokémon
NORMAL FLYING
Height: 3' 11"
Weight: 54.9lbs
The muscles in its wings and legs are very strong. It can easily fly while carrying a small Pokémon in its talons.
?!
WHAT'S THAT DEVICE FOR? LOOKS HANDY!
!!!
INCREDIBLE! IT EVEN HAS A PICTURE OF STARAPTOR'S FOOTPRINT!
LET ME SEE THAT! WHAT OTHER POKÉMON FOOTPRINTS DOES IT HAVE?!
FLAIL
DOCTOR, PLEASE! NOW IS NOT THE TIME!
FLAIL
ACK!
THIS DAY CAN'T GET ANY WORSE!
OH, DON'T BE SO DOWN IN THE MOUTH! AT LEAST I'VE COLLECTED SOME FOOTPRINTS!
...OR SHOULD I SAY "LANDING GEAR" PRINTS—SINCE THEY'RE FROM FLYING-TYPE POKÉMON!
I'M NOT LAUGHING!

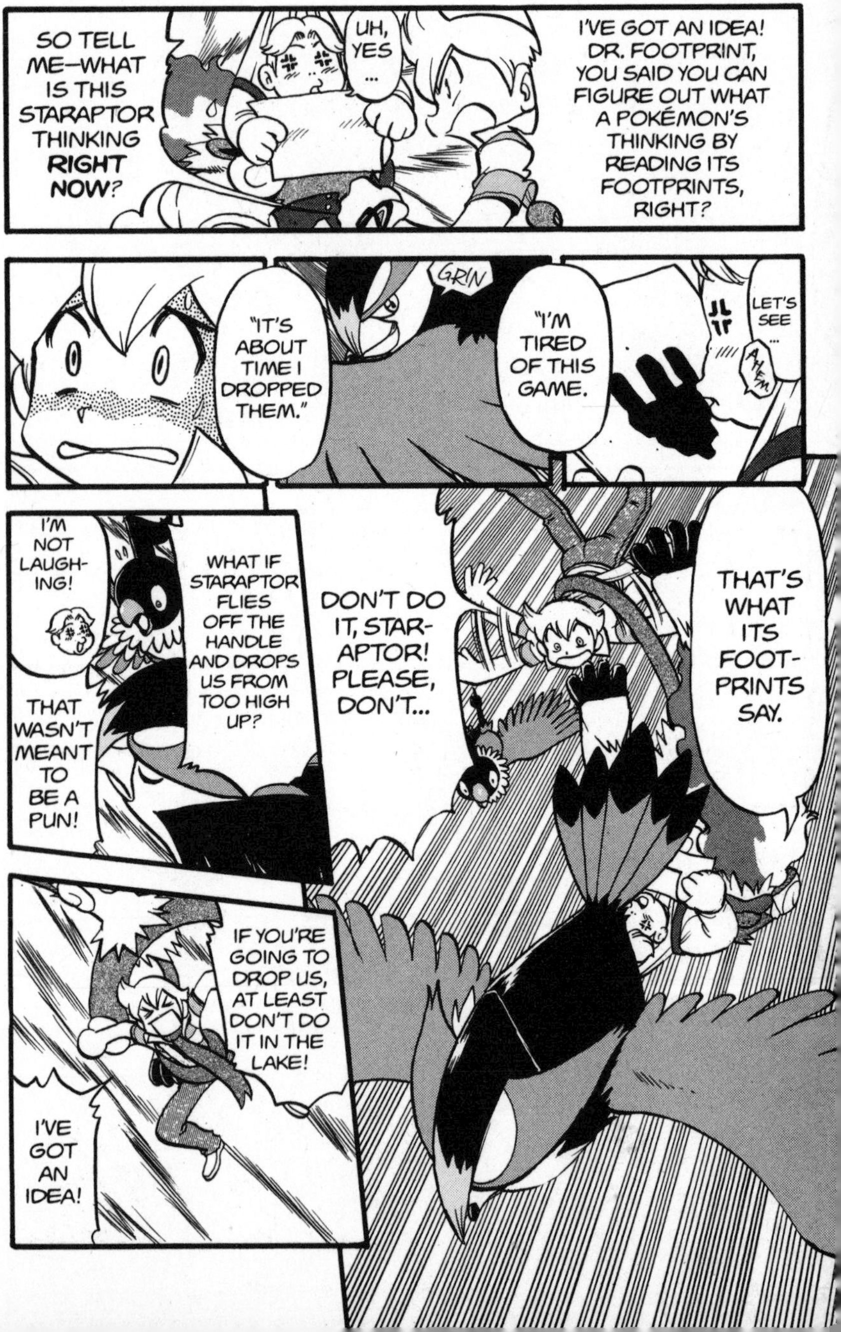
I'VE GOT AN IDEA! DR. FOOTPRINT, YOU SAID YOU CAN FIGURE OUT WHAT A POKÉMON'S THINKING BY READING ITS FOOTPRINTS, RIGHT?
UH, YES ...
SO TELL ME—WHAT IS THIS STARAPTOR THINKING RIGHT NOW?
LET'S SEE ...
AHEM
"I'M TIRED OF THIS GAME.
GRIN
"IT'S ABOUT TIME I DROPPED THEM."
THAT'S WHAT ITS FOOTPRINTS SAY.
DON'T DO IT, STARAPTOR! PLEASE, DON'T...
WHAT IF STARAPTOR FLIES OFF THE HANDLE AND DROPS US FROM TOO HIGH UP?
I'M NOT LAUGHING!
THAT WASN'T MEANT TO BE A PUN!
IF YOU'RE GOING TO DROP US, AT LEAST DON'T DO IT IN THE LAKE!
I'VE GOT AN IDEA!

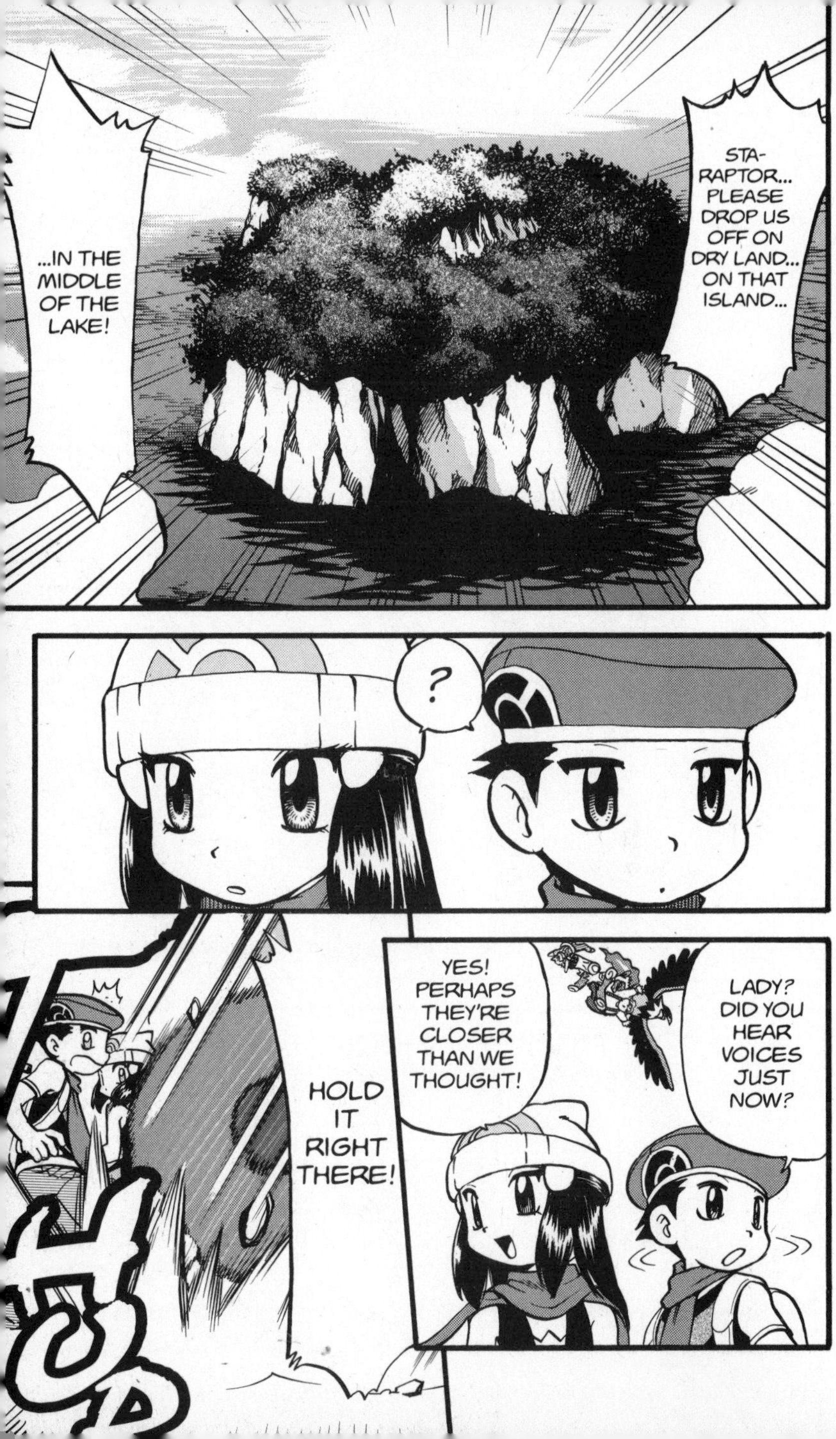
STA-RAPTOR... PLEASE DROP US OFF ON DRY LAND... ON THAT ISLAND...
...IN THE MIDDLE OF THE LAKE!
?
LADY? DID YOU HEAR VOICES JUST NOW?
YES! PERHAPS THEY'RE CLOSER THAN WE THOUGHT!
HOLD IT RIGHT THERE!

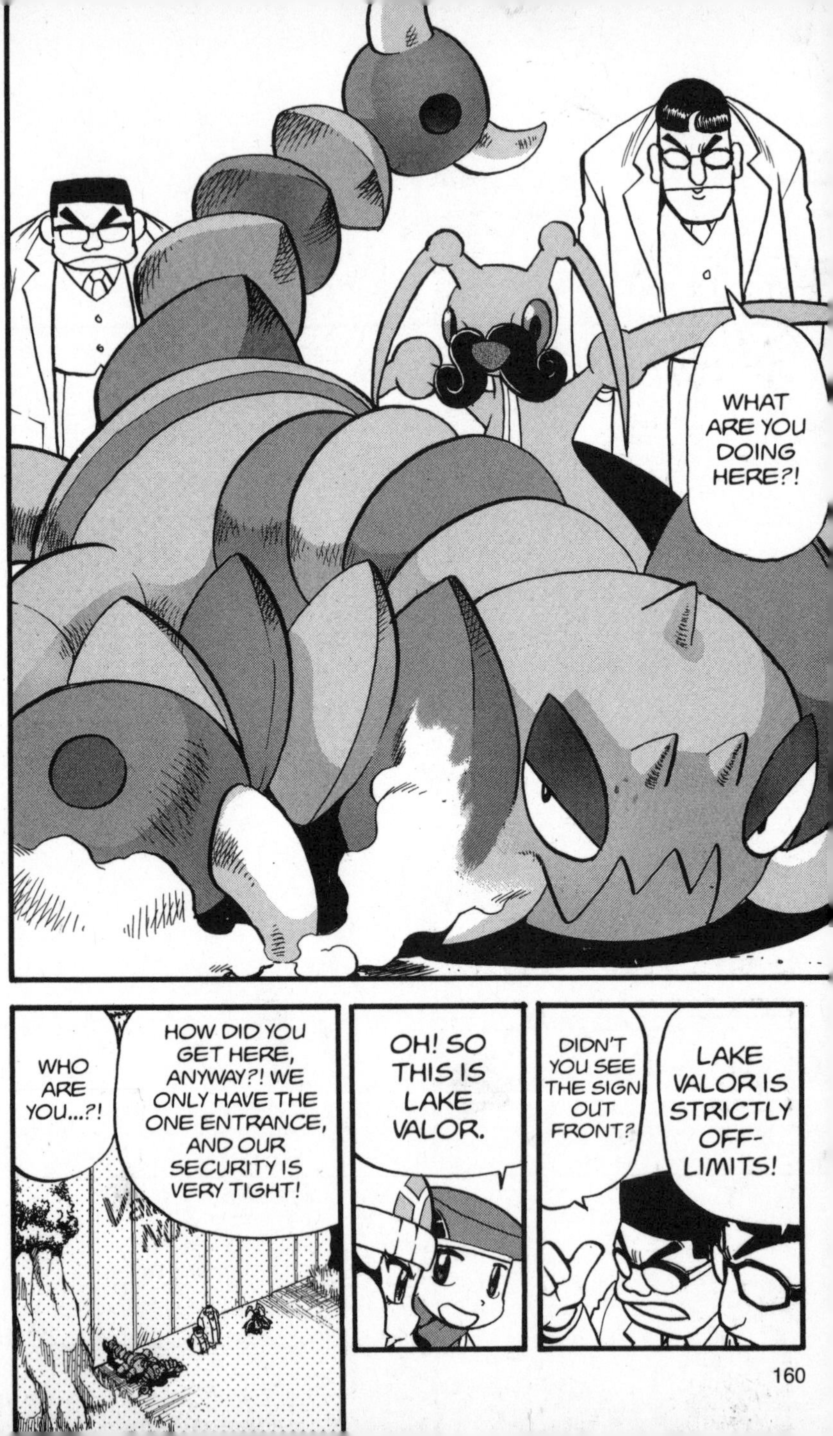
WHAT ARE YOU DOING HERE?!
LAKE VALOR IS STRICTLY OFF-LIMITS!
DIDN'T YOU SEE THE SIGN OUT FRONT?
OH! SO THIS IS LAKE VALOR.
HOW DID YOU GET HERE, ANYWAY?! WE ONLY HAVE THE ONE ENTRANCE, AND OUR SECURITY IS VERY TIGHT!
WHO ARE YOU...?!

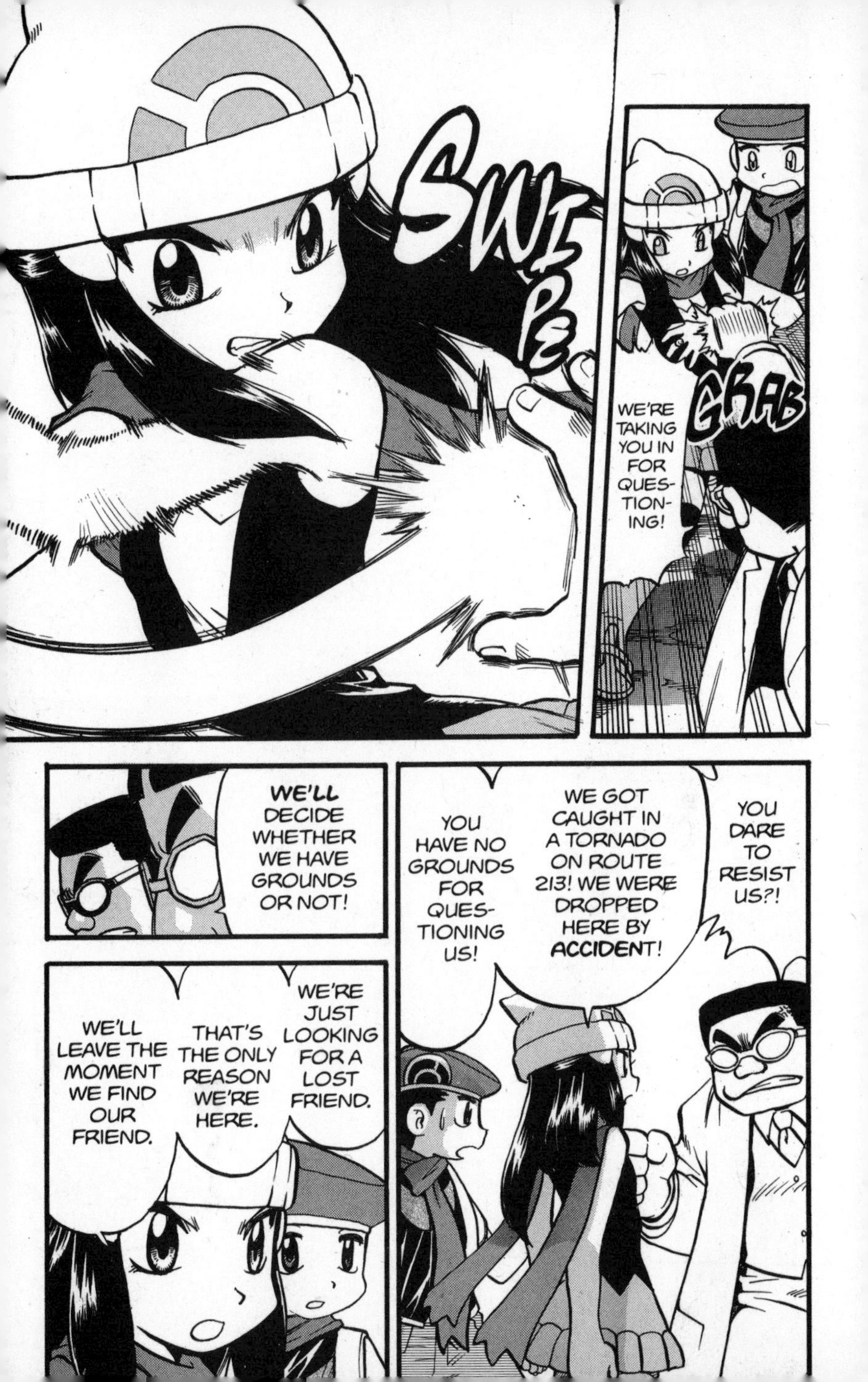

WE'RE TAKING YOU IN FOR QUES-TION-ING!
GRAB
SWIPE
YOU DARE TO RESIST US?!
WE GOT CAUGHT IN A TORNADO ON ROUTE 213! WE WERE DROPPED HERE BY **ACCIDENT**!
YOU HAVE NO GROUNDS FOR QUES-TIONING US!
WE'LL DECIDE WHETHER WE HAVE GROUNDS OR NOT!
WE'RE JUST LOOKING FOR A LOST FRIEND.
THAT'S THE ONLY REASON WE'RE HERE.
WE'LL LEAVE THE MOMENT WE FIND OUR FRIEND.

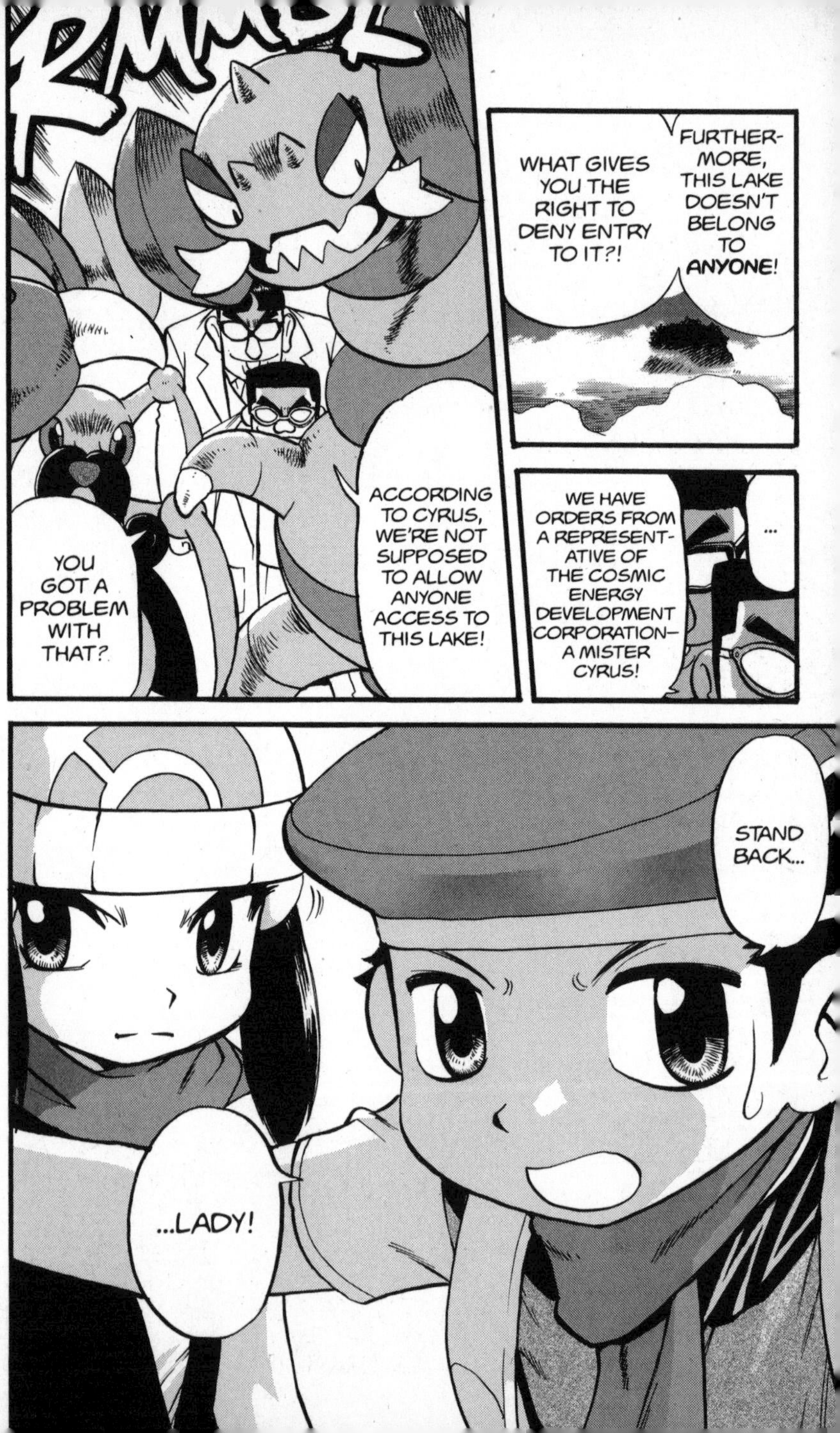
FURTHERMORE, THIS LAKE DOESN'T BELONG TO **ANYONE**!
WHAT GIVES YOU THE RIGHT TO DENY ENTRY TO IT?!
...
WE HAVE ORDERS FROM A REPRESENTATIVE OF THE COSMIC ENERGY DEVELOPMENT CORPORATION—A MISTER CYRUS!
ACCORDING TO CYRUS, WE'RE NOT SUPPOSED TO ALLOW ANYONE ACCESS TO THIS LAKE!
YOU GOT A PROBLEM WITH THAT?
STAND BACK...
...LADY!

ADVENTURE MAP

◄ Lake Valor ◄

Oreburgh VS Roark Coal Badge	Eterna VS Gardenia Forest Badge	Veilstone VS Maylene Cobble Badge					

LADY

DIAMOND

PEARL

▶ TRU

Torterra ♂

▶ LAX

Munchlax ♂

▶ CHIMLER

Infernape ♂

▶ CHATLER

Chatot ♂

▶ EMPOLEON

Empoleon ♀

▶ PONYTA

Ponyta ♂

26

Dramatic
Drapion
&
Crafty
Kricketune 2

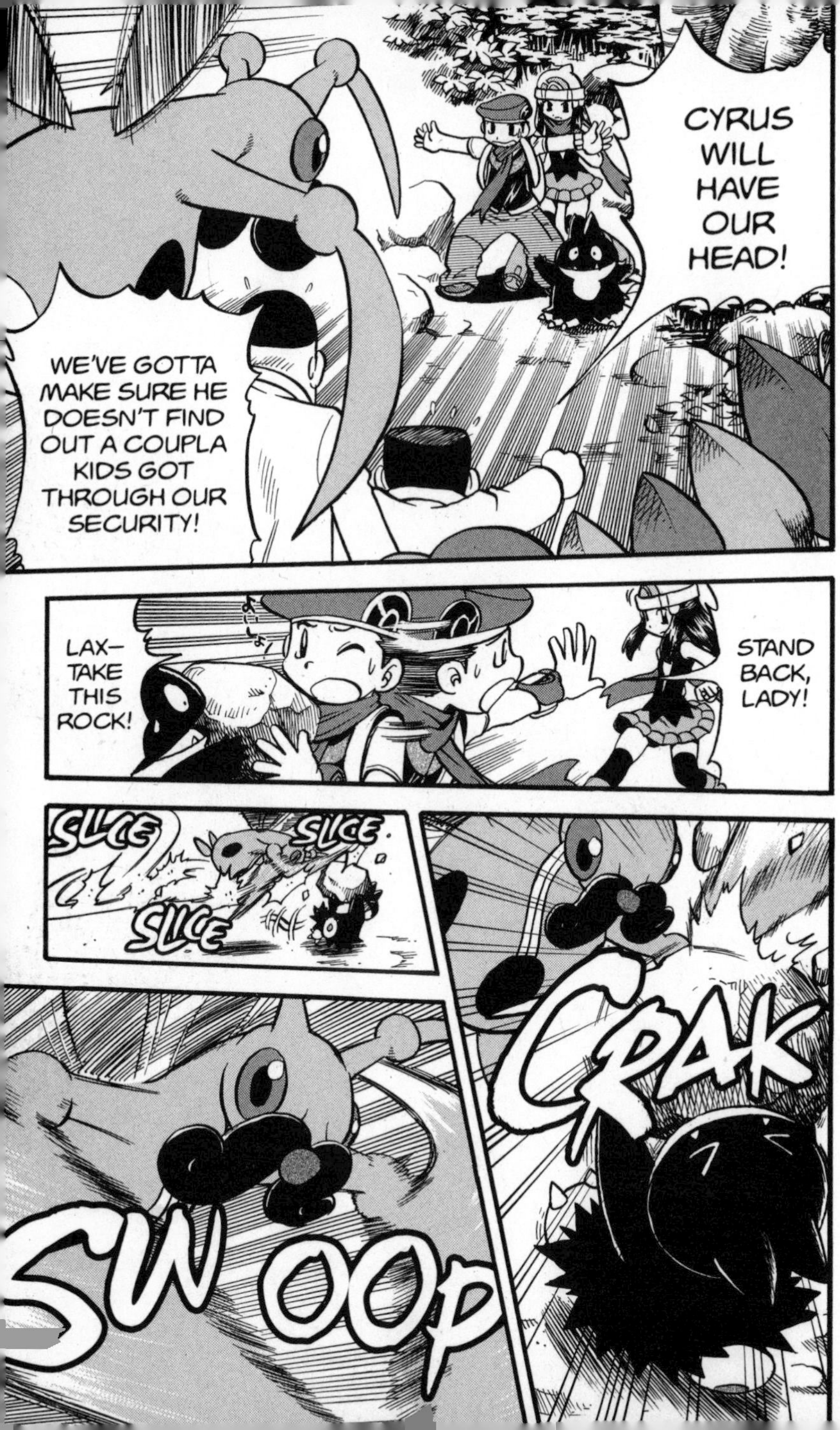
CYRUS WILL HAVE OUR HEAD!
WE'VE GOTTA MAKE SURE HE DOESN'T FIND OUT A COUPLA KIDS GOT THROUGH OUR SECURITY!
STAND BACK, LADY!
LAX—TAKE THIS ROCK!
CRAK
SLICE
SLICE
SLICE
SWOOP

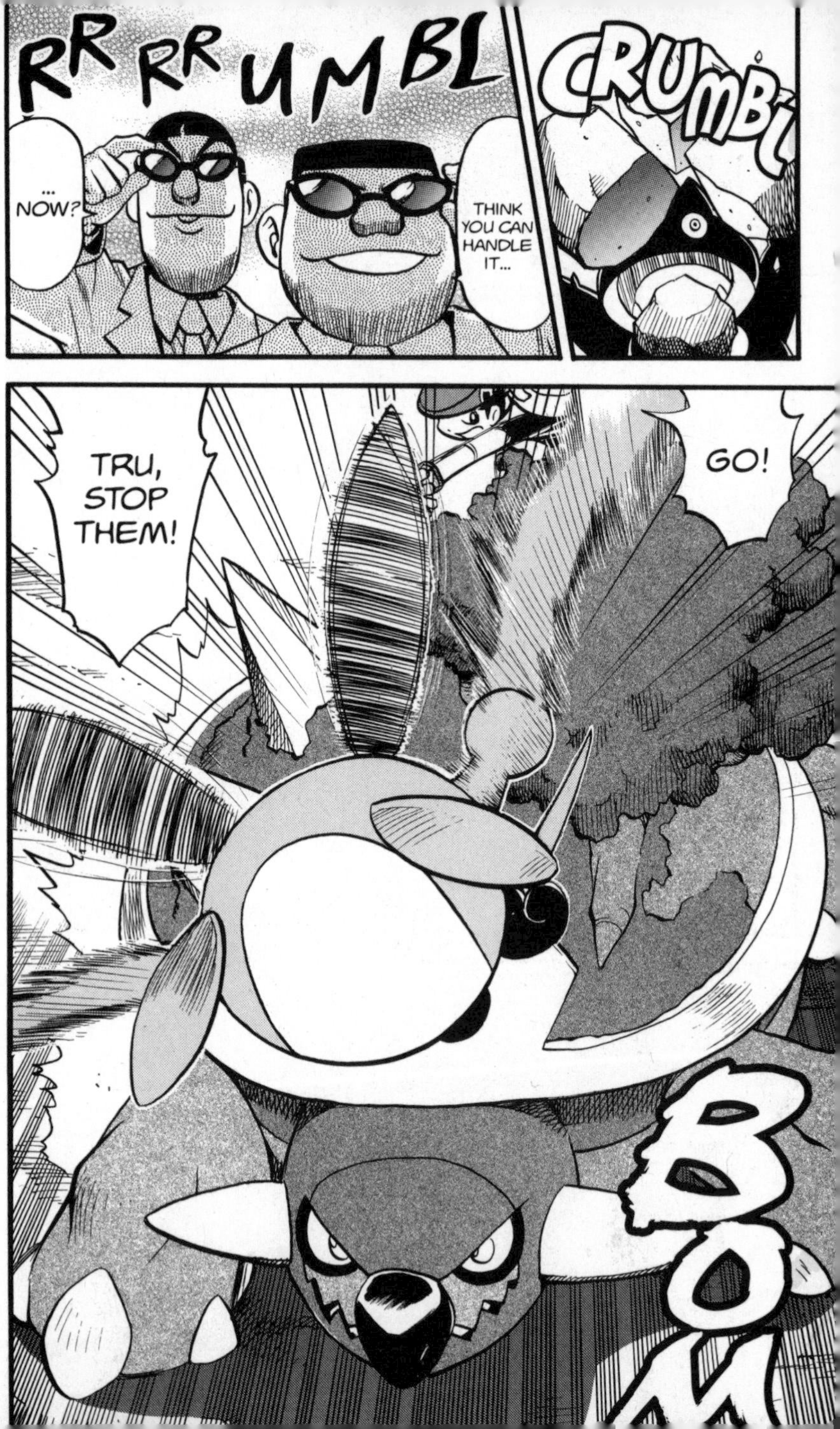
CRUMBL
RR RR UMBL
THINK YOU CAN HANDLE IT...
... NOW?
GO!
TRU, STOP THEM!
BOOM

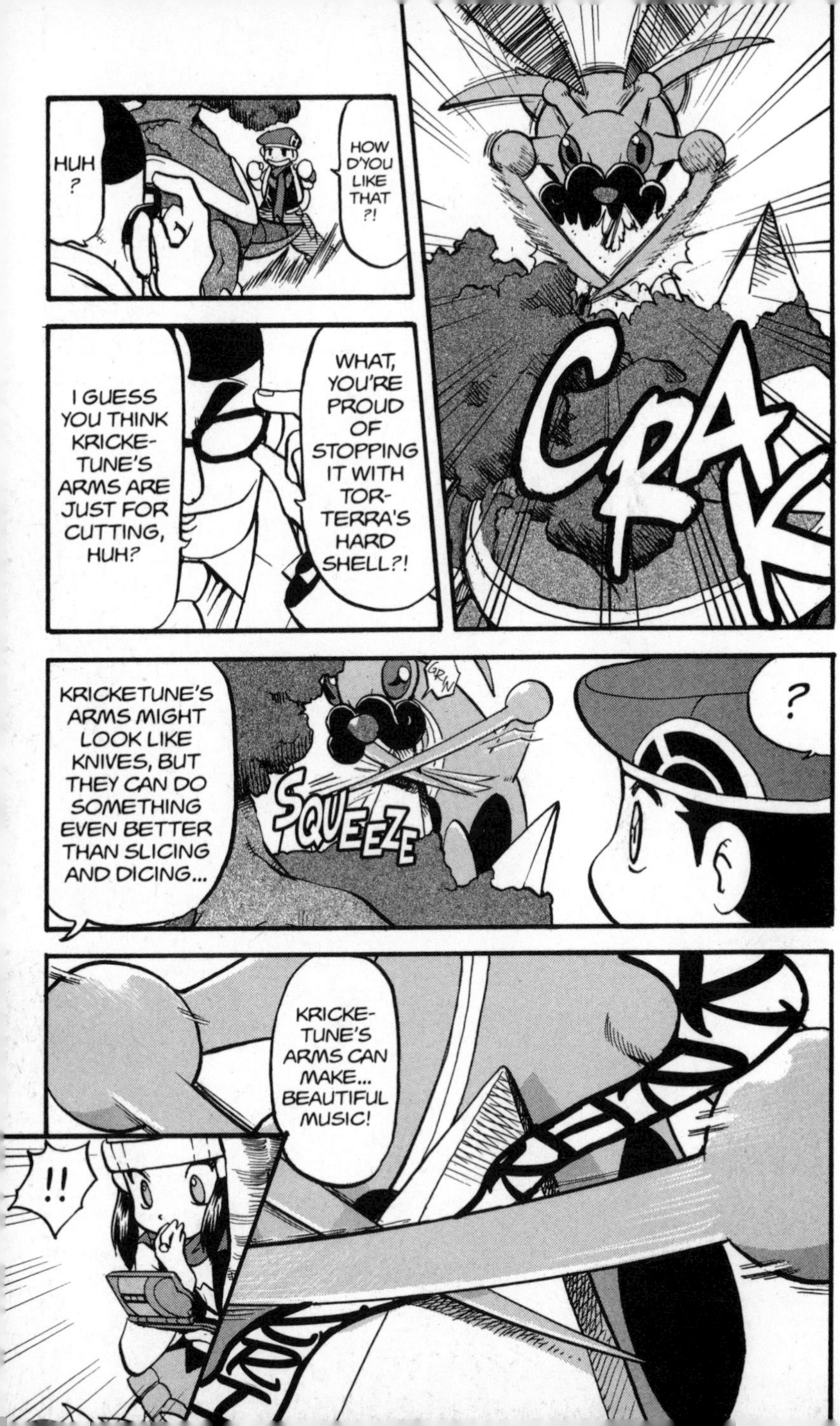
CRAK
HOW D'YOU LIKE THAT?!
HUH?
WHAT, YOU'RE PROUD OF STOPPING IT WITH TOR-TERRA'S HARD SHELL?!
I GUESS YOU THINK KRICKE-TUNE'S ARMS ARE JUST FOR CUTTING, HUH?
?
GRIN
SQUEEZE
KRICKETUNE'S ARMS MIGHT LOOK LIKE KNIVES, BUT THEY CAN DO SOMETHING EVEN BETTER THAN SLICING AND DICING...
KRICKE-TUNE'S ARMS CAN MAKE... BEAUTIFUL MUSIC!
!!

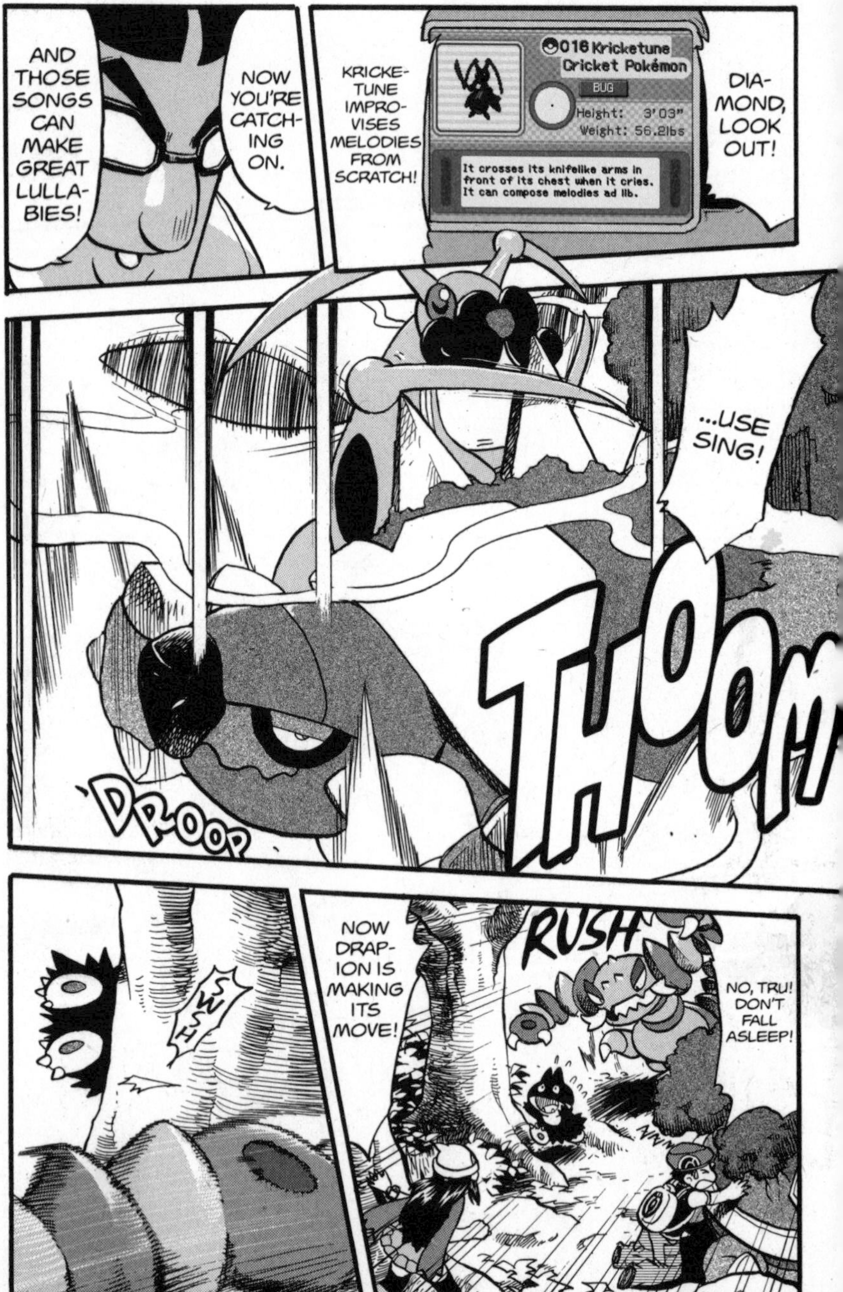
DIAMOND, LOOK OUT!
016 Kricketune
Cricket Pokémon
BUG
Height: 3'03"
Weight: 56.2lbs
It crosses its knifelike arms in front of its chest when it cries. It can compose melodies ad lib.
KRICKETUNE IMPROVISES MELODIES FROM SCRATCH!
NOW YOU'RE CATCHING ON.
AND THOSE SONGS CAN MAKE GREAT LULLABIES!
...USE SING!
THOOM
DROOP
NO, TRU! DON'T FALL ASLEEP!
RUSH
NOW DRAPION IS MAKING ITS MOVE!
SWSH

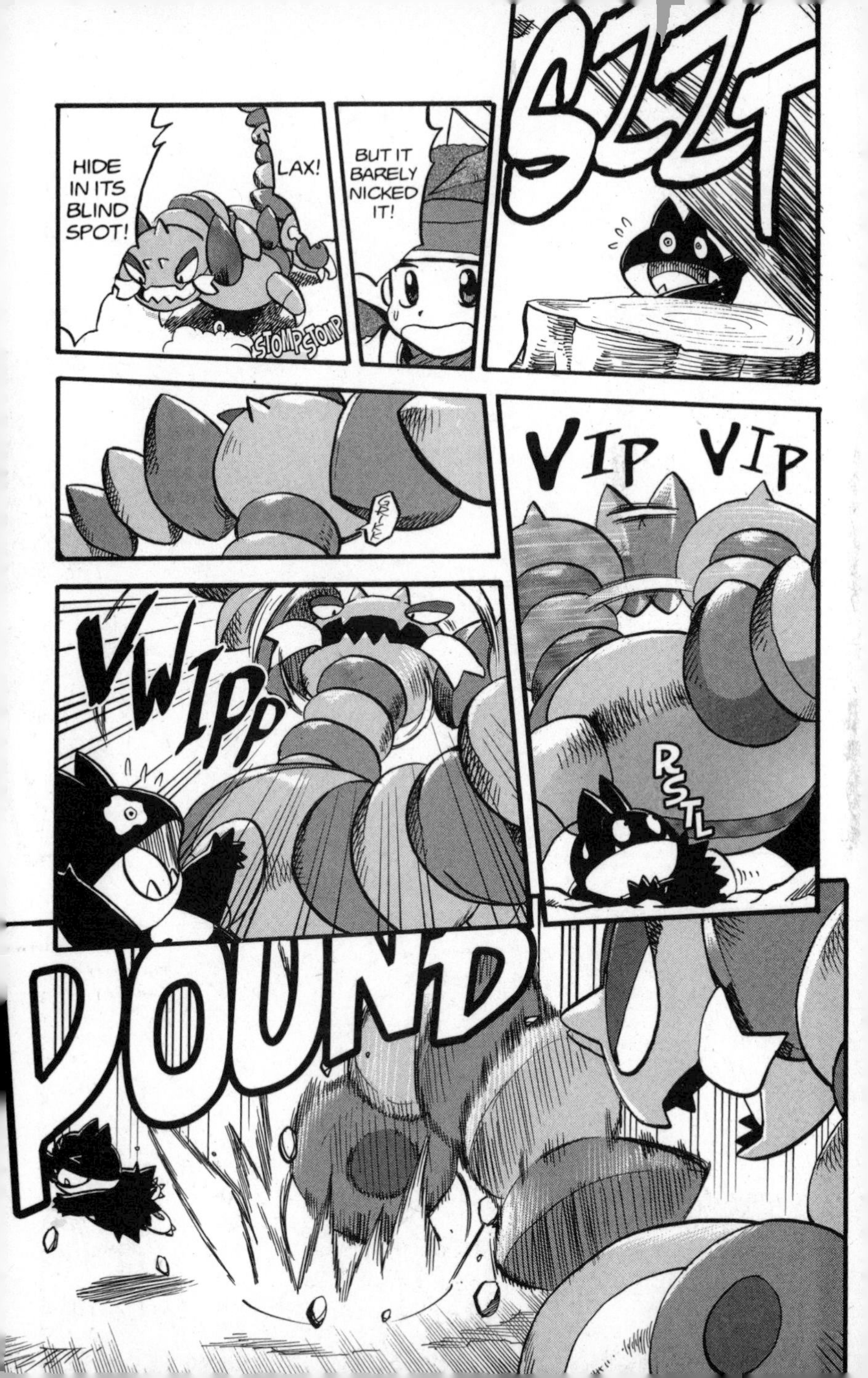
SZZT
BUT IT BARELY NICKED IT!
LAX!
HIDE IN ITS BLIND SPOT!
STOMP STOMP
VIP VIP
RSTL
GRIKK
VWIPP
POUND

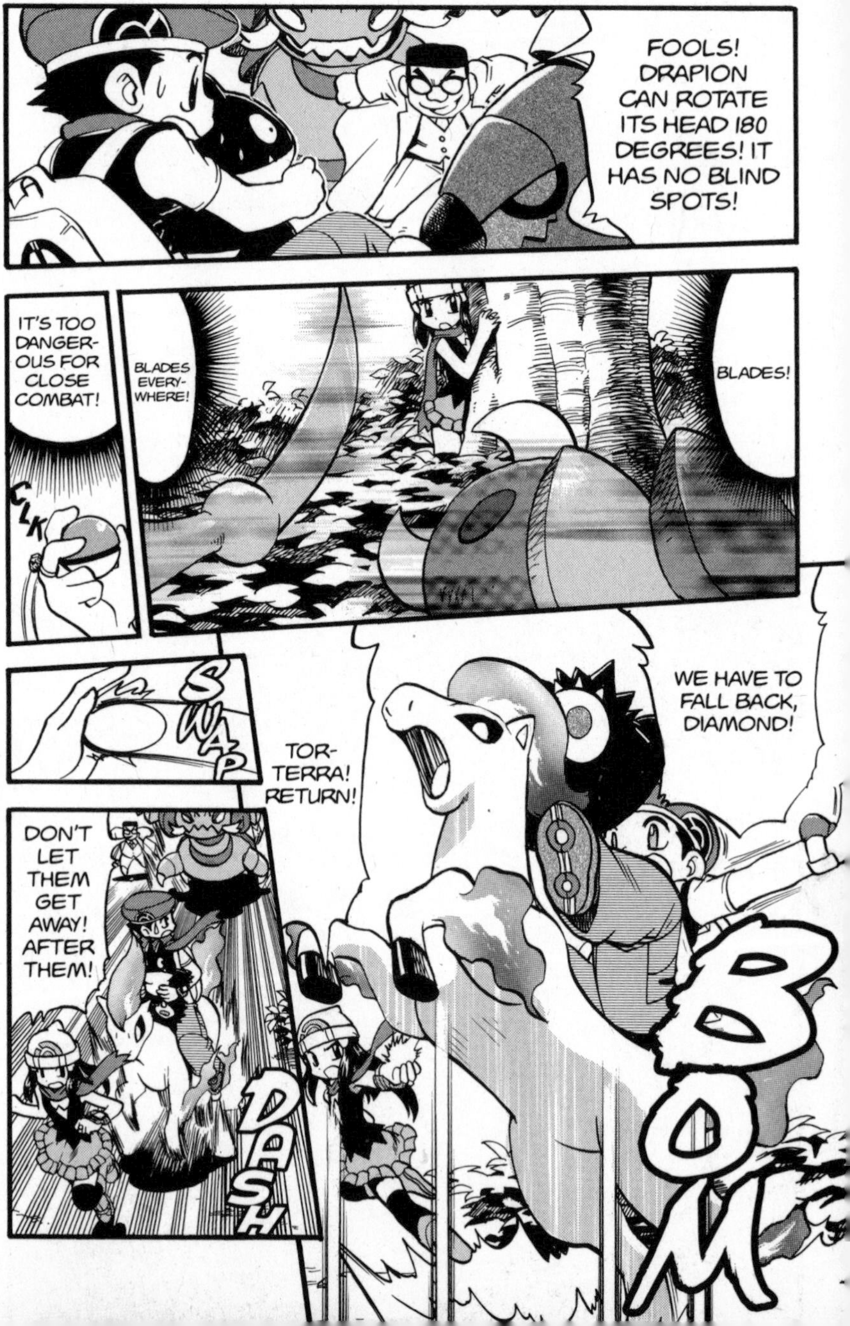
FOOLS! DRAPION CAN ROTATE ITS HEAD 180 DEGREES! IT HAS NO BLIND SPOTS!
BLADES!
BLADES EVERYWHERE!
IT'S TOO DANGEROUS FOR CLOSE COMBAT!
CLK
WE HAVE TO FALL BACK, DIAMOND!
TORTERRA! RETURN!
BOOM
SWAP
DON'T LET THEM GET AWAY! AFTER THEM!
DASH

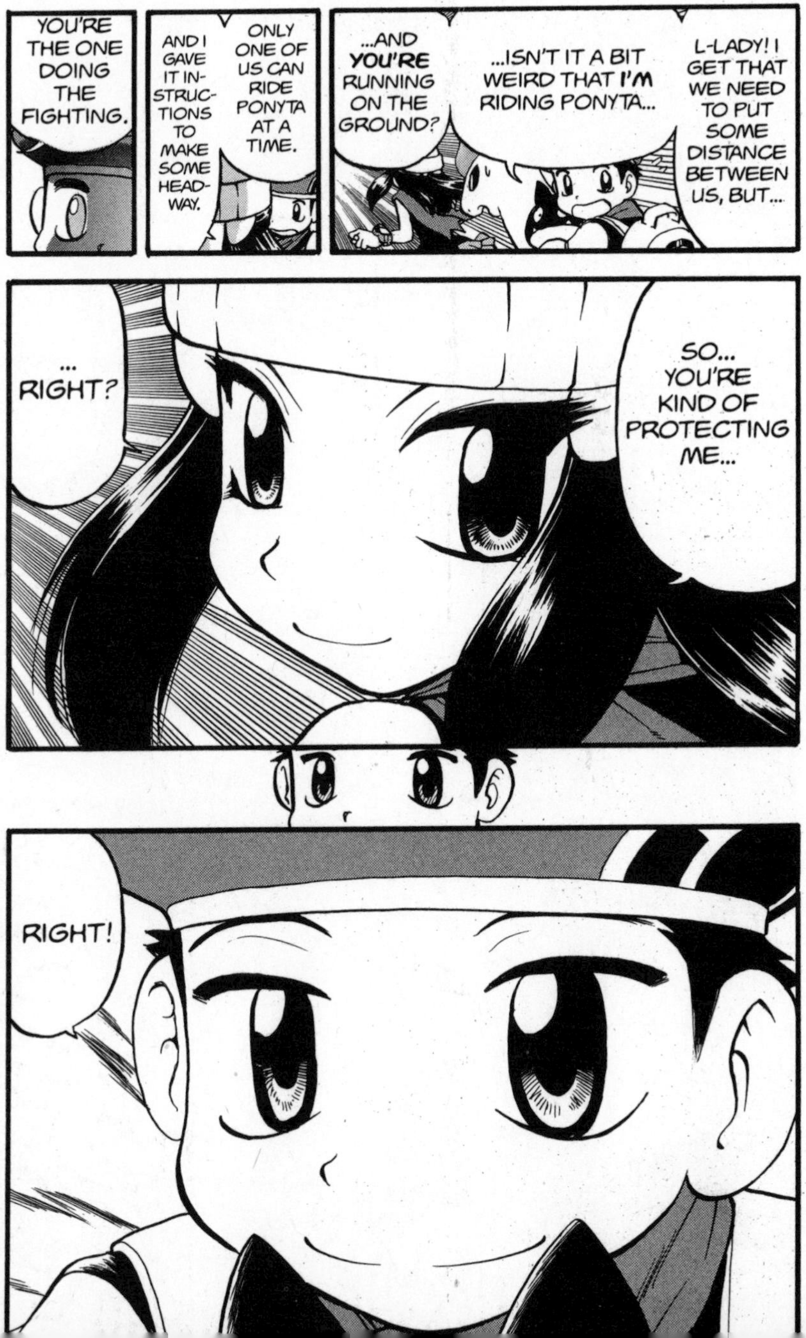
L-LADY! I GET THAT WE NEED TO PUT SOME DISTANCE BETWEEN US, BUT...
...ISN'T IT A BIT WEIRD THAT **I'M** RIDING PONYTA...
...AND **YOU'RE** RUNNING ON THE GROUND?
ONLY ONE OF US CAN RIDE PONYTA AT A TIME.
AND I GAVE IT INSTRUCTIONS TO MAKE SOME HEADWAY.
YOU'RE THE ONE DOING THE FIGHTING.
SO... YOU'RE KIND OF PROTECTING ME...
... RIGHT?
RIGHT!

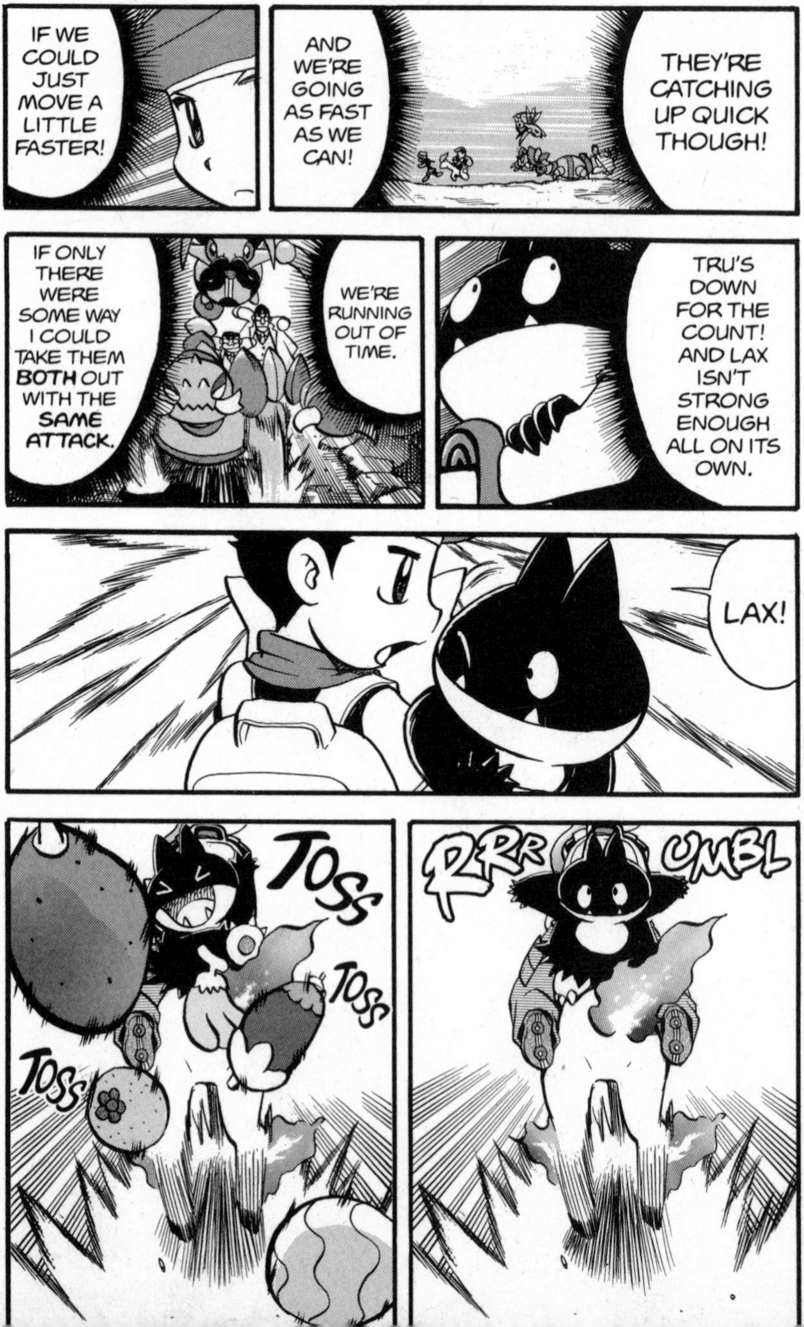
THEY'RE CATCHING UP QUICK THOUGH!
AND WE'RE GOING AS FAST AS WE CAN!
IF WE COULD JUST MOVE A LITTLE FASTER!
TRU'S DOWN FOR THE COUNT! AND LAX ISN'T STRONG ENOUGH ALL ON ITS OWN.
WE'RE RUNNING OUT OF TIME.
IF ONLY THERE WERE SOME WAY I COULD TAKE THEM **BOTH** OUT WITH THE **SAME** ATTACK.
LAX!
RRRUMBL
TOSS
TOSS
TOSS

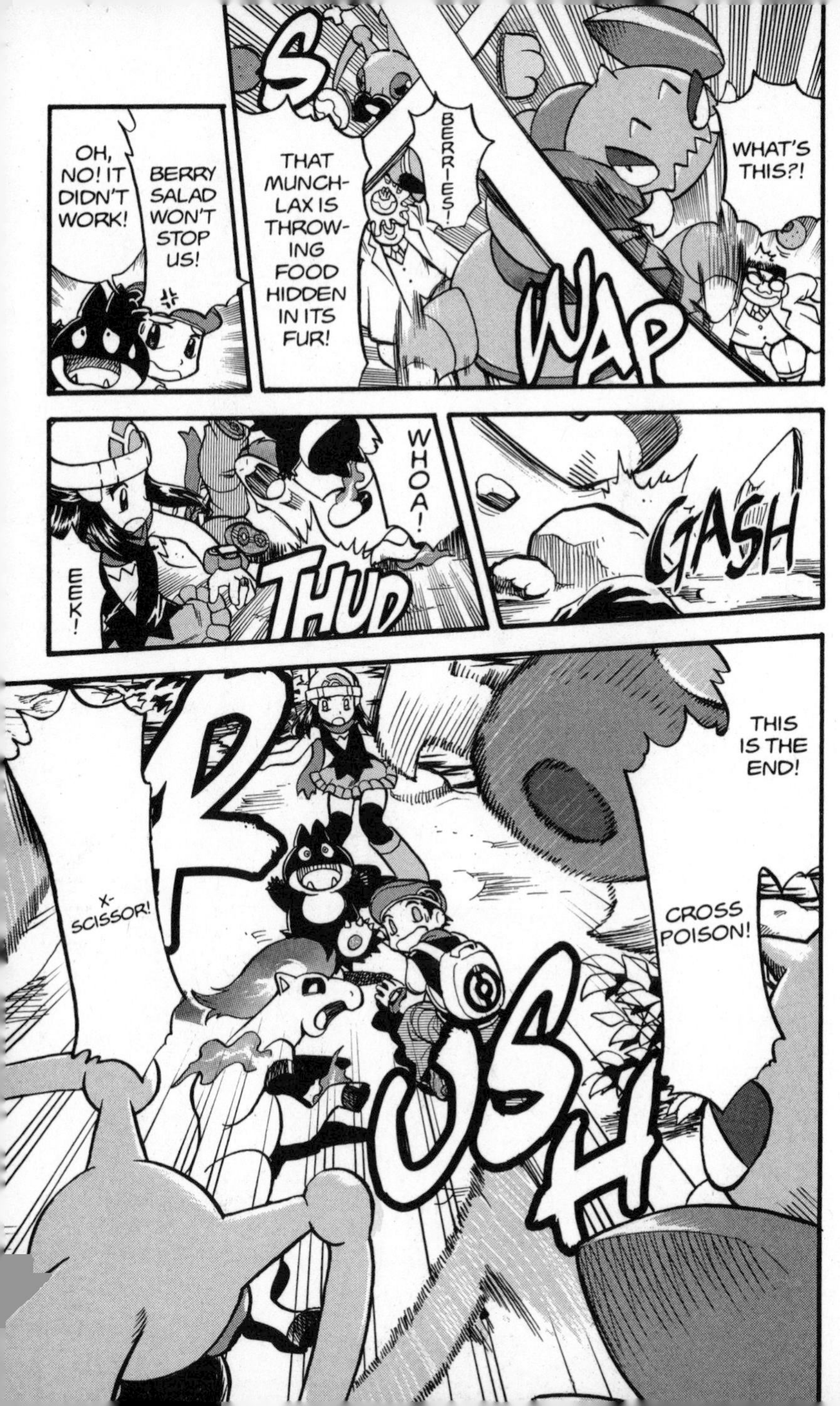
WHAT'S THIS?!
WAP
BERRIES!
S
THAT MUNCH-LAX IS THROW-ING FOOD HIDDEN IN ITS FUR!
BERRY SALAD WON'T STOP US!
OH, NO! IT DIDN'T WORK!
GASH
WHOA!
THUD
EEK!
THIS IS THE END!
CROSS POISON!
X-SCISSOR!
RUSH

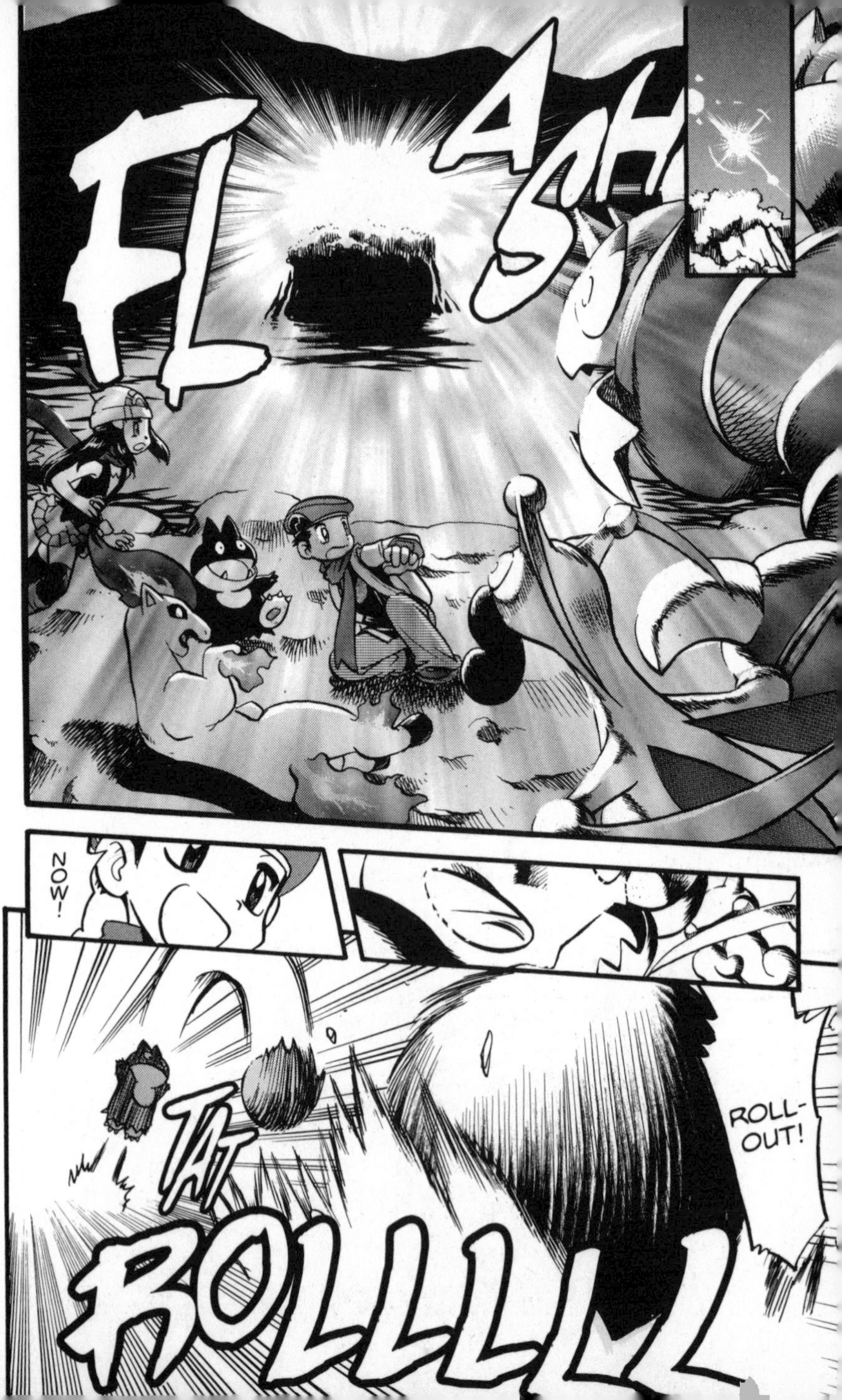
FLAASH
NOW!
ROLL-OUT!
TAT
ROLLLL

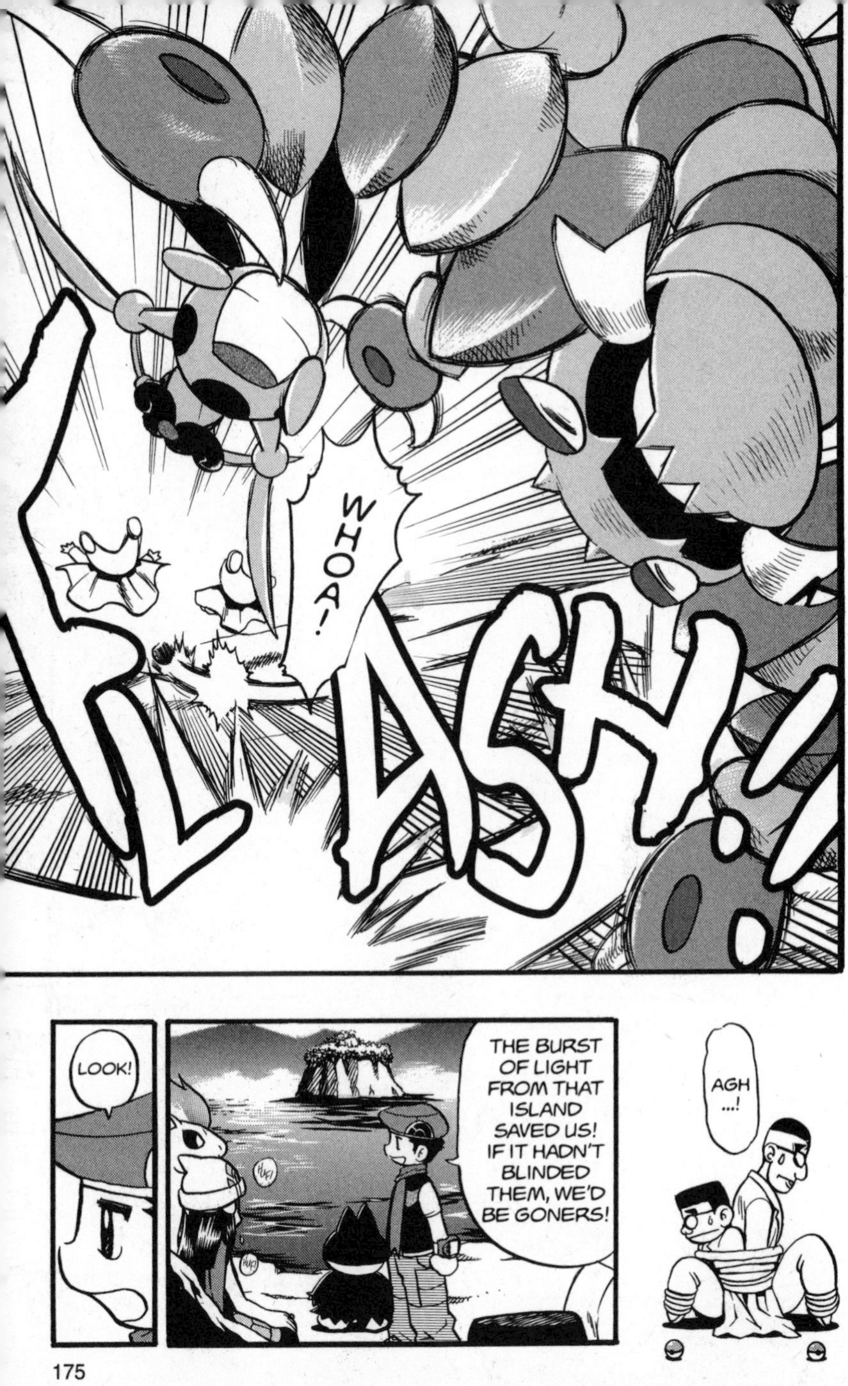
WHOA…!
FLASH!!
AGH…!
THE BURST OF LIGHT FROM THAT ISLAND SAVED US! IF IT HADN'T BLINDED THEM, WE'D BE GONERS!
LOOK!

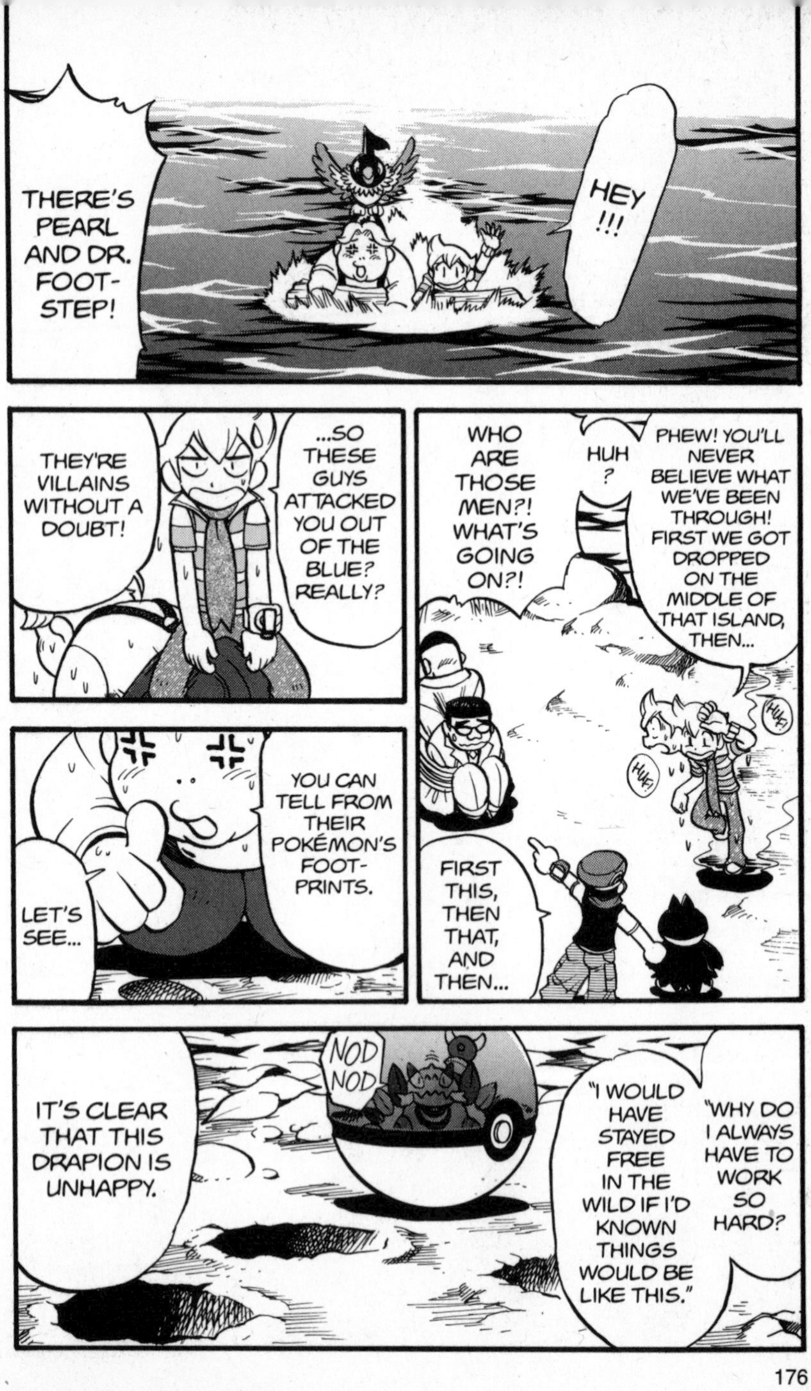
HEY !!!
THERE'S PEARL AND DR. FOOT-STEP!
PHEW! YOU'LL NEVER BELIEVE WHAT WE'VE BEEN THROUGH! FIRST WE GOT DROPPED ON THE MIDDLE OF THAT ISLAND, THEN...
HUH ?
WHO ARE THOSE MEN?! WHAT'S GOING ON?!
FIRST THIS, THEN THAT, AND THEN...
...SO THESE GUYS ATTACKED YOU OUT OF THE BLUE? REALLY?
THEY'RE VILLAINS WITHOUT A DOUBT!
YOU CAN TELL FROM THEIR POKÉMON'S FOOT-PRINTS.
LET'S SEE...
NOD NOD
"WHY DO I ALWAYS HAVE TO WORK SO HARD?
"I WOULD HAVE STAYED FREE IN THE WILD IF I'D KNOWN THINGS WOULD BE LIKE THIS."
IT'S CLEAR THAT THIS DRAPION IS UNHAPPY.

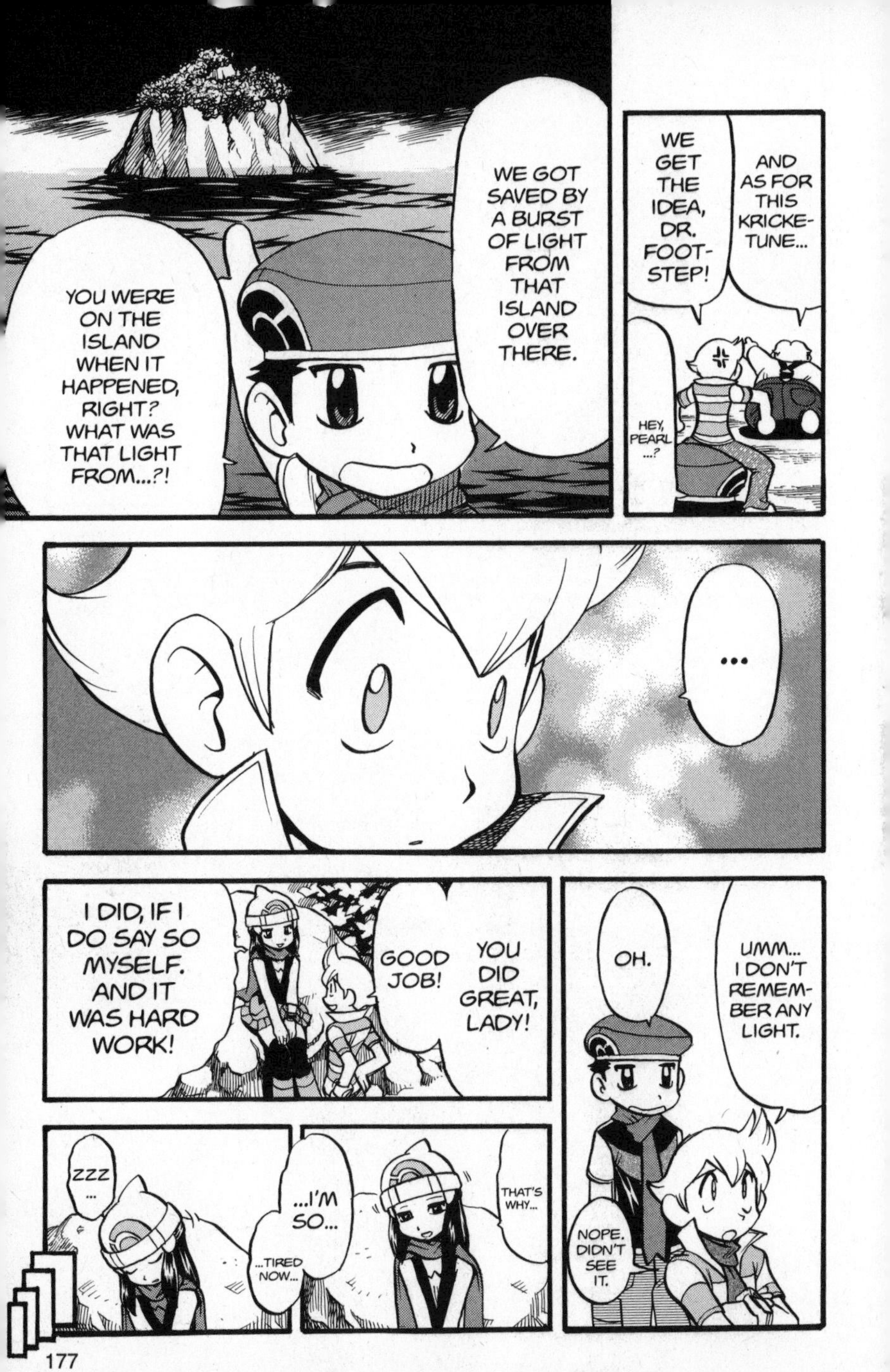
AND AS FOR THIS KRICKE-TUNE...
WE GET THE IDEA, DR. FOOT-STEP!
HEY, PEARL...?
WE GOT SAVED BY A BURST OF LIGHT FROM THAT ISLAND OVER THERE.
YOU WERE ON THE ISLAND WHEN IT HAPPENED, RIGHT? WHAT WAS THAT LIGHT FROM...?!
...
UMM... I DON'T REMEM-BER ANY LIGHT.
OH.
NOPE. DIDN'T SEE IT.
YOU DID GREAT, LADY!
GOOD JOB!
I DID, IF I DO SAY SO MYSELF. AND IT WAS HARD WORK!
THAT'S WHY...
...I'M SO...
...TIRED NOW...
ZZZ...

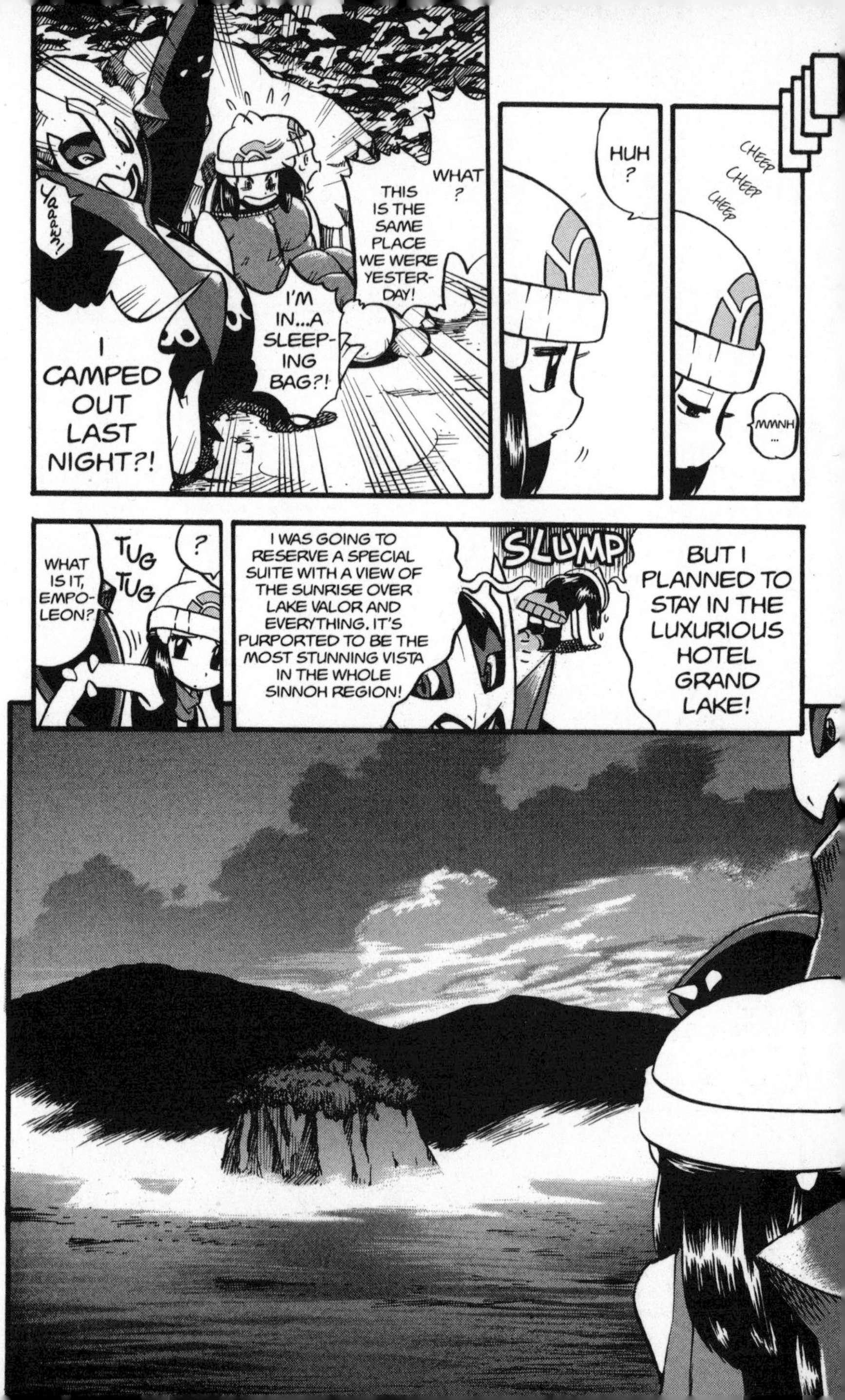
CHEEP CHEEP CHEEP
MMNH...
HUH?
WHAT?
THIS IS THE SAME PLACE WE WERE YESTERDAY!
I'M IN...A SLEEPING BAG?!
I CAMPED OUT LAST NIGHT?!
Yaaawn!
BUT I PLANNED TO STAY IN THE LUXURIOUS HOTEL GRAND LAKE!
SLUMP
I WAS GOING TO RESERVE A SPECIAL SUITE WITH A VIEW OF THE SUNRISE OVER LAKE VALOR AND EVERYTHING. IT'S PURPORTED TO BE THE MOST STUNNING VISTA IN THE WHOLE SINNOH REGION!
?
TUG TUG
WHAT IS IT, EMPOLEON?

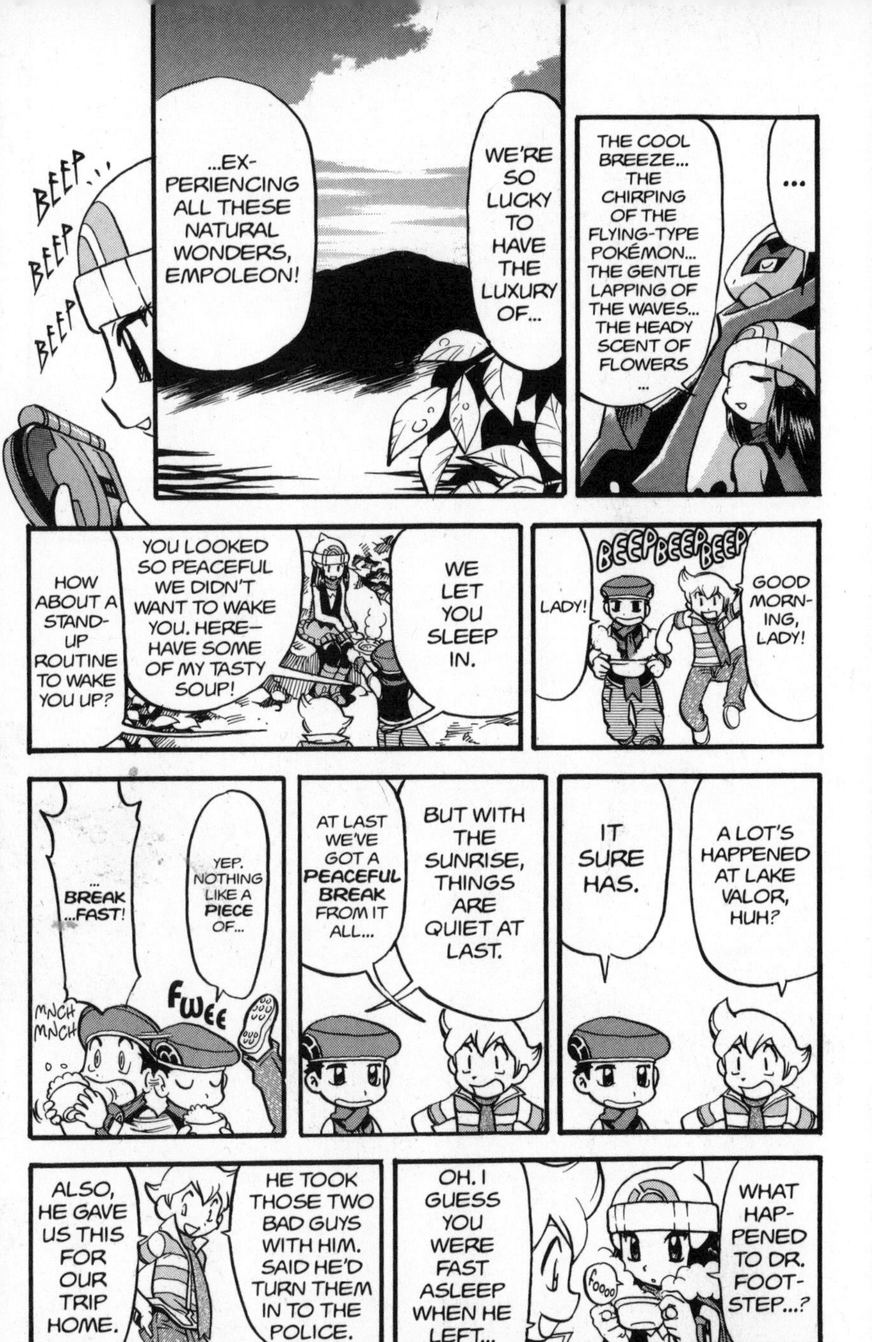
...
THE COOL BREEZE... THE CHIRPING OF THE FLYING-TYPE POKÉMON... THE GENTLE LAPPING OF THE WAVES... THE HEADY SCENT OF FLOWERS...
WE'RE SO LUCKY TO HAVE THE LUXURY OF...
...EX-PERIENCING ALL THESE NATURAL WONDERS, EMPOLEON!
BEEP... BEEP BEEP BEEP
GOOD MORN-ING, LADY!
BEEPBEEPBEEP
LADY!
WE LET YOU SLEEP IN.
YOU LOOKED SO PEACEFUL WE DIDN'T WANT TO WAKE YOU. HERE— HAVE SOME OF MY TASTY SOUP!
HOW ABOUT A STAND-UP ROUTINE TO WAKE YOU UP?
A LOT'S HAPPENED AT LAKE VALOR, HUH?
IT SURE HAS.
BUT WITH THE SUNRISE, THINGS ARE QUIET AT LAST.
AT LAST WE'VE GOT A **PEACEFUL BREAK** FROM IT ALL...
YEP. NOTHING LIKE A **PIECE** OF...
... **BREAK** ...**FAST**!
FWEE
MNCH MNCH
WHAT HAP-PENED TO DR. FOOT-STEP...?
Foooo
OH. I GUESS YOU WERE FAST ASLEEP WHEN HE LEFT...
HE TOOK THOSE TWO BAD GUYS WITH HIM. SAID HE'D TURN THEM IN TO THE POLICE.
ALSO, HE GAVE US THIS FOR OUR TRIP HOME.

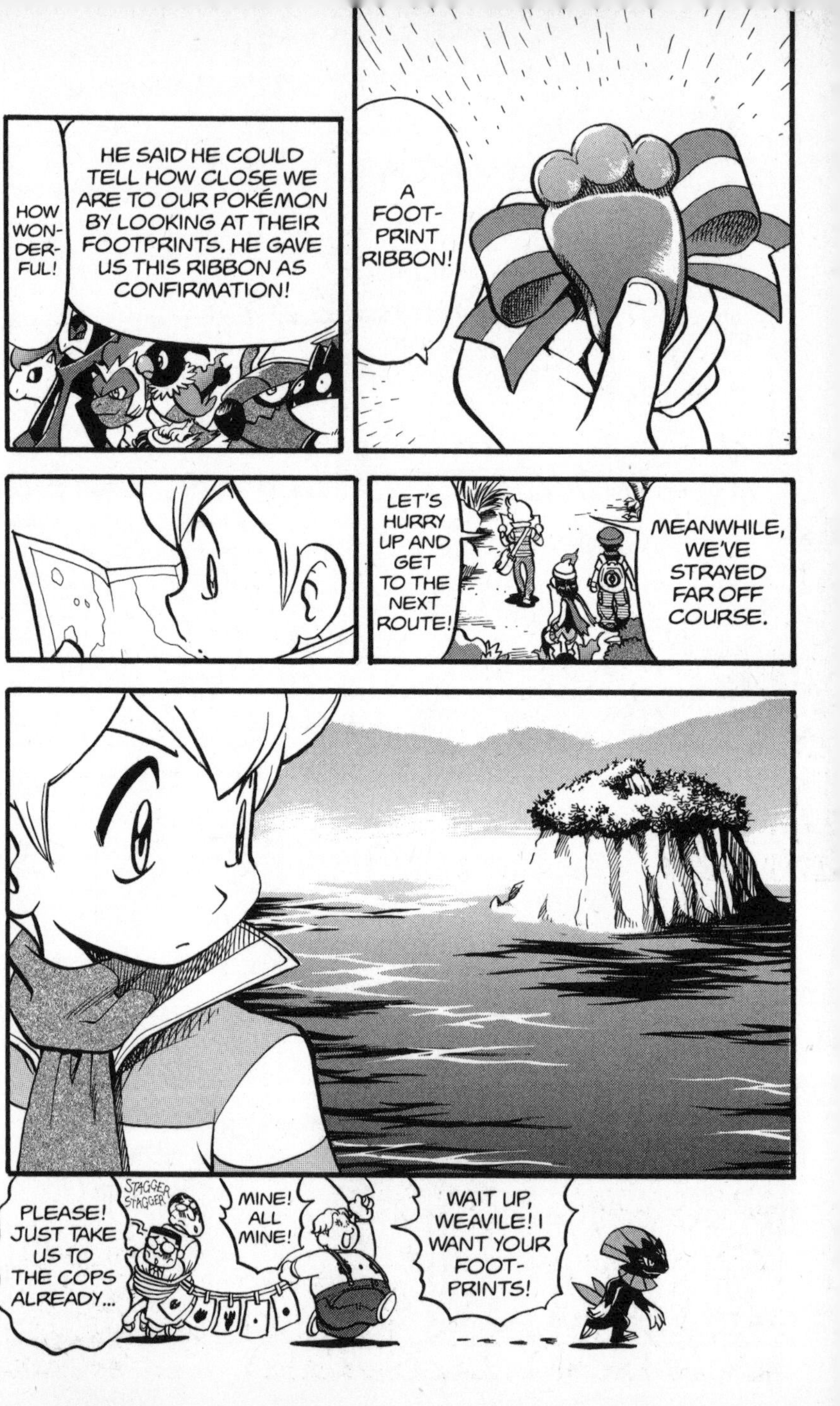
A FOOT-PRINT RIBBON!
HE SAID HE COULD TELL HOW CLOSE WE ARE TO OUR POKÉMON BY LOOKING AT THEIR FOOTPRINTS. HE GAVE US THIS RIBBON AS CONFIRMATION!
HOW WON-DER-FUL!
MEANWHILE, WE'VE STRAYED FAR OFF COURSE.
LET'S HURRY UP AND GET TO THE NEXT ROUTE!
WAIT UP, WEAVILE! I WANT YOUR FOOT-PRINTS!
MINE! ALL MINE!
STAGGER STAGGER
PLEASE! JUST TAKE US TO THE COPS ALREADY...

▶ Route 213 ◀

Oreburgh VS Roark Coal Badge	Eterna VS Gardenia Forest Badge	Veilstone VS Maylene Cobble Badge					

LADY

DIAMOND

PEARL

▶ TRU

Torterra ♂

▶ LAX

Munchlax ♂

▶ CHIMLER

Infernape ♂

▶ CHATLER

Chatot ♂

▶ EMPOLEON

Empoleon ♀

▶ PONYTA

Ponyta ♂

27

A
Skuffle
with
Skorupi

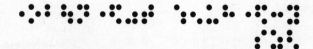

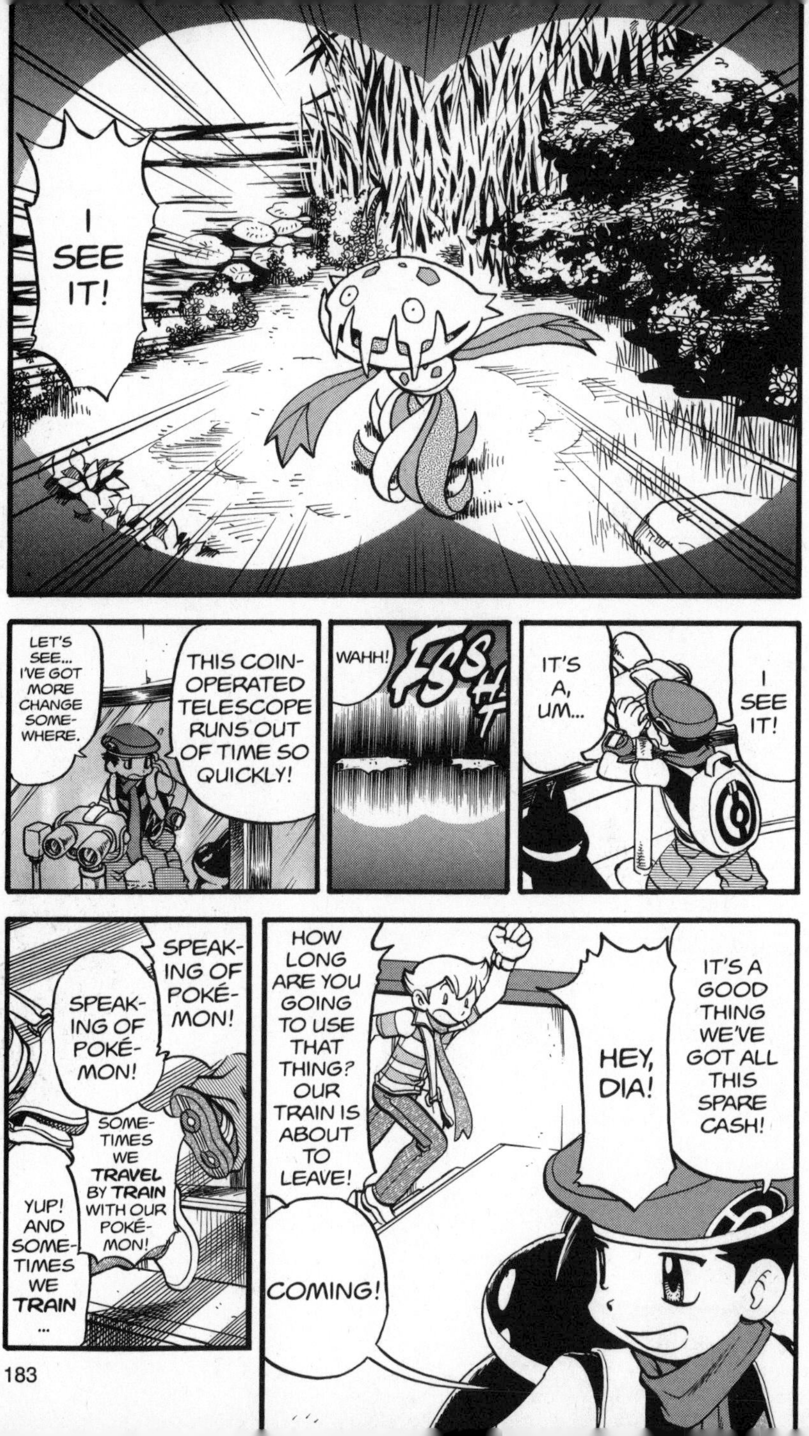
I SEE IT!
I SEE IT!
IT'S A, UM...
WAHH!
FSSHH
THIS COIN-OPERATED TELESCOPE RUNS OUT OF TIME SO QUICKLY!
LET'S SEE... I'VE GOT MORE CHANGE SOMEWHERE.
IT'S A GOOD THING WE'VE GOT ALL THIS SPARE CASH!
HEY, DIA!
HOW LONG ARE YOU GOING TO USE THAT THING? OUR TRAIN IS ABOUT TO LEAVE!
COMING!
SPEAKING OF POKÉMON!
SPEAKING OF POKÉMON!
SOMETIMES WE **TRAVEL** BY **TRAIN** WITH OUR POKÉMON!
YUP! AND SOMETIMES WE **TRAIN**...

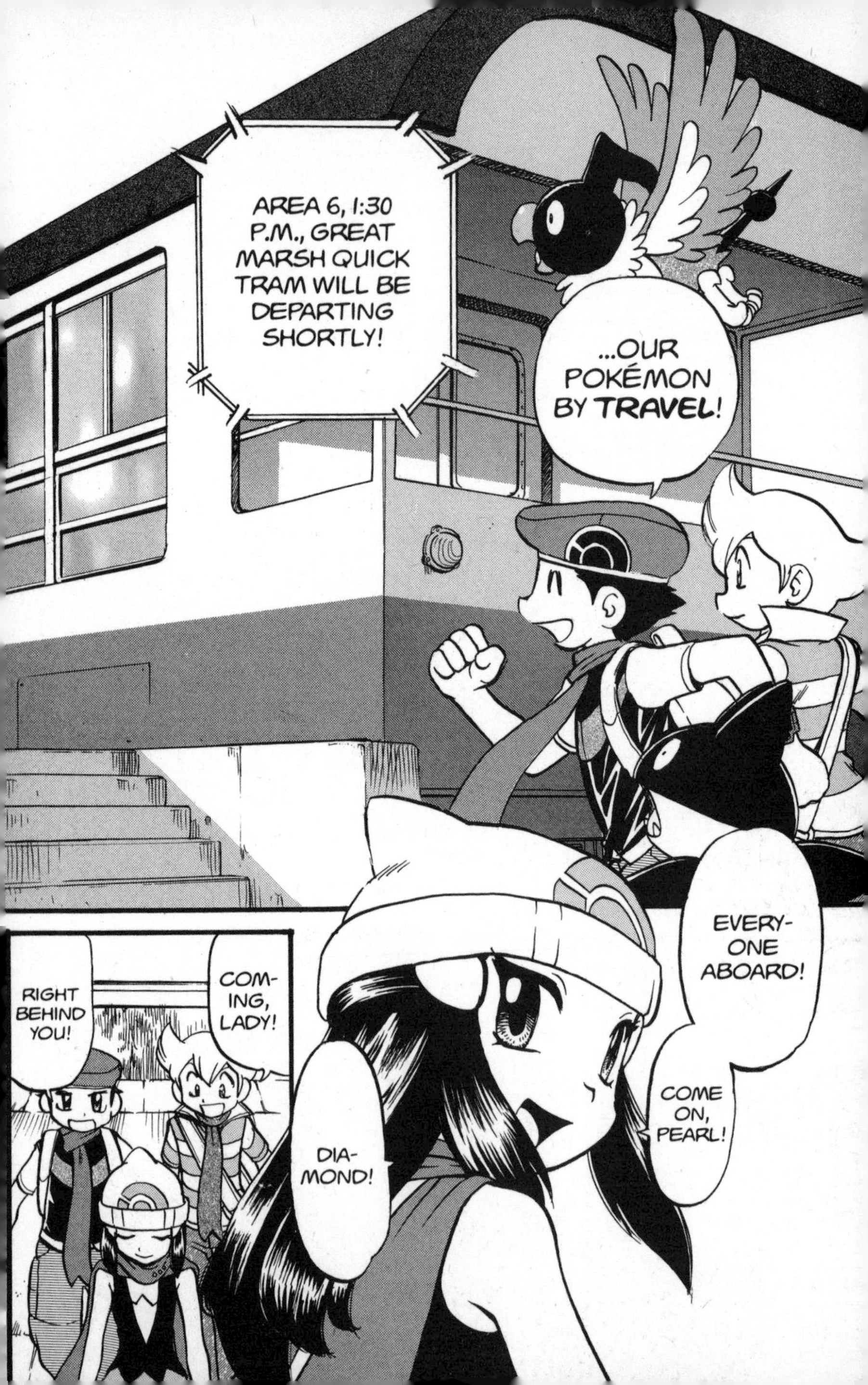
...OUR POKÉMON BY **TRAVEL**!
AREA 6, 1:30 P.M., GREAT MARSH QUICK TRAM WILL BE DEPARTING SHORTLY!
EVERY-ONE ABOARD!
COME ON, PEARL!
DIA-MOND!
COM-ING, LADY!
RIGHT BEHIND YOU!

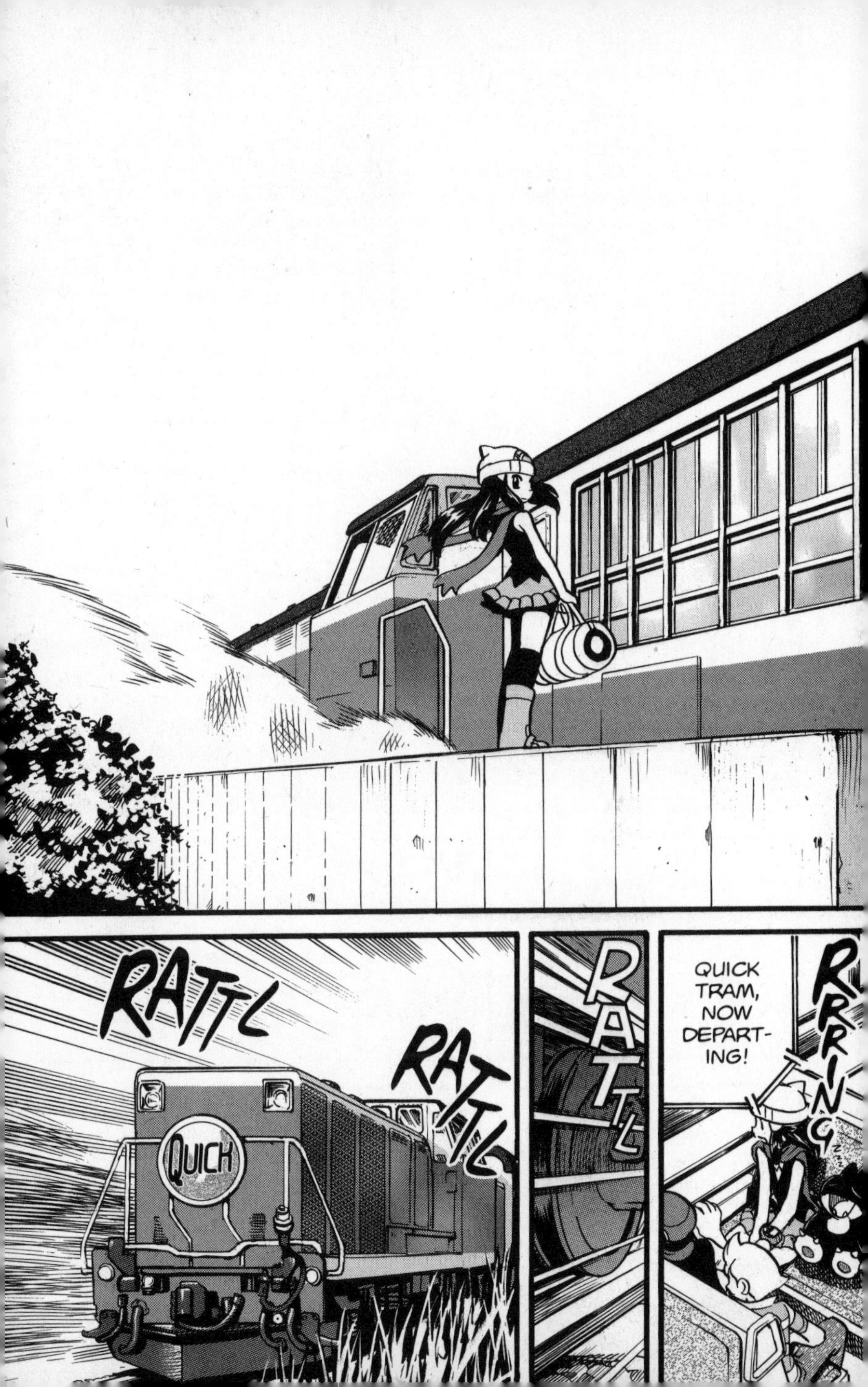
QUICK TRAM, NOW DEPART-ING!
RRRING
RATTL
RATTL
RATTL
QUICK

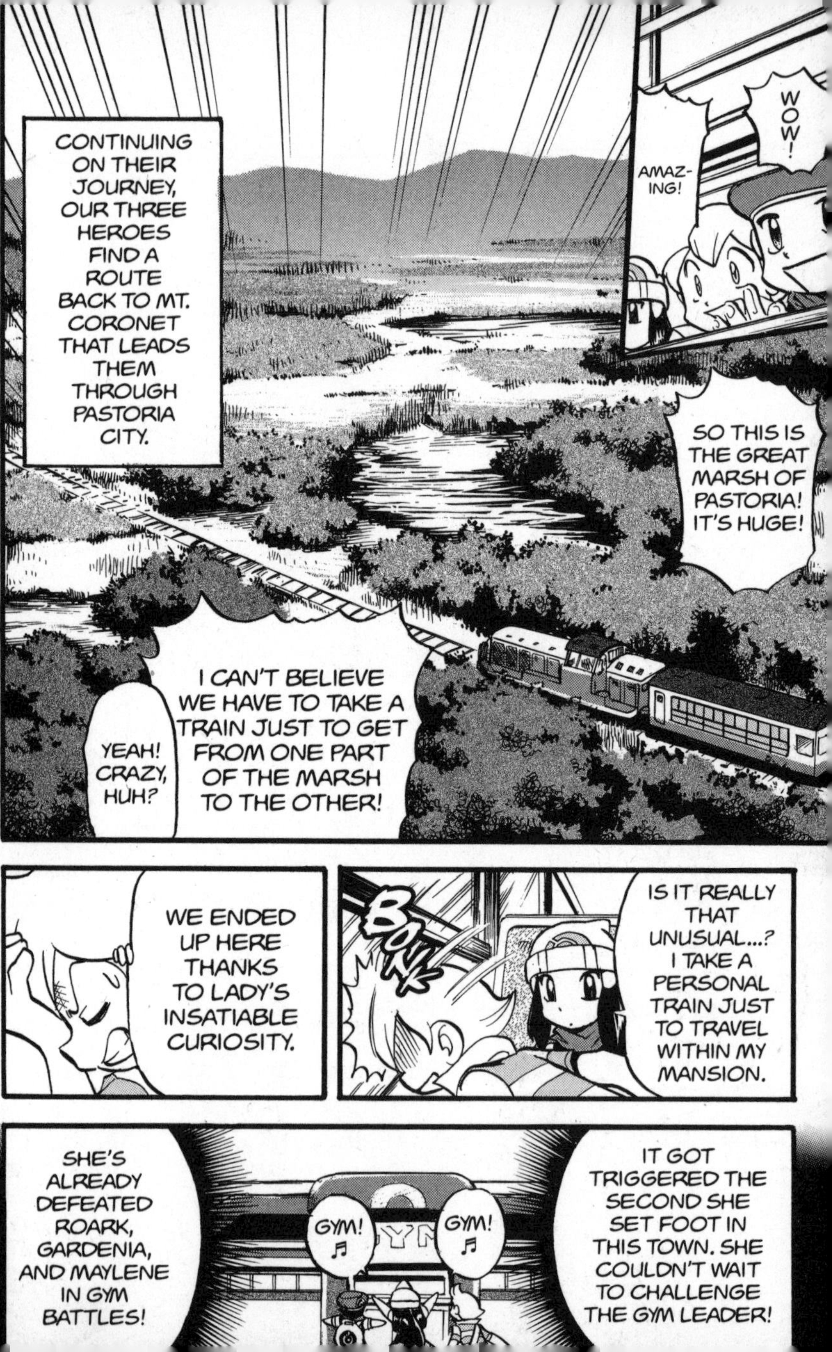
WOW!
AMAZ-ING!
CONTINUING ON THEIR JOURNEY, OUR THREE HEROES FIND A ROUTE BACK TO MT. CORONET THAT LEADS THEM THROUGH PASTORIA CITY.
SO THIS IS THE GREAT MARSH OF PASTORIA! IT'S HUGE!
I CAN'T BELIEVE WE HAVE TO TAKE A TRAIN JUST TO GET FROM ONE PART OF THE MARSH TO THE OTHER!
YEAH! CRAZY, HUH?
BONK
IS IT REALLY THAT UNUSUAL...? I TAKE A PERSONAL TRAIN JUST TO TRAVEL WITHIN MY MANSION.
WE ENDED UP HERE THANKS TO LADY'S INSATIABLE CURIOSITY.
IT GOT TRIGGERED THE SECOND SHE SET FOOT IN THIS TOWN. SHE COULDN'T WAIT TO CHALLENGE THE GYM LEADER!
GYM! ♪
GYM! ♪
SHE'S ALREADY DEFEATED ROARK, GARDENIA, AND MAYLENE IN GYM BATTLES!

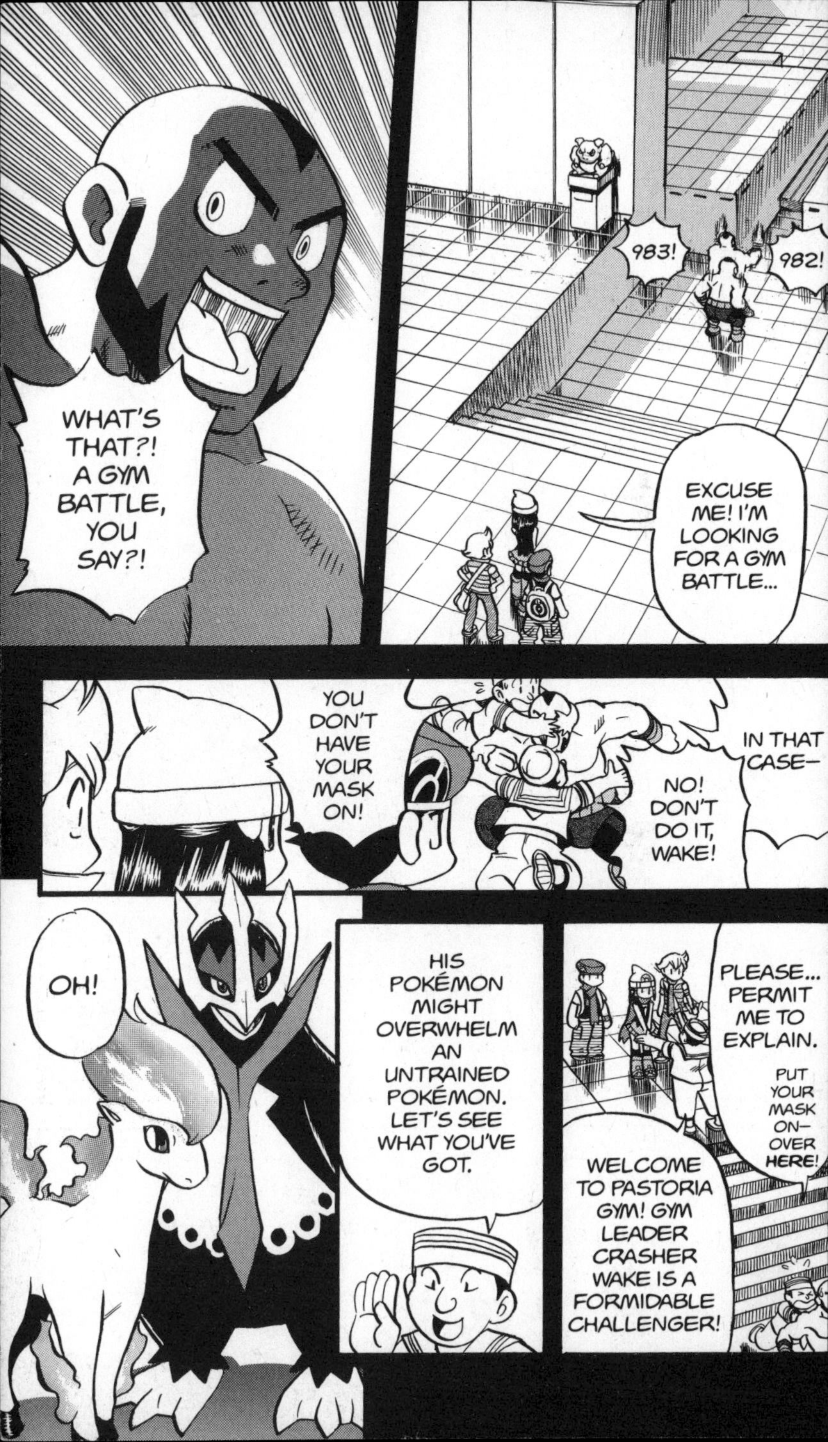
982!
983!
EXCUSE ME! I'M LOOKING FOR A GYM BATTLE...
WHAT'S THAT?! A GYM BATTLE, YOU SAY?!
IN THAT CASE—
NO! DON'T DO IT, WAKE!
YOU DON'T HAVE YOUR MASK ON!
PLEASE... PERMIT ME TO EXPLAIN.
PUT YOUR MASK ON— OVER HERE!
WELCOME TO PASTORIA GYM! GYM LEADER CRASHER WAKE IS A FORMIDABLE CHALLENGER!
HIS POKÉMON MIGHT OVERWHELM AN UNTRAINED POKÉMON. LET'S SEE WHAT YOU'VE GOT.
OH!

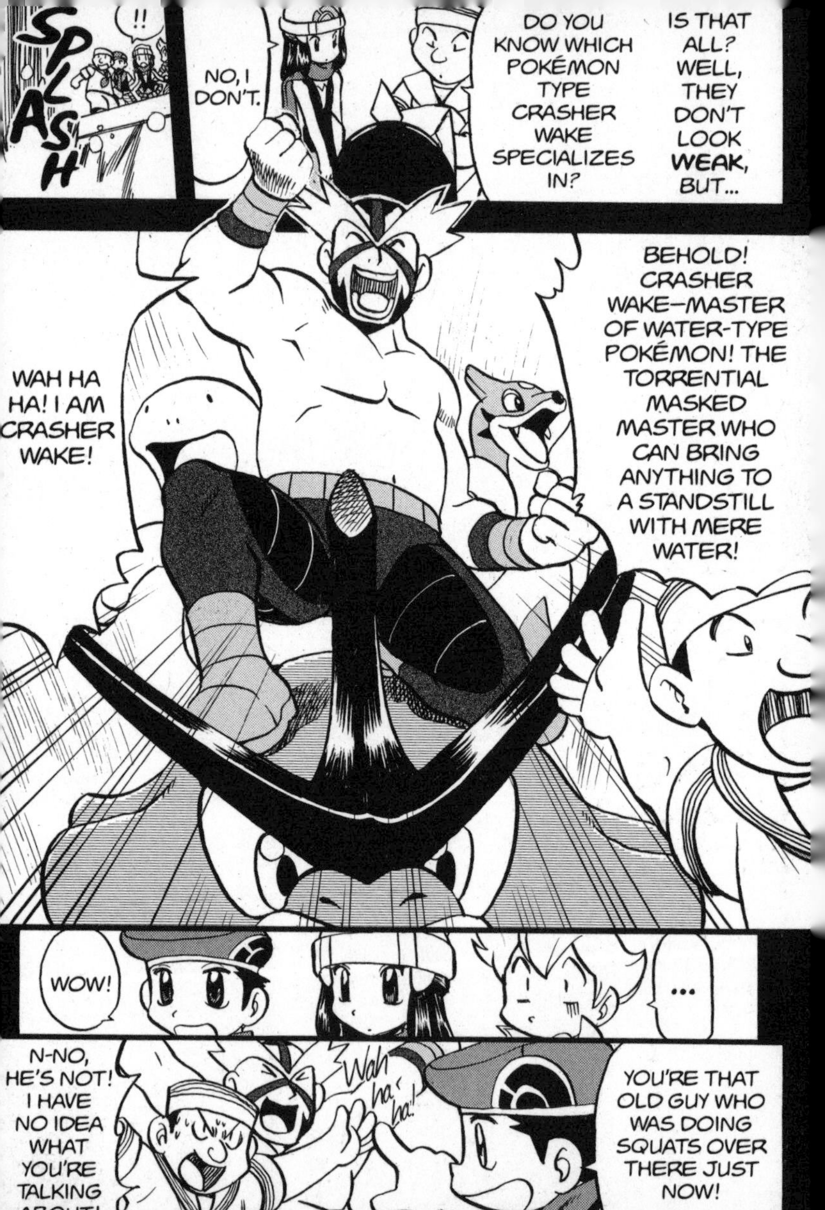
IS THAT ALL? WELL, THEY DON'T LOOK **WEAK**, BUT...
DO YOU KNOW WHICH POKÉMON TYPE CRASHER WAKE SPECIALIZES IN?
NO, I DON'T.
!!
SPLASH
BEHOLD! CRASHER WAKE—MASTER OF WATER-TYPE POKÉMON! THE TORRENTIAL MASKED MASTER WHO CAN BRING ANYTHING TO A STANDSTILL WITH MERE WATER!
WAH HA HA! I AM CRASHER WAKE!
...
WOW!
YOU'RE THAT OLD GUY WHO WAS DOING SQUATS OVER THERE JUST NOW!
Wah ha ha!
N-NO, HE'S NOT! I HAVE NO IDEA WHAT YOU'RE TALKING ABOUT!

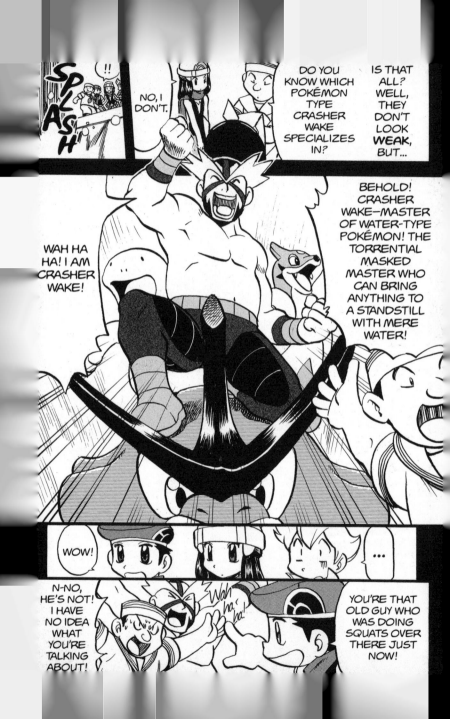

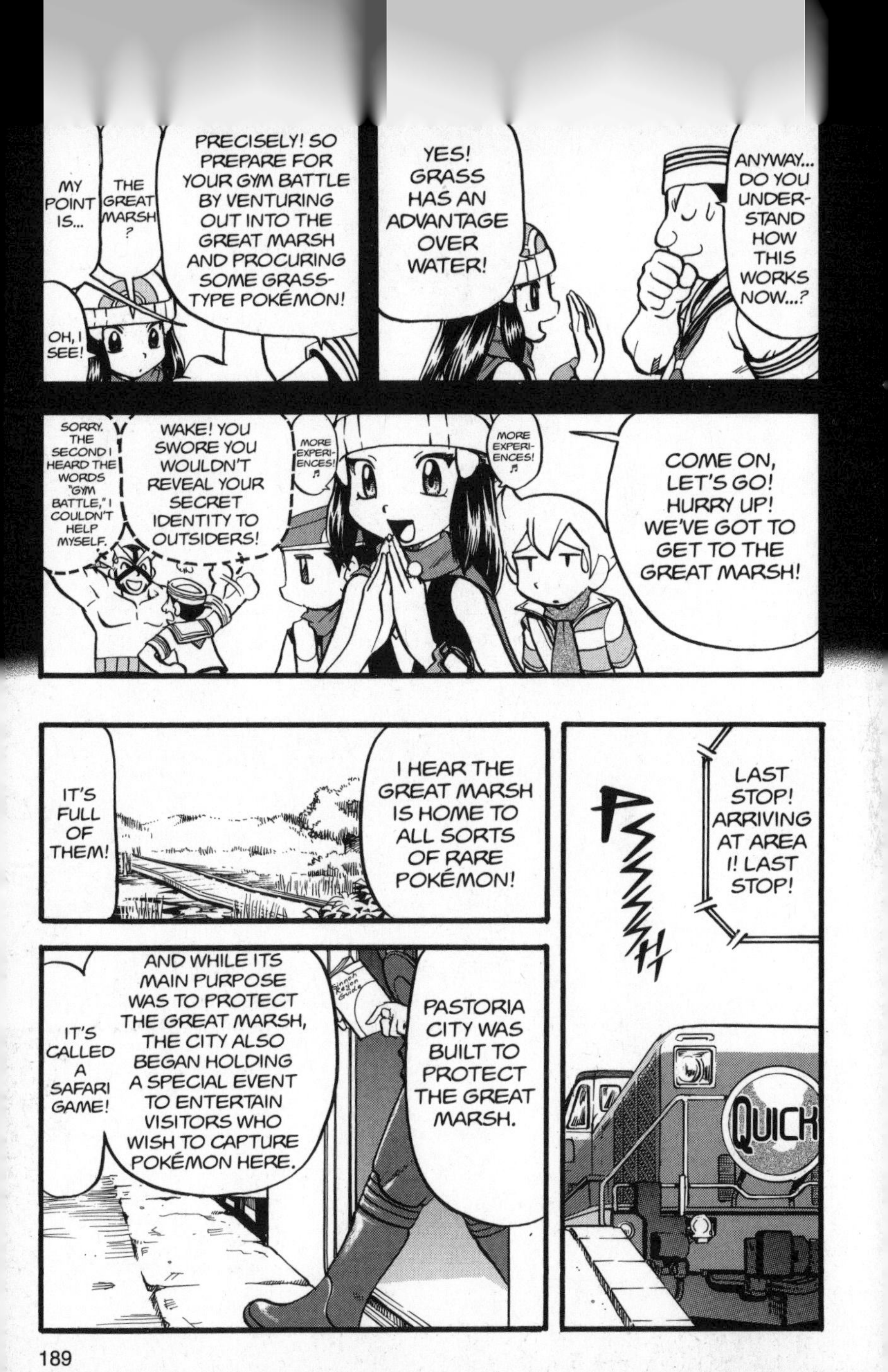
ANYWAY... DO YOU UNDERSTAND HOW THIS WORKS NOW...?
YES! GRASS HAS AN ADVANTAGE OVER WATER!
PRECISELY! SO PREPARE FOR YOUR GYM BATTLE BY VENTURING OUT INTO THE GREAT MARSH AND PROCURING SOME GRASS-TYPE POKÉMON!
THE GREAT MARSH?
MY POINT IS...
OH, I SEE!
COME ON, LET'S GO! HURRY UP! WE'VE GOT TO GET TO THE GREAT MARSH!
MORE EXPERIENCES! ♬
MORE EXPERIENCES! ♬
WAKE! YOU SWORE YOU WOULDN'T REVEAL YOUR SECRET IDENTITY TO OUTSIDERS!
SORRY. THE SECOND I HEARD THE WORDS "GYM BATTLE," I COULDN'T HELP MYSELF.
LAST STOP! ARRIVING AT AREA 1! LAST STOP!
QUICK
I HEAR THE GREAT MARSH IS HOME TO ALL SORTS OF RARE POKÉMON!
IT'S FULL OF THEM!
PASTORIA CITY WAS BUILT TO PROTECT THE GREAT MARSH.
Sinnoh Region Guide
AND WHILE ITS MAIN PURPOSE WAS TO PROTECT THE GREAT MARSH, THE CITY ALSO BEGAN HOLDING A SPECIAL EVENT TO ENTERTAIN VISITORS WHO WISH TO CAPTURE POKÉMON HERE.
IT'S CALLED A SAFARI GAME!

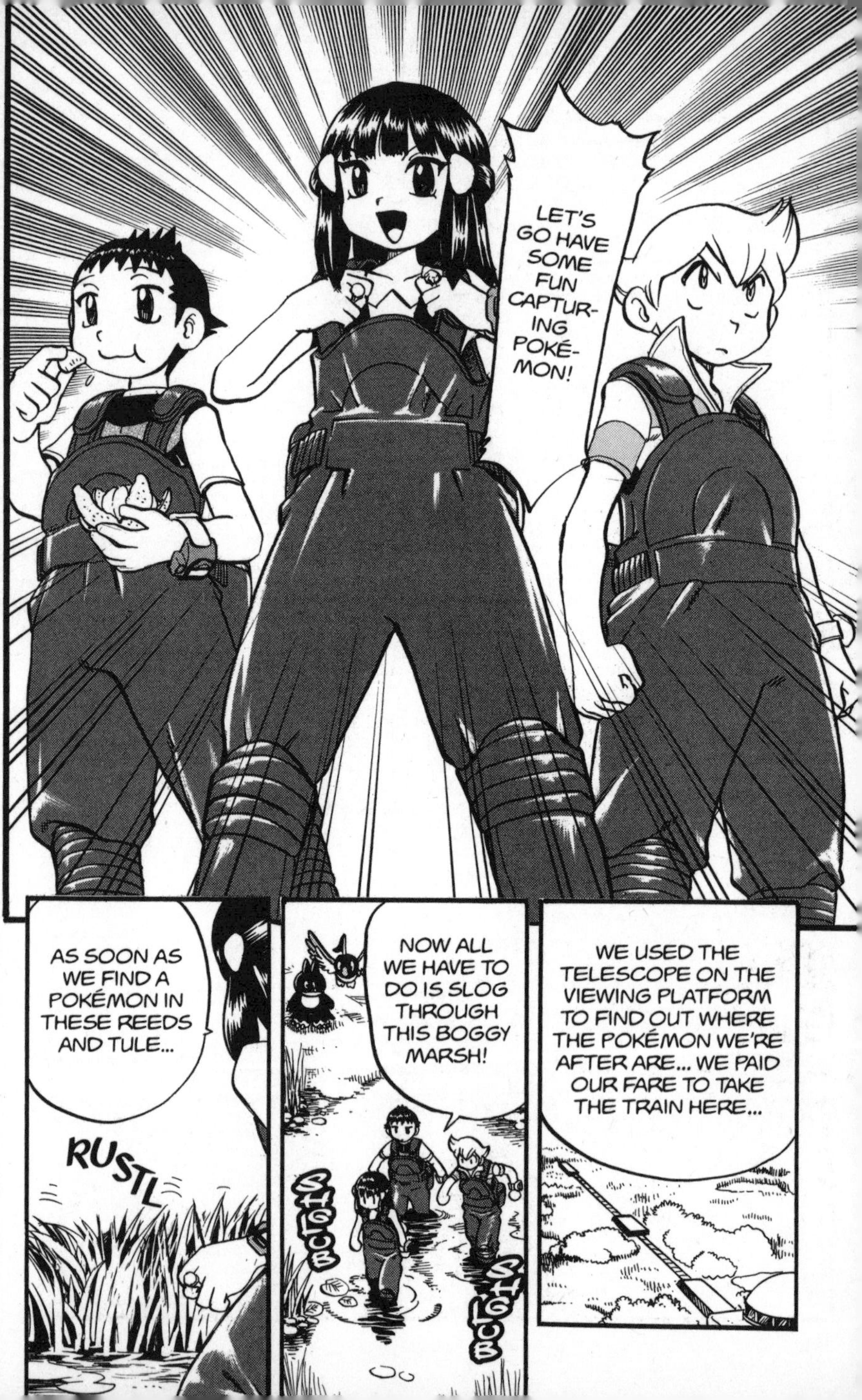
LET'S GO HAVE SOME FUN CAPTURING POKÉMON!
WE USED THE TELESCOPE ON THE VIEWING PLATFORM TO FIND OUT WHERE THE POKÉMON WE'RE AFTER ARE... WE PAID OUR FARE TO TAKE THE TRAIN HERE...
NOW ALL WE HAVE TO DO IS SLOG THROUGH THIS BOGGY MARSH!
SHGLUB
SHGLUB
AS SOON AS WE FIND A POKÉMON IN THESE REEDS AND TULE...
RUSTL

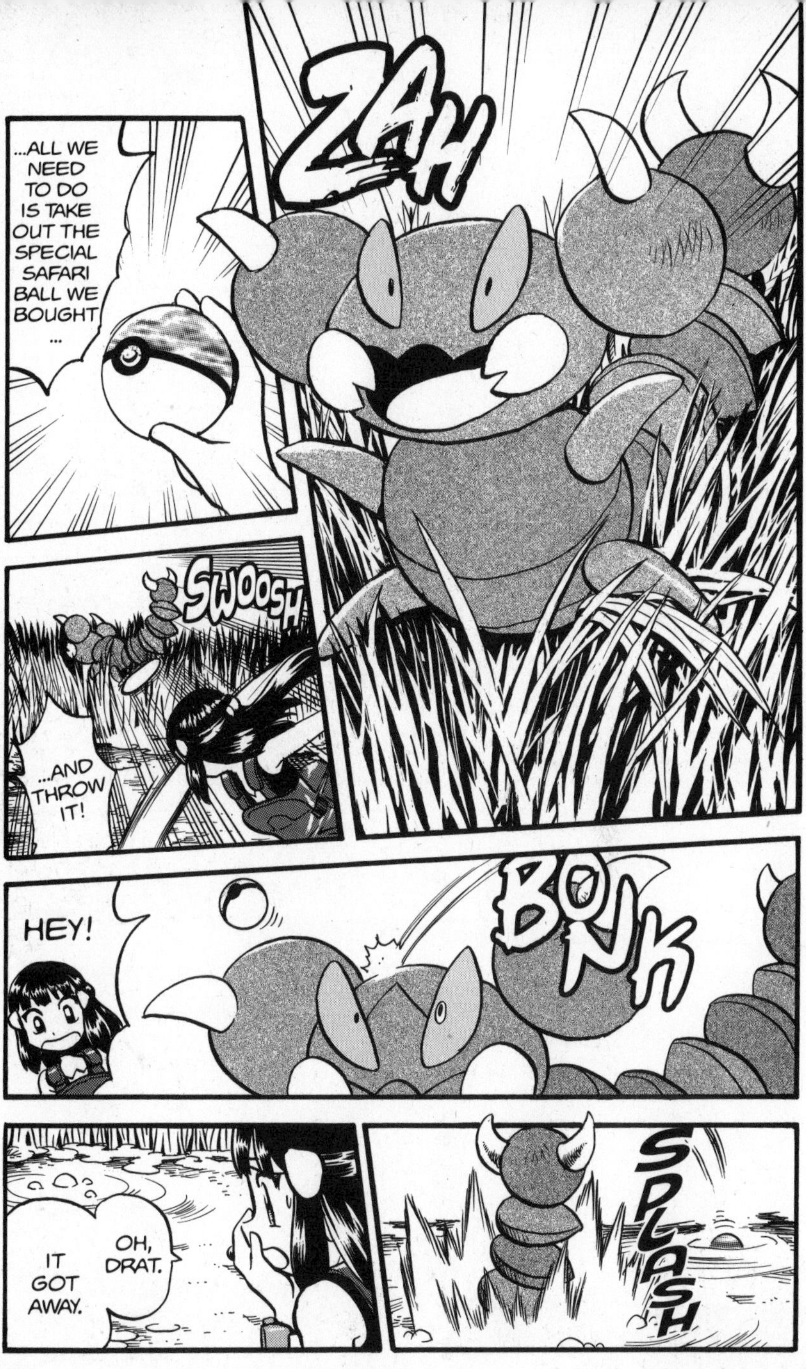
ZAH
...ALL WE NEED TO DO IS TAKE OUT THE SPECIAL SAFARI BALL WE BOUGHT...
SWOOSH
...AND THROW IT!
BONK
HEY!
SPLASH
OH, DRAT.
IT GOT AWAY.

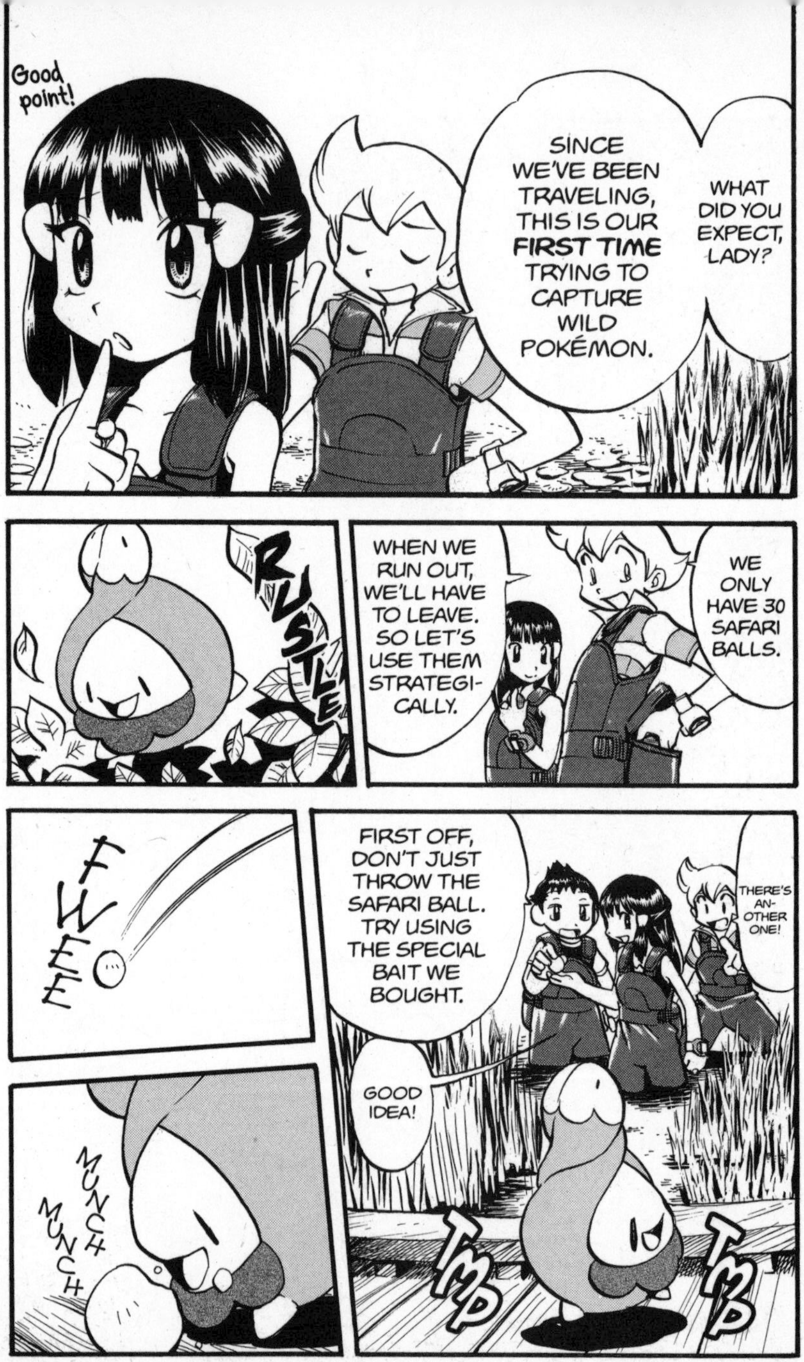
WHAT DID YOU EXPECT, LADY?
SINCE WE'VE BEEN TRAVELING, THIS IS OUR **FIRST TIME** TRYING TO CAPTURE WILD POKÉMON.
Good point!
WE ONLY HAVE 30 SAFARI BALLS.
WHEN WE RUN OUT, WE'LL HAVE TO LEAVE. SO LET'S USE THEM STRATEGICALLY.
RUSTLE
THERE'S ANOTHER ONE!
FIRST OFF, DON'T JUST THROW THE SAFARI BALL. TRY USING THE SPECIAL BAIT WE BOUGHT.
GOOD IDEA!
TMP
TMP
FWEE
MUNCH MUNCH

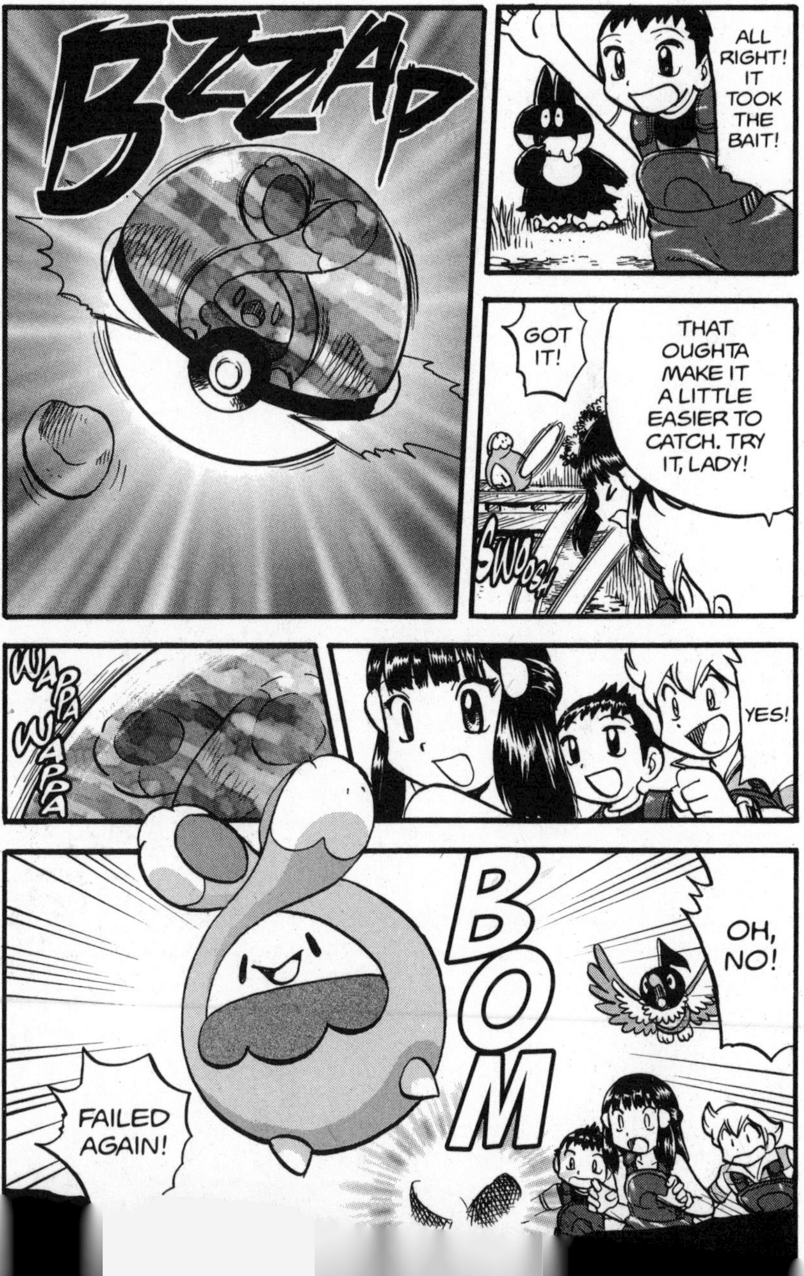
ALL RIGHT! IT TOOK THE BAIT!
THAT OUGHTA MAKE IT A LITTLE EASIER TO CATCH. TRY IT, LADY!
GOT IT!
SWOOSH
BZZAP
YES!
WAPPA WAPPA
OH, NO!
BOM
FAILED AGAIN!

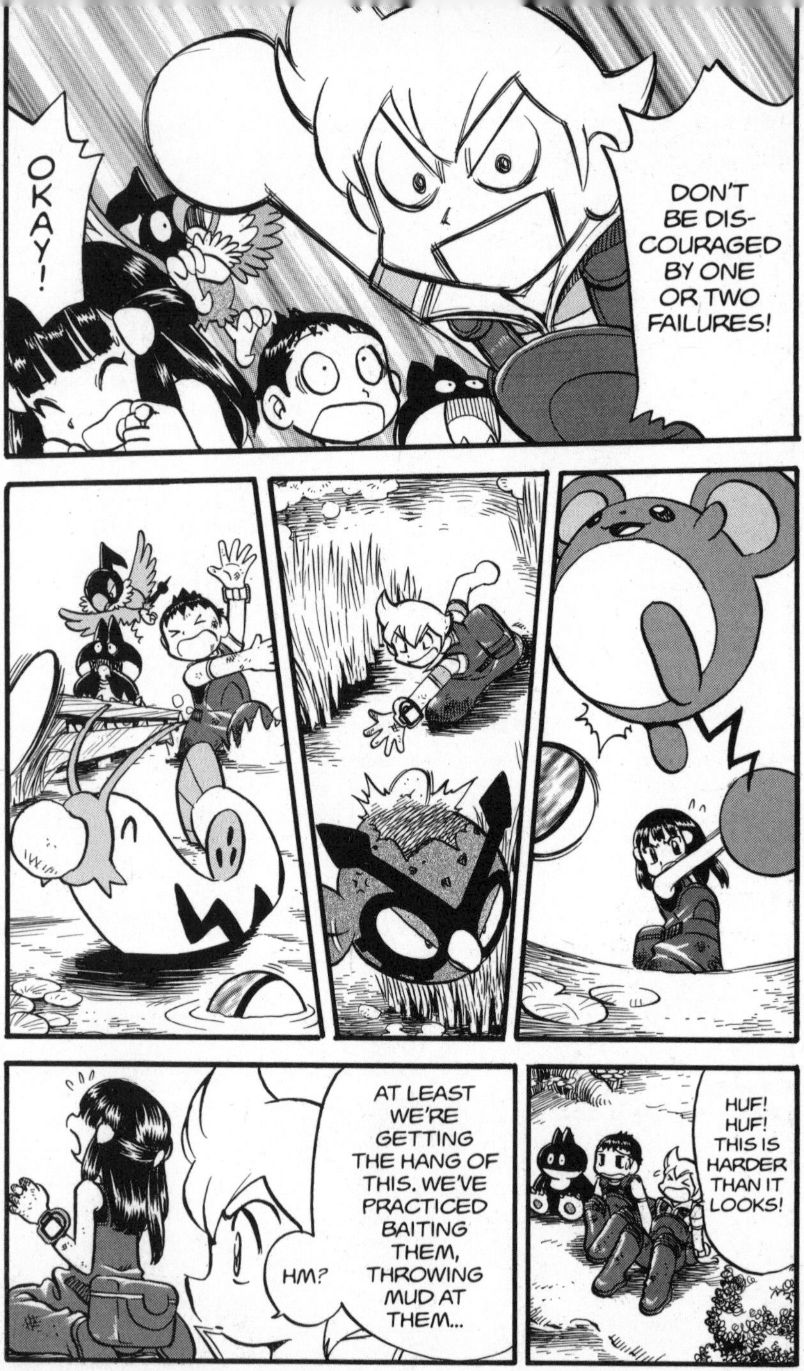
DON'T BE DIS-COURAGED BY ONE OR TWO FAILURES!
OKAY!
HUF! HUF! THIS IS HARDER THAN IT LOOKS!
AT LEAST WE'RE GETTING THE HANG OF THIS. WE'VE PRACTICED BAITING THEM, THROWING MUD AT THEM...
HM?

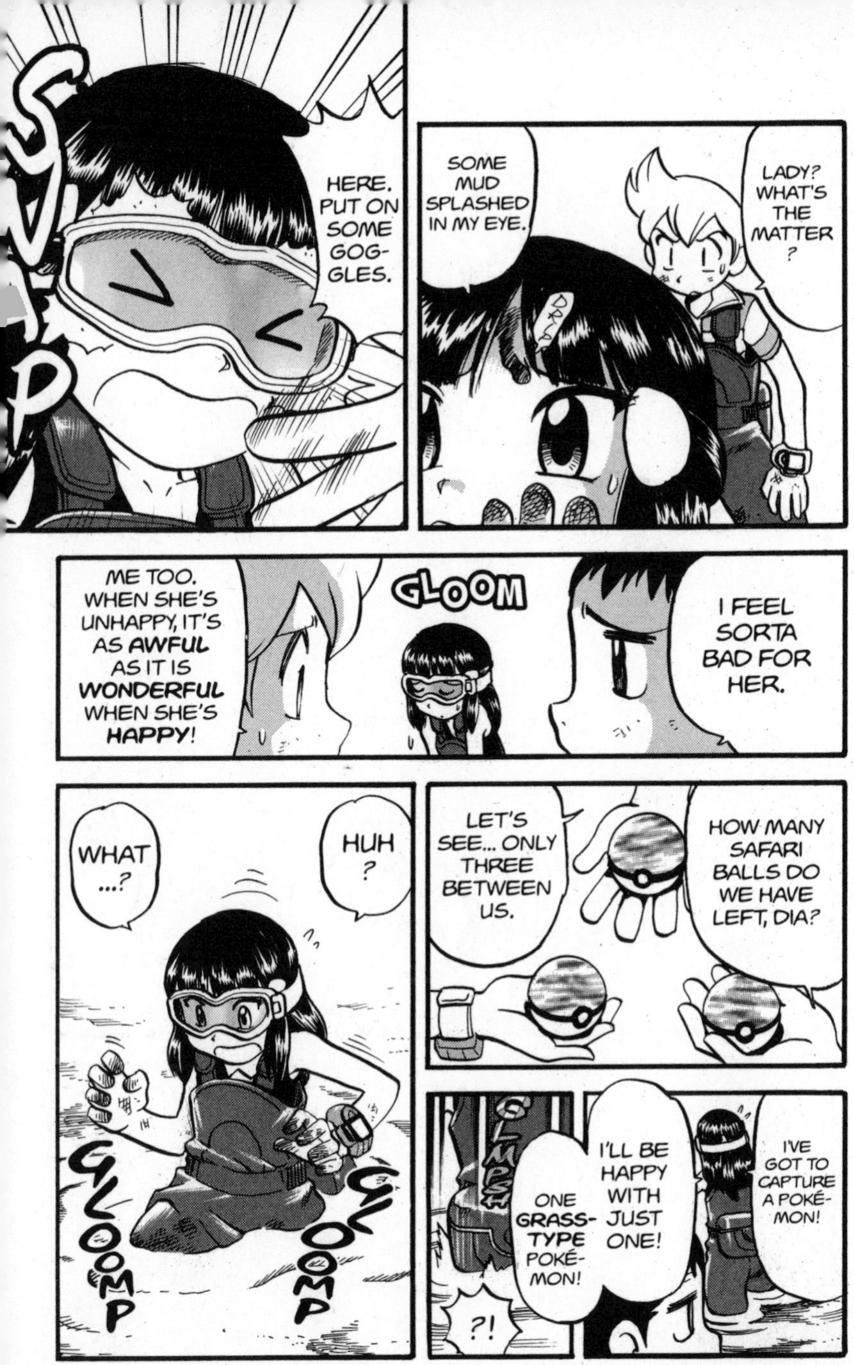
LADY? WHAT'S THE MATTER?
SOME MUD SPLASHED IN MY EYE.
DRIP
HERE. PUT ON SOME GOGGLES.
I FEEL SORTA BAD FOR HER.
GLOOM
ME TOO. WHEN SHE'S UNHAPPY, IT'S AS **AWFUL** AS IT IS **WONDERFUL** WHEN SHE'S **HAPPY**!
HOW MANY SAFARI BALLS DO WE HAVE LEFT, DIA?
LET'S SEE... ONLY THREE BETWEEN US.
I'VE GOT TO CAPTURE A POKÉMON!
I'LL BE HAPPY WITH JUST ONE!
ONE **GRASS-TYPE** POKÉMON!
?!
HUH?
WHAT...?
GLOOMP
GLOOMP

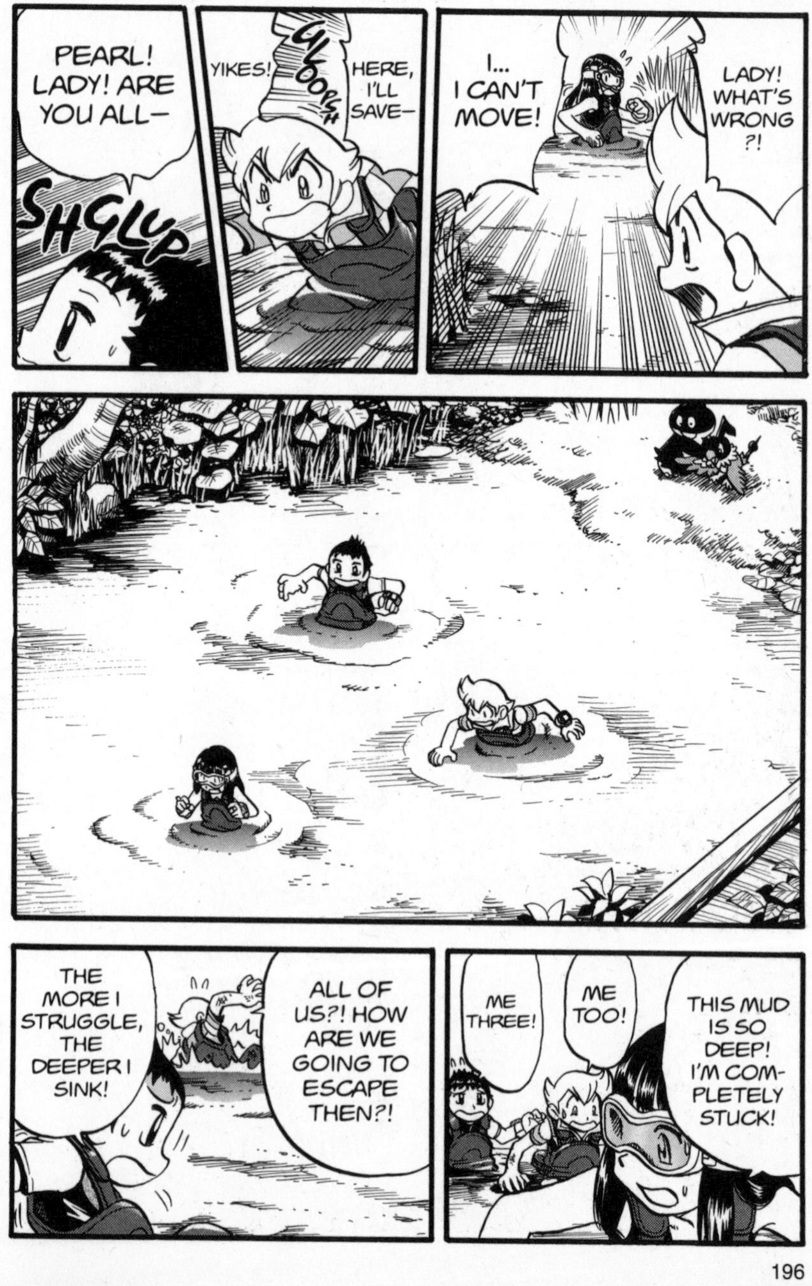
LADY! WHAT'S WRONG ?!
I... I CAN'T MOVE!
HERE, I'LL SAVE—
GLOOPSH
YIKES!
PEARL! LADY! ARE YOU ALL—
SHGLUP
THIS MUD IS SO DEEP! I'M COM-PLETELY STUCK!
ME TOO!
ME THREE!
ALL OF US?! HOW ARE WE GOING TO ESCAPE THEN?!
THE MORE I STRUGGLE, THE DEEPER I SINK!

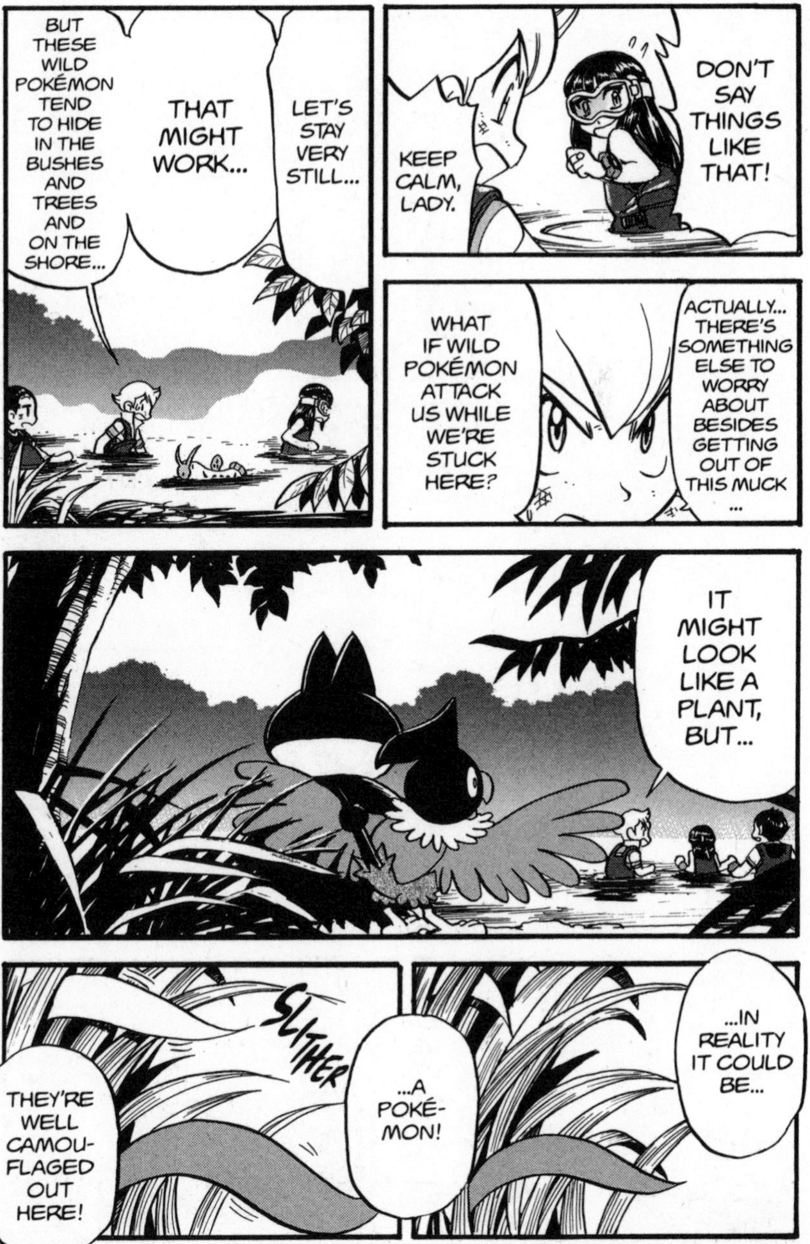
DON'T SAY THINGS LIKE THAT!
KEEP CALM, LADY.
ACTUALLY... THERE'S SOMETHING ELSE TO WORRY ABOUT BESIDES GETTING OUT OF THIS MUCK ...
WHAT IF WILD POKÉMON ATTACK US WHILE WE'RE STUCK HERE?
LET'S STAY VERY STILL...
THAT MIGHT WORK...
BUT THESE WILD POKÉMON TEND TO HIDE IN THE BUSHES AND TREES AND ON THE SHORE...
IT MIGHT LOOK LIKE A PLANT, BUT...
...IN REALITY IT COULD BE...
...A POKÉ-MON!
SLITHER
THEY'RE WELL CAMOU-FLAGED OUT HERE!

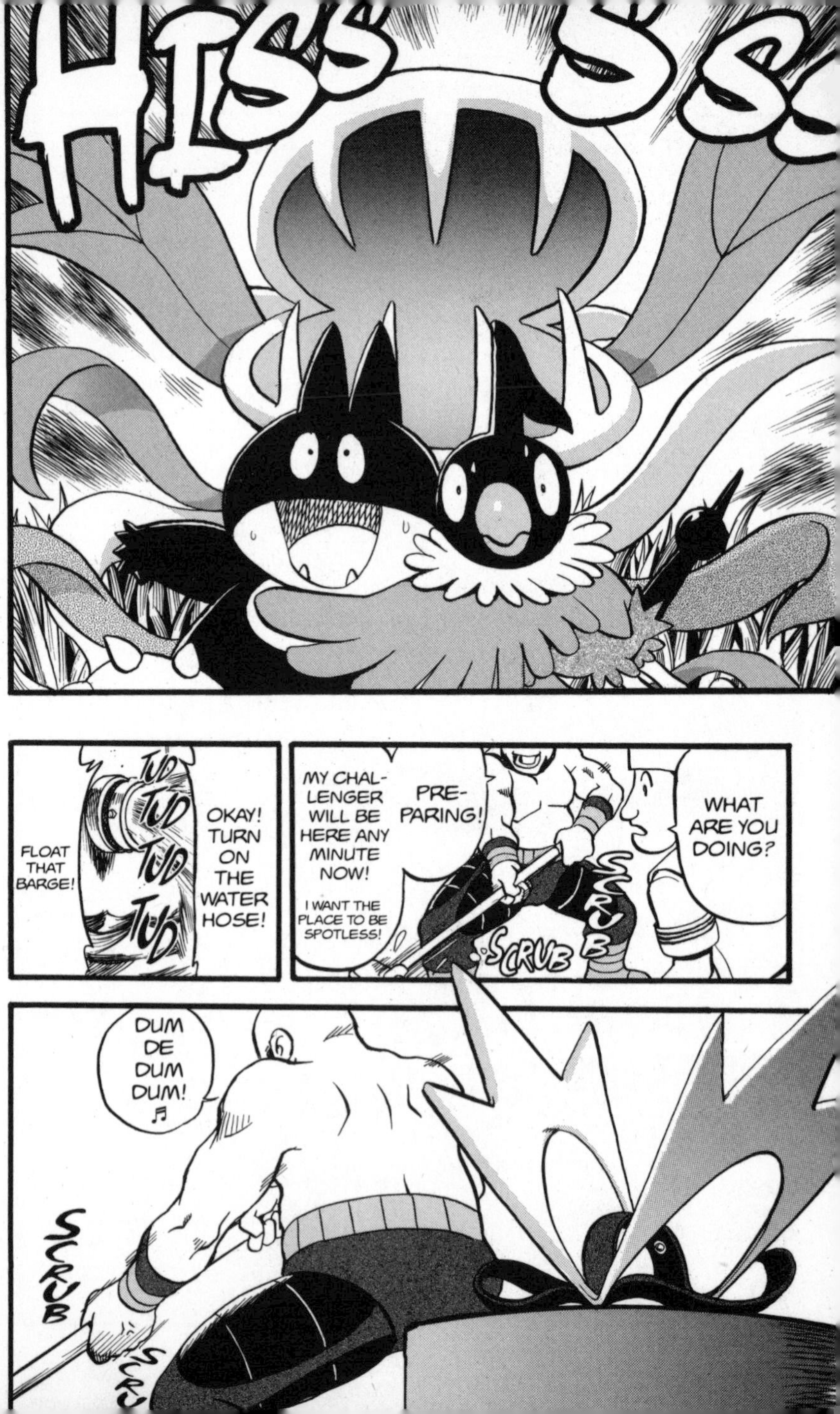
HISSS SS
WHAT ARE YOU DOING?
PRE-PARING!
MY CHAL-LENGER WILL BE HERE ANY MINUTE NOW!
I WANT THE PLACE TO BE SPOTLESS!
SCRUB
SCRUB
OKAY! TURN ON THE WATER HOSE!
TUD TUD TUD TUD
FLOAT THAT BARGE!
DUM DE DUM DUM! ♬
SCRUB
SCRU

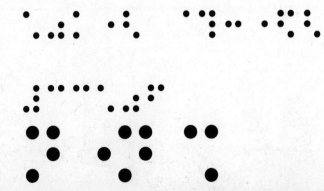

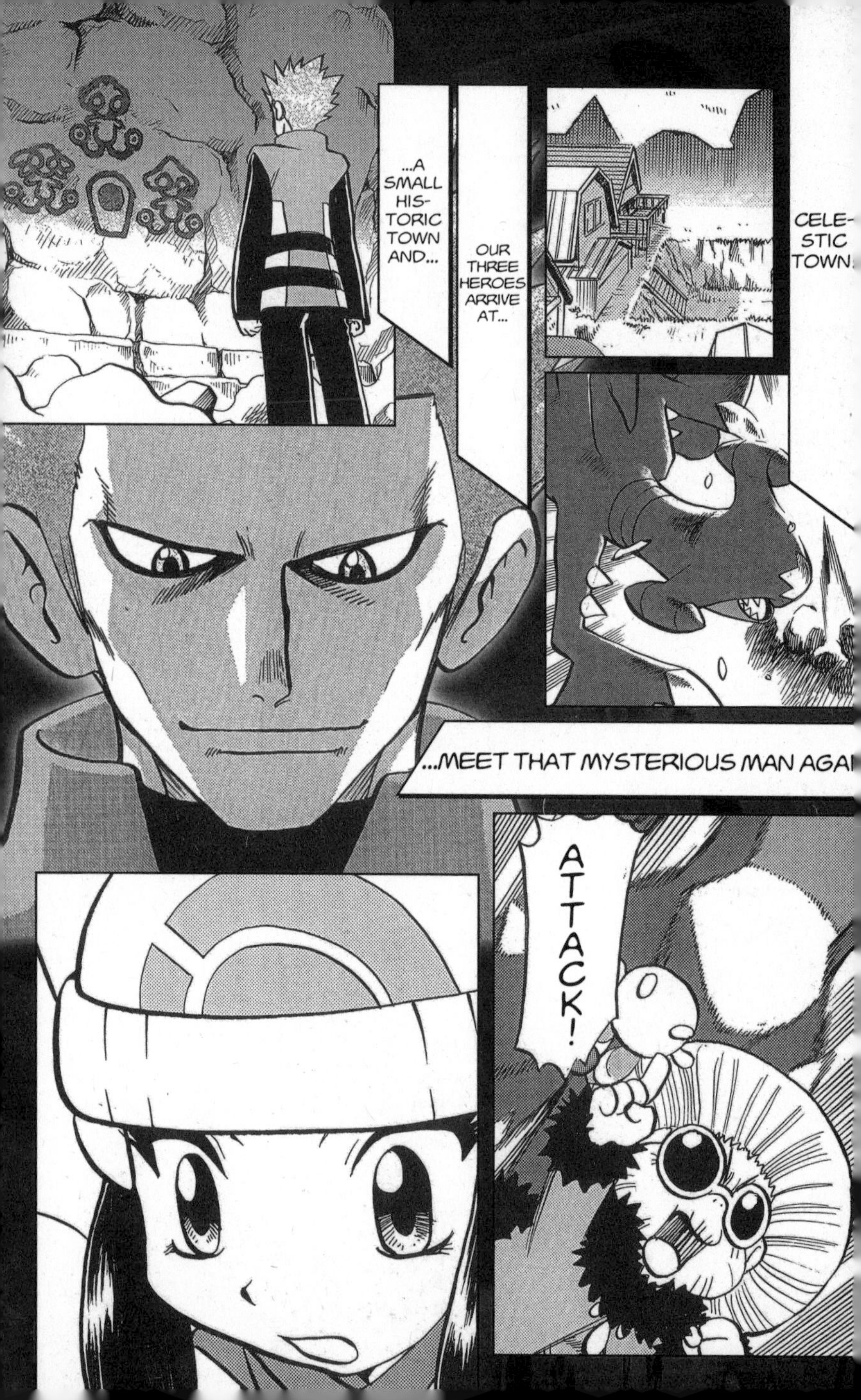
CELESTIC TOWN.
OUR THREE HEROES ARRIVE AT...
...A SMALL HISTORIC TOWN AND...
...MEET THAT MYSTERIOUS MAN AGA
ATTACK!

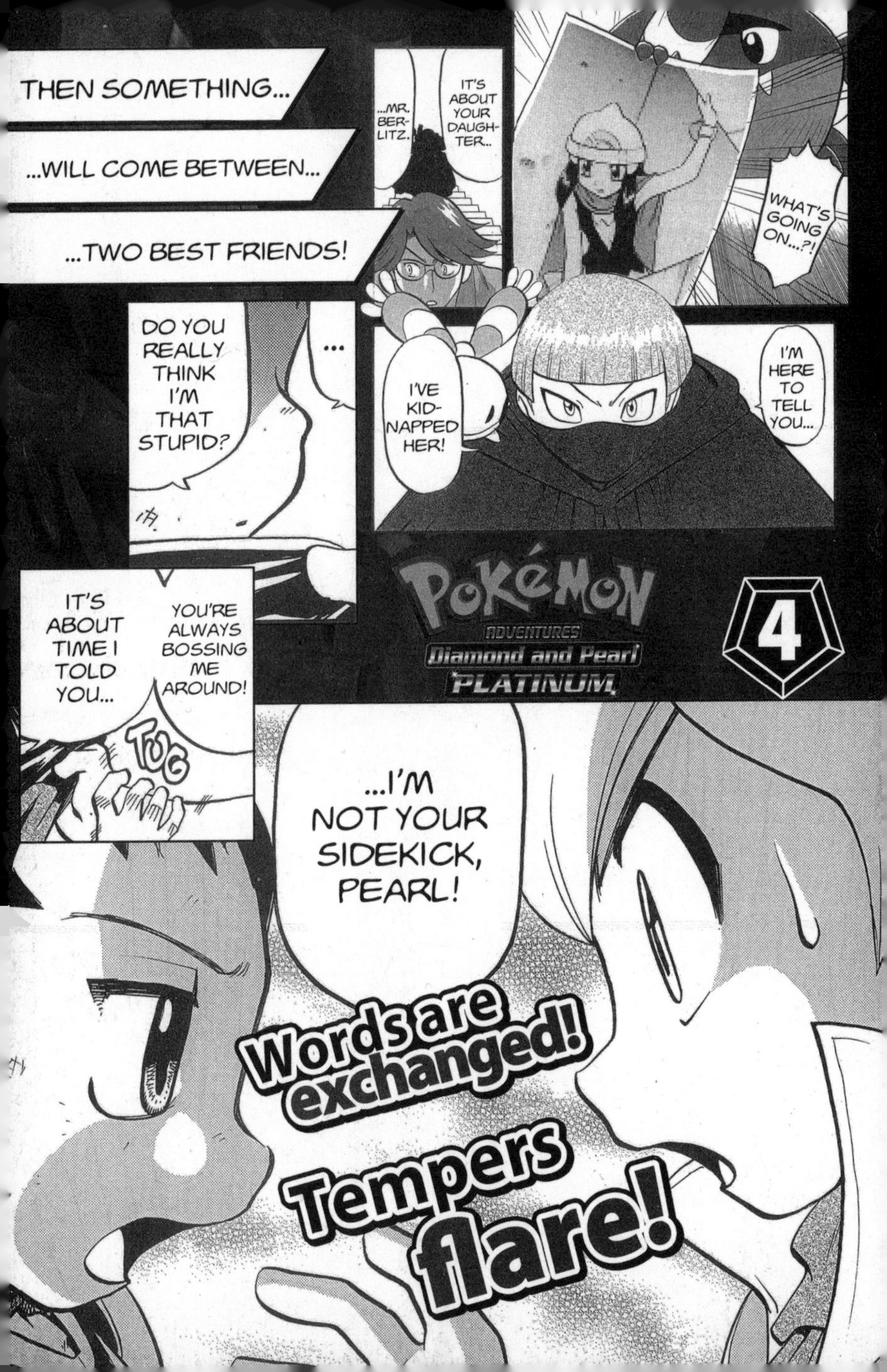
WHAT'S GOING ON...?!
IT'S ABOUT YOUR DAUGHTER...
...MR. BERLITZ.
THEN SOMETHING...
...WILL COME BETWEEN...
...TWO BEST FRIENDS!
I'M HERE TO TELL YOU...
I'VE KIDNAPPED HER!
...
DO YOU REALLY THINK I'M THAT STUPID?
POKÉMON ADVENTURES Diamond and Pearl PLATINUM
4
YOU'RE ALWAYS BOSSING ME AROUND!
IT'S ABOUT TIME I TOLD YOU...
TUG
...I'M NOT YOUR SIDEKICK, PEARL!
Words are exchanged!
Tempers flare!

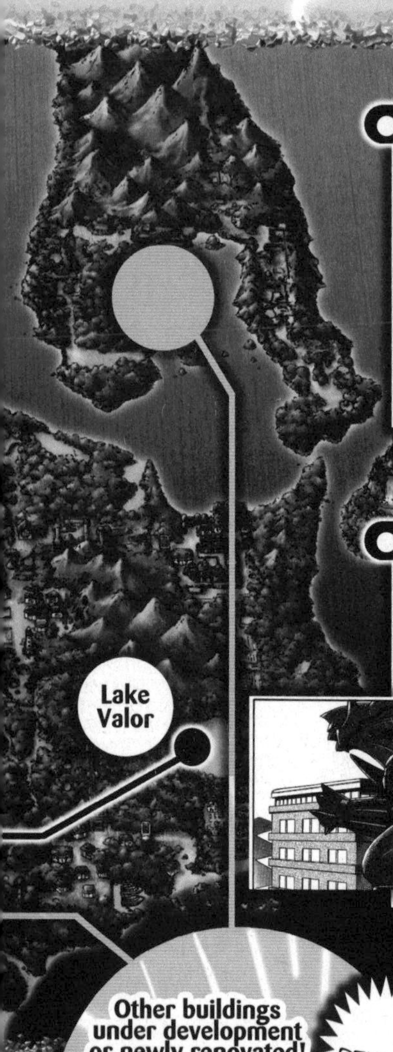
Lake
Valor

A treasure trove of legends and ruins.

Wall Paintings

THE HISTORICAL SITE THIS TOWN PROTECTS...

OF ALL THE SURVIVING ARCHEOLOGICAL RUINS IN THE SINNOH REGION, CELESTIC TOWN BOASTS THE MOST FAMOUS ONES. THE SECRET BEHIND THE RUINS' WALL PAINTINGS ARE PROTECTED BY THE ELDEST CLAN.

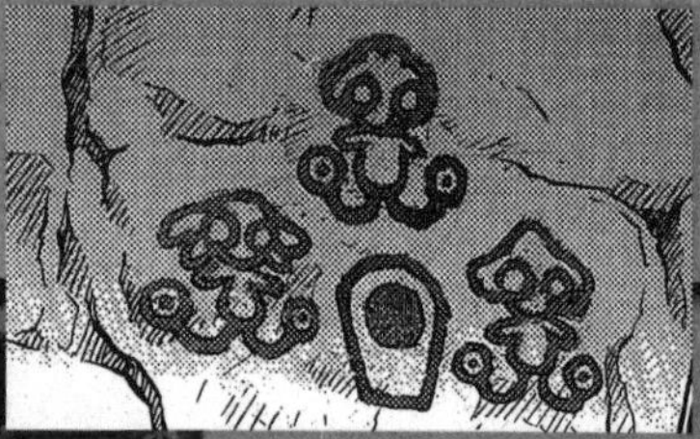
FEW ARE ALLOWED TO VIEW THEM

The Birth of This Land

WHAT DO THE FIGURES THAT REMAIN STANDING IN EACH REGION SIGNIFY?

THE STATUE IN ETERNA CITY AND SIMILAR IMAGES IN CELESTIC TOWN TELL THE STORY OF A TIME BEFORE THIS REGION EVEN EXISTED!

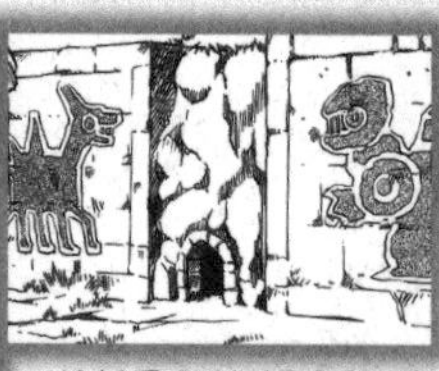
THE TWO FIGURES APPEAR TO BE FACING EACH OTHER.

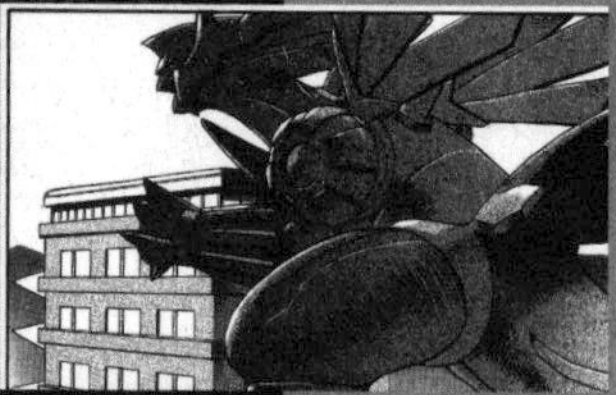
WHAT AN IMPOSING STATUE!

Literature

SCORES OF SCHOLARS EXPLORE THE ARCHIVES!

CANALAVE CITY IS FAMOUS FOR ITS EXTENSIVE COLLECTION OF ANCIENT LITERATURE. THE TOMES ARE STORED IN THIS LIBRARY FOR ANY VISITOR TO PERUSE.

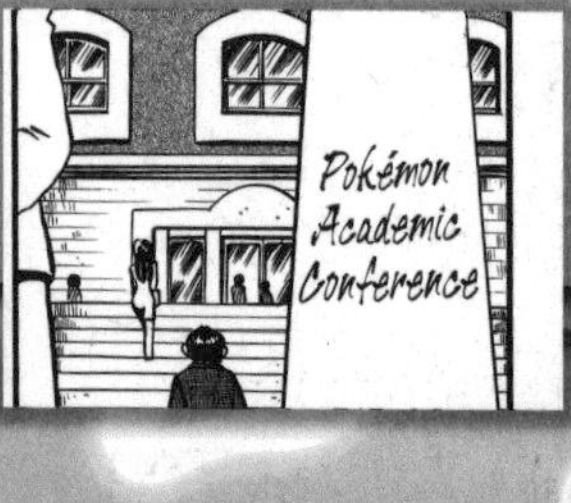
Pokémon
Academic
Conference
HOSTS A VARIETY OF EDUCATIONAL EVENTS.

Other buildings under development or newly renovated!

DEVELOPMENT!

WHILE SOME AREAS OF SINNOH ABOUND WITH NATURAL RESOURCES AND HISTORY, OTHERS ARE NEWLY DEVELOPED, MAKING IT A RICHLY VARIED REGION. THERE ARE ALSO PLANS FOR POKÉMON BATTLE ESTABLISHMENTS AND POKÉMON CAPTURING EXHIBITIONS! CAN'T WAIT TO SEE THEM!

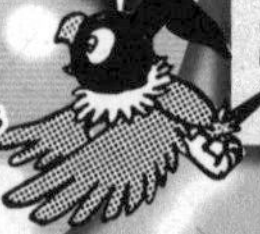

COMPLETE COLLECTION

DISCOVER The Sinnoh Region!!

ABUNDANT FORESTS AND MOUNTAIN RANGES! CLIMATES RANGING FROM HOT AND HUMID TO FREEZING! THIS IS THE SINNOH REGION, THE SETTING FOR OUR THREE HEROES' ADVENTURE! GAWK AT THE MYRIAD SIGHTS OF THE REGION, GASP AT ITS UNIQUE TOPOGRAPHY! THE KEY TO OUR TRIO'S QUEST MAY LIE IN THE LAND ITSELF—AS WELL AS ITS HISTORY!

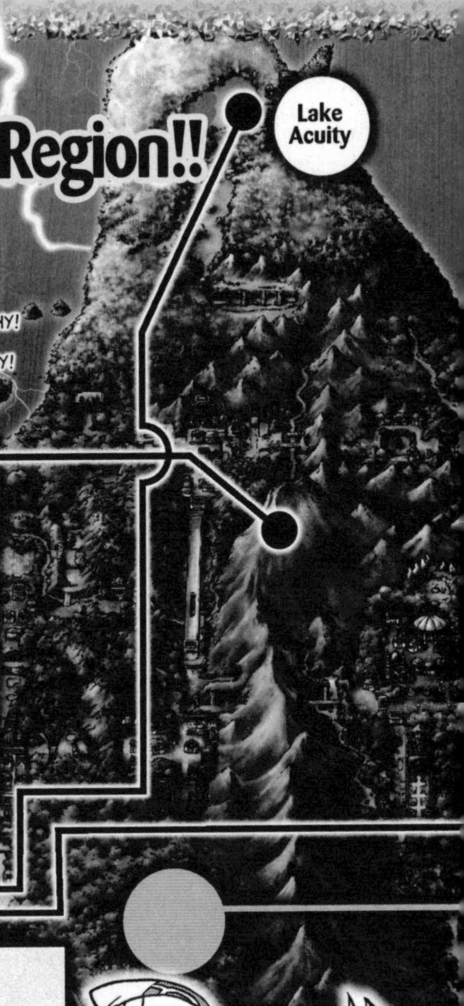
Lake Acuity
Lake Verity

Varied Nature

Mt. Coronet

OVERFLOWING WITH ENERGY AND NATURAL RESOURCES!

THIS GREAT AND IMPOSING MOUNTAIN DIVIDES THE SINNOH REGION STRAIGHT DOWN THE MIDDLE INTO EASTERN AND WESTERN HALVES. SOME SORT OF MYSTERIOUS ENERGY EXISTS WITHIN IT—AN ENERGY WITH THE POWER TO EVOLVE POKÉMON!

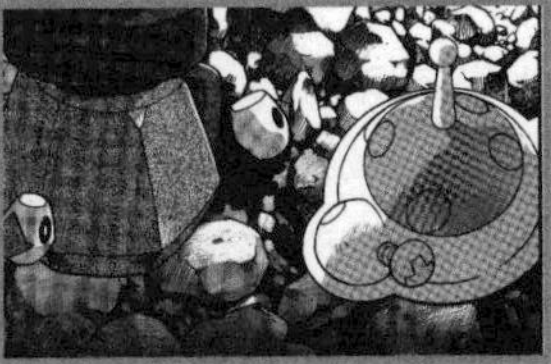

Three Great Lakes

THE SURFACE OF THESE BODIES OF WATER REFLECT THE SECRETS OF THE HEART!

IN THE NORTH, EAST, AND WEST OF THE SINNOH REGION, LIE THREE GREAT LAKES. EACH INSPIRES A STRANGE FEELING IN THE BEHOLDER... COULD SOMETHING MYSTICAL LIE BENEATH THEIR SPARKLING WAVES?

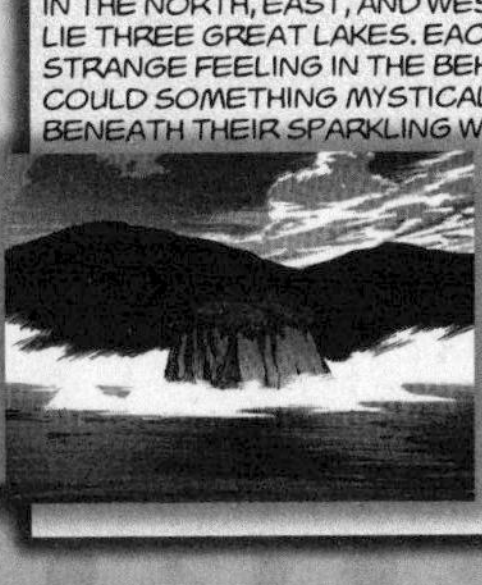

◀ ALSO KNOWN AS A GREAT SIGHT-SEEING AREA.

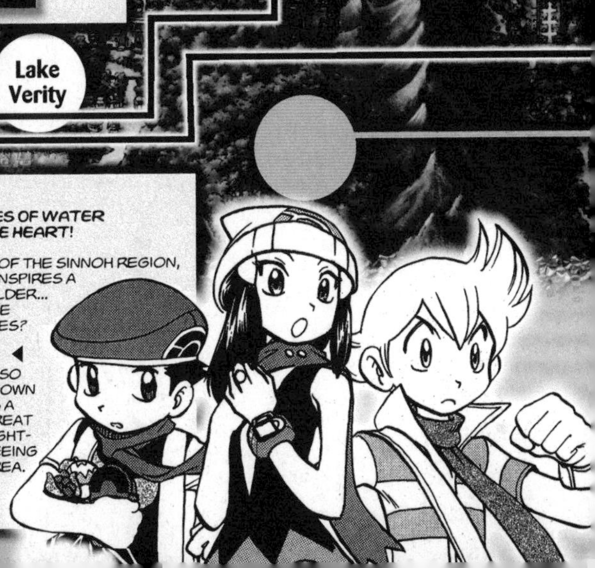

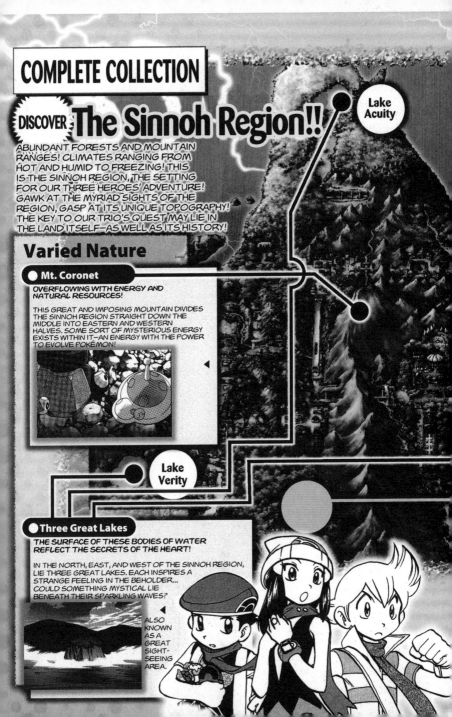

Message from

Hidenori Kusaka

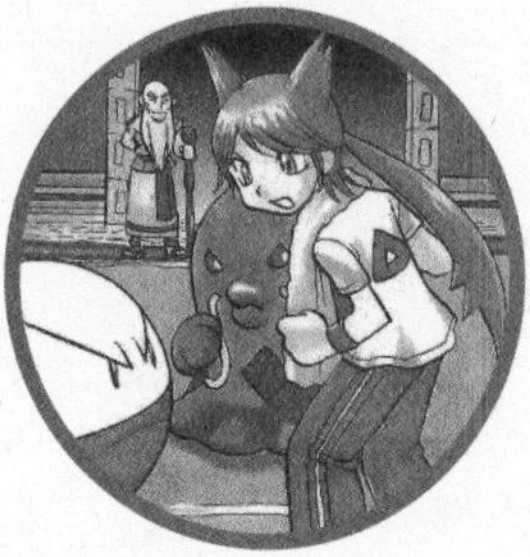

When I'm playing Pokémon on the DS, I play *FireRed* and *LeafGreen* when I want to play in the Kanto region. If I want to play in Hoenn, I play *Ruby*, *Sapphire*, and *Emerald*. And if I want to play in Sinnoh, I of course play *Diamond*, *Pearl*, and *Platinum Version*. Huh? One region is missing! I can't play Johto on my DS! But soon I won't be missing it anymore...because they're redoing the *Gold* and *Silver* games! I can't wait!

Message from

Satoshi Yamamoto

Pokémon Adventures gives a lot of side characters a place in the sun, but when they first appeared, I never imagined Paka and Uji would get so big. When this happens, I always think, "I should have made better character designs." But sometimes these things work out because the characters are so simply defined. (LOL)

More Adventures Coming Soon...

Mysteries abound when a Psyduck and a Pokémon researcher go missing. And Lady fights two epic Gym battles! If only Pearl and Diamond could stop fighting *each other*...!

Then, what secret does Cyrus, leader of Team Galactic, seek in the ruins and relics of Celestic Town...?

Plus, meet Carnivine, Floatzel, Magnezone, Drifblim, Mismagius, Bronzong and many more Sinnoh Pokémon friends!

AVAILABLE NOW!

POCKET COMICS

STORY & ART BY SANTA HARUKAZE

BLACK & WHITE
$9.99 US / $10.99 CAN

LEGENDARY POKÉMON
$9.99 US / $10.99 CAN

X•Y
$12.99 US / $13.99 CAN

A Pokémon pocket-sized book chock-full of four-panel gags, Pokémon trivia and fun quizzes based on the characters you know and love!

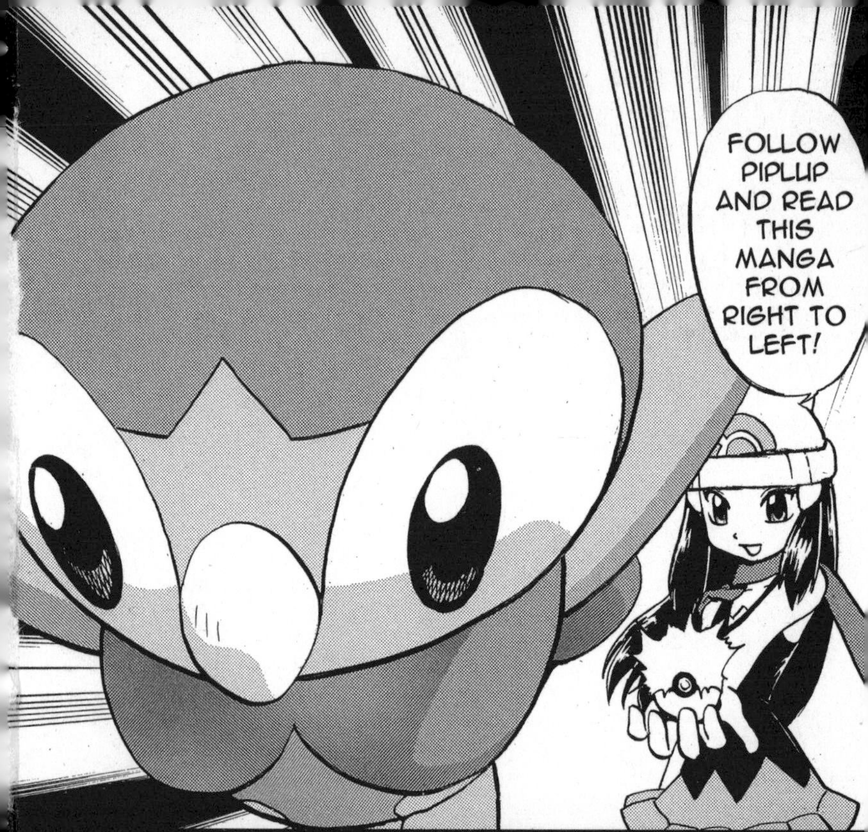
FOLLOW PIPLUP AND READ THIS MANGA FROM RIGHT TO LEFT!

THIS IS THE END OF THIS GRAPHIC NOVEL!

To properly enjoy this VIZ Media graphic novel, please turn it around and begin reading from right to left.

This book has been printed in the original Japanese format in order to preserve the orientation of the original artwork. Have fun with it!

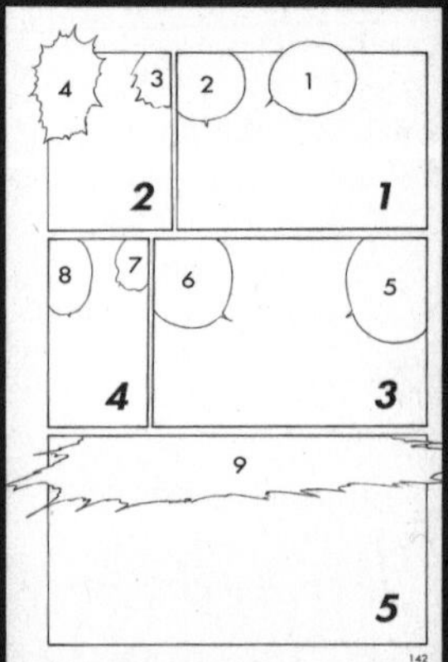